God, Send Sunday departs f_ Morrison's *Beloved* and Sherley Anne Williams' *Dessa Rose*. Like Morrison and Williams, Wheelock had to create a plot based on the evidence of history, but she puts a spotlight on the agency of the enslaved in shaping evidence which is often used sparingly by professional historians. Although the novel is immersed in black Christian thought, she wisely refuses to throw hush-puppies to the modern and somewhat passive Christian choir. Discerning readers will appreciate that.

— JERRY W. WARD, CO-EDITOR OF THE
*CAMBRIDGE HISTORY OF AFRICAN AMERICAN
LITERATURE*

I was totally mesmerized while reading *God, Send Sunday*. I laughed, cried, got angry, and put it down only to immediately pick it up again. I felt the pain of desertion, despair, desolation, and the sheer unadulterated joy of reunion. Jacqueline Wheelock has a gift for painting a picture so clearly that you are able to see each detail—from the buildings to the clothes to the facial features—with accuracy and clarity. Her writing is a welcome change in a world that seems devoid of civility and human compassion.

— PATRICIA WHITLOCK, RETIRED
UNIVERSITY OF MISSISSIPPI MEDICAL
CENTER PROFESSIONAL AND AVID READER
OF BLACK HISTORY

God, Send Sunday

JACQUELINE FREEMAN WHEELOCK

Scrivenings
PRESS
Quench your thirst for story.
www.ScriveningsPress.com

Published by Scrivenings Press LLC
15 Lucky Lane
Morrilton, Arkansas 72110
https://ScriveningsPress.com

Printed in the United States of America

Paperback ISBN 978-1-64917-226-6
eBook ISBN 978-1-64917-227-3

Cover by Linda Fulkerson, bookmarketinggraphics.com

All characters are fictional, and any resemblance to real people, either factual or historical, is purely coincidental.

All scriptures are taken from the KING JAMES VERSION (KJV): KING JAMES VERSION, public domain.

Published in association with Joyce Hart of Hartline Literary Agency, Pittsburgh, PA.

To all God's women who have bent their minds to settle for what their hearts neither desired nor deserved, Sunday dedicates her story to you.

ACKNOWLEDGMENTS

I want to thank Linda Fulkerson and Scrivenings Press for the opportunity to publish one of the books of my heart which I had long since dubbed a shelf novel. Equally, I want to thank my husband, children, their spouses and my grandchildren for loving me through it all.

AUTHOR'S NOTE: A CAVEAT

The word "nigger" was used regularly during the antebellum period. In an attempt to remain faithful to many of the conversations of that era, I have chosen to use the word in this novel. It should be noted, however, that the choice is solely mine and, in no sense, reflects the policies and leanings of Scrivenings Press. In my opinion, however, the neglect of its use in dialogue during the nineteenth century imposes a superficiality that does not serve a realistic image of certain pre-Civil War interactions.

I deeply appreciate Linda Fulkerson for her understanding, and my hope is simply that the novel provides readers with a slightly different perspective on slavery and the Christian walk during a painful segment of America's evolving history.

~ Jacqueline Freeman Wheelock

PROLOGUE

A county in southern Virginia
Sunday, July 7, 1846

Six-year-old Sunday Pennington stretched her legs along her father's solid lap. Back nestled against his chest, she felt the steady beat of his heart. Most mornings when he left for his shed, she was still asleep, so this Sabbath-Day pause, when the two of them lingered at the breakfast table and Mama quietly moved about tidying up, was a time young Sunday lived for.

Papa set down his empty coffee tin, gently tugged one of her thick wiry plaits, and pressed his whiskered chin against the part in her hair while she giggled and waited for the words she knew would come.

"All right, my little Sabbath girl. What world-famous drawing do you have for your papa today?"

His deep voice was as comforting and familiar and mysterious as the rapidly aging sunrise outside the window. Sunday shrugged her shoulders in mock modesty. Beneath her empty breakfast plate lay one of her pencil sketches, its crimped edges hidden from Papa. She eased the length of paper from underneath the dish and placed it in Papa's hands, her eager inquiry spilling forth before the sheet touched his palm.

"You like this one, Papa?"

Papa played the game with practiced ease. Angled the grease-spotted paper toward the sun. Took his time answering. "Best drawing you ever did."

He looked into her eyes as though he'd not made that declaration a thousand times before. And for the thousandth time, she believed him with all her heart.

"A drawing of your mama and me," he said, resettling her onto his lap. Suddenly his voice was small and shaky, his eyes wet. "You're gifted and beautiful, just like your mama, and one day you go'n be famous. Your papa go'n see to it."

Sunday snuggled in closer. That sadness in Papa's eyes—as though he dragged a big dark secret behind him whenever he spoke pretty words about Mama—didn't show up often. But each time it happened, it pulled hard at Sunday's feelings.

"Time to worship," he said as Mama quickly placed a greasy butcher knife in the dishwater basin, the tang of the bacon slabs she'd fried and served earlier still hanging in the tiny space of the kitchen.

"I'll wash it later," she mumbled to herself. Mama forced a smile. The one she used when she was nervous. "William, I wouldn't worry overmuch about all those slave speculator rumors running around. We've been on this spot of land for a good many years now, and not a single white man—except a few poor ones who tried to use their color to demand we sell—has set foot out here unless he truly wanted to buy something."

Papa frowned. Shot a rare mean look at Mama. "You sure about that, Sadie?"

Mama seemed scolded, like a naughty puppy. "Well ... that is ... *nearly* none."

Sunday studied her mother's words. Decided there was no

real trouble hiding in Papa's rather harsh correction. Summed it up as another one of those odd grown-folks things that happened every so often.

Contentment flooded Sunday as her mother slid into her special chair—the most beautiful piece Papa had ever carved—and waited for his special after-breakfast Sabbath prayer. There was no church for blacks out here, so Papa made his own. Sunday bowed her head. Mouthed the words along with her father.

"Most Holy One, we thank you for this Sabbath Day. A day after which my sweet girl here was named. A day in which we celebrate the gift of freedom which you have bestowed upon us."

He halted, throwing Sunday's silent recital out of rhythm. His voice trembled through the next part of the prayer.

"And, Father, we pray once more and again for our sisters and brothers out yonder not yet free, believing and knowing it's go'n happen one of these days. 'Til then, we remain your humble servants. Amen." Sunday's mama bustled up from the table, her voice full of its own weepiness.

"Mercy. I've got okra to cut before that sun gets too hot." She poured Papa a second steaming cup. Dabbed her eyes with her apron bib and enfolded her family with a quick hug. "Don't know what's taken hold of me." She swept up her garden basket and flew out the back door as Sunday pointed toward the basin on the work table.

"Mama done forgot her butcher knife."

Papa's shoulders shook with laughter. "Yep. Forgot to wash it too. When that garden of hers hits your mama's mind—"

Pounding, sharp and sudden, shut down Papa's laugh. "Horse's hooves. Who'd be wanting chairs made bad enough to come way out here on a Sunday?"

As abruptly as the sound rose, it ceased. Whinnying, mixed with Mama's "hello," struck through the silence.

"Yes, sir. What can we do for you?"

Sunday's stomach tumbled. Mama's voice was as thin and uncertain as Papa's had been moments ago. Was she still upset over Papa's correction?

"Where's your man?"

The words from the stranger were question words, but the sound was scary. Demanding. Papa's body stiffened underneath Sunday.

"A white man. Doesn't sound too friendly either."

Sunday had never met a white man in her life, Papa always making certain she was kept out of sight when he did his chair-making business. Fresh cup still in his hands, he nearly pushed her from his lap. He grabbed the greasy knife from the dishwater. Slid it into his shirt.

"Stay here. Don't move unless I say so."

"Papa?" She folded the sketch and slid it into the pocket Mama had stitched onto her dress. "Papa?"

Curiosity outstripping Papa's orders, she hovered in the shadow of the doorway and peered across the small grassless yard. Funny. The rider hadn't even bothered to tie his horse. Papa stepped off the porch and faced the man. Why had Papa said the man was white when he was clearly the loudest shade of pink Sunday had ever seen? Her insides took another dive. She couldn't tell what, but something was bad wrong.

"Help you, sir? Needing some chairs built today?"

"Ain't interested in none of your fancy chairs."

Papa said nothing. Just continued to stand with the coffee cup in his hand. The pink sweating man pulled something from his belt—a foreign looking thing with a handle and a short shiny pole pointing straight at Papa.

"I've got no personal quarrel with you, but you've been playing the big nigra long enough—building out here in the middle of nowhere, selling fancy made chairs like a white man. Mr. Duval is needing boys like you to work the tobacco fields over at Duval Plantation. I've been offered a right nice sum to haul you and your woman out there. And I intend to deliver."

Papa gestured toward one of his fine-looking rocking chairs at the edge of the porch. "'Fraid you got the wrong fella. Like you yourself said, I make chairs for a living. I'm a freeborn man. I don't work without pay. Don't try to hide that from anybody."

The man's laugh was clipped. "Free? Don't you know there ain't no such thing as a free black man in this country? Now put down that cup and let's go."

Papa continued to hold the cup—not loosely as he had at the table but with a death grip that made Sunday want to visit the outhouse. But she couldn't, not when the smell of fear had overpowered the bacon, nailing her to the spot.

"There's been some kind of mistake here. My wife and I have lived on this land nigh on to eight years."

"Not interested in your li'l make-believe nest out here nor how long you've lived in it."

From beneath his collar, the man produced a chain with a set of open circles at either end. *Click, click.* He fingered the handle of the metal pole.

"Put the cup down and turn around. No foolishness now, or I'll have to—"

"Nooooo!" Mama's scream echoed across the yard. "Don't let him do it, Lord!"

Now. It was time for Sunday to do something. She opened her mouth. Tried to warn Mama of the horse. But the words cowered inside, mute and cold as a log of green firewood.

"Don't hurt my husband. Please." Mama's tiny body hurtled toward the pink-white man like a falling star.

"Sadie, no. Stay back."

A fire curled the edges of Sunday's stomach as the horse whinnied and reared. Eyes flashing alarm, the animal pawed the air, the same space Mama was flying headlong into while Sunday's toes gripped the floor. *Thud.* Mama hit the ground, her eyes staring at the sky. Fixed in shock as though she'd never before seen the rising sun.

My mama.

A scream tried to push past the terror lodged in Sunday's throat, as Papa flung the coffee into the white man's face. Yelping like a scalded dog, the man dropped the metal pole as Papa pulled the knife from his shirt. Walking backwards towards Mama, he waved it toward the intruder.

"Get off my land, or you won't live to ride another day."

Papa knelt at Mama's side, just before the man bent toward the ground and grabbed the handle to his shiny pole.

Papaaa!

Papa turned. In a stretch of seconds, Sunday watched her father join her mother in the dirt, their faces to the sun, blood pumping from Papa's head faster than a body could milk a cow. Finally, Sunday moved from the shadows, the latent screams bursting forth like a spring freshet. Clear. Cold.

"Mamaaa! Papaa!"

Water and waste from her convulsing body made their way down her legs, Mama's words in hot pursuit.

"Remember, honey. Big girls don't soil their pants."

Sunday halted the screams. Breathed relief. That's what Mama would say when she woke up—when she and Papa got better and everything turned back to the way it was minutes ago.

Big girls don't soil their pants. Big girls don't ...

And if they should happen to do so now and again, they certainly didn't go outside wearing them. Slamming the door shut, Sunday flew toward the bedroom in search of fresh underpants.

Yes. That's what Mama would say. She'd be proud of Sunday when she woke up. Wouldn't she?

PART I

1

Thou shalt have no other gods before me.
~ Exodus 20:3

Saturday, March 16, 1861
Duval Plantation
A county on the southern border of Virginia

Sunday Duval rushed along the edge of the tobacco fields toward the door of her cabin, her son July in her arms, her husband Noah speaking too close to her ear.

"You don't understand, Sunny. I need you to trust me."

"Trust you?"

Had this man been sleeping on the same pallet with her for over three years, and still didn't know Sunday Pennington Duval trusted no one? Stepping over the threshold, she rounded on Noah. Glared up at him with all the defiance in her arsenal. She knew what he wanted, all right. Vowed she would never give it to him.

"It ain't about trust, Noah. I just won't do it."

Even suggesting such a thing was past what she could

understand. He knew what a homebody she was. Knew she'd not ventured from her world of field and cabin since she was six. Not even—for reasons too painful to admit—to mount the back steps of the big house. Why, then, was he asking her to join something as far-flung and cloudy and shapeless as the Underground Railroad? The very idea struck fear to Sunday's soul causing her to press the soft wool of July's head to her throat.

"And I plan for them to be my final words on the matter."

Squinting past her husband toward the westering sun, she looked out onto the dead tobacco fields that had been her life for so many years. She gathered her child closer. Moved deeper into the cabin. Waited and hoped for Noah's usual gentle concession to her demands, so that her life could regain its pulse of backbreaking work and loving July. And more back-breaking work.

But Noah didn't budge.

"Well? You go'n just stand there like a dumb oak 'til this time next week? Shut the door."

He didn't blink. Just held his place filling the doorway, giving free course to every bug in Virginia to invade her nest. The shock at her blunt refusal had marred his good-looking face which she knew every female fieldworker on Duval Plantation secretly wanted to touch. It was a wonder she hadn't gotten caught up in the sheer beauty of the man. But it had never been possible, since she'd married him for one reason and one reason only. To conceive July.

Her son. The only real joy she'd experienced since Mama and Papa. A joy trapped between the moment she had first laid her soft eager baby to her breast and that dreaded day when she would look at him and know he had become old enough for Handley Duval to sell.

Snatching the dusty rag from her head, she settled her son onto the dirt floor. She placed the smooth wooden ball Noah had made for him into his hand and locked eyes with her sweat-drenched husband.

"I ain't got no more time for this kind of addlebrained talking, Noah. I got to fix supper."

"Don't fix none for me. I got a sore throat."

Ignoring him, she removed a sack from behind the fire pit. Examined the last of this week's meal allowance. Poured the meal into her only frying pan. Long-buried horrors from her past popped and sizzled inside her head like the rancid hog fat she'd already used the last of. Bright pink and purple, the only two colors she despised, swarmed her brain. Muddled her thoughts. Tried to lock her tongue. *Am I about to fall dumb again?* As she'd been for years when she was an orphaned child living with Miss Tullie.

Wrong word. She had never been dumb. It had simply become too painful to talk.

"What in the world ails you, Sunny? Don't you even want to be free?"

Reminded of Papa's words, she winced at the accusation lurking in Noah's question. "Oughn't every drop of black blood in these United States be running toward a chance at freedom?" Papa used to say.

No, Papa. The image of her baby being snatched from some "railroad" wagon and thrown to a pack of howling dogs splayed itself across Sunday's mind. Stiffened her resolve. Sealed her lips until hopefully Noah would hush.

"I asked you a question, Sunny. And I ain't go'n be put off no more. Do you or don't you want us to have a new life of freedom—me, you, and July?"

A long, tired sigh escaped Sunday's chest. Eleven of her twenty-one years, she had known Noah Duval—gathered in tobacco from the fields with him, received the same rotten rations with him. Savored the night skies with him. Finally agreed before God and the other slaves to be his wife. Yet never once had she told him what she really thought about this thing called freedom—how it had deceived her, cowed her at those crucial minutes when she should have done something to save her mama and papa, jerked her around for five whole days afterward, until she'd landed at the brink of crazy and stayed there for years. Until Miss Tullie's kindness coaxed her tongue loose. After a back-wrenching day of clearing the final bit of land Handley Duval owned for a new tobacco field, the last thing she wanted to discuss was freedom.

Setting aside the idea of supper for a while, Sunday scooped her son up from the floor while Noah pressed a hand to his throat. A frisson of worry caused her to grip July. She backed up toward a bench against the wall of the cabin. Lifted her gaze to the space separating her from July's father.

"Noah, you feeling po'ly?"

Noah took a moment. Sized her up. "This about Silas, Sunny?"

Mr. Silas, he meant. Somehow things seemed always to crawl back around to that lowdown murderous man who stood between Handley Duval and the other slaves like a barely disguised sinkhole.

"You scared he'll find out and send Massa's hounds after us? 'Cause if that's all it is, you got to remember it won't be just us out there by ourselves fighting men like Silas. There's conductors and stations and—"

"Stop it, Noah. Will you just stop with all this railroad talk? Naw, it ain't Silas what's holding me back. Ain't seen that rascal for a while now. Wouldn't be scared of him if I did." *Lie.* Handley Duval's black driver had sparked fear in her since the days of that dreadful scarecrow.

But Silas didn't know that, and neither did Noah.

"Well if it ain't Silas, what's troubling you? What can a man do to make you understand that this our time, girl? Tomorrow night might be the only chance we ever get to leave this place. Make a better life for July."

"So you asking me to just pull up roots overnight? Strike out without even much 'lowing him to say bye to Miss Tullie who loves him nearly as much as I do? You'd ask me to do that to her, good as she's been to us?"

Noah rearranged himself in the door space, one hip leaned into the frame, his brow drawn into a scowl that disturbed her. "So now it's go'n be all about Mama Tullie, huh. Well, you might as well know. I already talked to her. She's all for us leaving."

Sunday pressed July into her chest until he whimpered. "I can't do it. I just can't."

Noah slammed shut the shabby vertical boards he had fashioned into a door, his steps eating up the space between them in three long strides. He leaned into Sunday with violent urgency she'd not seen before.

"Can't or won't?"

He pointed back toward the rope-hinged door that had crept back open, his half forefinger trembling with anger. Why had he never told her what happened to his fingers? Why had she never asked?

"Didn't I just explain to you, coming from the field, how all this works? These railroad folks want to help us. Free us. But it's got to be now, Sunny. Now!" His eyes settled back into a plea. He stepped away. Tamped down his voice.

"They ain't got time for this kind of foolish fence-riding, Sunny. Too many other slaves waiting in line. They know what they doing. Been doing it for years."

Turning away from her, he paced the cabin in long strides. His excitement building, charging the close space like lightning strikes. Desperation bled through every word. He stopped. Squatted before her and July.

"These white folks, they got it all laid out, just where they go'n take us and how they go'n get us there. Stations, they call them. Places where all different kinds of folks—rich and poor, farmers and city folk—hide whole families like me and you and July along the way. All the way up yonder to Canada."

Canada? Where in the world was that?

Noah's eyes continued to beg for what his mouth had stopped short of. The one thing she knew he'd craved these many years. Love. Sunday's heart tried to stutter into some uninvited feeling of warmth. She wouldn't allow it.

"Why it got to be tomorrow? Is there something you ain't telling me? Something I don't want to know? Who is these white folks you talking about, Noah? And if all you say be true and everything be lined up so easy like that, how come more slaves haven't left Duval Plantation long time ago—?"

"Don't chu go against me on this one, Sunny."

There it was in varying shades of purple. That hint of rage she'd seen while they'd walked from the fields, lurking at the edges of her husband's speech. Threatening the way she'd painfully set things up in her cabin all these years.

"You don't know how many nights I've spent thinking about this. Dreaming about how it would feel to make sure July grow up into a free man ..."

"One day you go'n be famous, Sunday. Your papa's go'n see to it ..."

Lies. All lies.

"Now, at last, I got me the push I been waiting for. I need you to be with me on this."

Noah slumped onto the bench next to her, leaned his head back against the wall—the pleading in his eyes now outrage as he massaged one of the finger stumps.

"If I don't take this chance for freedom, no telling what I might do to Handley Duval this very night. You hear me? No telling. I got that Nat Turner feeling on me, and it just ain't no telling."

Sunday sat forward. "You in some kind of trouble?"

"The leaving—I hadn't planned on it quite so soon. But something serious done come up. I got to leave. Right away."

"How come?"

One of the men in the field passed a word on to me today. Said Duval's land is just about wore out."

"Yeah? And?"

"Money done dried up. Might have to sell most of his slaves if he don't turn a profit soon. That's why he had you women out helping us clear the new field."

Moisture trickled alongside Sunday's neck down into her bosom. Somehow, she'd always known this day would come when she would have to choose between her husband's desires and her son's future. And, Lord help her, she'd always known which one would win.

"What? Why didn't you say that up front 'stead of all this talk about freedom?"

"'Cause the whole thing is about freedom, woman! Duval done already sold me to a speculator from up north. Said he's losing money on the sale, but he figured I'd bring him the best price of the lot of us men he still owned. It's just a matter of hours 'fore the man come looking to claim me." Sunday's arms slacked away from her son.

"Aw, Noah, naw."

"Just so happens I heard at the hush meeting that some-body from the Railroad go'n be near your creek 'round midnight tomorrow. Might not be back for months. Said the fellow'd be able to take up to eight passengers. Plenty 'nough room for me and you and July." Noah stroked his knuckles along July's cheek then pointed toward the top of the cabin. "Don't you see, Sunny? Somebody up there looking out for us."

God. He was talking about God again. Noah and Miss Tullie —always bringing Him up at the worse possible times. Sunday wasn't of a mind to hear anything about God tonight—the very

One who, when she was still on Papa's knee, had shown her just how treacherous freedom really was.

She searched her husband's profile. Despite how firmly she'd rejected his railroad idea, her heart was wooed. Noah Duval was a good man. Working twice as hard as any slave on the plantation, trying to get around the very thing that was about to happen—the auction block. He deserved better.

Better than you. Maybe. But that ingredient didn't belong in this mixing bowl of troubling thoughts.

In a stretch of seconds, she measured and weighed everything out in her mind. July was everything to her. The love of her life. She couldn't risk it. Simply could not. She felt a piece of herself detach as she watched her thoughts quickly form into a lie.

"Now you listen to me, Noah Duval. Me and July, we go'n be all right. We got Miss Tullie, and we got each other. You go on ahead with the white abolitionist. I want you to—truly I do."

She tapped Noah's forearm. Shushed a squirming July. Every nerve in her body strained under the weight of the treachery. Rarely had she lied to Noah outright. Never about anything this big, not even about her feelings for him when he'd begged her to marry him ...

"I ain't so sure about that thing y'all call love."

"Tell you what. I'll—me and July—we'll just catch the next 'train' that comes around. When you reach freedom land, you can wait for us. Then we'll all go to Canada together. How about that? That sound good to you? Just tell me where to look for you, and we'll be coming along 'fore you know it."

Noah opened his eyes. Bolted up straight. He rubbed his palms against the ragged britches covering his muscular thighs. "Going from station to station on the Underground Railroad ain't quite that simple. From what I hear, there ain't just no one or two routes. I can't tell you what the folks who run this train got planned nor where I'm go'n be at a particular time."

"I know, I know. But I'm strong and I'm well and we can do it, me and July. We'll find you soon as July gets well."

"Gets well? What's wrong with my son?"

"Oh, nothing much." That part of Sunday she still owned wondered how these lies were coming so fast. "Just a little fever last night, like young'uns will have. I didn't wake you, and Miss Tullie said not to tell you. Said a big good-looking hardworking man like you didn't need to hear every time his young'un take a head cold."

She held her breath, the balls of her feet tingling with fear and another feeling she'd not been touched by since July's birth. Hoping Noah was desperate enough to believe her, she startled when he laughed at the flirtatious words that sounded so much like Miss Tullie. He exhaled deeply, his eyes lighting up with hope.

"I don't know. But as I think on it, it might just work." Sunday bit her lip. Nodded for him to continue.

"I hear tell of folks who so caught up in wanting to help free slaves they actually come back down to get a man's family." He turned to look at her, cupped July's face. "Sunny, if y'all willing to do exactly what I tell you—"

"I will. I'll do anything you say."

She listened as he explained who it was that had put him on to this chance to escape, someone from another plantation who attended those hush harbor meetings. Noah would ask the man to keep her informed about the next opportunity. He would work hard to learn the railroad system and who would be coming back this way. And with God on his side, when he made it to a free state, he'd send word to her. Then he'd wait.

"I'll wait forever if I have to, Sunny, 'til you and July come. No matter how long it takes, I'm go'n wait—try to see if I can hear tell of us a little place somewhere in Canada where I can start my own woodshop and July can have a little yard to play in."

She watched the flicker of hope light Noah's eyes again as he searched her face for a reaction. Hoping it was enough to satisfy the longing she saw, she managed another smile. "I reckon that's a good plan, Noah."

"And in the meantime, you'll watch out for Silas, all right? You know that old lusty hound dog been after you since you was twelve." She smiled at Noah's description.

"I can handle Silas."

But knowing she had no intention of ever joining Noah in Canada or anywhere else, she put a label on that other feeling she'd been gripped by a moment ago.

Shame.

The same helpless shame she had felt when she'd just stood there and watched Papa and Mama die in the advancing sun.

2

Sunday night, March 17, 1861

Noah squatted behind a tree near the placid stream Sunday had always claimed as her own. His throat hurt from a developing cold. His very earlobes seemed weighted. He was that tired—that heightened—straining to hear the wagon wheels which would change his life. He didn't doubt it would be a wagon because Mama Tullie, who'd been the one to alert him to this chance, had told him so ... well ... at the least, she'd said *maybe*, and he'd not known the no-nonsense, nearly blind old woman to be wrong about a whole lot of things. Still, she had emphasized, maybe.

Maybe you go'n end up walking like you did the first time you run away.

Suddenly yesterday's argument with Sunday—the certainty with which he had described the workings of the Railroad—struck him as puny. Far-fetched. Misgivings about the whole idea of a white "conductor" who cared about him swooped down like a starving buzzard pecking away at his entrails.

"What chu really know about these people, man?" Noah

had taken to whispering to himself in order to stay alert. "What white man have you ever knowed to do such a thing?"

He cracked his knuckles—a habit Sunny hated—nearly losing his balance. He shook his head. "Uh-uh. Too late to think like that."

He righted himself. Shifted from one of the many cramped positions he'd held for hours. Wondered if he should stand up for a while and stretch. He settled on squatting as the wisest way to mask his height while remaining ready to flee at a moment's notice. For the last twenty-four hours, Noah had waged war against sleep. Gut clenched the whole time. Brain constantly making the lap around the bloody memory of Handley Duval's "Reclaiming" Noah's thirteen-year-old self after he had run away and stayed gone for five years. He thumbed over one of his hacked-off fingers. Remembered the countless remaining scars.

"I ain't going back to that reclaiming again. Rather be put up under the dirt first ... What the—"

He jumped at the scurrying sound of an animal he reckoned ought to be asleep somewhere this time of night. "Get hold of yourself, man. You ain't no pitiful boy like you was back then." After tonight, Duval would just be a rotten memory. "Nobody go'n ever make you do nothing again, save the Lord and yourself. That's it. Steady now. Just try to keep your mind out of the ditch and on the middle of that road there. Ain't this what you been praying for all your life?"

Truth told, that failed attempt at the age of eight—along with the shattered promise Noah had made to his five-year-old cousin Clayton to return for him—had become a double-barreled gun blasting Noah at each sunrise ever since. Where was Clayton now? Was he still alive, and did he even much remember Noah?

Bits of Noah had died over his failure to free Clayton until all that was left was a fistful of well-contained rage. Lord, how he had needed to talk to someone about his little cousin. Speak to someone of the unspeakable.

"Why did I never tell Sunny?"

His eyelids drew down of their own volition, teasing him with the idea of a five-minute nap, only to fly open to another barrage of old thoughts. Memories dragged him back between the tobacco rows that night sixteen years ago in '45 when he made his first run for freedom. The wonder of finally escaping Handley Duval's whip. The ecstasy of fleeing. The hope that he would soon return for Clayton. Then the hunger that made him crazy after a few days of vicious insects and vengeful snakes and polluted water. The glare of a strange tall white man's lantern, scalding Noah's eyes—*"Wonder who he belongs to, honey?"* A religious man who, as it turned out, was kind enough, housing Noah for five years.

Until the Reclaiming from Massa Duval—a beating so raw that Noah reckoned himself to have joined Mama Tullie's heavenly angels in some kind of blue twilight. The utter humiliation of having his nakedness dragged back to the Duval plantation behind a horse. Then the scorching despair when the hope that little Clayton still waited for him was snuffed out.

Noah slapped away a mosquito. Shuddered. His large calloused hands clammy from the memory, his brain shouting new accusations of a second desertion.

Is it true? Is that what I'm doing? Dumping Sunny and July?

"Naw. Naw, t'aint. I ain't shaking off Sunday and July with the same kind of promise I made to Clayton. They could've come if they'd a mind to." And why was he talking about them as though they were one? His son had no say in this.

Noah searched the heavens for the time. *Past midnight.* Sunday would have long since put July to bed after acting out one of her many made-up stories with their son on her lap. It was a sight he never tired of, so tender it made him weep from time to time.

Sweat ran between his shoulder blades at the thought of how much he would miss them—how many times he had already left them alone, pretending to seek God at the hush harbor, when what he was really after was news of someone's successful run.

He swallowed down a determined yawn. Forced his eyeballs to search the woods once more. Had the conductor changed his mind? Noah hadn't attended the meeting last night. Instead, he'd sat up all night with the child in his arms, trying to satisfy himself that July's mysterious fever was gone. Thankfully, it hadn't flared. Thigh muscles aching like a rotted tooth, he adjusted his squat once more. Had Mama Tullie somehow gotten wrong the meeting place? Doubt pressed into his chest like the hooves of a beast.

"Wonder what it's go'n feel like to give yourself over to a strange white man when all your life you been fighting against doing just that?"

Something cold and firm—a metal pipe if he'd had to guess—pressed against the nape of his neck. He froze at the sound of a woman's voice.

"Well, you ain't apt to find out tonight, is you? Now, say the name."

Relief rushed from Noah's lungs at the voice he knew as well as his own. It had been a while since he'd heard it, but unless the last two days of sleepless nights had scuttled his brain more than he imagined, that voice belonged to—

"What's the name, I say?"

He scrambled to remember the code name Mama Tullie had whispered to him hours earlier. It was a Bible name. That much he knew.

Midian? Simeon? Goshen? The barrel dug deeper into his neck, rescuing his flailing memory.

"Gideon."

The woman said nothing. Simply continued to push the

gun against his neck. Must be trying to decide if he'd taken too long to answer. His dreams of freedom being rapidly sucked up by the threat of the barrel, Noah decided to take a chance.

"Miss Maggie?"

"What chu say?" The woman stepped around to face him, a look of surprise and a touch of fear showing up even in the darkness. She motioned toward him with the pistol's barrel. "Git to your feet, boy. How you know my name?" Noah willed his sore muscles to push him to his feet.

"I'd know your voice anywhere, Miss Maggie. Me and Clayton, we took enough biscuits from your hands when we was young'uns to feed Pharaoh's army." The renewed stretch of quiet unnerved Noah. Made him wonder if memory had failed him. A line of perfect white teeth pierced the darkness.

"Li'l Noah? That you? Aw, yeah, yeah! Ain't you a sight for the sore eye, though? And if the darkness ain't foolin' these old peepers, you done turned into some kinda good looker too."

A big soft squeeze followed, gun dangling from Miss Maggie's hand. Noah felt the heat of embarrassment. Sometimes—especially at a moment like this when a likely loaded gun hung around his neck while he was trying to escape a lifelong hell like Duval's plantation—he wished women wouldn't take such notice.

"Uh, thank you ma'am."

"Reckon I ain't see'd you over a half-dozen times since Handley brung you back some years ago."

True. And thank God the quarters had been built a good ways down from the big house which Noah, until this moment, had thought Miss Maggie never left. After the horror of the Reclaiming, he rarely went near the place, not even for the celebrations allowed at Christmas and the Fourth of July. Not even to sample Miss Maggie's cooking. Sunday and July—the cabin and the whittling knife Handley Duval had dropped during the Reclaiming—that was enough plantation life for Noah until he could make another try at freedom.

"I often wondered what become of li'l Clayton. Looked around one day and he was gone, just like when you took off. Everything about his leaving was hush-hush too. Everybody scared to mention it, same as with yours."

Panic eclipsed the embarrassment of a moment ago. How would he go about voicing to this good woman why he had failed Clayton, without crushing the flimsy will he clung to in order to leave his wife and child? A twig snapped a few feet away erasing all thoughts of everything except survival. He shoved Miss Maggie behind him, one of his truncated fingers spitefully shooting back and forth with the memory of the Reclaiming.

"What's the trouble here?"

Another woman? This one, Noah was sure he'd never heard. He angled toward the side of the tree, Miss Maggie side-stepping his unspoken directions. But the strange woman was already upon him—a stealthy litheness about her, the likes of which he had never witnessed. Slave? Indian? Slave *and* Indian? Even in the darkness, it was easy to see she was beautiful, but she sounded neither black nor red. The question came before he could stop it.

"Who you—?"

"Beg pardon, Miss Gideon." Maggie interrupted, her answer directed toward the tiny woman, her hale voice reduced to sheepishness.

Gideon? He had thought that the code word. What kind of crazy name was that for a woman?

"When I saw it was Noah, here, I got kind of carried off by years gone by. Forgot for a minute how well you keep things on track." She let loose a robust laugh. "I slipped this boy and his cousin more of Massa's bread than Massa and his family could eat in a year. She passed the pistol to the woman called Gideon. "Put your mind to ease 'bout this one. He ain't no colored spy trying to trip us up like old Silas been rumoring about and doing all these years." Noah took a step. Stumbled at the mention of Silas Duval's name. The stranger seemed not to notice as she questioned Miss Maggie.

"Where are the other passengers? I was led to believe there would be at least five."

"Don't know. Probably all this talk about secesh and war done scared 'em off. But that shouldn't keep y'all from being on your way." Miss Maggie chuckled. "Just keep this one fed good, and he be all right."

Say what? Follow a woman? One who sounded like she'd never even seen a slave before? Let alone rescued one. The story he'd heard once about somebody called Moses was one thing. This little pretty-pretty was something else. Noah's shoulders tightened. He would be shot before he let himself be sold again ... *but I ain't about to follow no li'l skinny woman either.* He backed up toward Sunny's stream thinking he would make a run for it across the creek if he had to. It wouldn't be the first time. He held up his hand.

"W-wait a minute. Where the real conductor at?"

"You're looking at her, sir. Now let's go."

The conductor. This little sapling-switch of a woman, who talked like she ought to have her own big house, was one of the conductors in this big undertaking called the Underground Railroad?

"You crazy? Go where? And where's that wagon we was promised?"

"I don't know anything about a wagon, but I can tell you this. With the war looming, the train probably won't be back soon. You have five minutes to make up your mind." She raised the pistol to hip level. "And if you decide to go, there'll be no turning back."

Noah said nothing. Being told what to do sounded too much like another form of slavery.

"I learned that principle from Moses. I find it works. I'll shoot you myself before I allow you to turn back and jeopardize the chance for others."

Noah stared at the woman, continuing to size her up as much as the night would allow. He turned his back to her—and Maggie, who'd gone stone cold quiet—and looked out into the darkness beyond the stream. He could probably carry this so-called conductor across his shoulder as easily as a tobacco sheaf. And she was supposed to protect *him*?

"Your time has expired, sir."

Still holding the gun, the conductor spoke to Miss Maggie in low-pitched tones of instruction then gathered her into a quick embrace, Noah listening intently. *They've done this before.*

The woman turned and walked along the stream. So noise-lessly until had Noah not caught a whiff of her tempting scent, he might have thought her a ghost. He could not have explained it if she had put the gun to his ear. But in that moment, he saw strength. He decided to trust this little whisper of a woman with his life, at least for a while. He had to leave this place, and he reckoned one reckless chance was as good as another. Somehow, he would get his family back. If not with this train, then another. He would not fail Sunny and July as he had Clayton. He fell in step behind a woman whose real name he didn't even know yet. Turned to take a step back.

"Miss Maggie?"

"What is it, child?"

"Could you be watching for word from me, so's you could let my wife—her name Sunday—know where I be settled?" The older woman flashed her unforgettable smile.

"I know Sunday, leastways I know her story."

"And say bye to Mama Tullie for me."

"Sir, we have miles to cover before the dawning is upon us."

"Coming."

Noah smiled into the darkness. *Man, I wish I could learn to talk like this here woman.* He hesitated. Glanced over his shoulder one last time.

Wonder what *was* his wife's story—the whole story? Dread of something other than Handley Duval's dogs struck him. He'd not pushed hard enough to find out.

Now, there's a fair chance you ain't never go'n know.

3

Sunday March 24, 1861, just before sundown

The buckets were placed next to her ankles as Sunday stood before her little creek, about to collect the water for July's bath. Thankfully, *Mr.* Silas Duval—nasty old wrinkled rascal who had already started worrying her about moving in with her—had been sent into another county for a few days, affording her the safety to escape for a few minutes to the stream she had named after herself years ago. The Sunday Stream.

But how I'm go'n keep fending Silas off when he do get back?

She quickly filled her buckets and turned back toward the grove of slippery elm where she'd left Mama's basket, full of herbs. Positioning it onto her head, she sensed another unwanted thought pushing its way past her lips into the advancing dusk.

"Wonder if Noah be needing some bark tea tonight for that sore throat of his?"

She wouldn't allow her mind to open the image of her

husband, dragged back to Duval Plantation by the posse that had volunteered to run him down.

"How dare that nigger try a trick like this," one of them had yelled outside her cabin door, "and him already paid for by the speculator."

Goodness. She tightened her grip around the bucket handles. Felt a rush of cool sweat along her ribcage. *Why you keep thinking 'bout Noah when you got July? Ain't this what chu wanted?*

"Don't know," she answered herself aloud. Sunday lived for these Sabbath evening twilight escapes when most of the other slaves, including Noah before he left, sneaked away to be with their God and left her alone with her creek, the only place where she could savor the idea of what she loved almost as much as she loved July—drawing pictures.

She lowered her pails back to the ground along with Mama's perfectly weaved basket, then walked back to drink in her own image shimmering in the water. Sunday had never so much as held a looking glass in her hand. But since her parents' death, this quiet-spoken stream had consistently mirrored her, showing her a gradually evolving face with hints of the same purple as the rest of her body. An offshoot of the family of hateful hues which covered that tight belfry space all those years ago, hours after Mama and Papa were killed.

Hateful. Yet for fifteen summers, Sunday had been willing to put up with this shocking wrong-side-out color of her face just to see the changes and to let her mind fly free at the end of every Sabbath. She lifted her head to the few bold stars above the horizon. What distant sky, at this very moment, might hold captive another woman or man with the same bloodline that had laid upon Sunday's shoulders this wonderful burden to draw pictures? She smiled. One thing was for certain. No matter the origin of the desire to draw, her outward self was all Mama's.

You the spit of your mama. Not a speck of poor Papa's looks about her.

Thin arms spread like dragonfly wings, she backed away from the stream. Twirled around and around. Closed her eyes and painted herself in swaths of the bold yellows, reds, and oranges her brain had borrowed moments ago from the dying sun. She fashioned herself queen of her long-deceased mother's land, a painting tool of some kind in her hand. She slowed. Shrugged her shoulders as a string of giggles popped out like a rash.

"Queen, my foot. You too scared to even look toward the big house let alone be somebody's queen."

In truth, Sunday had mostly stripped her mind of such dizzying dreams—both the hand-clapping, foot-stomping hush-harbor religion that offered freedom in the by-and-by *and* that here-and-now kind of liberty freedom that Noah and the other slaves so craved. Until a week ago when Noah's probing words, "Don't you want to be free?" had found feeling in a nerve Sunday thought was dead. Why, oh why, did he have to haul off like that and mark up her carefully drawn picture of a world hopeless of respect for her and her kind?

She sighed into the stillness that swallowed up the cricket sounds. She rebalanced the basket of herbs onto her head as Mama had taught her and reached for her pails. Time she got back to the cabin before the path home turned as dark as her thinking. Further, she needed to get back to July whom she had loosely tied to the cabin's bench leg while he napped. Miss Tullie had offered many times to take him to worship with her on these Sunday evenings, but Sunday would never allow her child inside that world of empty hope that had landed her bare backside on a pink-white man's horse, when she was but a baby herself, and ultimately into a lonely purple belfry to "consider her ways."

A wayward thought chilled Sunday's blood. July might

wriggle loose from the cabin bench or ... *What if Silas come back early and find my baby by his self and ...*

"Naw, now. None of that ain't happening."

Shaken by this new downturn in her thinking, she pushed her bare feet up the slope and onto the path leading back to the row of slave cabins. Fear dogged her steps, urging her to scan the pathway she had traveled countless times. Snakes, anthills —most anything—could latch onto her feet—

"Ouch!"

Stubbing her toe against a root as familiar as July's cry, she pitched forward—the basket tumbling to the path. Prized herbs and worrisome thoughts alike scattering to the wind. She fought to keep from losing her handle on the sloshing pails. Then felt a roughened hand lustily intrude upon her waist from behind.

"Take your hands off me!"

"Evening to ya, li'l pretty."

Silas. Black slave driver and spy for the Duval Tobacco Plantation—his whip coiling against the band of his grimy pants— stepped around in front of her. "Help you with something?"

Sunday's brain ticked off the possibilities of true help. Noah? Gone. Miss Tullie and every other slave on Duval's plantation? Singing and shouting in a hush harbor miles away.

Face it, girl. She was alone in the woods with the nastiest vilest man between here and that big ocean to the east which she'd heard of but never would see.

You done for.

Dawn, the same day

NOAH WATCHED as Gideon settled onto her side, her slender body curled into itself, her back to him signaling a demand for privacy. Instantly she slept, last night's travel having been especially hard, blowing rain challenging their every step. A half hour earlier, he'd wondered out loud how she had known where they were headed without seeing the heavens. Munching on dried apples, she had slipped the now-familiar book from her pocket.

"Moses taught me," was all she answered. Where did she always find the strength to use the advancing daylight to read each morning before falling asleep?

The same way you would if you knowed the meaning of one single mark on a piece of paper.

Noah yawned. Stretched. So many things he wanted to know about this woman who refused to admit to any name other than that of Gideon from a Bible story. But now that the sun had bested last night's clouds, it was time for him, too, to sleep—though, he would take the time to study her a bit longer. She was so small, too tiny to be taking on something like this, yet she handled her assignment like a six-foot soldier. Intrigued by every inch of her, Noah had whispered her name before he knew it.

"Gideon."

As quickly as she'd fallen asleep, she was awake, pistol in hand. "Yes? What's the matter?"

Noah's insides shrank. What was he to say now? That he was studying her form while she slept?

"Nothing. Just wondering h-how you know when to say 'was' and when to say 'were.' What make you change up like that when you talking?"

Sunlight flecking her face as she lowered her weapon, she propped herself up on her elbow. Stared at him a long moment then smiled.

"Why, No-wuh, I didn't know you had an interest in grammar."

Noah. It was the first time she'd called him anything except sir, and the sound of it rang with a fresh exhilarating separateness he'd never felt before, as though the name was suddenly attached to a single person and not a piece of property. She pronounced it No-wuh, hitting both parts with equal strength.

"How many arms do you have, No-wuh?"

Noah's defenses flared. Did she think him completely stupid? "Two. Like most everybody else, I reckon."

"Yes. You have two arms which, by the way, you just counted."

Noah looked the other direction. In fact, when it came to ciphering, he *was* stupid. Wouldn't Gideon be shocked to know he could barely stumble to the number twenty? And that, only because he had listened for years to the counting of the barrels of tobacco for market each season.

"Truth is—"

She raised her hand to prevent him. "I know what you're thinking, but even counting to two counts." She laughed out loud at her own obviously unintended turn of phrase. "It's a start. And being able to know the difference between one and more than one is to know the difference between 'was' and 'were.' If you speak about one person or thing, you use 'was.' If you speak about two of more, you use 'were,' unless, of course, you're dealing with the word 'you.'"

He fell silent—his manhood a bit frayed by this unexpected schoolboy lesson. Intrigue aside, he didn't like feeling this exposed by a woman. Hadn't the Lord put women here to be cherished, protected, *taught*? The latter of which Sunday had never allowed him to do—not that he knew very much to teach.

But he'd never met a woman like Gideon. And at this moment, his longing to know was pushing past his pride.

"That easy, huh?"

"That easy."

A softness he'd not heard before had crept into her voice. She sat up straight, her unbound braids swaying with the quick movement. Suddenly, Noah wanted—needed—to run. To get away from this woman who overwhelmed his senses just by the toss of her hair. She jutted the tattered book in the air.

"I could teach you if you like—how to read and how to improve your speech." She scooted to his tree. Placed a soft palm over his fisted hand. Forced him to look into her eyes.

"Don't you want to learn to read?"

What ails you, Sunny? Don't you want to be free?

His words to his wife—that black-or-white, yes-or-no answer he had demanded a week ago—slammed into him like a wagonload of rocks. Might Sunday have had something in her past that kept her on the fence? Just as the idea of being taught by a woman was halting him now? Body heat outstripping that of the climbing sun, Noah struggled to make sense of this odd pull-and-push he felt toward Gideon, somewhere between attraction and trepidation.

"I'm thinking maybe the answer to your question ain't that easy to come by."

Yes, he wanted to read, almost as much as he wanted to breathe. But it wasn't quite so simple. He wanted knowledge, but he also wanted his pride. And the way Gideon was looking at him—the sultry way she called him No-wuh—it was mixing him up. Making him wonder if they were about to cross some kind of ungodly line.

"Gideon. I 'preciate what you trying to do, but I reckon I don't think we ought to—"

"Hush!" Noah could almost see Gideon's ears pricking up. "You hear that?"

Snatching her hand from atop his and resting it on her pistol, she switched into the terse fearless guide Noah had followed for days.

"I hear it."

The sounds of baying hounds bloomed from the southeast, not quite as terrifying as Noah's memory had stored them from years ago but strong enough to set his heart to racing. Gideon readied herself like a man of war.

"Here. Rub this asafetida on your feet."

He did as he was told, the pungent odor nearly taking his breath away. While Gideon quickly picked up every scrap of evidence and covered where she had lain with a new layer of sodden leaves, he finished getting into what was left of his shoes. Noah looked up and balked. Gideon was headed back in the direction from which they had come.

"You sure you know what chu doing? You was just bringing us from that way."

She spared him a moment's glare, all softness from minutes ago gone from her face. "I'm sure. And the clause you want is 'you were,' not 'you was.' Now move."

Noah fell to the path behind his guide. Now she'd really confused him with the "you was" lesson.

But whatever he had to swallow, for the short time he was with Gideon, he would learn all he could. Noah Duval was not going through the rest of his life being cut down simply because of the way he talked.

"NAW, Silas. You can't help me with nothing." Sunday tried bypassing him, but Silas was too quick. "And if you here again to try to talk me into letting you sleep with me just 'cause Noah ain't here—"

He shook her, one strong whiplash until she wondered if her neck bones had cracked.

"'*Mr.* Silas,' to you, and you best to be shutting up. For a woman who never been much of a talker, you sure is jabbering a lot since Noah left." Silas's eyes had turned deadly cold.

"I hates to be the one to bring this to you. But the overseer just laid it on me, so I'm bound to tell you."

"Tell me what?"

"Noah dead."

A heaviness settled in Sunday's legs, swirls of purple and deep blue sweeping away all the vibrancy of the sunset. She stooped to grip the handles of her pails and waited to see if her own heart was still beating or if she, too, had died.

"Now, just hold on there, li'l pretty. You done gone to trembling like—"

"Don't chu ... Git cho hands off me." She tried to breathe. Couldn't. Instead, she struggled toward the ability to think things through. A psalm from her years with Miss Tullie came unbidden. *"What time I am afraid, I will trust in thee ..."*

No—no, no. No Bible verses. She must think for herself. Mustn't let anybody decide for her. She would, in her own safe wisdom, not that of the hush harbor, think this through until she knew what to do. *When you most afraid, Sunday, you got to look way inside your own self.* She felt her lungs fill up again. Better. *All right, all right, then.* She relished the idea that her mind was surging with its own energy. *We cookin' now.*

"You a lie, Silas. Noah might be caught somewhere, but he ain't dead. I know he ain't. Not in no one-week's time. Not July's papa. He too smart to—"

"Shot. Before he even made it to the middle of Virginie. Thought I'd catch you whilst you having your own li'l upside down church service out here and everybody else gone to the *north* woods."

Sunday froze, his words tunneling into a sharp point. That's where Mama Tullie 'nem's group was meeting tonight. How did this devil know?

All these years, Silas had to have known there were meetings. The slaves had been careful, though, all the time scheming to throw him off. But something about the way he'd hit down on the word "north" scrambled Sunday's confidence. *He bluffing.* If Silas ever found out exactly where the slaves were worshiping, he'd tell the overseer as fast as his next breath. Which is why the poor Jesus-worshipers were always changing their meeting places.

"You one fine looking woman, Sunday. And the way I figure, now that Noah been kil't, you go'n need some strong, man-type company."

"You ain't got enough man left in you to count."

"Got more'n that buzzard-picked man of yours."

Sunday sucked in another heaping of air, willing herself to ignore the image of July's father's beautiful body left to the palates of buzzards. She could no more believe Silas than ...

But what if it was true? It was possible, after all, if the Underground Railroad was the big fuzzy unproven idea she believed it to be. Noah could be dead. Picked to the bone like Silas said.

And if he was, she'd had a hand in it.

It had been a week since Noah had sealed their separation with a cold kiss against her forehead and vanished into the dark. Why now was the idea of harm coming to him causing her to hold her breath as though it were her last?

You know you ain't never loved him. You just married him to get July.

Her legs. Not only did they feel like two logs of green firewood, but now her very soul seemed dragging behind her. As though it had been snatched from the colorfully wrapped body she'd envisioned minutes ago near the stream and pinned to the hem of her shift.

"Move out of my way, Silas. I ain't go'n stand here no longer, listening to this mess."

"It was really the dogs took up where the bullet in Noah's

head left off. Made hash out of him. If you don't believe me, I can get the overseer out here."

Surely the false god of freedom that she had tried to truce with all these years wouldn't injure her this way a second time, first causing her mama to try to reason with that white man then leading Papa to believe he could argue with him. Then sucking her husband into the belief that there was somewhere called Canada.

"So what chu complaining 'bout?" An accusing voice using her own speech whispered to her. *"Ain't this just what you expected? Maybe hoped for just a little bit when Noah left—so you'd be proved right?"*

Not like this. She hadn't wanted to be "right" like this. Hadn't wanted July's father dead. She took a step backward. Felt the buckets tremble. Forced a glaring look. *Just go'n have to leave Mama's basket.*

"I ain't trying to see no overseer, and I don't want to see no more of you. Git away from me, Silas. Right now." Silas moved in closer.

"Don't say things you'll be sorry for, li'l pretty. I can make life hard for you and that young'un of yours, or I can make it easy. I might even could get you out of the fields for good if you'd be willing to let me warm your bed ever now and then."

"I'd rather bed with a copperhead."

"Any more of your sass and you might have to."

Water leapt from the wooden pails Noah had made for her —one of the many first-year-married gifts he'd handcrafted for her—as she flung the icy liquid in Silas's face. A face that crawled sideways in a vindictive smile.

"'Fraid you done gone and crossed the line, li'l pretty. Can't nobody do that to old Silas and get away with it. Fact is, I'd show you right now how much man I got left if I didn't have to make a li'l appearance at that hush harbor."

Fear curled up inside her belly like a fat worm. For the first time since she'd seen Silas do what he'd done to that baby so long ago, Sunday's dread of him pushed through full-grown. She heard herself scream as she flew down the path, leaving in her wake the basket and buckets, along with a half-sneer she'd not soon forget.

4

S unday stared at the hush harbor. Struggled to even out her
breaths. Stroked July's back.

"Little fellow ain't good and woke yet," she whispered. Even
after she'd untied him from that bench and run through the
woods like a fire in a drought.

She laid her cheek to his forehead. Hot to the touch,
reminding her of the lie she'd sold Noah about July's being
puny. A chill seized her, as though trying to counter the spiking
heat of her son, but it was failing. Instead, the heat clung to her.
Lingering. *What I'm s'pose to do now?*

Only a few steps and she could be behind the quilts
warning the slaves about Silas. There'd been no difficulty in
finding her people. On any given Sunday, she knew where
these worshipers were. Though Noah never had, Miss Tullie
always told her of the place in case July or Sunday needed her.
And now Miss Tullie needed *her*.

But a vow was a vow. And Sunday Duval had vowed never
to cross the threshold of a place of worship again. Not after the
horror of her parents' death and the pain of the purple belfry.

She hoisted her little boy further up her side. Tucked his

damp forehead beneath her chin as her bare feet marked out little circles on the forest floor.

"July? You agree with me, honey?"

But then ... no telling what ugliness would happen if Silas brought that overseer out here, especially after Handley Duval had warned the slaves never to meet. No time. Nowhere.

The sound of an owl drew her attention, the screech mimicking Massa's raspy laugh. "At the least, he go'n beat the guts out of 'em. And po' Miss Tullie in there somewhere, blind as a bat. Probably praying her heart out about who-knows-what. She can't stand up under no more whippings. I got to warn them."

Her frantic words fell apart against a rising wind, the sudden angry gusts causing her thin shift to cling to the backs of her knees like a spanked child. Silas was near. She could smell him. She slipped farther back into the woods, every heartbeat pounding out Silas's footsteps.

Moans came in waves from behind the suspended quilts that marked the place of worship. Low slow barely discernible music, straight from the slaves' lips. That ageless pensive plea to their God that seeped into the marrow. The harmony might have split the moonless sky had it not been for the sodden tattered hangings spread over the poles of the temporary praying ground to keep the noised hushed. Sunday startled at July's voice.

"Ma-ma got to warm them?"

"'Warn,' baby. Not warm."

Her son whimpered. Nodded drowsily. "Uh huh. Got to warm Ma-ma Tullie. She cold."

The child's words stopped her. Moved her from indecision to another place. Made her realize just how much she didn't want Miss Tullie to ever be cold. Sunday thought of the time she'd been taken from a scarecrow field and thrown into the arms of the older woman—hot yet shivering from shock. Miss Tullie was younger then, her bosom warm and inviting.

"Where Mama Tullie? I want Mama Tullie." July's abrupt whining startled her.

"Shhh." She eased him to the other hip, fighting a budding resentment at his persistence these days in calling Miss Tullie "Mama." Yet it had been Miss Tullie who'd swung her up and kissed Sunday's finger that day. A child with a voice so utterly dead that Miss Tullie rejoiced when a splinter in her thumb brought about the little girl's first lusty cry since coming to Duval Plantation.

"I just hope I'm wrong. I just hope Silas don't know where—"

The sound of footsteps coming from the west pushed Sunday's attention toward the meeting, panic saturating every pore. Please. Please—

"Sun-dee? That chu, baby?"

Miss Tullie, her shrunken form shuffling and tapping its way across the flattened grass, called to her. How did this woman who had lost most of her sight over the last year continue to manage so beautifully? Sunday flew out of the woods. Stumbled into a small hole. Caught herself before she and July fell onto the old woman.

"How'd you know I was out here?"

Miss Tullie managed to hold her stance. "The Spirit told me."

The words soothed. Like a balm that at once burns and cools, the old woman's Bible words dulled the pain—brought back the countless times Sunday had climbed into Miss Tullie's lap during those years when she'd been so shocked by what freedom had done to her mama and papa that she didn't say a word for four years. *The Spirit's with you, Sugar,* Miss Tullie would say. Truth was, Sunday wanted to crawl into Miss Tullie's lap right now.

"He's really moving in there, honey. Why don't you come on in—see if He might move in you tonight?"

Eying the sagging quilts as July reached for the old slave who'd kept him since birth while she worked the fields, Sunday drew her son in closer.

"It's too tight up in there for me. A body wouldn't be able to breathe. Anyhow, I feel the spirit just fine. Right out here where I am." Miss Tullie grunted. Leaned heavily on her stick.

"You saying you done finally felt His presence?"

"No, ma'am. I reckon I ain't. Not in the way you mean. The spirit I feel comes from the beauty lying all around. Like the colors of the sun."

"And where you think them colors come from? Just happened up on their own? Remember, honey, you ain't allowed to have no other gods before you. That's God's law. Wrongheaded folks worship trees and rivers and sky and such." The older woman let that sink in. Straightened her spine. Touched her walking stick to Sunday's shoulder.

"Jesus loves you, honey. But He hates idols. He'll hurt cho feelings 'bout taking on idols 'stead of Him. Oh, yes, He will."

Miss Tullie had just laid down a warning. One so full of pain that Sunday nearly cried out. "Miss Tullie, I need to tell you something. I don't know how to say it 'cept Noah dead."

"Hush." The older woman lashed out at her with her cane then rattled on toward another subject as though Sunday had said nothing. "So much talk going on 'bout this secesh. White folks real mad. Some of 'em more scared than mad. The secesh, I tell you. That's what you need to be thinking 'bout. That's what everybody praying and moaning 'bout in there now. Trying to 'cern whether this be the time the good Lord go'n set us free."

The moans swelling from behind the quilts pulled Sunday back to the urgency. "Miss Tullie, you got to listen. The preacher. All y'all. Y'all need to be getting out of here quick. Silas on his way out here right now. You just said how scared white folks is these days. No telling what Massa Duval'll do if he catches y'all. And even if he don't, if Silas finds out, you as good as catched!"

Sunday handed July to Miss Tullie—a peace offering of sorts. She studied the earth and hugged herself. "I'm sorry I sprung that news of Noah on you like that. It's just that—"

"I don't believe it nohow. The Lord ain't ready for Noah yet, not in the way He ready for me. If you was tuned in to the Lord, you'd know that."

"Ma-ma?"

Sunday pivoted, the sound of July's voice at once steadying and unraveling her. Even in the dark, his eyes—the mold of his chin—his very self was a miniature Noah. Without another thought, she wrapped July and Miss Tullie in her arms, her world seemingly tilting upright as soon as the circle closed. This was where she belonged. Noah had been a good man. But it was July and Miss Tullie that truly mattered. She checked the tears threatening to overwhelm her.

"I did the right thing, Miss Tullie, didn't I? Staying here?"

"When the time is right," Miss Tullie's bony fingers gently tapped against her back, "the Lord will let you know." Sunday's hand slipped from the circle.

"Well, that'll be a change, now won't it? Since He ain't never cared enough to give me no kind of warning before—"

"Like I ain't warning you right now, lil pretty?"

"Mercy, Lord. Ha'mercy on us."

"Did you really think old Silas wasn't go'n track you?"

Miss Tullie took to humming, her voice mixing flawlessly with the mournful sounds coming from behind the quilts. Shaking out her hands as though flinging off a mat of bees, Sunday backed away from her baby and Miss Tullie. She tore the rag from her head. Began stripping herself of her slave-issue shift.

"Take me, Silas. It's me you want. Leave July and Miss Tullie be."

"No, ma'am!" Miss Tullie's voice turned dissonant, desperate. "I ain't raised you like that. I ain't raised you to be soiled by the likes of Silas Duval."

Silas seemed a bit stunned before nodding toward the woods—a hot, knowing leer overruling what he had obviously meant to be a smile. "Hur' up, then. We ain't got long."

Long before what? Had he already told Massa where these poor people were? Pain shot from her elbow as Silas wrenched her arm upwards behind her back and shoved her toward the thicket. "Just do like I say 'fore I lose my appetite."

No telling what Handley Duval would do to the slaves if he caught them out here. To hear Noah tell it, Massa could be more of an animal than his wife had been with that purple church.

"No, ma'am. No ma'am." Miss Tullie continued her lamentation. With her free arm, Sunday tried to nudge her back.

"You think you can find your way to my cabin?"

Silence.

"Please, Miss Tullie. For July's sake. You want him to see what Silas do to women like me? At least this way he won't see me hurt. Maybe I even get back to y'all 'fore Massa get hol't to me."

Driven by Silas, Sunday stumbled into the woods. There was no time in which to wonder if she was right. Not a second to hope this near-blind old woman could find her way back to safety and Silas might be somehow prevented from finally having his way. Silas's scratchy palm came at her face with the force of a twister, pushing her down to the cool earth. Beginning to finish what she herself had started moments ago.

Miss Tullie's footsteps faded into the distance, July eerily quiet. For a moment, the sweet strains of music from behind the quilts lulled Sunday as she looked up at the forested ceiling. The hope that there could be a God who cared for her flickered and soon died along with the heavenly songs. Silas kneed her, then hesitated.

"Something wrong here. Slaves done gone too quiet."

They here. Instinct took hold. For better or worse, the overseer—maybe even Handley Duval himself—had finally found the meeting place.

"No need for to get too happy, li'l pretty. I reckon Massa 'nem in there now. We mays well finish what we started. One mo grunt out of you and I'll squeeze your li'l throat. Hear me?"

Sunday nodded a lie. She'd fight this little bantam rooster until her blood cried from the ground.

5

Silas was wearing her down, the strength she had mustered minutes earlier slipping fast.

"Go'n show you jes how much man I got left in me."

Though easily twice Sunday's twenty-one years, he was still strong. And to her shock, his suspicion that Duval was behind those quilts hadn't meant he was giving up their deal. She tried one last push to lift herself to her elbows. But to no avail. Silas leaned in until he mixed his breath with hers.

"More man than you reckoned, huh."

Lips swollen, head pounding, Sunday silently congratulated herself on a good fight. One she had lost, but ... July was safe. All that matters. *My baby is safe. My baby is ...*

But what if Miss Tullie had lost her way? A new shot of strength infused her. She lifted her head and bit Silas's tobacco-fouled lip until she tasted blood.

"This be one steal you won't enjoy, old man."

Silas yelped before he spat blood in her eye, his howl quickly descending into a laugh. "Oh, yeah. Just what I figured it would be like all these years." He bore his knee into her stomach. Harder this time. "Been waiting for this since way before you married that pretty boy. And after you did, it made thinking 'bout this night mo sweeter." Silas grunted as Sunday's last spurt of strength fluttered and died.

"You a frisky one. I give you that. But old Silas here is still a man—"

"Silas!" Handley's Duval's drawl saturated the darkness, rolling over Sunday like a poisoned fog. Though she'd only heard his voice a few times over the years, the slow scratchy meanness that had crossed her ears could belong to no one else.

"You out there, boy?"

Silas leapt to his feet. "Don't. Chu. Move. Or I'll catch you and stomp you to death along with that young'un of yours."

Sunday said nothing. Just lay there—her mind trying to protect itself with questions. Why would Duval come out here? No matter his decree, why would he even cut into his Sunday evening, risking mosquito bites and limbs slapping his head to look upon a bunch of misguided slaves, when he had long since left this kind of dirty work to his overseer and Silas?

"You hear me, gal?"

She would have smiled had her swollen mouth allowed. "W-w-what happened t-to 'li'l pretty?' Ain't I pr-pretty no more?" She would have enjoyed the obvious fear in Silas had Miss Tullie's words not reached out and answered her questions about Duval.

Secesh. That's what had the plantation master out here. Fear of what the secesh meant in the minds of his slaves. She lay still as Silas trotted into the open. Willed her heart to slow its beat. Listened while the smell of kerosene assaulted her. She would wait a few minutes before trying to make her escape. She needed to get her bearings to remember the shortcut she'd used to get here, but her thoughts kept getting in the way.

What is secesh, anyhow? She would ask when she got back to the safety of the quarters. Back to where Noah ...

She touched a finger to the teardrop sliding from the corner of her eye. Noah would have known. He always kept up with things like that. A heap of mottled screams lit up the night. Piled up on each other like so many living, breathing rocks. Men, women, children—pleading and crying out to their God.

"Help us, O Holy One of Israel."

"Naw, Massa! We be but praying. That's all. We ain't trying to start no trouble."

All amidst the regulated and cold fall of the whip, as fire—goaded by coal oil—caught hold of the wet quilts and sent heavy choking smoke to join the other clouds of night.

Sunday, April 7, two weeks later

THE ROAD SEEMED ABNORMALLY QUIET, stirring up Sunday's self-talk. *It was your place to warn the people.* Not Miss Tullie's. It had been all the older woman could do, blind and near breathless, to get July safely to the cabin. Now every field-hand and house-slave Sunday sighted shunned her. They hadn't liked her in the first place. Said she was a stuck-up heathen. But now that Silas had told them how she'd stood outside the arbor "near-'bout" an hour and not said a word, the not-liking had crystalized into pure hate.

Sunday halted. Stared down the dusty road squeezed between miles of tobacco fields toward Miss Tullie's cabin, guilt and confusion washing over her.

You should'a told them. Went behind them quilts like a woman and warned them ...

A faint vibration quickened her. She felt it before she saw it. Felt, too, the damp bundle shift on her head as she turned back toward the roadbed she'd just covered, seconds before a white man driving a green wagonload of slaves—Duval slaves?—

rounded the bend. She sucked in her breath. Would the angry slaves she labored with every day finally attack her? Let go of the globs seemingly gathered in their mouths for two weeks and plaster her with vengeful spit?

No. The little swell of her belly, left over from July's birth, relaxed. The nearer the wagon came, the surer she was it didn't carry Duval slaves. Had she not been so guilty over the beatings she had allowed, she'd have immediately known they didn't belong to Duval simply by the fact they were riding in a wagon. Duval never allowed his slaves to ride unless they were being sold.

Like poor Noah was likely about to be.

She stepped to the side of the road to let the wagon pass. Raised her arms to adjust her wash load when a set of hands clamped her shoulders from behind. She swiveled her neck as far as she could, a slew of wet rags flying from atop her head.

"Afternoon, li'l pretty."

Silas. Again.

"Get your paws off me, Silas!" Managing to free herself, she struck at his hands, chest, head. "You here to try to ravish me again, or did you decide to bring me some more of that made-up news of yours about Noah? Miss Tullie said you ain't nothing but a nasty lying wonder, and I believe her." She snatched a wet rag from her shoulder and popped his face.

"Do." *Pop.* "You." *Slap.* "Really plan to try to take me again right here? With that white man coming down the road and his load of slaves looking on? You lowdown, nasty old devil, you."

She continued to sting him with the wet clothes while, seemingly amused, he ducked and danced. She didn't have time for another wrestling match with Silas, especially after she had promised to pick up July early so Miss Tullie could rest before she and a few other brave souls attempted the first secret meeting since the beatings. Still insisting on keeping July, Miss Tullie had been ailing lately. Sunday was worried—

Mercy. Silas had somehow managed to subdue her arms, squeeze them as though he were testing a warm baked sweet potato. He leaned in to kiss her. Heaven help her, she had not lain on the forest floor while the other slaves took a thrashing that likely saved her guilty backside in order to allow Silas to get the best of her now. She wriggled back and rammed a fist into his jaw.

Whack! Silas laid the hit right back on her, blinding her for a moment as he captured her wrists. "That be enough, li'l pretty. You got by last time, but I guarantee you won't get away today—"

"That will do, Silas."

The man driving the green wagon spoke a tenuous authority. Turning toward him, Sunday wondered what white man was saving her from Silas for the second time in as many weeks. Didn't matter. She was thankful, albeit the man's way of talking was strange. Clipped. Hurried—as he took a moment to assess her, causing Sunday to feel like a big hairy tongue had just ascended the length of her body.

Stop it. You just spooked, that's all. Everybody ain't like Silas.

"Violence isn't called for, Silas. Just restrain her."

Restrain? Sunday squinted at the hard-sounding word— what little learning she had garnered as a child having soaked into the soil of the tobacco fields. Satisfaction flickered across Silas's face as he dropped his hold on her. The odd-sounding man on the wagon seat, his face shaded by an enormous hat, threw a length of chain toward Silas.

"Put the manacles on her, if you please."

Understanding bloomed alongside a choking dread. Her body swayed. Kind of like she'd heard tell sometimes happened amongst white women when they demanded attention. Problem was, attention was the last thing Sunday wanted right now.

Wet clothes strewn everywhere—wisps of hair shooting out

from the edge of her head handkerchief, she backed away toward a nearby sapling. The strange man thumbed his hat backward. Suddenly Sunday's world lost all vibrancy. Except the shock of one of the two colors she hated.

Deep Pink.

His neck a sweating column, the man gazed at her, his eyes flashing with something much too close, too familiar. *Papa, Mama. It's him.* Except for the pink, he looked nothing like the killer who had cut down her parents all those years ago. But it was the same man. Different time, different body. But the same unsteady arrogance, as though he were doing something somebody told him he had a right to do but really didn't know how. She stared right back, hoping he could see through her eyes right down to the sickened pit of her stomach. Miss Tullie's words tried to edge into her thoughts. *Pray, chile. You ought to be praying.*

Not now.

Too late to run, she ran anyway. Until the click-click of a warning halted her steps. Images of blood shooting from her father's head stopped her in midflight. Only that one time in '46 had she seen a pistol, but once was enough to make her understand that the difference between life and death—free and slave—lay within that short silver pole she knew was pointed straight at her. She turned. Blinked back the nightmares, old and new. Spoke under her breath.

"I hate pink."

"What was that?" The man shot a look toward Silas then back toward her. "What did you say?"

Sunday swallowed down a shouting repeat of what had slipped from her lips. Instead, she shook her head side to side.

"Then if you'd be so kind as to put your wrists together." He waved his pistol toward Silas. "What are you waiting for? Do your job. I've paid for her already."

What to do? What should I do?

Fear invaded her like a swarm of locusts, stripping her ability to think what to do. The clanking of the metal dangling from Silas's hand reminded her of a newly purchased slave she'd once glimpsed near her cabin, branded with what must have been his former master's name. So who he b'long to now? She had thought at the time. She stared at the length of iron in front of her.

"W-what you fixin' to do, Silas? What you go'n do to me?"

"What's it look like? You 'bout to be hauled off from here and resold at a good profit." He gestured his head toward the green wagon. "Just like them there fellows. Just like that high and mighty husband of yours would 'a been if he hadn't got his self kil't."

Hauled off? *Hauled off*. No, no. This couldn't be happening. It couldn't be that she'd fought so hard to keep July safe only to end up shackled to a wagon maybe even far less safe than any Underground Railroad.

"B-but what about my baby? What about July?" Silas ignored her, clicked the manacles onto her wrists. Of an instant, the white man seemed more surefooted.

"Now I don't really know much about you people down here, black or white. But in Ohio, I was reared to be a gentleman. And, as such, I'm going to keep you, Sunday—that is your name, isn't it?—I'm going to keep you detached from the rest of the coffle. Since they're all males, I'm letting you ride the edge of the wagon bed. Swing your legs over the gate if you like, at least for a while, and depending upon your behavior, I might bring you up here with me."

Was ... was he expecting her to thank him for that? *Crazy.* The man was old-fashioned everyday crazy.

"Silas? You didn't say anything about July."

"Cease!" The man shouted straight down the roadway, refusing to look at her. "I don't know who July is, but I have no plans to purchase another slave right now."

Sunday's knees wanted to let her go—stop supporting her like Mama's, Papa's, and now even Noah's had done. But she would remain straight of form. No time to collapse. Maybe she could outfox this man who struck her as knowing about as much about the absolute power of a slaveholder as July himself. Before she even spoke it, she imagined the disgusting pleading about to show up in her voice. Like Mama's all those years ago when she begged for Papa's life.

"My-my baby, sir. I got a little boy waiting for me, depending on me." Thoughts of her plans to begin taking July to the creek with her stormed her. Tears she had neither planned for nor imagined spilled over. "Please. Can't I just take him with me? I'll work hard—do anything you say—if you'll just let me have my baby to take 'long with me."

The man laughed nervously, whitening up parts of his face, rendering the rest beet red. "You'll do anything I say no matter what."

Silas grinned. "Now you talking, suh." He tried to capture Sunday's gaze. She resisted. "That li'l spoilt young'un of yours and Noah's, he just go'n have to find another mama. Fend for hisself like you did, li'l pretty."

Sunday heaved her body at Silas only to be reminded of her wrists, the chains keeping them bound jangling offkey. She felt herself hoisted up, her knees hitting the floor of the wagon, torn skin stinging from the splinters of the bed as Silas pushed her against the wagon's side. Then changing his will, he lifted her and dropped her onto her backside, straddling her while the other slaves, except for a wide-eyed overgrown boy who gasped and stared straight at her, behaved as though she wasn't there.

She closed her eyes, the urge to hold July swelling inside her chest like mother's milk. She wasn't going to be able to stand this. She wasn't going to be able to survive if—

Wait, wait, wait, Sunday, she thought. *You have to survive.*

Until you can find a way to get back to July. You have to stand it, girl. You have to.

NOAH SQUINTED UPWARD AND SMILED. Even though the journey of sleeping days and running nights had caused his brain to scramble the days of the week, today his heart told him it was Sabbath Day—that glorious gift from God that seemed to own a special sunshine. And, to Noah, had ever been tied to the essence of his wife.

Gazing through the stand of magnolias Gideon had chosen for today's sleeping place, he savored the dappling of the morning sun. One day closer to freedom. He abandoned the bed of piled-up leaves he'd just finished making. Stretched his limbs and yawned. Turned and caught Gideon staring at him. Absentmindedly, she touched the corner of her mouth.

Maybe it was the beauty of the dawn—or maybe it was simply *her* beauty—but suddenly Noah felt playful, like he wanted to tease her. He spread his arms in mock ignorance.

"What? Part of my breakfast left on my face or something?"

She averted her eyes. Offered a rare smile, blossoming into the striking woman beneath the constant fierceness.

"You look fine. I was just thinking of how quickly you learn."

Noah's chest swelled. Was she finally acknowledging his progress with letters and numbers?

"I got a fine teacher." *And a real good scout.* Why was it so hard for him to admit that too?

Navigating the state of Virginia like the expert she had proven to be, she had jarred every one of Noah's waking moments with her skill. He'd watched her shake off that pack of blood hounds back there like a housefly. But he couldn't bring himself to say it. The fact that he was running through the woods trying to keep up with a body not even half his weight—placing his life in her hands—had reached his head but not his heart. In truth, it chafed him to the core.

"May be," she said, aloofness seeping back into her voice. "I had the finest of teachers myself, without whose navigation skills I and my cargo would have perished in these woods long ago." She scooped up her book, lowered herself to her pallet, her hat still in place. "We still have lots of miles to conquer. I suggest you get some sleep."

There it was again. That feeling she sparked in Noah of his being a perpetual boy with a slave master, or in this case, a mistress. Arms crossed over his chest, he set a wide-legged stance.

"If you got to know, I really wasn't praising your railroad knowledge. I was talking 'bout your book learning."

Her back stiffened. He had hit a nerve. Obviously, she'd known what he referred to and chosen to ignore it.

"I suppose I should thank you, but if I had to choose which I'm most proud of, it would be that 'railroad knowledge' you seem to slight."

Noah flinched. "And why's that?"

"Because of my teacher. I am no Moses, but I know what I know. I'm good at what I do, and the knowledge I learned about the Railroad, I learned from her."

"Her?"

Noah's mind revisited the scores of hush harbor meetings where Moses from the Bible was revered for leading the Hebrew slaves out of Egypt. Anybody with sense knew the name was reserved for a man, and hopefully a good man at that.

"What kind of mama would be crazy enough to name her li'l girl Moses?"

"The same kind of 'mama' who would choose a name like Gideon, I suppose." She stood from her bed of leaves, obviously deciding whether to dress him down or have pity. "Have you never even heard of Harriet Tubman?"

Noah barely restrained a yell. "No, ma'am."

She seized him up for a moment. "And I'm guessing you know little about northern cities."

"Reckon not."

Gideon rested her back against a nearby tree. She massaged the bridge of her nose and removed her hat, allowing a cascade of shiny tresses to fall past her shoulders. Like Noah himself, she likely had something besides Africa in her blood.

"Well, if we're going to navigate these so-called 'free' cities we're headed toward, I'm thinking it's time you know what they're like."

"So-called? What chu mean by that?"

She ignored the interruption. "Ten years ago, I had worked my way into becoming a headmistress in a school for orphan girls of color in Philadelphia. Having been born in Canada to a light-skinned black man and an Indian woman, I'd always felt a pull to enter the states and help the children of my bloodlines. One day during recess I was abducted." Her voice faltered at the memory.

"'Smile,' the man said, as I was forced at knifepoint from the schoolyard. 'No need to start a ruckus among the pickaninnies if we don't have to.'

"I pleaded with him, tried to tell him I was free—had always been. Had a lineage of black and red that had managed to escape a single enslavement on this continent." She paused, a rare bit of defeat seemingly escaping her resolve. "I was wrong. No family of color completely escapes, even when it thinks it has."

Noah eased to the ground, silently pitching scoldings at himself. He didn't like the direction this was going. Didn't want to dig into another horror story to add to the many he already possessed.

"The children never knew what happened. I determined to die before I brought injury to a single one of them. The man showed me a daguerreotype of a Negro woman—clearly not me, the only shared features being light skin and glossy hair. I continued to try to reason with him—even told him I'd give him what little money I had accumulated."

Realizing for the first time that he'd not even asked about her home, her family, Noah listened. So focused on his own freedom, he'd forgotten common decency.

"But the man was unmoved. Said his bread and butter depended on nigger-catching, and he had wasted enough time searching for the woman in the picture. He wagered it wouldn't matter much to the man who hired him. I was pretty enough to make my new master shelve the difference and strong enough to work the fields and add to the number of slaves my abductor's employer needed to make a good crop. He forced me to the Eastern Shore of Maryland. And, true enough, I added to my master's number. Four babies in a little over five years."

Noah wanted to curse. Stomp. Howl. But the rage rendered him speechless. Could this kind of thing happen in a distant place like Maryland? Likely near the promised land he'd always imagined as a reflection of the real Moses' story? He longed to offer some kind of comfort, but he couldn't move—frozen on a new rung of fright.

He managed to flex his fingers, more aware of the dearth of words in his head than ever before. He choked on his own ignorance, longed for a fight with someone to counter it. Instead, he managed to pray. Lord Jesus, help me to know what to say.

Just listen. She needs an ear.

"Then one day out of the blue, Harriet Tubman, a little woman whom I came to know as Moses, appeared behind my cabin. Head rag soundly in place, teeth missing, she could not have stood more than five feet, but I've seen few equal her strength and agility.

"She said she had heard about me, and though her story had not been exactly mine, she could relate to my plight. She said she had room for me on 'God's train to Canaan.' Said I could even take my babies if I wanted to. I wanted to, and I did. We traveled by foot, hiding and sleeping during the day, traveling at night. In all my years as an educator, I'd never seen that kind of intelligence. And not only did she know exactly when to run, when to walk, when to feign, when to pray, she always had exactly the right kind of medicine to calm my August when he ran a fever—"

"August?"

"My son. August. Odd name, I know."

"Not so much. My wife's name is Sunday. My baby is July."

It was the first time he had mentioned his family. Gideon seemed momentarily put aside. But then she continued as if he hadn't said a word.

"I vowed if I made it to Canada, I'd come back into slave states as Moses did, as she still does, as often as I could leave my babies. For the last four years, I've not missed a year. My babies are in western New York where they and I now live with my mother." A bemused look shadowed her fatigue. "This is the first trip where I've brought back less than five souls."

"The plan of God, I'd think."

Gideon nodded. "Yes, maybe. But it's probably time I told you I won't be surprised any time I hear President Lincoln has declared war on the secessionist."

"What? What makes you think that?"

"I have my reasons."

"Wouldn't that be a good thing—I mean, for us?"

"Perhaps. But I, for one, don't believe it will be an easy outcome, nor do I think everyone in the north will suddenly side with the Union. There'll be northern whites who are embittered by having to fight for a war over slavery, not to mention the desperate slave bounty hunters and speculators who'll want to capture and sell off as many blacks as they can before things get too complicated." Gideon reached for her book. Turned her back. Noah didn't know what to say.

"All right, then. I'll let you get to sleep."

"I'll sleep a lot sounder when we get through Pittsburgh and New York City."

"So-called free cities," she'd said earlier. The first hint of a tainted dream dug into Noah's consciousness. Tried to seed his thoughts. But he clung to the vision of Sunday and July and the freedom waiting for them if he continued to keep up with this strange woman. Surely God hadn't meant him to come this far only to run into some kind of slavecatcher in a free city. Taking a deep breath, he scraped up all the words his pitiful reservoir could offer.

"I sho' do hate to hear what happened to you, Gideon. I sho' do."

"I thank you," she replied, a near imperceptible break in her voice.

Noah swallowed. Gideon had done so much for him already, never even mentioning any kind of pay. An urge to comfort her nearly drove him to her pallet. *Too dangerous.* Like jumping off into a quick-moving river.

As the hush-harbor preacher liked to say, Noah was going to have to "guard his heart."

6

S unday sat at the edge of the wagon, her bound wrists surrendered to her lap, her feet not quite touching the earth while one knee bounced furiously at will. Always, within her limited sphere, she'd been able to think her way out of dark places, but right now her thoughts were a bed of stinging ants. No. That was only the feel. The *look* was a round of purple swirls. If she could just rid her head of the purple.

What poor Miss Tullie go'n think when I don't show up?

She struggled against the manacles. Managed to press her fingertips against her temples. Felt a continuous shaking. Why was the wagon trembling so?

"Oh, Lord. My baby."

"Did you say something, ma'am?"

Her insides leapt. She hadn't realized she'd spoken aloud. Had forgotten the men were behind her while the white man talked to Silas.

"You feeling chilly, ma'am? You shaking something awful."

"Huh? N-naw." She looked back over her shoulder. The man's eyes were kind. Papa had had kind eyes. Would have been about his age now. "I mean, n-no, sir."

"Name's Jess. What's yours?"

"Sunday."

"Like the Lord's-Day kind of Sunday?"

If Sunday believed in prayer, she'd be begging now for this man to be hushed. "Reckon so."

A smile lit Jess's eyes, smoothing years from his face. He worked his feet side to side, wiggled the toes pushing through his worn boots. "Well, looks like to me you've been doubly blessed, to own a name like that and to be spared these nice ankle bracelets."

Sunday frowned. She was sick to the bone of hearing slaves talk about blessings. There was nothing blessed about her life except her baby. And he was not a blessing—something bestowed upon her. He was her own creation carried by her own body. *He my life.*

She sucked in a helping of air, afraid if she answered, she'd hurt a well-meaning old man whom she wouldn't be bothered with very long anyway. After all, it was just a matter of hours—days if she had to try more than once—before she would get back to July. Thankfully, they were headed right past Miss Tullie's cabin, Sunday's first chance to rescue her child.

The white man climbed back into the driver's seat, a look of stupid detachment on his face. He'd chosen to say no more to her, and she hoped it would stay that way. He flicked the reins while Silas came around to the back, jumped onto the wagon bed and jammed himself so close against her that his stink nearly overwhelmed her. She shrank back while Silas laughed. Where did he think he was going? Surely Massa would have him skinned as quickly as the next slave if he didn't get back to the plantation before sundown unless Duval himself had sent him to do some kind of devil work.

The wagon lurched forward, sending her slamming into a knot of shackled ripe-smelling men. She tried to balance herself with her arms, finally maneuvering to the side, as far from Silas as the wagon's edge allowed while he grinned with spiteful pleasure.

"I knows what you thinking, li'l pretty. But you might want to know Massa done already got paid for my services. Done sent me 'long with this man to make sure y'all gets to the Ohio River." He grabbed Sunday's arm and yanked her back toward him, his breath so hot it nearly melted her ear. "Next time a hardworking man like myself offers to take care of you, you might see things a li'l clearer."

Splinters spearing her thighs, Sunday managed to land an elbow into Silas's ribs. Silas cursed. The wagon halted. The white man turned around.

"What's going on back there? I thought I already made it clear. I wasn't raised to this kind of uncouth life." Sunday swiveled to face the man.

"What kind of life makes a man steal a mama from her young'un?"

Soon as the words were out, Sunday felt lightheaded. The youth with the wide eyes and legs nearly as long as her body, gasped again. *Ha' mercy.* When had she started questioning white men? When in her grown years had she ever talked to a white man at all? Terror lit up the green wagon. Even Silas looked scared.

The man cleared his throat. No white man—north or south —would put up with that kind of sass. He laid a hand on his pistol as he barely spoke above a whisper.

"I made a fair and legal purchase precipitated by a fair offer. Are you thinking otherwise, *Miss* Sunday?"

Thinking just how seriously she had overstepped, Sunday wondered if she would ever hear July laugh again. She waited next to Silas as the man's footsteps neared the wagon's gate. Lips primped, sweat dripping from beneath his chin, he pointed the gun at her again.

"Would you care to continue this conversation?"

CLAYTON DUVAL CRUSHED a mosquito against his grimy neck. Having been bitten by every insect species in North Carolina, he longed for time away from the woods. No matter he could smell the nearness of the plantation that had been the hellhole of his Virginia childhood, he was tired of walking through thick forests alone and lonely. Sick of traveling in the dark of night as he made his way northward where he would find a way to build his own plantation—live free outside of the Dismal Swamp he had lived in for years. Be a man the only way a man truly could be in the South: by owning slaves.

Knowing full well the patter-rollers were edgy these days because of all the war talk, he had somehow made it as far as Virginia. And now he would reward himself by flirting with the open road in broad daylight. The same road that ran alongside and through the fields of the Duval Plantation from which he'd fled when he was ten. The place whose memory of Noah as his only kin and protector had now congealed into a mass of life-sustaining hate. He had loved Noah. They had been destined to stick together—had literally been drawn from the same hat—two pieces of paper that decided they were a pair that wouldn't be sold.

Words from Handley Duval taunted Clayton's steps. Made him stumble under the memory of the whip ...

"Where is he? Where'd Noah tell you he was going?" *Crack!* "Don't you know that little sneaky cousin of yours lied to you? He's having the time of his life while you try to protect him." *Crack!* "Ain't never coming back for you like he promised. Done joined up with the nigger lovers. Getting closer to Canada every day while you take the beatings that's rightfully his ..."

Clayton halted, the sound of distant horse hooves colliding with a cry so faint that Clayton wondered if he'd heard it at all. He flattened his body to the earth. Tried to shield himself in the sparsely forested space. A wounded animal, maybe? Some poor runaway captured by patter-rollers?

He ordered his thoughts to quiet. No time to cloak his fear with wild guesses. It was the undeniable sound of horses headed his way. Surely the horses would be carrying trouble for him if he was discovered. He imagined Buck Riley's cat-o-nine poised for him like a coiled rattler, waiting to lay open the pattern of stripes that had bloomed willy-nilly across his back over the years.

Sweat beads formed along his forearms like blisters while he strained to hear. There were two of them, young white men, the sound of their carefree voices growing steadily. Following the direction in which they traveled, he spotted a small cabin across the road, dwarfed by two giant oaks—its boards so weathered it almost looked like a huge stump. A woman sat in a chair holding a child as the two young men reined in their horses.

"I'd wager it's the old granny from Duval Plantation in that chair. I don't know who the little one is, but its cry sounds like a wild animal in distress."

"Hard to tell the difference," said the second rider, "since they mostly share the same brain type anyway." They laughed at the clever comparison.

"Want to have a closer look?"

"Sure. Why not? Never could stand to see a poor animal suffer."

The two finely dressed men swung down and sauntered up to the cabin, partly obstructing Clayton's view of the woman and child. They couldn't be patter-rollers. They spoke too well. Probably out for a Sunday ride. Planter class, he was sure. He felt the familiar bitterness that rode him as expertly as the men rode their horses. He might have owned his own plantation by now—maybe a few well-treated slaves—if Noah hadn't left him to fend for himself.

"Auntie?"

Nothing. Except for the mewling sound of the child, every now and then muttering something about "Tullie" needing to be warmed.

"Yep. It's Aunt Tullie, all right. I'd know her anywhere. Duval's place is about a mile or so from here. I used to play with his children when I was younger." The first speaker poked the woman's shoulder with his cane. "Auntie?"

Clayton pinched his nostrils to keep from sneezing and perhaps swearing against the offhanded way the men were treating the old lady.

"Well, Jove! I believe she's dead."

"Dead? Then what're we going to do with Duval's little property here?"

The leader shrugged. "According to my daddy, it wouldn't make much difference where Duval's plantation is concerned. It's about to go under for the last time. I can't see how rescuing this little darkie would do him any good." Silence reigned as the men seemed to think on what to do next.

"Hey, I have an idea. What say we cross over to the creek, take our shoes off and wade in like we did when we were boys?"

The second speaker didn't seem comfortable with simply leaving the child, but clearly his wouldn't be the last word. Clayton stiffened. No way they would miss him if they crossed that road. Unless maybe he could overpower them. But there were two. And they weren't small men. He hadn't prayed much since he left these acres, but a prayer passed his lips as easily as slurping Miss Maggie's warm syrup.

Heavenly Father, I done come too far to be caught. Plain and simple.

The child stepped up its screaming, recapturing the men's attention and offering Clayton a slim chance to ease down the incline toward the creek. But the creek was the same to which the men were heading, its surroundings not exactly thick with trees. Where would he find a place to hide?

"Like I said, Lord. You go'n have to handle this. Plain and simple."

————

Sunday kept her head lowered—saw from the corner of her eye Jess shake his head ever so slightly, warning her to tread lightly.

"Naw suh. Ain't got no thoughts otherwise than yours."

"How about questions? Any more of those?"

Hundreds. But she wouldn't ask them, seeing the man's move for the dare it was. "Naw suh. Sometimes I gets a li'l too curious. A li'l too quick about the lip."

The slave dealer was quiet for a long time, as if he was trying to figure out what a real slave owner would do about this kind of sass.

"Indeed," he finally muttered. "Don't let it happen again. And boys, I'm charging you not to misbehave back here. Leave the girl be."

She saw the half-shocked, half-tickled looks in the men's eyes. What kind of slave monger would let something like this go? And even if they wanted to "misbehave" toward her—and a few of them looked as though they did—what could they do, yoked to each other like so many oxen? Silas posed the only misbehaving threat right now. Without another word, the man returned to the wagon seat.

Sunday fought to calm herself, measuring each breath by the rocking motion they'd fallen into. She would get a chance to see July and Miss Tullie if the wagon stayed on this road. More's the point, they would see *her* as the wagon passed the cabin. No matter how awful, they would know the fix she'd been thrown into. Know she hadn't simply run off. But how?

How would Miss Tullie, blind as she was, recognize Sunday hanging off the gate of a wagon full of slaves? The poor old thing could hardly see her hand before her face anymore, let alone figure out who Sunday was, squeezed between Silas and the wagon side. Mercy. *What's I'm go'n do?* If only—

No. *No Noah-thoughts.* She concentrated on the wagon's rhythm, reminding herself that she hadn't been muzzled. Still had the use of her lungs. Could still scream.

This time of day, Miss Tullie would be sitting in her chair underneath one of the oaks with July in her arms, most likely trying to get him to fall asleep. July was getting to be a handful —didn't appreciate his naps as much as he used to. What if, this once, they weren't in the yard? All Sunday needed to do was shout loudly enough. Let Miss Tullie know she would come back for July no matter what. She'd have to be quick—before Silas had a chance to stop her. He had turned deadly quiet. She suspected she'd shamed him back there, and, more than most, she knew Silas had no soul—had seen what he did to that baby when Sunday herself was little more than a tot.

The wagon cleared a bend, and affection flared as Sunday spotted Miss Tullie sitting in her vine chair. Oh, but the woman was so proud of that chair. Noah had made it and given it to her. His way of thanking her for keeping July every day. It was going to be all Sunday could do to keep from catapulting herself from that wagon into Miss Tullie's yard. But the slave dealer would surely shoot her this time, leaving July without a mother.

Then above the din of the wagon, she heard a cry. She shivered with anticipation. Had her child spotted his mama already? But ... this was no sweet sound. More like a scared, confused wailing. Her baby was ... scared? Why would he be scared? The wagon creaked to within several hogshead lengths of the yard, and Sunday saw July's little arms stretched straight toward her, Miss Tullie's wrinkled limbs loosely wrapped around him. Something about the slump of Miss Tullie's body rattled Sunday's senses. Why wasn't her old friend tending July? A fly landed and re-landed above the woman's open mouth. Was she asleep? Then why hadn't July's piercing cries awakened her?

"Mama Tullie cold. She need warm."

A different cold swept through Sunday's bones as July—screaming, snot and tears glistening beneath his tiny nostrils—reached for her.

"July! What's the matter, baby?"

For some reason her baby decided to turn away, snuggling back against Miss Tullie, as though he sensed that the hellish trap he had found himself in might be better than the one his mama was in. Sunday leaned forward, willing herself to fall sideways into the dust.

"Mama's coming, July! I'm coming!"

The shock of Silas's fist connecting to her temple was the last thing Sunday heard before she entered a hole of pitch.

FROM A THICK ISOLATED stand of bamboo saplings at the creek's edge, Clayton had heard the two future planters mount their horses and ride back in the direction from which they'd come, the leader having remembered promising his little sister her own Sunday evening ride. He was certain they hadn't spared a backward glance. *Selfish swine.* The both of them. What about that crying baby? One selfish act had cost Clayton his chance for freedom—long before he escaped Duval, was captured by Buck Riley then fled to the Dismal Swamp—and he would never forgive the one responsible.

Cousin Noah Duval.

But now—having decided to remain hidden from a second visit to the dead woman and the child—he listened as the wagon wheels crunched away from the cabin. Minutes ago, a woman's cries had overpowered those of the child. There'd been screams. Some type of scuffle. Then nothing. Too near the creek, he had not been able to make out at first if the company was black or white, but a woman's complaints, her screams, had finally said everything. She could only be one more slave forced to do the thing she most detested—leave her child. Clayton fought against the sudden nausea. "I won't be treating my slaves like that."

He belly-crawled to the edge of the road and stayed low until he could no longer hear the wagon wheels, then trotted over to the front of the cabin. The old woman, cold dead, stared across the yard, the child in her arms—his cry now so weak and comfortless that Clayton was near compelled to mix in his own weeping. *Weeping?* What was wrong with him, and what was he supposed to do about this?

The least he could do was to see if the child, who couldn't be much more than a year or two, would eat some of the berries staining Clayton's pocket. Making one last scan of the road, he reached to remove the child—a little boy—only to find the old woman's arms firmly set around him, the child's head against her sagging bosom.

"Pa-pa?"

Clayton's gut tightened. "No, no. Not your papa." He drew the baby from the stiff arms of the old woman. He would move her before sundown, but now he had to see what he could do for the child. "No, li'l one, I ain't your papa, but I do wonder where he is."

The windowless cabin was nearly nighttime dark, smelling of old folks and sour baby, but it was a place for the exhausted tot to sleep. The miraculously quieted baby in arms, Clayton dug into his pocket and sat down in the lone chair.

"Here you go, li'l fellow. These go'n make you feel better."

The little one tried to ratchet up his holler, spitting back the berries as fast as Clayton forced them in. But his strength was gone, no doubt previous screaming having stolen it. Clayton ransacked his mind trying to think of a way to get a few berries into the child. Remembering a trick Noah had taught him, he eased the boy to a floor pallet and sat across from him. Cross-legged, he faced him, the plump berries spread out between them. He tilted his head back, tossed up a berry and caught it in his mouth. Once. Twice. The little guy stared. Giggled. Grabbed a berry and tried to pop it in his mouth, only to have it fall to the quilt. Clayton made as if he would snatch it.

"Mine!"

"Better hur' up, or I'm go'n take it."

The boy grabbed a fistful and crammed them into his mouth. Pleased with himself, he scooped another helping, leveled a wily grin and reached for Clayton. Clayton's eyes moistened.

"Pa-pa," the child said, chasing away the darkness.

"Yeah, little fellow. I might have been a father by now, living free somewhere if Noah had kept his promise." The child brightened again—even laughed a bit and looked toward the door.

"Papa Noah come?"

"Naw. And be thankful for it. He'd just be real nice to you then leave you with a bunch of promises he wouldn't keep."

The child rubbed his eyes as Clayton stood and searched for something to replace the sopping sack on the baby's behind. He found several fresh ones neatly folded and lying on a corner crate. Returning to the pallet, he gently nudged the boy's back to the floor.

"Ain't too good at this, my man, but we go'n make it work, hmmm?" Clayton paused at the overly large, heart-shaped birth mark. "Got a heart on your hiney, huh. Good sign."

Within seconds, the boy was out, affording Clayton a chance to revisit the front yard. He was tired past bodily strength. His very thoughts were exhausted, but he had to do something about the old woman. At the least, he could move her around back. Spotting a homespun ancient shawl, he threw it across his shoulder and, lifting the chair and the woman as one, he deposited them against a doorless wall in the back yard and draped the musty shawl over her thin frame.

"I hate this, ma'am, but it's got to do 'til I can figure out what's next."

Task completed, Clayton stepped back around into the cabin. Yawned. Looked at the pallet. Knowing where he was—whose land he poached upon—should he?

He lay down next to the baby, pulled the little fellow onto his chest and stretched his long body past the limits of the quilt. Today was a day of chance-taking. He positioned the child's head snugly beneath his chin and joined him in a sound sleep.

7

Late April, eastern Kentucky
Near an isolated farmhouse at predawn

The clank of chains brought Sunday to full wakefulness. Pools of colors swirling in the midst of a dull headache while Silas's whip cuts on her back protested her every move. She and the rest of the slaves had been bumping along in the green wagon for days, maybe weeks, staring past curiosity seekers like straw-filled scarecrows.

Like that awful thing Silas had made her into when she was six. She blinked at the colors. *If only I had a way to draw something.*

Perhaps she could bear the separation from her son if she could sketch out the pictures piling up in her head. In the darkness, she flexed her fingers to fight the panicky feeling that nearly took her under each time she knew again that her wrists were bound. And now her feet. The "gentleman" had changed his mind about leaving her partly unshackled after she had tried to rescue July. For some reason, he'd felt the need to explain.

"I hadn't planned on taking on a female," he'd said not looking her in the eye, "at least not this soon. But the slave called Noah—the one I'd already paid Duval for—fled the plantation before I could claim him. So it seems I'm saddled with you as a replacement."

She flinched at the word "saddled," something soiled and dubious in its delivery. Instantly, he tried to recover.

"Understand this, Miss Sunday. I am a gentleman, but I won't have your disrespect. I'll have Silas train you as often as need be."

Why Silas? Why didn't he "train" her himself and save the cost of paying Duval extra for Silas's services? She hadn't—wouldn't—ask. Not anymore. Not with the recent memory of Silas's whip slicing through the hollow of her lower back. Her head throbbed. Neck hurt. She spoke sidelong to the older man named Jess to whose ankles hers were now bound.

"Where we at now, Mr. Jess?"

"Somewhere west of the state line is all I can tell you." He motioned his head toward the front of the wagon where Silas now drove. "A real warm brotherly type, that one, huh? Seems to love to wrap people up in the heat of that whip of his."

The possibility of Silas's whip, set loose on her again, threatened to overwhelm her. Though her fingers had tested the upbraided flesh on Noah's back a few times, she herself had never quite been whipped like this. How had her husband survived it and still believe there was a God out there on his side? How could he still hope for a thing called freedom?

She couldn't straighten things out in her head. Worries skittered to and fro, bumping into each other at break-neck speed. Where was July? Who, if anyone, had found poor Miss Tullie?

The youth in the coffle, whose long robust body did nothing to mask his innocence, pressed in toward her, his timid smile pushing back against the darkness in her mind.

"Your baby okay."

Not a question. He was *telling* her that July was well.

"And how would you be knowing?" When all he ever did was gasp and smile.

"God, He told me."

Sunday groaned.

The boy looked pained. "Miss Sunday?"

"It's all right, Georgie," said Jess. "Miss Sunday is all right."

The boy's God-talk made her jumpy. She closed her eyes and allowed her grief to come striding back. Her baby was miles behind, imprisoned in a dead woman's arms. Many times these last several days she had sketched him in her head. The lines of his feet when first he was born. The gloss of the half-straight hair he had inherited from Noah. The clenched fists, the dimples beneath his tiny knuckles. Needing release from the pain digging into her neck and pressing out from her temples, she deliberately leaned from side to side just before the wagon swerved onto a lane in an open field and her sight strained toward a shadowy farmhouse.

"We 'bout to call on these people before the sun even rises?"

It was the youth speaking again. They'd only been back on the road since shortly before midnight. Could this be a place where they might get some relief from the wagon for a stretch of days? A hot meal, maybe? She touched Jess's arm.

"What in the world could Mr. Ohio be thinking bothering these people this time of morning?"

"Don't know, but my guess is this whole speculating thing is a game he don't know nothing about. Spending money on a loud-colored wagon in the middle of all this war talk—even got a string of manacles special made with locks where one key can open them all—is a mark of don't-know-what-I'm-about. Now he's running out of cash." Jess's mouth went sideways with a chuckle. "Starting to look about as starved as the rest of us. Some of these fellows from up north just plain don't count up the cost before they come barreling down here thinking to make a bunch of money on buying and stealing God's people."

"What chu mean? I always thought folks from the North was on our side. Leastways that's what my husband said. And just what is this 'speculating thing' anyhow?"

Mr. Jess smiled at her the way her father used to when she'd stumbled onto questions to which only grown folks were privy.

"You really don't know, do you?"

"Know what?"

"Lots of money to be made in selling slaves to the lower South, and greed don't know no state lines. Charleston, New Orleans, Memphis, Natchez, and all in between, just waiting on deals no matter where they come from. Fellows from Virginia, Pennsylvania, Ohio, even New York, on the lookout for slaves— plantation-bound and runaways—hoping to turn a big profit when they reach them slave-hungry cotton planters down in the lower South."

The wagon dipped, Sunday's heart right along with it. After all these years, she was finally able to put a label to her parents' killer. A speculator. So that's what the pink murderer had been —just as mama had hinted—although he had made a deal with a devil named Handley Duval, much closer than the cotton states.

"They go after free people too."

Jess mistook her words for an inquiry. "Yes, of course. They buy and steal free people too. How you think I got to be amongst these po' fellas?" Jess lifted his cuffed hands and scratched at his whiskers. "Beatingest thing I ever saw in my life. One day I was a free man. Had my own shop in Charleston. Next thing I knew I'd been knocked in the back of my head with a weapon I never even got a chance to put a name to. Dragged off by a bunch of hooligans without a word to the wife and children. Sold to this fellow who'd just bought himself a silly looking green wagon."

Cramps seized Sunday's gut. "So you was Mr. Ohio's first slave?"

She felt a hand clumsily searching for hers, stilling the tremors that had set in.

"You all right, honey? Didn't mean to get you all trembly like this."

"I'm all right. It's just that ... freedom. Only fools dabble in it."

As one, the coffle turned toward her, Georgie reining in his gasp. Jess gave her the same you-must-be-crazy scowl Noah had given her weeks before. "Pardon me?"

"You heard what I said. Ain't no such thing as a free black person in this here country. I ought to know since, for the first six years of my life, I thought I was free, only to be kicked by a horse and shot in the head until I died."

"What?—"

"Seems like an awful lot of jabbering going on back there!"

The white man's shout commanded silence. Caught up in her past, Sunday hadn't felt the wagon slowing. Hadn't noticed it stopping yards from the door of the farmhouse. She felt the unrest of her fellow bondsmen who'd been drawn into her story.

"Yes, suh, I'll get 'em straight," said Silas, jumping down off the wagon seat. "Fall out of there, you bunch of worthless horse flesh."

Sunday lowered her head. She hated she'd rattled the coffle's nerves then left them hanging. But she had meant what she said. Jess's abduction was just one more page in a storybook of free fools, offering proof to anyone who would listen of how useless was the desire of a black person to live free in this country. She would never seek freedom again. All she wanted was July back in her arms. It didn't matter which patch of soil she occupied as long as they were together.

Feeling a nudge of hope she couldn't account for, she lifted her eyes to a smile so bright—so sunshiny and starry and moonlit, all in one—it stunned her.

"Georgie?"

"Don't chu worry, Miss Sunday. God's got him. And you go'n see him soon. Just you wait and see."

"How'd you know I was …?"

Stopped by the boy's spooky words, Sunday hushed. Rested her chin to her chest. Tried to strike a one-sided bargain with Miss Tullie's God for the first time since just after she had been booted from her father's lap during that ill-fated breakfast fifteen years ago.

You show me my boy is all right, and I just might start praying again.

Eastern Kentucky

CLAYTON LAY SPRAWLED on a different pallet on a different floor, gazing at the dark ceiling—his attempt to bury the stiffened old woman holding fast to a corner of his mind.

"It was the best I could do," he whispered.

It wouldn't be long before daylight. How had he gotten stuck with the little boy in the next room, cute as he was? Days and nights had melded into one long stretch of nerves since he'd found the child, but finally he had run into a "train" on the Underground Railroad and made his way in record time to the house of a woman across the state line. Eliza Borden was her name, someone he had been told helped blacks from time to time. Depending on her mood at the moment.

She'd proven a crazy one, this Miss Borden. Always dressed in men's britches and colorful cotton shirts, she looked to be about twice Clayton's age. He didn't know anything about how white women dressed their hair, but hers looked like whatever they usually did hadn't been done to hers in a mighty long time. Groups of long gray snarled strands stood separate from each other like prison guards. Still, she had answered the conductor's knock, taken him and the child in with a creepy kind of glee.

Got to find a way out of here soon.

He glanced toward Miss Borden's bedroom where she had put the little one down for the night in an old rickety crib next to her bed. The grin with which she had closed her door had niggled at Clayton. But now his body's need for sleep was besting every worry.

A sound invaded, barely past a scratch. Clayton shot to a sitting position. Leapt to his feet and scrambled toward the larder Miss Borden had pointed out in case of trouble. The woman was out of her bedroom in an instant shuffling toward the door.

"Who knocks?"

He held his breath. Prayed the baby wouldn't awaken. Wondered if the woman was crazy enough to open the door without knowledge of who was behind it.

"I asked who disturbs my rest before sunrise. Answer or take a bullet through the door."

The voice of a Yankee white man penetrated the wood. "The name's Hartley, Jed Hartley. I'm afraid I'm in need of a little help."

"What kind of help?"

"Well, I've been traveling since the Carolinas, and my supplies are getting low. I have a wagon, nicely painted and in good condition. I would like to trade it for food supplies that will last until I can reach the Ohio River."

"You alone?"

"Uh, not exactly. But I promise you no one in my party will do you harm."

Clayton heard the woman open the door. Not good. Not this

time of morning and not with a flimsy reason like needing supplies. If the wagon was in such good condition, wouldn't the man be likely to have money? And how was it the man hadn't sold the wagon before now if he was in such shape as to have to wake someone at dawn in order to sell it? And why had he chosen a desolate farmhouse in the middle of nowhere?

The door closed. Had she let the man inside? Had this refuge been some kind of trap to capture Clayton? His breathing thinned to a tenuous thing. *The back door.* He was leaving. Now. But what about the baby? *You can't just leave the baby ...*

"Noah? You coming back for me?" *Noah stuck his chest out. Looked down at Clayton. Would Clayton ever grow that tall?*

"I'll be back. Just you be ready when I come."

Aw, shoot. Clayton was go'n cry, and he didn't want to. Wanted to act like a man—like Noah.

"Noah, I'm scared. Please don't leave me ..."

Voices from the other side of the door slowed Clayton's heartbeat. They were beneath the stoop. He ticked off seconds in his mind then crept from the cupboard across the floor. He placed his ear to the door—only to hear the sound of metal clinking in the distance. Chains! He stepped back from the door. He'd know that sound anywhere. Had seen many people run into the Swamp with chains still dangling. He measured off a few more seconds. Talked to himself.

"Now, hold on, Clayton. Folks use chains for lots of reason."

No need to lose his mind over the common sound of metal. A streak of sunlight stole through the window as Miss Borden's voice turned from rankled to hard-edged.

"You're not welcome here."

"That's a rather quick decision, isn't it? Where's your husband? Wait." The man's voice rose with suspicion. "You're not one of *them*, are you?"

"Depends on what you mean by 'them.'"

"I would think everybody in the South knows—"

If you're talking about the abolitionists, I'm one when I choose to be and not one when I don't. And whenever that happens to be is no concern of yours."

The sound of a bullet stabbed the air. "Now git, you murdering thief! And take that hideous wagon along with you 'fore I mingle you with the morning dew."

Clayton's chest caved with a sigh of relief. Right along with the piercing screams of the toddler in the next room.

8

The most brilliant sunrise she had ever seen lit the elements, at once startling and delightful. Words of hope, buried along with her parents, bobbed up with the sun.

"The heavens declare the glory of God." If only Sunday could recapture the simple faith of that six-year-old sitting on Papa's knee.

A popping sound shattered the sacred memory. Georgie gasped, arousing in Sunday a need to shelter the beautiful innocent boy. A woman standing near a set of sun-washed steps shouted orders.

"Git, you murdering thief!"

The speculator stood stock still, his features locked in amazement, as though to be called a murdering thief was so far beneath him as to mark the wild-looking woman insane. Sunday moved closer to Jess, tension spreading along the coffle like lightning up a tree trunk. The men ducked and shifted. What if the woman *was* crazy—decided to shoot down all of them including the speculator? *I can't die now. I have to find July—*

A child's cry floated out from the farmhouse. So sweet, the

feel of it so real, Sunday thought she might reach out and touch it. Her whole body flushed. Could Georgie be right? Could God have spoken through that simple boy? It couldn't be—

The cry again. Hungry. Wet. Scared. *July.*

"July! That's my baby! That's July!"

Sunday surged in the direction of the house that stood shimmering in the sunrise. Strength she didn't recognize lashed the coffle back and forth like an overseer's whip.

"My baby. I know it. I know it is!"

The woman brandished the gun, her eyes suddenly clouded with fear, her long gray hair glistening with the sun's rays. The speculator yelled over his shoulder.

"Shut her up."

Sunday froze, images of a child kneeling near a purple belfry playing out in rapid succession. Hands chained to the underside of a wooden altar block. Head drooped. Thick braids, not combed for days, seemingly as heavy as a piece of Papa's chair wood. Underpants so soiled they stuck to her buttocks.

"Where's Mama ...?"

Thoughts scrambling back to the shimmering yard, Sunday tried to swallow. But her throat was closing in on itself, a lump the size of July's fist cutting off her air. In seconds she would no longer be able to breathe, to save her child. She had to let Jess know, tell somebody.

"He's go'n die in the purple! My baby's go'n die! I have to get him out."

She watched the speculator, hands toward the sky, back away from the woman and her smoking gun. "What's all this talk about purple, Silas? Shut her up before she gets us all killed."

Sunday sensed Silas advancing on her from behind. She continued trying to push the words through. Terror severing her ability to reason, shutting off her speech.

"He ... mine ... July ... mine. Have ... to take care of him ... or they lock him up. Try ... to make ... him pray."

Jess's opposing weight tugged at her, hinting to her jumbled mind at the fruitlessness of the struggle toward her child. He yanked her toward him whispering through clenched teeth.

"Hush up, now. That ain't cho baby. All babies sound alike, don't cha know? And even if it is your boy, you don't want Silas to find that out, do you?"

No. Silas hated crying babies. That much she knew.

"But it *is* her baby." Georgie smiled contentedly, as though they had all just sat down to a savory breakfast of ham and grits and eggs. Jess looked at the boy with patient silencing.

"Can't pay Georgie no mind right now. Now settle down before you get us all whipped."

Sunday clamped her mouth shut. Breathed through the brain fog as her mind clambered toward another way. Someway. Somehow.

The speculator spoke conspiratorially to the woman whose gun was now aimed straight at his heart. Looking completely bewildered, he gestured toward Sunday.

"Pardon all this ruckus. I'm afraid I might have taken on an idiot in that one."

The woman backed up the steps toward the door, never losing aim. "I got no quarrel with her. Just keep her quiet and away from my baby 'til you get off my property."

Sunday steeled herself. Heard the door slam behind the silver-haired woman. Just before Silas ran past the coffle onto the porch and kicked open the door.

His brain was afire. Thoughts of being chained to a line of slaves—one that included a mother obviously separated from her child on some auction block—were pushing Clayton himself into crazy. This was not what he had planned. Not the fulfillment of the picture of himself running his own plantation with his own well-cared-for slaves. Not how he would get even with Noah for abandoning him.

"I got to shut that baby up. I ain't clawed my way toward freedom for the last eleven years to be herded off by some sorry slave dealer who can't even keep his slaves fed long enough to sell 'em off."

Crossing the space toward the bedroom, he stopped. Was that quiet he was hearing? Glory be. The crying had stopped.

He backed away from the bedroom door. His usually steady heartbeat did a funny little leap as Miss Borden rushed in closing the door behind her—just before a black man kicked it in, knocking her to the floor before she could draw half a breath. A head shorter than Clayton, the man scrambled toward the pistol that flew from Miss Borden's hand and set a foot upon it. Clayton's heart slowed in relief. A freeman, happened up to help him.

"Man, am I glad to see you. How'd you get past that slave dealer out there?"

The man ignored him. Dug the toe of his muddy shoe into Miss Borden's side. "Git up."

"No need to treat her rough. She on our side."

Leveling the gun at Clayton, the man chuckled. "That so? Who you b'longst to, boy?"

Boy?

A thousand thoughts crowded into that one word— images of torture, caused by Noah's escape, repossessing him ...

"BOY, you know where your cousin is?" Master Duval pressed his forehead to within an inch of Clayton's. A slight tobacco stain beneath his lower lip looked like a half moon. "Don't tell me you don't know. That's not what I'm wanting to hear ..."

Clayton watched as the man stood over Miss Borden, gun in

hand. "This your nigger, ma'am? Or could it be you hiding him out." The woman struggled to regain her footing.

"I don't see that what I do is anything to a glob of spit like you."

"Yes, m'am, but it is. Strong young fellow like this looks like just the kind that would try to run away from his master. And the kind to turn a right sweet profit, too, if he was to be returned or sold. He could bring Mr. Hartley out there real happiness when we git to the auction block, you see. And my aim on this trip is to make Mr. Hartley happy." He waved the gun in the direction of the Clayton. "So let's go outside, see if we can start making some happiness."

Sounds of a child awakening arrested everyone. Clayton could only guess at what Miss Borden meant to do, given how she'd taken an unnatural shine to the little fellow. He also knew everyone would be better served if the other crazy woman outside didn't get to screaming again when she heard the baby's cry. Miss Borden made a tentative step.

"I'm needing to see about the baby."

The man seemed amused and quite satisfied. "I was just waiting. Knowed you'd ask."

"Except I ain't asking your permission. I'm telling you I'm going to see about the child." Miss Borden made a step. The man clicked the gun.

"Not 'til I find out what's in it for me."

Miss Borden studied him for a moment. "Well, it could very well calm that woman down outside to see that the baby is not hers." Her eyes glanced off Clayton. "The plain truth is, the baby is mine."

Hers? Not only was Clayton's hope in this man snuffed out. Something truly off-balance was going on in Miss Borden's head.

"Might work," said the man. "Be worth watching Miss Sunday suffer a bit more when she sees the brat ain't hers." He waved the gun toward the bedroom. "Be unkind of you, ma'am, to do something foolish in there."

It seemed hours before Miss Borden returned with the hungry little boy in her arms. The man lit up with malice, eyes stretched to the size of a kneecap.

"Well, ain't this my day. Ain't this just old Mr. Silas's day."

Naw. This here is a crazy day. Clayton's fingers flexed, instinct warning him something was eternally twisted inside this little cocky man. Something far worse than he'd sensed earlier in Eliza Borden.

Got to find a way to get away from here or my chance for freedom is forever shot.

SUNDAY'S EYELIDS fluttered against the sun. Was that ... a baby in Silas's arms?

Mercy. It was July.

If there was a Creator like Miss Tullie said, a being that loved so completely He gave up His only Son, He wouldn't allow a man like Silas to touch her only little boy. Why would God answer her prayer—show her July like Georgie said—then shove him into Silas's arms?

This had to be a bad vision. Sometimes these pictures in her head were so far-fetched they astounded even her. Yet there he stood, Silas Duval, meanness dripping from him like blood from an open wound, with July in his arms. She opened her mouth to scream, but nothing came. Georgie tugged at the coffle chain.

"Easy, Miss Sunday. Real easy. Yo' Father's got you."

My Father. She'd heard Him called God, heard him called Lord—even heard Miss Tullie call Him a Rock in a weary land. But she'd never heard Him called Father. Not like this. It soothed, dripped balm into places that had been laid bare more years than she cared to remember. Oh, how she needed a father right now. Someone to stand up for her against Silas and all the Silases in the world. But she had traveled the road of following a father's leading before. She wouldn't risk that false protection again. There was no one she could trust except herself.

"Ma-ma."

July had spotted her, flooding her with something so sweet it actually hurt. She pressed her hand to her heart. "My baby."

Jess looked at her, pity in his eyes while July—his curls grown wild and beautiful—stuck his thumb in his mouth and sucked fiercely. He would probably look much like Georgie did now when he grew up. But at this moment he was in Silas's arms. Her whole life resting on the forearm of a killer. She willed her body to remain upright. Though she didn't know Silas's plan, for certain it meant more pain for her. July on one side and the drawn pistol on the other, Silas moved toward the speculator while Jess whispered through barely moving lips.

"Did you know that clown had a gun?"

"No. Only the whip."

"Well, there you go. Flunky slaves don't usually have guns. Probably don't even know how to use it."

"Yes, but with a sorry massa like the one we got, who knows what Silas might try?"

Jess snorted. "Point taken."

The speculator, who had barely moved since Silas entered the house, snatched the gun. "Now I want everyone to listen." He trained the gun onto a black man standing in the doorway. "You, there. Get over here next to the girl."

Sunday thought the man would break and run, his features a writhing mix of fear and hatred. Instead, while the speculator spoke to Silas, who'd handed off July to the woman, the man seemingly willed himself calm. He took his time making it across the yard as Silas lashed his back from one shoulder to the opposite rib cage. He scarcely flinched as Silas flaunted the master key that opened every manacle the speculator owned. Silas shackled the man's wrists then pulled a new chain from a toolbox on the wagon and fastened the man's ankle to Sunday's.

"Got chu a new man, li'l pretty."

"Please, Silas. C-can I just touch my son? Can I just put his hair right a bit?"

"Say, 'Please, *Mr.* Silas.'"

Sunday swallowed down the hate, so potent she could actually taste the vinegar of it on her tongue. "P-please, Mr. Silas."

"Naw. The boy stays with the woman. She'll fix his hair. And you might want to know. She's plenty crazy. Thinks he b'longst to her."

He swaggered back over to the speculator, as loathing coursed through Sunday's veins. She watched as the woman took July back into the house while Silas brought out as much food as the wagon could handle with the load of slaves. Once again, Sunday was about to be forced to leave July. First with a dead woman. Now with a crazy one. Hatred emerged as a hard-won whisper.

"One d-day I'll ... m-make Silas pay."

"No," said the new man next to her. "That'll be my job."

She stared at him for a long moment. Something about his voice, his profile, was familiar. Then as she tried to utter her next protest, she found her voice was completely gone. Vanished. Just as it had on the day she was sent to the purple belfry.

9

Mid-May, Pittsburgh, Pennsylvania

Noah followed Gideon toward the river's edge. Only chirping birds and the scampering of furry animals punctuated the quiet woods, yet everything around them seemed stiller than moments ago, waiting for the sunrise that never failed. They were nearing a body of water with the strange yet beautiful name of Monongahela. "A flowing name like the river itself," Gideon had said days ago when she'd first mentioned it.

"We're not very far from the point. The Monongahela and the Allegheny are about to bow to the majesty of the Ohio," she whispered in the darkness.

Gideon had a way of lapsing into pretty ways of saying things that, at once, puzzled and drew Noah. When it came to her job of leading strangers to freedom, she was as good as, if not better than, any man he could imagine. How she must be missing that school she talked about, not to mention her little ones.

They strained toward what appeared an uneven skyline.

Pittsburgh? To Noah, it looked like a huge wedge carved out of several waters, buzzing with commerce. Did people really live that close together anywhere on God's earth without going crazy? Missing Gideon's sudden swerve to the left, Noah banged into a dense pile of branches stacked against a tree.

"What in the ...?"

"This is it, sir." Gideon's voice was tinged with mischief. "Our own stately river transport."

A small upended raft took shape as Gideon tugged at the dead limbs, its appearance so shabby he was certain his heart would plummet to the river's bottom before he traveled a handbreadth on that collection of weathered boards. Barely hiding a chuckle, Gideon made a pitiful attempt to console.

"I know. It should have been tossed for fuel long ago. Obviously, we've had more passengers than usual waiting for transport."

A tall skinny baby-faced youth, his bare white feet perpetually moving, materialized with the dawn, a wooden sign in one of his hands and two sacks in the other, one with a faint bready smell.

"Hank. You're right on time. It's good to see you." She reached into the first sack the boy handed her and pulled out a folded sheet of paper. Scanning it quickly, she turned back to Noah. "You all right, No-wuh?"

Noah bristled at the hint of his ineptness. "Never better."

"Hank, this is No-wuh. No-wuh, Hank."

The youth nodded—endless motion commandeering his thin frame. His way of speaking was stranger even than Gideon's.

"Thou will wait here, Gideon." He turned toward the raft. "Are thou ready, then, Noah?"

"Ready for what?" Surely Gideon didn't mean to send him across that river on this shaky-looking pallet of poles with this boy. Reading his confusion, she moved closer.

"You're a large man, No-wuh. Too risky for all three of us to board, so the two of you will go first. Hank is skilled. It will be quick."

The trip or my death?

Gideon's eyes twinkled in the morning light, Noah guessing she had read his thoughts. She dumped a wad of clothing from the bag that had held the note.

"Here, put these on. We don't have time to waste."

Noah flinched. "Right here?"

He had never undressed before a woman except Sunday, and he wasn't about to do so now.

Sighing a lack of patience, Gideon turned away while he slid into a pair of clean britches. Scratchy and much too short.

"Hank will set you up as a freeman, a vendor." Noah hiked an eyebrow.

"Forgive me, a *seller*," she said. "You will sell pretzels in the safest spot you're allowed in the city. Be careful with them. I'm sure they were hard to come by."

He'd never heard of a pretzel. "What about you?"

"Hank will return for me. Keep busy until I come for you. Whatever you do, do not assume you're not being watched. Keep to mind what we've already eluded."

"Listen, Gideon, I—"

"Pittsburgh has a good many free blacks. Simply carry yourself like one of them. Can you do that for a little while?"

Was she funning with him again? How could a fieldhand who'd only tasted liberty for a few days when he was eight act like a free and settled man?

"Well, uh, Yes. I can do it. Ain't no hardship for me."

"So be it, Mr. Duval." Gideon laughed out loud. "And best of luck."

Freshly-Baked Pretzels! Still Warm!

NOAH STARED at the wooden sign he couldn't read, praying it said what Hank had instructed him to say. He propped it against the wall of an alley along with the bag of pretzels, which he'd never heard of in his life.

"The Lord be with thee," the boy had said. "I pray thou will not be bothered again with the fellow who seemed to be tailing us a while back."

Now, Noah shadowed the entrance to the alley. He'd not sold a thing. Hank had been gone long enough to cross that river several times. He lengthened his breaths to gain control of his nerves. Since his escape, his body had been puckered with mosquito bites from lower Virginia to the top of Maryland, last year's slave-issue clothing barely hanging on to his frame. But nothing had rattled him like being set loose as a seller among a stream of unfamiliar people—black, white, red, and yellow—without the backup of Gideon's wisdom. How would he be able to sell? Why, he'd barely learned how to count to one hundred!

So far, his idea of an adventure on the Underground Railroad had taken a beating. There'd been no wagon-wielding conductor waiting for him at the edge of Duval Plantation. No stern face of abolition. No outstretched arm of white righteousness.

Only a female named Gideon.

And speaking of wagons, the sole wagon he had come near since he'd wrapped July in a final embrace and pecked a kiss on Sunday's forehead was a high-sided contraption on the day of his escape, parked close to the Duval Plantation home just before sundown, painted such a loud startling green that he'd wanted to place his fingers in his ears. A smile threatened his nasty mood. Sunday would've cherished that loud green.

He backed further into the alley. Slumped against the hot

brick wall of what Hank had called an apothecary. Closed his eyes and drifted into …

Sunday. Crazy beautiful, and she didn't even know it. Why couldn't she just be his pretty wife? Let him be the man like other women did for their men? *Oh, you mean like Gideon's been letting you run things ever since y'all left the plantation?*

Noah's shoulders shook with quiet laughter. True enough, Gideon was his match. Challenging him to meet her strength. So why not his wife? Why had Sunday's strength perpetually aggravated him while he grew more dependent on Gideon by the day? Always he had known that trying to force Sunny to do what she'd set her mind against was pointless. But he had been angry when he left—her refusal to follow his dream cutting deep. Gideon, on the other hand, intrigued him. Still, when he lay down in the same space with Gideon each night, it was Sunday and July who owned his thoughts.

And truth be told, little Clayton.

Noah pressed further into the wall, the feel of being trapped inside Duval's circle of dogs beginning to flourish. Hoping he'd finally shaken the man who had dogged his and Hank's steps for more than an hour after they had cleared the river, Noah glanced at the sign whose words Hank had read to him. It was time to move to the streets of Pittsburgh.

Same day

CLAYTON SQUINTED toward the noonday sun wondering what part of Kentucky they traveled. The runt called Silas strutted in the distance, leading the coffle, while Jed Hartley brought up the rear on a horse they'd stolen from Eliza Borden. Hartley had sold that awful green wagon a day after they'd left Eliza's, and now the entire company of half-naked men—and a woman who hadn't parted her lips except to eat a few dried kernels of corn and take a sip of water—walked toward the Ohio River.

Clayton glanced at the chain which had bound him to the woman called Sunday for the better part of three weeks. Though they'd walked together, stumbled together, skirted snake pits and graves together—even slept together—there hadn't been words enough between them to equal the sum of his fingers and toes, the handful that had been spoken all his: "Wake up. Watch out for Silas. Step lightly, snake."

Still, he didn't believe the child they'd left behind belonged to this girl.

He eyed her profile. Craziness aside, her nearness was bothersome—an unsolicited, undeserved distraction. Perfectly formed nose and high cheekbones. Black-velvet skin. Thick springy braids. No question, she was a comely woman, but he had no time for that. All he need think of was that his single good deed, since he'd left the Swamp, may have cost him his chance for freedom. A thriving plantation with his own slaves. His last opportunity to get revenge on Noah.

"Miss Sunday?" The man called Jess who'd tried each day to unlock the woman's speech was trying again. "When you go'n finish your say about black folks and freedom? How about tonight when Silas and Hartley will likely knock themselves out with liquor? Remember, weeks ago you said, as a black person, only fools dabble in freedom. Can't just leave us hanging like that."

The man was rankling Clayton. Couldn't he see it was too hot for anybody, much less a mute, to unravel the rambling line of questions sure to follow a discussion like that? He stared ahead at Silas, his thoughts running toward how easy it would be to overpower him and Hartley if Clayton could get full consent from the rest of the men. That was what they needed to be discussing. Not freedom. *Get back to your own dream, man.*

Maybe ... maybe *he* could just keep them—Jess and all—for himself. For his own plantation.

He recoiled. The idea of owning these particular men made his flesh crawl. He needed to find men he didn't know. Hadn't yet suffered with. He'd be forced to put the fear of God into them at first—not like Duval or Buck Riley, of course—but enough to let them know he wasn't just any black man. He was the master. All his life, he'd heard slaves and ex-slaves talk against another black man owning slaves, but what did they know? What did they have to show for the talk? Owning men and women was the pattern for money in this country, one that worked best if a man wanted to get rich quick.

"Me and the rest of the men, we waiting to hear what you got against freedom," continued Jess, "and why you said you got kicked in the head and died. Didn't make a lot of sense to us, Sunday. Why don't you take us out of our misery about what you meant?"

Clayton focused on the horizon. Fancied he smelled the river. They wouldn't make it today, but the surrounding scape affirmed his sense of approaching water. What then? Surely this stupid speculator didn't expect to get a herd of slaves on a boat with no money in his pocket. And if he did, where would—

"Why did she have to die?"

Sunday's voice—haunting. Sweet. Reminding him of Miss Maggie's molasses. Arresting his silent grousing.

The coffle came to a military halt, soft sobs following Sunday's vague shocking whisper.

"Miss Tullie, sh-she the only mama I had after my real mama. W-why couldn't I ever call her *Mama* Tullie like every-body else? Why she have to die and leave me without another mama? Why come my July have to get caught in her dead arms?"

Dead arms?

A chill stroked Clayton's spine. Coincidence? Or just a part of that untold story that had roped Jess and the others in before this hellish coffle claimed Clayton's plan for a self-styled freedom and revenge?

"What's she talking about, Jess?"

"Can't say, but the child, he *did* call Sunday 'mama—'"

"Hush up!"

Clayton jumped. Swerved to look at Sunday who was staring at both men.

"Hush up! Both of you. Talking about me like I ain't here. Yes, he called me mama, which I am. And you ain't never go'n be. A mama know her own baby. Yes, she do."

———

SUNDAY HAD FELT the breach coming the moment she saw Silas's hands on her baby, her speech pulling away from her thoughts as cleanly as on the day Papa and Mama died. And when that strange-acting woman back there shut the door with July in her arms, Sunday felt her tongue completely locking down, storing the resentment and the uselessness of her pleas, just as it had with Mistress Duval all those years ago when she'd been taken to the Duval plantation.

But this talk about July had reconnected parts of her, just as Miss Tullie's loving care had done during those earlier years of muteness. She blinked back the tears, finding herself the center of discussion. As if she wasn't there at all—

"What's the matter with the two of y'all? You think I'm deaf and dumb?"

The man named Clayton, eyes so familiar they set her heart racing, stared at her. "Your baby, do he cry sometime in his sleep?"

Sunday swallowed down a sob. Nodded.

"A-and do he got a heart on his behind?"

"Yes. Yes, he do."

Sunday's stomach muscles contracted. She wondered if she would be able to contain her bowels while she watched the fierceness of a battle play out on the man's face.

"I-I'm sorry, ma'am. But that was your July back there."

As if she hadn't known.

10

"Must be through with you," Noah whispered. "Done got you to freedom. Reckon she figure that be enough."

He stepped from the alley. Positioned the pretzels sign in the spot where young Hank had told him to. Confusion grabbed a hold while people, from glorious to tattered, bustled and pushed with purpose as intense as any tobacco harvest before the threat of a storm. Transports of every sort imaginable rocked and jostled as boats stood proud and tall against the banks of the Monongahela.

How would he ever make a living in a city like this?

Images of Sunday working alongside him in the Duval tobacco fields, July barely a month old tied to her back, rushed upon him. She had worked as hard as he, and in the midst of it all, delivered him a son. He missed home and hated it all at the same time.

A noise from behind him cut his musing. He turned, his eyes probing the far end of the alley. And there, her back to him, looking as though about to prepare a meal, was Sunday herself. *Sunny? July?* Had they caught up with him already?

She was studying the corner, her precious burden strapped to her bosom. The nape of her long perfect neck and shoulders forming a silhouette even her own magnificent drawings could never capture. Joy sucked up all his scattered thoughts as he dropped the sign and headed back into the alley. In several strides he caught up to her. Touched her shoulder.

"Sunny? That you? I ain't even had time yet to let you know—"

Fear and defiance slammed him along with the smell of mother's milk. "Who you? You one of them black bounties come to fetch me, ain't chu?" The woman spat past him. A warning of sorts. "Reckon you need to know you got your hands full. I jes made it to the city this morning. I won't go easy."

Noah's hands went up in surrender. "Wait, now. You mistake me. I'm one of your kind." He locked his eyes onto hers, praying she would see the truth in them. He lowered his arms then cradled them before her. "Why don't you let me help you with the little one. I thought you was my Sunny—"

"Hey, boy!"

Noah's heart skipped out of rhythm, the slow twangy hard-edged accent of the man in shadow echoing all he had ever feared and despised.

"Told you that was him. That's Duval's nigger."

"And I'm thinking here's another runaway in here with him."

Two of them—the dreaded slavecatchers the woman had thought him to be a part of. Odd. The fear he'd known as a boy of thirteen, when Duval had strung his thin limbs from a swine-killing crosstree, wasn't there. Instead, motion seized him, moving against his own reasoning, his feet moving forward toward the men yet backward through every nightmare he had ever lived. The same inevitable desperate flight, only in reverse, knowing—expecting—the horrible degrading end.

Wonder how long it'll take them to get me back to Duval? Would they follow Gideon's route? Was Sunny right, after all? Was freedom just a foolish dream?

"That your woman?"

"Nawsuh."

"Then how come y'all was all bunched up in the corner like that?"

Good question, though Noah and the woman weren't exactly "bunched up." Obviously, it was Noah they were looking for, and it was Noah they would get—albeit a dead Noah, for he would not go back to Duval. But what about this poor woman? Must she die, too, because of another of his hasty selfish choices? Noah chanced a lustful eye toward the defiant woman, hoping she would catch on to his ruse.

"Well, uh ruh, she was just trying to see ... you know ... just trying to see if I had a coin or two—to help take care of her and her baby." He shifted his eyes to the ground. "I told her I reckon there'd be a price."

The man doing most of the talking stared at Noah. He held a gun. Glanced at his partner.

"See? I told you. Dogs. The whole lot of 'em. Propositioning her right here with the pickaninny in her arms."

The second man seemed embarrassed. "Can we just get on with it?"

"And some of these crazies in the north willing to fight a war to force a country with no slaves. Some talking 'bout turning darkies plum loose on the Lord's chosen folks."

Noah felt the urge to laugh. Last he'd heard, the Jews were God's chosen people. He tensed as the quieter of the two struggled to put the cuffs on his wrists. The other one moved closer. Leveled his gun toward Noah's heart.

"Don't 'preciate this kind of treatment, do you?" He backhanded Noah so violently he swore his brain shook. "That what you trying to tell us with that grin?"

Noah hadn't realized he was grinning—his senses too over-powered with the long-ago smell of hog and scalded hair on Duval's crosstree from which he hung. His thirteen-year-old back running blood so fast that he felt it down to his ankle. Trying to grin defiantly was the only way he'd known to handle the pain.

His brain reset. Blood wasn't coming from his back this time. It was gushing from beneath one of his teeth. He growled with rage, spitting the tooth to the ground and provoking a fist to his empty stomach.

"If I hadn't been promised wages enough to get me and the wife through the next winter, I'd finish you off right here. I've a mind to do it anyways."

"Just a minute, now." The other man still fumbled with the manacles, obviously trying to engage the lock. "We don't want to lose everything we've been chasing all these weeks."

Noah glanced toward where the woman had stood seconds ago, the leader-apparent following his sightline. She had vanished as noiselessly as she'd appeared. *Thank Jesus.*

"Where'd that woman go, huh? I know she belongs to somebody."

Noah's stomach jerked. The plain foolishness of it all. The notion that this woman, whoever she was, belonged to anybody other than herself in a nation built on individual rights pushed him past a line he had peered over but never crossed. The laughter came up from his belly. Untethered. Out loud—his voice rolling through the alley like thunder.

"Did you just laugh at me? There's no amount of money in the world that's worth you laughing at me and staying alive to tell it. Why, you—"

"Come on, then. Drop that gun and fight like a man." Noah charged. Shock and outrage coloring the slavecatcher man, before a third man appeared near the alley's front. *Hank?* The gunman turned.

"Hank! Watch out, man! He got a gun."

The last thing Noah heard was Hank's primal yell and the leader's wild holler of triumph. "Who's tickled now?"

Lord, I'm headed back to Duval.

"WE BE STOPPING FOR A SPELL."

Silas led them deep into a thicket, and the coffle lowered their bodies to the ground. Bone tired, Sunday fell against the trunk of a tree. Wanted to shout like a hush-harbor worshiper. There was not a word of talk as they shared greedily from the tin of water. Ate the uncooked cornmeal. Tried to flex their toes. Thankfully, Silas and Hartley lost no time searching out the bottle, drinking and trading jokes that quickly faded into loud snores. Sunday leaned forward, lowering her voice to the hearing range of only Jess, Georgie, and Clayton.

"Why come we don't make a run for it?" Jess and Clayton came alert, Georgie's face, as much as she could tell, remaining unmoved. "Noah told me once that slaves find ways to run all the time. Sometimes they just get the best of whoever is over them. Said the Underground was the best way to run but not the only—"

Clayton yanked the chain as though fire had shot through it, cutting into Sunday's already torn flesh.

"What's the matter with you, boy?"

"Nothing."

"You about tore my arm off just now." Sunday glared, determined to make him open up. "Now what is it?"

"Okay, it's just that I knowed someone by that name once, and he wasn't a very nice person."

"What name you talking about?"

"Noah."

Sunday knew raw hatred when she saw it, and the flash of

heat coming from this man was as bound to pure hate as her limbs were to his. He had tried to be nice to her on this awful journey. He deserved to know there was at least one fine upstanding Noah—not at all like the man disturbing him so.

"Then, you ought to meet my Noah. He'll put a fresh taste in your mouth."

Both men sat up straight, Jess with a smile on his face. Was she sounding that girlish about Noah? No matter. *Noah a good man. Deserve better than I give him.*

"Truth is ... I heard tell Noah is dead."

Jess's sympathy rose as rock solid as ever. "Was Noah your man? How'd he die?"

"He was my husband, and he died trying to run away to freedom a few months ago." Georgie shook his head, denying the truth of her words as Jess pressed on.

"How'd he come to be by himself?"

"Why didn't he take you and your baby?" Clayton's question was filled with the same ire from moments ago. "What kind of husband and father would do something like that?"

"Oh, he wanted to take us—begged and reckoned with me about the Underground Railroad and how it was go'n take us to Canada."

"Then why didn't you go," said Jess. "It couldn't have been any worse than this."

"Wudn't her time," said Georgie.

Lord, to be able to explain. To open out the cocoon she had built these last eleven years. Never going near the big house and its attendant chapel with the belfry. Beating back the ravages of freedom-talk like it was a brushfire. Delighting in the fact that her body could produce the only thing in the world she could own as a black woman.

Oh, she knew of plenty slave women whose ideas butted heads with hers. Women who bought into that warning that as soon as the child slipped from the womb he belonged to Massa.

Women who would rather kill their babies than have them grow up slaves. But strange as it was, these were women who still had hope—women who, in spite of themselves, knelt and prayed that life would get better one day so that black children born to a future time wouldn't have to be murdered to have a chance at freedom.

She kept up her prattle. Best to ignore Georgie. "Noah, he was some kinda man, all right. Got a hold of a knife from somewhere, long before we tried and failed to jump the broom."

A chuckle stole Sunday's words. The memory of how they had tripped over the broom handle and fallen to the ground—Noah putting his arm around her as they stared up at the other slaves—warming her.

"That man could whittle out any image you could think of with that knife. Good looking too, that Noah boy. But them big feets of his got tangled when we tried to jump."

"Did you love him?"

Sunday's head snapped back against the tree, Georgie's word reopening the wound Miss Tullie had probed a while back. Folks just didn't understand. She didn't know that kind of love.

"Naw. Seemed the only thing we had to talk about, once the field let go our hides each day, were the pictures in our heads. The ones he whittled and the ones I wanted to draw. And July. We both loved to talk about July." She laughed again. "Look like July was carved right out of Noah's side."

Lifting his chained wrist, Jess attempted to scratch his head. Failed. "How many years did you say you spent with him?"

"Three."

"Sounds to me like you collected more memories in three years than most of us do in a lifetime."

"Yeah, may be. Noah Duval made good memories. Just dreamt too much is all."

CLAYTON'S NERVES crawled with happy disbelief and unmitigated rage. Did she just say ... *Yes.* She had just said Noah's full name. Clear as an Easter morn.

Yes, ma'am. You got that right. All Noah ever did was dream.

Perspiration trailed Clayton's spine. Being able to comfortably wipe it away had become its own dream. But could a man get any luckier? He hadn't mentioned the name Duval to a soul, but he felt the need to say something. Else his very countenance might betray him. He managed to squeak out a few words sounding like a buck on the edge of manhood.

"Noah *Duval,* did you say?"

Noah's pretty wife perked up. "Yeah. Why you ask? You know anybody named Duval?"

Clayton looked away. "Oh, no. No-no-no. Just find that name kind of inter-resting. That's all. Like it may have come from some folks I met from Louisiana in the Great Dismal Swamp." Clayton's efforts to untie himself from the lie hung in midair, finally saved by Jess.

"Tell us more about this Great Dismal Swamp."

Blessed relief. A chance to rattle on about the log-sized snakes and thumb-sized mosquitoes and bears and panthers and mud and briars in the mystical swamp of slave refugees in lower Virginia and upper North Carolina until Silas's cryptic laugh. Nothing for it now but to wait for sleep.

Clayton rested his head against his spot on the tree. Seemed Cousin Noah was still the selfish pretty boy he'd always been, abandoning those who depended on him. All right, so maybe he hadn't been living the good life all this time like Massa Duval had hammered into Clayton's head. Still, he had turned out to be the same old Noah with a mouth full of promises and a heart full of lies.

Maybe he ought to feel different, now that Noah was dead.

But the hatred for his cousin was too old to let go of that easily. The need to blame someone for what life had handed him too deep. Now more than ever, he had to find a way to free himself and Sunday and July. Then he would marry Noah's beautiful wife and claim his cousin's son as his own. A perfect ending to a tale of revenge.

Until Silas crept up and unlocked Georgie.

11

Late May, 1861

The warm rain could easily have been snow. Hartley's abrupt sale of Georgie had left Sunday barely able to feel heat or cold.

She moved along in her place near the coffle's end—half-pushed, half-pulled, half-protected by Jess and Clayton. The group had been walking since dawn, the rain-shrouded sun having set hours ago. She took advantage of the darkness and the downpour to whisper a complaint to Jess.

"Hartley planning on driving us 'til the next sunrise?"

"Looks like it."

"I'd give anything to know what became of Georgie." It was the first anyone had mentioned him.

"He doesn't do so well in wet weather," said Jess, what with that wheezing and all. And his being sold as a man when he is only fourteen years."

"Y'all don't know Silas like I do. He would sell his mama dressed up like a boy if he thought he could turn a white man a profit and gain favor."

A lone two-story structure rose from the darkness, a man galloping across the field as though he'd been summoned to review the troops, shutting down Sunday's lament and causing her to slam against Jess's back. The stranger swung a lantern back and forth along an arc until its yellow beam landed on Hartley. Sunday masked her whisper with a cough.

"Reckon he found the color he looking for?"

Jess chuckled. "Reckon so."

"Evenin' to you, sir. You needin' a keepin' place for your property for a few days?" The man stretched his neck toward Hartley, water dripping from his hat brim. "Hey, don't I know you? Ain't you the fellow what come through here some months back searching out the location of a holding pen?"

"I suppose you could call my little reconnaissance something like that, yes."

"Re-*what?*" whispered Jess. "Never seen a pair britches that full of hot wind in my life before."

Sunday giggled. "That's the honest truth. Full of more stanky air talk than a body who just ate a mess of rotten collard greens."

The man's horse stepped impatiently. "What can I do for you?"

Sunday watched as Hartley unfurled some of the cash she supposed he had made from the sale of Georgie.

"I can't say how long I'll be needing your services, but this deposit should be sufficient for now."

The man moved his lantern closer. Whistled his appreciation. "Yes sir, I believe it is. Glad you didn't offer the new Confederate money. Been having a little problem with that this close to the lines." He looked sidelong at Silas. "There's a room out back for him if you've a mind for it. I'll be your guard for the night. If you're wantin' to get yourself a nice room at a hotel, you're in luck. There's one more ferry trip across the Ohio tonight."

He trotted across the field and slid from his horse. Reins in one hand, lantern hanging near his knee, he led them into what Sunday assumed a barn—stench hitting like a crop of live outhouses, setting off in her a line of rapid-fire sneezing. She shuddered and coughed so hard the entire coffle rattled.

"Quit that hacking!" yelled Silas.

"B-beg pardon," she offered the rest of the coffle, recalling the manners her mama had taught her a lifetime ago. Unable to bring the edge of her shredded shift to her face, she tried to curb the sneezing with her forearm, only to butt her forehead into Jess's shoulder. She tendered another apology. Sneezed again and backed into Clayton. Clayton? Had he changed into a chunk of sullen silence?

"Slave pen," he whispered.

Two words—*slave pen*—caused an uptick in the putrid air. *What?* A holding and selling pen like that Franklin and Armfield place in Alexandria Jess had told her about? Was that stink she smelled in fact not the waste of animals but the outhouse kind? Sketches of men and women—maybe even boys and girls the age of Georgie—pushed through. A picture of July on the edge of manhood—herded in before her—cut off Clayton's words.

"Can't happen," she said.

"And how you think you go'n stop it?"

"Careful." Jess spoke a warning over his shoulder. "That white boy seems mild enough right now, but we don't know yet what we dealing with."

"Yeah, and ain't that always the case with this hellish life called slavery?" Jess's words took on a knife's edge. "Hush up, Clayton."

He scared, thought Sunday.

The rain turned demanding against the high leaky roof while Silas lit another lantern. Sunday set her face against his smirk and tried to take in the surroundings closest to her.

Chinked split logs—interspersed with gaping holes—rose from a hay-strewn floor and ended with a loft sectioned off against the far right wall. But for its lack of stalls, it might have been the inside of any number of falling-down deserted barns she had seen during this awful trip.

Wait. Not just missing stalls. *Them's shackles spaced 'long the wall boards like nooses.*

"Mr. Jess?"

"Shhhh!"

"Mr. Jess! I ain't go'n let my baby end up in a place like this. You hear me?"

But hadn't Sunday's papa declared the same thing about her, the very morning he was murdered and she was taken to Mistress Duval to be placed next to the purple belfry?

Help me.

The life's plan she had so carefully crafted was crumbling before her eyes. And it seemed there was not a soul who walked on dirt that could help her. She struggled to corral the anguish. She needed to release it to someone stronger.

Help me.

THE GUARD WAS ALREADY asleep in the loft as Silas locked each man to a separate iron loop, saving Sunday until last. She spoke under the cover of the rain.

"Silas, it's been two days without a bite. These men, they been starving a lot longer than me. They ain't go'n sell if y'all don't start feeding them."

Offering nothing of food or what else was to come, Silas stepped back toward the door, past the pouring eave where Hartley must have waited. Long minutes ticked by, the captors' voices lost to the pounding on the roof. Finally, Silas re-crossed the threshold, Hartley at his heels. For the first time in Sunday's memory, Silas seemed unsure of what to say.

"Uh, Massa Hartley and me, we goin' off a piece."

The words flew out of Sunday's mouth before she could stop them. "And leave us without even a piece of bread?"

Hartley snatched the lantern from Silas. Lifted it to reveal his eyebrows arched beneath the syrupy light. "Sorry to see me go, Sunday? Would you want to come along?"

The catch in Sunday's belly matched the stiffening she sensed in Clayton's body, the space around her pulsing with the unspoken question. *"What chu want with Sunday?"*

But no one asked.

"Naw suh. I reckon I be pleased to stay right here."

She braced for the whip. Blessedly, Silas followed Hartley out the door. Facing the wall, she tried to settle in, but sporadic drops from the leaky roof pelted her. And as she huddled against the floor, the straw beneath her—lumped with the feel and smell of what her mind refused to take in—canceled her hope of sleep. Turning, she stared at the feet of the man she had been chained to for weeks. *I need to thank him. He the reason I even know where my child at.*

From the moment she had learned what happened at Miss Tullie's cabin—how Clayton had fed July, found a spot behind the cabin and buried Miss Tullie beneath twigs and all the dirt he could muster with Miss Tullie's axe—part of her had wanted to throw her arms around him and hug that seething hate out of him.

She reached her free hand toward him. Pulled back, prompted toward the older man at her feet whom she'd come to depend on.

"Jess?"

"Yes, ma'am."

"I get the feeling we pretty close to a river. You feel that way too?"

117

"I do."

"Jess?"

"Yes, ma'am."

"Did you say it's true that sometimes slaves are sold right out of pens like this here?"

Jess reached up to pat her hand. Couldn't quite get there. "Best not to think about. Best to trust God we'll be put on a boat like Silas said. Don't forget there's a war brewing. Each minute we remain unsold is a minute we might be graced with a way to run."

But right now, they had no way to know if they would ever get away. If a war was brewing, Hartley would want to cash in on them as quickly as possible. Sunday thought of how selfish she had been these weeks past. Other than Jess and Clayton, not even bothering to learn the names of the men lined ahead of her against the wall. *If one of these men be sold tomorrow, I won't even know his name.*

"Jess?"

"Yes, ma'am."

"I want to know the names of the other men."

"Right now?"

"Yes, sir. If you please."

"I'm not even sure I know all their names. Some have chosen to talk hardly at all."

"Please."

"All right, sugar. I'll try." Jess's chain clanked too loudly as he sat up, but the rain noise covered. He whispered along the wall.

"Amos."

"Huh?"

"Tell the men Miss Sunday say will they please say their names, starting at the line's end."

"What!? You crazy?"

"Just do like I say, gather them in your heads, and send them back down the line."

Sunday couldn't make out the rest of the whispers. Only that Amos whispered something to the one next to him who whispered to the next one until the message returned, each man whispering the collection of names until all ten members of the maddening line of chained human beings were known to Sunday.

Amos. Dickson. Theodore. Dewey. Eugene. Corbett. Frank. Peter. Jessie. Clayton. Nobody mentioned Georgie.

More soothed than she had felt since the sale of Georgie, Sunday leaned her head against the block of wood that held the iron loops and fell into dreams of a family of protective brothers.

―――――――

"GIT UP."

Something prodded her. Sunday lurched as far as the manacle allowed. Shrank back from the lantern light.

"What chu want now?"

A hush fell over the snoring men who had offered their names an hour ago. Eyes adjusting, Sunday recognized the whip in his hand. She heaved a long breath. "Oh, no, you don't."

She would fight him with everything she still owned—the spit of her mouth, the butt of her forehead—until she died. But then ... what of July? She stilled as he held the lantern to the key loose in his hand, the first time she'd ever seen it detached from his person. Was he about to unbind her? Sell her? Her breaths sped up. His hands shook.

"Silas?"

"Shut your face and let's go."

EVERY INCH of Clayton's body was put on notice as he, along with the rest of the men, heard Silas Duval poke Sunday awake. How twisted that he shared a name with a man like this. A man he had never seen during his time on Duval's plantation. For half a moment, Clayton allowed himself to wonder what his name would have been had he been born in Africa. Wondered if someday someone would find a means to trace the roots of people like him. He gave himself a mental shake. No time for this kind of soft thinking when Sunday was likely about to be ravished.

By Silas or Hartley. *Or both.*

To Sunday's credit, she was offering Silas about as much respect as she would a cockroach.

"I said, what chu doing, Silas?" Slap. Spit. Kick. "Get from over me! I ain't going with you."

The fight was to be admired. But Clayton guessed her insides were curdling like clabber. And her husband—good old Cousin Noah, dead or alive—was to blame for it all.

He kept his back turned. No need to cause this animal to become more riled than he already was. Clayton sensed Silas had pulled her to her feet, having somehow managed to get Sunday's wrist manacle unlocked in the midst of her scrapping. He sneaked a glance. She still bit and clawed, the dangling iron resounding to the roof.

"Shoot me. Go 'head, kill me Silas like you kil't that po' baby on the plantation and Lord knows how many others."

Clayton's jaw clinched until the pain shot down the side of his neck. *Killed a baby? What was she talking about?*

"You thought nobody saw you when you smothered that little half-sick crying angel because she was taking up too much of her mother's field time, whilst that overseer looked the other way, pleased to have one of his best workers free from nursing just when it was time for harvest. But I, the li'l *scarecrow*, saw—"

Silas's slap echoed around the pen shortly before an ear-shattering shock of thunder. What was that clinking sound? *Some of all these manacles, man. What else?* Sunday barely flinched from the slap, but the sting of it seemed to hang in the air along with the entrenched smell of human waste and the receding roll of thunder. Rapid bumbling footsteps from the loft scattered Clayton's anger.

"What's the trouble down here?"

The guard must have had a bottle or two stashed away up there, for it was all he could do to remain upright. The lantern he had somehow managed to light wobbled like a spinning top.

"Can't a man get a night's sleep without a bunch of darkie ruckus?"

Silence. All eyes on that swinging lantern. *Lord, don't let him set this place afire.*

Sunday's scrapping had winded Silas. He breathed so hard it surely could be heard across that mysterious river out there. Clayton chanced a whispered question.

"Reckon what happened to that easygoing fellow that loped across the field to welcome us a few hours ago, Jess?"

"Don't know, but this business of owning folks makes men into those same beasts they claim slaves to be."

Silas answered the guard in a monotone. "Massa Hartley, he said bring her outside."

Clayton's fists turned hard while Jess sucked in his breath. "Easy, Clayton. Raging won't help her. Right now, you can't do anything but make it worse."

The guard scratched his whiskers, his speech as slurred as a man who'd been struck with apoplexy. "Is that all? Then whatcha waiting for? Git her on out of here." He laughed to himself. "Wouldn't mind having a go at her myself."

He staggered back up the stairs, while Silas—seemingly

still shaken by what Sunday had said about that baby—wrestled to subdue her. Fending off her continued attempts at blows, he dragged her out into the rain. Not knowing why he cared, Clayton prayed.

If You're there, help her.

12

Jed Hartley rested atop his stolen horse. The rain having slowed to a light drizzle, he sat tall. Self-important. It had been a full two hours or more since he and Silas had tied her beneath the eave and gone off together somewhere. Now they were back, something suspicious bouncing between them. Hartley spoke, uneasiness marking his speech.

"Are you very cold, Sunday? We hadn't thought to be so long."

Cold? It was May. The dark of the night would make the spring rain chilly. But *very* cold?

"Suh?"

"I asked if you were cold. Why don't you come up here? Let me warm you?"

"Naw suh. I be fine." Silas untied her. She had no idea why he'd decided to rope her this time. Hartley did a throat-clearing.

"Well, then, gentleman that I am, I'm going to offer you a choice."

The sucking sound of Silas's shoes blended with the drizzle

as he moved closer. "Uh ruh, Massa? Could I have a few more words with you?"

Hartley held a steady aloof gaze. Had he not heard Silas?

"July or not July."

Sunday said nothing. Hartley couldn't be talking about her baby. Maybe he spoke of selling her in the month of July?

"I'm offering you a hot meal. A bath, fresh clothing, and a warm bed in Cincinnati. Tonight. In addition to your son July."

She had never heard of Cincinnati. But at the sound of her child's name, she herself started to feel like a babe. If her cramping stomach was any indication, she would lose control of herself at any moment as she had done near another pink white man so long ago.

"July? You got my July close by?"

What if he was lying? *What if he's not?* What if she was being offered her life back? July was her life. She didn't stand a chance of breathing much longer without him. Miss Tullie's stern warning from their meeting at the hush harbor came raining down on Sunday's head. *"No other gods, Sunday. No other gods before Me."*

But July ain't nobody's god. He my baby!

Shifting, Hartley seemed to test his saddle. Grabbing hold to the horns, he answered her. "Yes, I have him. He's being looked after in the hotel as we speak."

Sunday exhaled, dizzy with the possibility. Pleased that her ability to think past Miss Tullie's warnings still served her—

"I'll deliver him to you first thing in the morning if you consent to ... spending time with me. I've been out here for months now, trying to improve the lot of my family and myself. My father was a Kentucky planter, so I'm part of the aristocracy. But a man gets a little lonely, you know." He paused as though Sunday was expected to feel something for his plight. "Though it is within my rights, I'll not force you."

Realization spread like a plague, her saturated braids

feeling like coils of rope fitted for her neck. She sank a bit under the weight of the choice this man was imposing upon her.

"Truly, I don't think that be the thing. Suh—"

"You'd be able to take the child with you to Mississippi. Maybe even keep him in the big house with you while you serve as a maid." Silas shook his head furiously. Sunday ignored him.

Mississippi? The last thing Sunday wanted was to run in behind some white lady in a "big house" in the heart of cotton country. She would prefer death by sunstroke in a hundred-acre field of tobacco to serving someone like Mistress Duval who had tried to cleanse her of the notion of "acting deaf and dumb," when Sunday didn't even know the meaning of the phrase. Maybe Silas was telling the truth for once. Hartley couldn't be planning to sell her as a maid.

Silas continued to signal "no" to her. When it came to knowing how best to sell the skills of slaves, Sunday would take Silas's word over Hartley's anytime. Yet if it ever came to that—slaving inside a big house—she would do it to have July near her again.

Anything? Even give yourself to the man who left July in the arms of a corpse?

A verse the preacher used when she and Noah tried to jump the broom floated in. "Know ye not that your body is the temple of the Holy Ghost?" Sunday's teeth banged together, not from the rain but from the cold lonely place between yes and no.

"C-can I see July—I mean, just look at him before we ...?"

Silas interrupted. "Done got pretty late. I wouldn't count on—"

"I suppose that could be arranged." Again, Hartley reached down for her, his gloved hand wet. She looked over her shoulder at the ugly pen. What would Jess think? Clayton?

Don't matter. July my life.

She offered her hand, and in an awkward scramble, managed to climb up behind a man she despised. Having never sat a horse before, it felt strange, terrifying—like the soggy body of the man before her as they trotted toward the river, leaving Silas looking as though he had finally become one with darkness itself. From tethering the horse to the ferry, to the bright lights of a hotel, Sunday moved through a maze of nightmares. Finally at the threshold of a room, the likes of which she had never imagined, she paused.

Anything for my child, as she stepped across and heard Hartley shut the door behind her.

NOAH STRUGGLED to open both his eyes, one flatly refusing to cooperate. The other, its lashes pushing up against what felt like molasses, finally able to scan the yellow walls of an unfamiliar room. What part of Duval Plantation was this?

One short window touched the ceiling—its stingy light signaling he was below ground. He tried to think. *Miss Maggie's cellar?* But why would he be here by himself? Where was his little shadow, Clayton?

His mind as scattered as November leaves, he allowed his lids to relax against his burning eyes. He tried to flex his fingers—much larger than the eight-year-old fingers that would soon be reaching for Miss Maggie's jam. He forced his good eye open again, a killing kind of dread popping out in beads of sweat. Was he thirteen now instead of eight, waiting for the rest of the Reclaiming? *Is this before or after I be put on the crosstree?*

He tried to raise the large unfamiliar frame that housed the childish mind, the pain in his midsection so excruciating he slumped back, barely holding down the scream of the eight-year-old he had first thought he was. *Must be after the Reclaiming ...*

Hair like black corn silk trailed along his jaw, catapulting him into manhood. "Sunny?"

"It's Gideon."

Noah's mind flipped right side up. It was his scout, and he had mistakenly called her Sunny—the pet name he used for his wife. He felt the need to apologize, but the pain, from earlobe to toenail, quickly erased that notion. He heard himself groan.

"W-where am I?"

"You're at a station, No-wuh, once run by a Mr. John B. Vashon, a businessman in Pittsburgh."

"How long I been ... out like this?"

Gideon's eyes twinkled. "Too long. In fact, you're wearing out your welcome."

Noah spotted the faces of three men and one woman, all snickering good-humoredly. Slaves? *Ha'mercy.* Did they think he and Gideon were mates?

"That mean I'm go'n live long enough to leave?"

"Looks that way." Gideon chuckled. "This might be the only time in your life when the backbreaking work you've done all these years has paid off. You were shot in your chest. You fell, hitting your head against a brick left by someone in the alley. But you've managed to fight admirably."

Noah lifted his brow—a mistake quickly paid for by another sharp pain through his eye.

"I ain't—*I'm not*—understanding."

"Simple. Your strong muscular body saw you through."

"I'd rather believe it was the good Lord."

Gideon didn't answer. Images of an alley—a woman and a child—crowded out the silence. Again, Noah tried to lift himself to his elbows.

"Hank? What happened to Hank?" He sank back, Gideon

hurrying to him with more pillows. He didn't like the helpless feel of this. Too much like the Reclaiming.

"Gideon?"

She primped her lips. Dabbed a damp cloth to his forehead, cheeks, neck. "Not yet time for you to worry about Hank, sir, or anyone else."

Back to calling me sir. Was it because he'd just called her Sunny? Or was it something she wasn't telling him. Something he didn't want to hear.

"But there was a woman, a baby. From behind, she looked so much like—"

"Like the woman and babe over there?"

Noah's eye found the cradle near the room's only window, a thin woman with a fighting visage sitting beside it. He listened to the story of how Gideon had searched for him after she couldn't find him on the street with his selling sign. Of how she ran headlong into a woman with a baby in her arms. Babbling. Begging. Insisting Gideon help a man who had saved her life and was likely dying right then in an alley nearby. Of how Gideon had wavered. But then, overwhelmed by the woman's pleas, had followed her back to the alley, only to have Hank sprawled at the other end. Still, he must have somehow knocked the leader unconscious, while the second man fled. With the help of the woman, Gideon got Noah to the street where a kindly Quaker took Noah to the station. After seeing to Hank, Gideon quickly followed. Now, her face was mottled, her eyes glistening with what Noah knew were not the first of her recent tears.

"No-wuh, I'm so sorry—"

"Stop. I ain't wanting to hear no more." He turned his back to what she would say about Hank, but it was too late. Like the edges of one of Miss Maggie's hot biscuits, a piece of Noah's dream fell to the ground.

Lord. So You sayin' Pittsburgh ain't altogether free for a black man, either? And even a kind white boy can be kil't trying to help him?

Gideon smoothed the back of his hand. "Canada is waiting for us."

Noah's brain registered the full force of someone dying for him. *She talkin' crazy.*

"I'll give you another five to seven days, sir, and we're headed to Canada. Time to rest now. You'll be hungry when next you awaken, and Miss Maggie said to keep you fed." She entwined her small fingers with his. Noah squeezed back.

"No-wuh." She smiled as though he had just given her a sparkling gem. "I ..."

But her soft words faded before he could count past twenty as she had taught him.

SUNDAY PACED THE HOTEL ROOM. Waiting for the laugh, the feel, the smell of her baby. Sinking inside from the thought of the price she yet had to pay. What would Noah think if he knew that she had let herself get separated from their son? That she hadn't laid eyes on him since early April—weeks of soul-numbing despair ending in a trade of her soul to get him back?

She smoothed the bottom half of her filthy shift and glanced at the remaining food Hartley had sent up before he left to gamble or do whatever men did downstairs in a place like this. The man behind the desk had frowned when Hartley brought her out of the shadows, but an extra coin or two convinced him to look the other way. Wrenching her mind back around to July, she smiled and tingled with renewed hope.

"Will he still know me? What's the little fellow's time been like with that addled woman in Kentucky?"

True to his word, Hartley had had a tub of warm soapy water sent up. She peeled the soiled clothing away and eased her trembling body into the lukewarm water. Beautiful clothes lay on a bed in a room full of heavy furniture. All paid for by the sale of a fourteen-year-old boy who happened to be too big and healthy looking for his own good.

"Georgie. Po' little fellow."

She hung her head over the side of the tub and emptied the bit of dinner she had eaten onto the floor.

THE DOORKNOB CLICKED Hartley's arrival before he staggered into the room, his pistol butt above his waistband, his pores dripping lust. Relocking the door and slipping the key into his vest pocket, he turned to face her, the dictates of strong drink muddling his words.

"You smell so goo'."

She simply watched, every nerve in her body standing on end while he moved unsteadily toward where she sat, freshly bathed, on the poster bed. *For July. For my baby.*

"You ready, then, Miss Z-zunday."

Never would Sunday be ready for this. But she would do it. For July. For his future. Hartley's breath stank of pork and liquor and some kind of sickening mint that made her already-emptied stomach fold in on itself. Obviously, the fine liquor in Cincinnati had the same effect as the still liquor on the Duval plantation.

She heard the clink of a chain. The color of Hartley's face racing past its usual pinkness to a bright red, holding forth all the way down to his collar as he dropped the locked circle of a set of wrist manacles over a bedpost. Eyes bugged out with doggish determination, he shoved her toward the bedpost before she had time to collect her wits. She lunged. The gun clicked.

"Don't fight, now, or I'll have to silence you. I'm still a married gentleman with a reputation to protect."

Her teeth rattled as he slid her wrist into the remaining circle and fastened it. She had only been with one man in her life. And though she hadn't married Noah for love, he had always handled her like costly glass.

While he fumbled with his clothing like a two-year-old, she looked away, curled in toward the bed's edge, her locked wrist stretched toward the ceiling. Hartley fell upon her with the force of a windstorm.

"None of that woman stuff, now. We've a deal."

"No. No, we don't. Y-you promised to let me see July first. You promised—"

"You're the most ek ... ek ...zotically beautiful woman I've ever seen."

She didn't know why, but she didn't like the sound of "ek-zotic." She'd never thought herself beautiful. But the way he said it made her feel outside the limits of normal beauty—as though there was *true* beauty and then there was *exotic* beauty.

"W-where my baby?"

"Shush. Let's not worry about little what's-his-name right now."

"But you promised—"

"Hush. I sold a valuable boy for you. Could have gotten far more for him downriver, but I couldn't bear the idea of the long boat ride down the Ohio and Mississippi rivers without having you."

"B-but you said ... you said we had a deal—"

He waved an arc across the surrounding space. "This *is* the deal, woman! Haven't I set you up in a manner most slave wenches would die for?"

Deep purple filled every corner of her mind. "Did you ... have you even seen my baby since we left the farmhouse? Do you even know if he's ..." The words were a cord of wood in her throat. "Do you know if he yet lives?"

Hartley stared at her, a flicker of guilt racing across his brow. "Come on, now. No need to waste the night in regret."

Hope ran from her insides like the water from a pregnant woman's broken sac, the coming pain of what lay ahead offering no hope for delivery. Thoughts of Noah—his constant tries at tenderness—assailed her. Was Noah in Canada by now? *Could he maybe save July?*

The man's scent circled her like a pack of wolves as she clung to the pitiful hope that Noah was still out there somewhere. Praying to his God. Feeling her pain. Somehow, he would rescue their son. She held her breath to keep from dry-heaving. And then she laughed. A harsh laugh devoid of the smile that always accompanied true humor. Once again, freedom had made a fool of Sunday Pennington Duval. Keeping her heart free to cherish only July, she had barely tolerated Noah's love. And now she had lost them both. How would she ever survive this night?

She gripped the bedpost. And waited for Miss Tullie's God to bring on the relief of dying.

13

A rapping on the door of the hotel room joined the sounds of Sunday's weeping. Hartley fisted a pillow and shouted.

"Whadda you want!"

"It's me, suh. Silas."

Silas? *Would he have his turn too? Had he and Hartley struck some kind of horrible deal—with her at the core?*

"Go away, boy. I don't need you right now."

Silas knocked harder. "Sorry to bother you, Massa Hartley, but my conscience wouldn't let me leave."

Conscience? When had Silas cut one of those? For him that was like cutting a third set of teeth.

"There's something you oughta know 'fore you ..."

Hartley rolled out of the bed not even bothering to put on his robe. Clutching the sheet to her neck, Sunday sat up as he threw open the door. He said nothing. Just stood there breathing quiet fury, glaring at Silas who held a set of manacles in his hand.

"I reckon I'd best get to the point."

"I *reckon* you'd better."

Silas took the liberty of moving past the threshold, his eyes every whit as lecherous as Hartley's. But something more. As though he'd been inspired with new treachery.

"That girl there. You don't want to be with her. Hope it ain't too late. She got the clap."

Hartley whirled on her. "The clap? As in the disease?"

Sunday's thoughts swung between hope and confusion. What was the clap, and why was Silas trying to save her? Silas studied the rug, sliding into place his best slave mask. "Yes, suh. 'Fraid so. Old Silas shoulda been told you, but he didn't think it would come to this here." Head down, he crept toward the bed, wrist manacle dangling.

"She done messed up a heap of slave men already. I'll just be taking her on back to the holding pen for you."

"No."

"Suh?"

"I said, no."

Sunday struggled to move to the side of the bed. What was happening here? What was Silas truly after? The man's serpent-like movements reminded her of the heated talk between him and Sunday not so very long ago ...

"I'd rather bed with a copperhead."

"Before this is over with, you might have to ..."

Her eyes raced between the two men, finally coming to rest on the manacles that rendered her helpless. Since the time Miss Tullie's love had finally coaxed her into talking, she had sworn she would protect herself from human pain. She would renounce hope. She would control her outcomes by expecting nothing except to be a slave. Yet here she was. Even after she'd seen her child in peril, she told herself she would figure a way to rescue him. But now she faced the end of herself. The end of her wits. Both these men had aimed to use her for pleasure. Power. But it wasn't just her physical wholeness that was near an end. It was her ability to think her way out. If Sunday

Pennington Duval was to emerge from this room unscathed, she must have help.

She leaned against the richly-carved headboard and felt a release from trying to figure things out. Music from the hush harbor flooded her thoughts. Placed her on Papa's lap that Sunday morning. Georgie's words reached out to her. *The Father got chu—*

"I said leave, Silas. Time you remembered who's doling out sustenance here, and don't even consider telling what I'm about to say. Go down and tell the barkeeper I've turned ill. He's to find another client. Send him up. Neither of them is to know what you just told me. I'll rent the girl to the client and split the cost with the barkeeper. That way, I won't lose all my investment. I don't have money to throw away, but with a wife and children, I can't afford to taint myself either."

Sunday watched in horror as Silas left the room. Fear returned in full force. It seemed the Lord of the hush harbor had failed her again.

CLAYTON LOOKED up at the dripping rafters and tried to settle his nerves.

"God, please. Send Sunday back."

Sighing deeply, he looked to the floor. A tiny flash of metal caught his eye. A key. In front of Sunday's space lay ... *a key?* He yanked at his chain.

"Mr. Jess. Mr. Jess, wake up."

"Nobody's asleep except that fellow upstairs."

"Mr. Jess. What Sunday said about Silas killing babies must have really shook him, 'cause I do believe he done got careless —hauled off and left us our freedom."

"Are you sure she belongs to you?"

Hartley frowned at the new client's question. "I'm a man of my word. You need never question me."

Sunday watched him count the money he'd just made on renting her. *A man of his word.* Still, he would rent her believing she had a bad disease.

"A half hour," he said.

"But what about the ... the wrist iron?"

Hartley regained his ugliest pink. "My apologies, but it remains" he said, before closing the door.

Sunday's new ravisher was so thin she wondered if he could survive a windy day. Wondered, too, at the involuntary jerking of her legs. The man's voice brought her to attention.

"W-would you like something to drink?"

"Naw—suh."

"You're a mighty pretty girl."

Sunday couldn't believe her ears. He'd neither called her a good looking "thang" nor singled her out as a pretty *black* girl. Simply a pretty girl. She dared to look at him. Yes. Sincerity flowed from this man. He was somehow making her feel not exotic but ... innocent. Worthwhile.

Naw. Keep your wits about chu. She ducked her head, not knowing what to say. She couldn't believe what she finally did say.

"I ... well ... I reckon I ought to thank you for that."

The young man pulled at his struggling beard. He couldn't have been more than twenty. He eased into a chair.

"I'm finding myself not in a hurry after all. Mind telling me how you got here?"

Yes. She minded right down to her marrow. She did a hasty turnaround in her mind as to how she felt about this man. Who was he to dig into her past? Yet scraps of her childhood bobbed up unbidden like the occasional debris on her stream in Virginia. Grabbing the first thoughts that drifted by, she spoke.

"Umm. Well. Massa Duval had been married once before, dontcha know ... that is, before the speculator brung me there. A good-hearted woman, they tell me. But she hadn't lasted long under Massa's meanness—just long enough to see her chapel built where she had already started 'lowing slaves to go to worship her God before she died. She had a purplish room built in the little chapel—up in the air, right next to what Miss Tullie called a belfry which was painted inside with the same color. Miss Tullie said the color purple meant royalty. Odd looking getup if you ask me.

"She called it the 'throne room.' A place where folks could pray and not be troubled with anybody else. I reckon she meant to do the right thing. Miss Tullie said the room that held the belfry was where she—Miss Tullie—got her soul saved. But for me, all that room did was mark the end of my peace, all whilst I stared up at that bell." Sunday paused. Glared at the bedpost holding her wrist.

"I was six by the time I got to the plantation, and Massa's good wife was dead. The new wife was still showing her way of running things, so she had me shackled, sort of like this." Sunday looked to the manacle. "To a bench in that throne room. My knees was bent and my legs bound in place so I couldn't get myself up from kneeling. I was ordered to pray for forgiveness for not answering the new mistress in the way I'd been told. But the truth was, I had lost how to talk. Tongue just quit on me. From time to time, the man who put me in there came with water and to see if I was ready to say the words my mistress told me to. But I wasn't. Couldn't. So he left me there some more hours. Days. I don't know exactly how long. Still I couldn't pray the prayer my missus wanted."

Sunday sensed her story hitting a wall as they sat in silence —the man in the chair, the gaudy furnishings—all stock still, seemingly holding their breath, waiting for the rest of her story. But that had been the only whole piece her mind had seized for the moment. Finally, the man stood and walked to the window.

"I don't believe I'm going to be able to do this." His words rushed in on a near-adolescent crackle. "I want to be a writer, you know."

"A writer? What they do?"

He scratched his forehead. Combed long fingers through thin blond hair. "Hard question. All I can tell you is they write. From their heart and soul, they write, and if the words don't come from there ... well, that's how you tell the difference between a writer and a wordsmith.

"Anyhow, Daddy's a preacher. Mama, she's practically a saint except she worries about me—always trying to make me feel more like a man's man. I never could gain weight, you see— tried eating a loaf of bread and a dozen eggs a day to fill out like the rest of the boys I know, so the girls would pay more attention. I just get so tired of being teased." He sighed, sounding much more like July than a grown man. "I thought ... I thought *this* would give me more confidence about myself. Be something I could crow about. But I just can't do it."

Sunday ignored the wetness on her face. "You already more man than most I've seen and a far truer gentleman than the scoundrel who just took your money."

He slipped her a coin before quietly leaving. "Thank you, ma'am. That's about the nicest thing anybody's ever said to me."

ON THE KENTUCKY side of the Ohio River, Clayton listened as Jess took another stab at voicing an opinion Clayton didn't want to hear.

"I'm sorry I ever told you Hartley made that deal to sell

Sunday to Vicksburg. You'll never find her, not on this side of Jordan."

"It ain't the Jordan I'm concerned about. It's that Ohio River there and another one called the Mississippi. That's how I'm go'n find her."

"No, you won't. Do you know where Vicksburg is, son? It don't get no deeper in cotton-picking territory than Mississippi. Plus the war is on now. A real honest-to-goodness war. White folks down there probably madder than a sore-headed bear. You'll never make it before they catch you and slap you onto a plantation."

Jess's words bounced off Clayton like pelts of rain. The man simply didn't understand. He had to have this woman. *Noah's* woman.

"So you figuring we just let that Silas dog have her? That what you thinking? They just over the river there. Silas ain't left yet for Mississippi. Remember, he thinks he got to come up with that key before the speculator demands it."

"Tell me this. How's it go'n help for you to be caught and chained to Sunday again? That's what's going to happen, you know. Did you notice that not a single one of those slaves we just said our farewells to said anything about staying in Cincinnati? They heading for places further north. There's a reason for that. Don't believe it, ask somebody about the terrible attacks Cincinnati put on black folks in '29."

"A long time ago, and I had you pegged for more than a man what deserts a poor female."

Clayton didn't have time to argue with Jess about the history of black folks in this country. He wished he'd gone on ahead by himself. If he'd been thinking straight, he'd have left them all in chains. Searched the city of Cincinnati until he found Sunday then come back and got them to help him build the plantation he'd always dreamed of.

Oh, he would never let himself be boiled down to the animal Silas had become. Didn't have it in him. He'd be a kind master but a master, nonetheless. Georgie's smile sat on him, innocent eyes begging Clayton for help. He slapped it away. He'd got caught up in that kind of mushy trust once before, believing Noah would come back to get him. No more. War or no war, there was no way the South would be giving up slavery any time soon, and if buying folks was the way to get ahead in this world—and it was—then that's what he would do when the time came.

"If you really want to do what's sensible and right—"

Who said Clayton wanted to do everything right? Just because he'd saved the little boy, that didn't mean—

"You'd go back and get little July from that crazy woman."

Clayton's mind churned with the idea—*the bad idea*. The time it would take—the risk it would be—for him to backtrack to that part of Kentucky amidst the outbreak of war ... but if he could find the little boy and show up in Vicksburg with him ... What better way to convince her of the marriage offer he planned?

And to hammer that final nail in his cousin's pine box.

"I'll even go to the farmhouse with you before I try to find a way back to my own family." Jess roughed up his hair more than it already was. "It won't be easy, two black men traveling without a master, but that's the least we can do for Sunday."

PART II

14

September, 1861, Vicksburg, Mississippi

The wagon scaled a steep incline in a place called Vicksburg. Sunday tried to calm herself. After all, she was rid of Silas. Didn't know what became of him. Didn't care. All she knew was, he'd released her in a city called Memphis to another man who had guarded her until they reached Vicksburg, Mississippi.

She was keeping her distance from the tiny light-skinned girl named Nonnie sitting next to her in the wagon—or perhaps it was the girl who was keeping *her* distance, since Sunday couldn't recall the last time she'd had a chance to wash herself. Back at the waterfront, she'd noticed the girl had a slight limp. But seemingly it did nothing to dampen her delight in just being alive. Their backs to the driver, they rocked along on the soft seat while the girl laughed and pointed at the silliest things.

"Looka yonder! That squirrel put me in mind of a puppy chasing its own tail."

Sunday lifted a brow. "Umm."

"You ever see'd a September sky this here deep before? Why, I thought peoples only see'd skies this blue in the month of October. Oh!" The girl gasped as though she'd been blessed with a long sought-after revelation. "Maybe that's cause I ain't never took time to look at the sky in September. Too busy preparing for cotton-picking—"

"Uh, tell me something, Nonnie. What kind of plantation massa would send two slaves and a padded wagon to fetch another slave he done bought?" If the girl wouldn't hush, Sunday would force her to talk about something worthwhile. "Must be some real contented slaves here in Mississippi not to take a chance like this to run away."

Nonnie slapped her palm to her mouth and smothered a giggle. "Massa just a little bit different is all."

Either that or he had scared his slaves to the point where they would never think to cross him with something crazy like trying to escape in his wagon.

Looking down at the Mississippi River from which she had just disembarked, Sunday massaged her tender wrists, avoiding the places too stubborn to heal. She'd been living for the day when the manacles on her hands and feet were removed, and an hour ago, Pete—the man driving the wagon—led her to this soft seat without a scrap of metal clanging against her body. Why did she feel more bound than ever?

Thoughts of her Sunday afternoons back in Virginia rushed her. She closed her eyes, allowing herself to be lulled by the clop of horses and the noise of the street, blocking out the infernal weariness to come once she was thrown into the unfamiliar cotton fields. She startled at Nonnie's touch. The way the girl looked said Sunday must be frowning something fierce.

"Begging your pardon, looks like you got a lot on your mind. I was just wondering what you was thinking about Vicksburg, so far. You like it?"

Sunday mustered the decency to answer. "I reckon it's all right."

"Just all right? Most folks see the town as right pretty—with the bluffs and hills and all."

"I been riding the river since a place called Cincinnati—the Ohio then the Mississippi. Never dreamed I'd end up in a hilly place next to a snaky river that just won't quit being there. I always pictured cotton land flat."

Nonnie smiled, revealing a set of white, if slightly crooked, teeth. She pointed toward a series of steps that must lead to a breath-stopping view of the river and its town.

"That there's Sky Parlor Hill where the white womens go to fun themselves and gossip. I always wanted to go up there— just me and Pete."

"You and Pete, y'all together?"

The girl lowered her chin, her face a mixture of hope and anguish. "We was, 'fore Massa Gillie sent me off'n the plantation, over here to work for Massa Johns."

"Who is Massa Johns?"

"Massa Johnston Smithmore. He the oldest and the one what most everything b'longst to—on the plantation and here in town. Massa Gillie be his brother what runs the plantation." Nonnie stopped. Heaved a breath. "Pete and me, we had our own little hill behind the quarters where we could dream about marrying one day and having babies. And being free—"

Sunday held up her hand. She thought she just might scream. Not two hours in Vicksburg and already here was a slave talking about being free. A set of invisible chains started to reclaim her. Would it ever end?

"Such a peaceful-lookin' place, Sky Parlor Hill." Nonnie listed sideways for a better view. "Reckon that's how come I been wantin' to climb up there. But a slave best have somebody white with her if she go up yonder, and the missus here in town ain't one for pleasuring her slaves."

Though Sunday knew the impossibility of it, the thought of having a white mistress direct her every move—as in those first hours at Duval Plantation—twisted her gut. Stitched her to the cushioned bench while she took slow marked breaths and managed to keep from jumping off the wagon and running for her life. Thank heavens she already knew she'd be working the fields, Sunday wouldn't have to deal with Nonnie's mistress. Would never have to see her.

She leaned forward. Started to relax a bit. Took in every angle of the view, her mind beginning to sketch what she'd seen while still on the boat. No matter what she had said to Nonnie, it was a comely town.

"Which way is the cotton fields?"

Pain easily missed, had Sunday not seen it so often, touched the girl's brow. "Don't you worry none. Plenty of them around. They just ain't always jammed up against that river down there. Like I was saying, I come over from the Smithmore Plantation about a year ago. Had to leave my Pete, but at least I get to see him now and again." She turned and smiled at the driver's rigid back. "On days like today whenever Massa Johns sends for him."

Sunday closed her eyes again and felt the horses braving another steep hill. Unnerved, she risked a peek hoping for a miraculous bit of flat land. But the drop-off and the scary river she had been forced to travel were still there guarding the town like the walls and moats of castle keeps that Mama used to tell her about.

"Harumph!" Nonnie made a show of clearing her throat. "So you was wondering hard on why Massa Johns sent us to meet you."

"I didn't say I had put all *that* much into it—"

"I don't blame you. I'd be wondering, too, if I was you." Nonnie folded her small work-worn hands atop her lap. "Well, here's the trouble. Massa's hoping I'll be able to kind of soften you up for the missus. You see, she ain't what you would call the pleasant sort. Says she deserves one of them lady's maids like rich people have in a place called England, but she claim slaves too emptyheaded to learn to pretty up a lady. Done got rid of more maids over the years than a bird its feathers at shedding time. But I reckon she can be managed by a few God-appointed souls."

Sunday bolted upwards. "Why you telling me this?"

"Lord knows I've tried—worked hours trying to satisfy her with silly hairdos and gowns with enough cloth for four womens—all the while trying to figure out what colors she likes and what ones she don't. I just wish somebody would tell me this. How you go'n set your feets to go out and have a gown made if you hates the color from the start? I ain't cut out for such. Give me a house to clean with nobody telling me what to do all the livelong time, and I'll give you a job you can brag about. But this kind of maid job I'm about to hand over to you—"

Rocking the wagon bed and nearly tumbling over the edge, Sunday shot to her feet. "To me? What maid job you talking 'bout?"

Bewilderment clouded Nonnie's smile. "The man what sent you down here, he didn't tell you? He was paid months ago to find Massa a trained house maid what can mostly serve his wife."

"Hadn't planned on taking on a female, at least not this soon. Hartley had always known she'd end up in Vicksburg as a house servant.

Nonnie glanced around as though someone might be within earshot. "I probably shouldn't be saying this, but I overheard the missus tell visiting kin that Gillie's cotton yield didn't do as good a year or so ago as Massa wanted. In the middle of that, two of the house girls here took the yellow jack fever and died. Missus had a fit not having enough help, so a few months back, when Massa run upon this northerner in New Orleans who said he was going speculating up in the Carolinas and Virginia and would be charging cheap if he could get the money up front, Massa Johns hired him on the spot to bring back a healthy young woman—one what already been a house worker somewhere—while Missus made do with me. 'Course, now the war is on, Massa's gun-making business here in town done picked up. So he can afford easy—mind you, he ain't never got nowhere near poor—that lady's maid Missus be wantin'."

Sunday ignored that last piece of talk. Didn't know what a gun-making business was no how. "But I can't ... I don't know how ... I was stolen right off the road. Right next to the tobacco fields I worked most of my life. I hardly know a corset from a petticoat 'cept for the little bit Miss Tullie told me. Wouldn't know the right shift to choose if my life depended on it."

Nonnie laughed. "They don't call 'em shifts. They call 'em gowns."

The wagon crested the hill and turned east onto a street lined with houses far too big for a body's comfort.

"This here's the street where you'll be living." Nonnie pointed a finger. "And that there is the house."

Pete swung into a graveled drive and around to the back of a white three-storied mansion. Nonnie reached for Sunday's hand—much the way Miss Tullie had all those years ago when a newly purchased slave named Silas delivered Sunday to Miss Tullie's cabin.

"Well, we here. Come on, let's get outta this wagon."

Sunday shook her head. "No."

"Come on now, pretty lady. You want to get cleaned up 'fore we present you to the missus?"

Sunday glared at the girl. Tried to blink back the memory. Failed.

"A stubborn little thing, aren't you?"

The room was wider than three of Mama's gardens. Way, way, way higher than Papa standing up. She'd been shoved to the front of the pink-white man who'd killed her parents, her bloomers soiled. Stinky. Partly dried out from the hard ride away from Mama and Papa left lying on the ground. She looked up into the gray eyes of a woman standing across from her. White. Tall as a loblolly pine, as her papa used to say. A startling sting to Sunday's cheek sent her reeling backward.

"Keep your eyes to the floor."

Sunday bowed her head, begging the Lord to help her not soil herself again. But it came anyway, saturating the tall room with the foul smell of her undigested breakfast.

"What is your name?"

"Sunday! Sunday!" Her mind shouted at her. But try as she may, she couldn't get her tongue moving.

"I asked you your name, and ... what is that smell?"

The woman would kill her now, like the pink man had killed her papa and the man's horse had killed her mother. Still, her tongue was a door, slammed and bolted—guarding between her thoughts and her ability to say them. The shiny hem of the woman's long flowing shift swung toward the other direction. She picked up a candlestick.

"How old are you?"

Hope flickered. Papa had taught Sunday her age and her numbers. All the way to fifty. Inside her head, she pushed once more to get her tongue to answer—to say it, "six." But it refused. Locked up as tight as Papa's tools in his shed. Locked down same as her feet earlier when she had watched her parents die but hadn't moved to help. Thinking maybe this would do, she held up all the shaky fingers of her right hand and the thumb on her left.

"Don't you throw signs at me, you little she-devil!" The woman swatted down Sunday's thumb with the candlestick causing it to throb like a bellyache. "Answer me!"

Nothing came except stunted tries.

"As you will, then. Perhaps a few days on your knees before God

will help you see the light. It has certainly worked for other little stubborn darkies in the past." She turned her back to Sunday who stood beneath something she'd heard her papa describe as a chandelier. "*Take her away from me. She stinks something terrible ...*"

"We got to go, now. Can't keep the missus waiting."

Sunday pushed off from the wagon seat, her laced fingers pressed to her middle, the mansion before her suddenly surrounded by tobacco fields, the girl in front of her a stranger.

Her head pounded from the sounds of glass. Cut to perfection. Dangling over her head as the mistress of Duval Plantation dismissed her with the stamp of her foot. "*Take her to the chapel.*" Sunday stared at the light-skinned stranger.

"Get away from me, whoever you is. I ain't going in there. I ain't never going back in there."

HE HAD BEEN desperate when he did it, trusting a scrap of money to a pompous northern stranger in New Orleans just so he could shut Lelia's mouth about a so-called lady's maid. Not that young female slaves were that hard to come by, but the ones he had seen in the New Orleans market who might possibly satisfy Lelia were a bit expensive for his taste.

He had never been insolvent, but the late fifties had not been kind to Johnston Smithmore, offering up a chunk of nasty debt looming over him like a specter. Cotton factors avoiding him. Bankers warning him. Both implicitly threatening his precious art pieces if he didn't recover soon. It was the only time in the twenty years he had been married to Lelia Rose that he was thankful they had never had children, at least not children who survived. He passed his forefinger over a locket in his vest pocket, one he had bought his daughter Ellen hours after she was born. He couldn't have stood it if his Ellen—whom the Lord had only allowed twenty-four hours' worth of breaths—

had lived to suffer social ruin. But now that the war had fired up, and with it a demand for not only his cotton but the new rifled cannons of his foundry, those concerns were but a fading nightmare.

He peered through the window of his ornate carriage, *too* ornate for him really—one of Lelia Rose's society ideas—at a woman on the street shifting her baby to the opposite hip. Not altogether gentry but not lowlife either. She reminded him of his brother's wife and all those wonderful rambunctious babies she'd had during the last fifteen years. He fought hard to keep from envying his brother, Gilliam. After all, if it wasn't for Gillie —manning the plantation home, keeping the slaves honest, producing the vital cotton crops—Johnston wouldn't be able to live in town, oversee the foundry business. Continue to purchase his beloved art.

Avoid the ugly demands of being a slave master.

But it was hard, the not envying part. Though Johnston had always been told he was by far the better looking of the two, Gillie had a wife whose bubbly optimism rivaled that of the servant girl, Nonnie, plus a passel of glowing children. All Johnston had ever really wanted was a loving wife and children. Children, and to be an art teacher. The relief he'd felt about being childless during his money misfortunes had been swift, the pain of wanting a son or daughter having now returned blade-sharp and persistent.

He expelled a long slow breath and studied the velvety ceiling of the carriage. No question but Lelia Rose's barrenness had made her brittle. Pushed her to insist on luxury beyond her innate ambition. Made her near impossible to touch. Yet he loved her as fiercely as he had at twenty-four when he had taken her as his bride. Maybe, just maybe, this latest maid would help calm her guilt about the childlessness, help soften her into the woman he thought he had married.

The footman guided the horses to the center of the drive

that followed the curved front of Johnston's three-storied structure. As always, the house looked stark. Uninviting with its unbroken white exterior, another of Lelia Rose's demands. Johnston jumped onto the gravel before the carriage completely stopped.

"Did Pete return yet?" The footman looked at him in dismay.

"Uh, I reckon I don't know, sir."

Johnston felt his neck heat up. Good Heavens. Was he losing his mind? How could his driver know if Pete—borrowed from the plantation for today only—had fetched the new girl, when the man had been chauffeuring Johnston himself around all day?

He nodded his head, unwilling to acknowledge the embarrassing moment. This uneasiness about the transaction with the northerner who had telegrammed Johnston of the girl's expected arrival was getting the best of him. He would be glad to get the whole foolish risky thing behind him. A shout from around the back of the house pierced his musings.

"No! Don't chu come near me, I said, or I'll knock what li'l black you got in that yellow skin of yours outta you. I ain't never going back in there. Never."

The voice of Lelia Rose's temporary girl, Nonnie—part upstairs maid, part lady's maid—countered with a half-laugh. "But you ain't never been in there before, honey."

Silence.

"Aw now. It's all right. You just lost your bearings there for a minute. That's all. It's go'n be all right, though. You'll see. Come on with Nonnie. You just been spooked by all these changes is all. Didn't you say you come all the way from Virginny?"

Johnston halted a few yards from the wagon he had ordered to the docking place. Pete, smoothing the sides of the restless horse, looked in the opposite direction. Nonnie stood in the wagon, while a soot-black girl, her carriage regal and rigid, looked toward the back verandah.

"What's the trouble here?"

Nonnie startled. Blanched near white while the new purchase became a frozen sculpture. He never had gotten quite used to provoking that kind of fear. "Everything all right, Nonnie? Pete?"

Pete studied his feet as Nonnie struggled against her lameness to get down from the wagon. "Massa Johns, we didn't hear you come up. Uh ruh, this here's the girl you sent Pete and me to fetch, but something's got her rattled. I ... I mean, Pete and me ... we can't get her to move outten the wagon."

The new girl swiveled her neck and stared at Johnston dead on. Somehow she seemed to mock him with a murky kinship. She had a comely face for someone as dark-skinned as she. Thick braids sloping from her head, nostrils flared and eyes wide, she looked like she'd been carved out of a midnight sky. He knew Gillie would never allow her to look at him directly this way—knew as lord of the manor he should bark or slap or something. But he had never mastered that type of thing. Odd how his thoughts ran to Ellen. She would have been about this girl's age had she lived, her milky coloring perhaps the polar opposite from the property who stood before him. A smile for what might have been—had Ellen lived—manifested itself before Johnston could stop it. He moved closer to the wagon.

"I'm Master Johns. What seems to be the problem?" He saw her hands trembling, saw the still-raw places around her wrists. "What's your name?"

"Sunday. My name Sunday. And my baby's name July."

"Fine names, both. Now suppose you tell me what's wrong here."

THE WHITE MAN fisted his hands against his hips and smiled as Sunday's confusion receded into a dark distant place. As best she could, she whispered soothing thoughts to herself.

Not Duval Plantation. Not six years old. Not go'n put me in the purple room. Not go'n make me a scarecrow.

Like Noah the night before he left, the man appeared to be trying to get her to trust him. Fine. She could excuse this strange master for that. He couldn't know her the way Noah should have. Had no inkling that she fully recognized trust for the treacherous bloody thing it was. The way Noah should have. She retreated from the man's stare. Looked at the galloping colors of the backyard still alive in September. Reds, yellows, blues ...

"Didn't know I was supposed to work in the house."

"Oh?" The man seemed amused. "Well, where'd you think you'd be working?"

"In the fields."

Confusion flickered across his brow before he righted himself. "Then all is well. Serving here in town should be an improvement."

Dread of the looming mansion outstripped all master-slave rules, as Sunday looked straight into his blue eyes again. "To tell the truth, suh, I'd rather be in the fields."

"But why? Why would you choose the fields when you could enjoy the comfort inside a home?"

Sunday struggled against a laugh. *There ain't no such thing as comfort near white folks.* She swallowed back the gagging answer. "I can draw between the rows."

"Draw? Draw what?"

"Anything, suh. When I'm in the fields, I can draw most anything in the dirt. But mostly I like drawing July." Sunday could almost see the light go off in his head. Had he thought she meant drawing water or something?

"Ohhh. I see what you mean now."

Anger flared. How dare he look at her like she was a pickled-brain child. "Yes, sir. Pictures. All I need is a stick—or maybe even a sharp rock—and I can get the pictures out of my head. They ain't the best, but I get 'em out of my head. I'm a real good field worker 'most all the time. But I can work even better when I get the pictures out of my head." She stopped to catch her breath. She was talking as much as Nonnie. "I-I mean to say the pictures come right regular."

The white man studied her for a long minute—his eyes thoroughly engaged, albeit insulting. "Now, where'd you say you come from?" She hadn't said.

"Virginia."

Had she imagined it? Or did the man seem troubled by the word Virginia. "Tobacco, I imagine."

Sunday's heart thumped against her chest. He was trying to decide what to do with her. *Anything, Lord. Anything but go up in there where I know there's a white woman waiting for me.*

"Yes, sir. Worked the fields most of my life."

The man crossed his arms and paced a short distance. He swore beneath his breath. "My fault. Mine entirely. Should never have trusted that Yankee. I specifically ordered a trained house servant, one with the temperament to work with Lelia Rose." He turned to Nonnie. "Take her on up to the attic rooms where y'all sleep. Gillie'll be here tomorrow. I'll see what I can do."

15

September 1861, New York City

Noah snorted his discontent. Gideon was as stubborn as ever about her timing rules. Viewing it from a distance last night, New York City had seemed a shiny kettle continuously on the boil, and now that Noah was only minutes away from the next Underground station, Gideon had insisted they wait beneath a shabby stoop.

"The cover of night is crucial to your safety and that of the couple who run the next station," she repeated for the tenth time. At last, she poked his ribs.

"Let's go."

No longer footsore as he'd been when he arrived in Pittsburgh, he sauntered along beside her, transfixed by the carriages and languages, shops and bakeries—stylish clothing and ... manure? He laughed at himself. *Thought there'd be horses 'thout manure around somewhere?*

They entered a busier section. Testing his ability to flaunt his new freedom, he looked a white couple in the eye.

"Evening to you, sir. Nice night, ain't it, ma'am?"

"No-wuh! Keep your head down."

He laughed once more, this time out loud. "I declare, Gideon. You starting to sound more like Sunny every day. Bossier with every breath."

Gideon frowned, as she always did when he mentioned the woman he was married to.

"Try to remember. I'm not 'Sunny.' I'm only trying to get you safely to Canada. Even though the war is on and many people believe it all comes down to freeing the slaves, still you can never be too careful when it concerns someone trying to make a dollar through the Fugitive Slave Law. Don't ever think New York is any better than Pittsburgh. The climate for tolerating Negroes here is cloudy at best, stormy at worst. Taking care is vital."

Noah smiled, still captivated by her ability to talk white. Obviously put out with him, she started to throw up her hands in frustration then abruptly stopped.

"How did you ever get the notion that every white person you see in the north is in love with you? How am I ever going to get that idea out of your head? I would've thought after Pittsburgh—"

"Aw, c'mon, Gideon. Ain't I nearly 'bout done everything you said so far?"

"Nearly 'bout," she mimicked.

Noah felt chastened. His speech was improving, but right now it was tumbling out in the way he'd heard all his life. She didn't have to make fun of him. "You know what I mean—"

"'Preciate it if you both would go ahead and put your hands in the air."

In the twilight, a man leaned against a storefront wall, black hat brim drawn low, one hand slid into a dark vest—the origin of his drawl a familiar nightmare. "Figured you'd come my way one of these nights. Now git moving."

Noah slammed into a Negro family halted a foot or two in

front of him. Unlike Noah's hands still inching upward, this man's hands shot up like a rocket, New Yorkers making a wide arc around the entire group as though they were part of a bad street play. The family man's voice trembled violently.

"W-what is it you after, m-mister?" "I ain't got no money worth talking about, but I can give you what I got."

"This ain't no robbery, and you know it. I come to haul you back down to your master in Alabama. Can't seem to do without you, now the war is on."

A Reclaiming? Right out here on the streets of New York. The very sound of the word in Noah's head sent his senses barreling toward Duval's crosstree and the smell of hog. Without thinking, he yelled, "Run, brother!"

As though he had been waiting to hear the words, the man and his family struck out in the direction from whence they'd come, weaving through the crowd, the slavecatcher—pistol in plain view—momentarily trapped by the evening rush. The woman, crushing a small child to her bosom, tried to keep up with the man Noah assumed was her husband. Then she stopped abruptly.

"Help us! Won't somebody help us?" before running again. Like the images Noah had heard about—planting themselves front and center at the moment of one's death—the swamps, the insects, the terrain Noah had endured since Virginia flashed before him. All for this? *Ain't this the North?* Why wasn't somebody helping these people?

He took out behind them, maneuvering around a half block of pedestrians and losing the slavecatcher, before Gideon overtook him placing herself squarely in front of him.

"What chu think you doing, woman?"

She grasped the muscles of his arms. Pulled him into a mercantile. "I can't let you do it. I can't."

He stared. This from a woman who had dedicated herself to the redemption of slaves? She seemed about to cry. "Don't you see the danger? My heart breaks for that family, but sometimes one has to make a choice between two horrors. When Hank met us at the river, he handed me a note asking for help with a runaway who'd just been delivered of twins. I'm a mother, Noah, so rather than join you in town, I chose to help her first. I risked sending you into the city, hoping there was more safety for you on the street than in the chance you'd be caught alone in the woods. From the urgency of the note, I dared not take you with me. My calculation was wrong, but I got lucky, and you survived." Noah watched the tears win out, streaming with abandon.

"This time I choose you." She heaved a breath. "Don't you see? If I allow you to save that couple, you very likely lose yourself."

Hush-harbor Scripture Noah had nearly closed his mind to opened itself to him. *"For whosoever will save his life shall lose it: and whosoever will lose his life for my sake shall find it."*

Noah scooped Gideon up and set her down on a bench outside the mercantile door. "Stay there." Sprinting, he nearly laid low a line of vendors about to wrap up their wares, only to find the space, as far as he could see in the waning light, bereft of the family.

Help me, Lord.

A faint keening came from around a corner. He slowed. Allowed the evening strollers to surge ahead—a duplicate of the crowd that had paid no attention to the plight of the man and his family minutes ago. The slavecatcher's back was yards away, his hat a dead giveaway, his pistol cocked and high. He seemed disoriented. Maybe his first slavecatching job. *Good.* Noah made the corner and turned into a narrow, paved walkway between two rows of side-street businesses. Counting on the thoroughfare noise to mask the sounds of his feet, he ran until he reached the sporadic cries. He spoke as loudly as he dared.

"Easy, now. This here a friend. A slave just like you."

Huddled with his family in one of two encased corners that winged a set of double doors, the man stepped out onto the passageway, wife and child following, his features near lost in the darkness. Except his eyes. Stretched. Shouting silent terror. Noah shook his head. Held a finger to his lips, praying the man would trust him.

The woman shot past Noah. *She going the wrong way. Done got turnt around.*

"Get down!"

The slavecatcher turned into the strip, firing through the darkness toward mother and child before Noah could feel his next heartbeat. In a strange half-second of reliving the torture of the crosstree, he stretched his body past its limits, knocking the slavecatcher to the pavement.

And the baby from the mother's arms.

The gun popped off beneath the slavecatcher's chin, stopping the forming crowd and Noah's heart right along with it. Had Noah knocked the little one from the mother's arms? Was the baby ...? The child was too still. The parents stymied in horror. Their baby—a little girlchild, was it?—lay sprawled on the ground, her small frame jammed against the slavecatcher's head. Blood soaking her light-colored tatty clothing. The mother's scream split the alley as the father rushed to lift the motionless child.

Dear Lord. I done killed somebody's child?

A woman's voice rose from the main the street. "Help! Someone help! I saw the whole thing." She spoke loudly above the crowd. "That's a runaway slave in there. And another nigger who's interfering with the law."

Noah turned to find Gideon by his side. An absurd question slipped from his thoughts.

"She just say '*nigger*?'" In New York?

Gideon looked at him, anger clouding her features. "Don't

talk. Move. Now." Carefully, she coaxed the child from the stunned father. "Run!"

"But—"

"No 'buts,' sir. You must trust me. I know what I'm doing. Run to the other end. Left to the next alley on the right. Wait there."

Noah stood back as Gideon looked over her shoulder at the child's mother, her knees dug into the street. Sounds of grief coming from her chest.

"Give me my baby! I want to die with my child."

"Shhhh! You will have your baby. Tonight. I promise. I'm a mother, too, trained to do this by Moses." Noah watched the man's eyes flicker understanding.

"Go!" repeated Gideon. "Carry your wife in your arms, if you must, but go!" The man, wife in arms, fled.

Noah grabbed the little girl before Gideon could object. Crowd swelling at the entrance to the promenade, he followed her. Pumped his legs harder than he had since running from Duval Plantation as a boy, policemen yelling in their wake.

Minutes later they were inside an alley, the light from the streetlamps revealing scores of tightly-packed barrels along the walls. Space hardly large enough for Noah alone to navigate, they skidded through layers of slick refuse, barely able to stop —before slamming into at least a dozen more barrels rowed up crosswise. Just shy of the barricade was the babe's father still carrying his wife.

Noah reviewed their choices. Clearly, the crowd was turning into a mob. He glanced at Gideon who surely read his thoughts. Quick removal of the centered barrels was the only way—a noisy risk-filled way—but they could ill afford to become hemmed in.

Releasing his wife from his arms, the child's father moved a barrel toward the crowd noise, the sound tumbling down a slope toward the escape route. Noah placed the baby into the mother's arms as Gideon began helping.

"That's it. Push them barrels toward the crowd. Noise don't matter no more. Then run. I'll be right behind you."

"No-wuh?" He knew her fear. The mob would kill him if he didn't move now. But likely he had killed a child tonight. The way he saw it, his death would be a life for a life. He must slow the angry crowd. Make time for Gideon, the parents, and the baby to get away before the mob could block the exit.

"Go on, now."

Though the set of Gideon's mouth said she was desperate to argue, she didn't. Instead, she guided the disoriented mother through whatever space she found as the father rolled a few barrels toward Noah and escaped into the open air with the others.

The first "nigger" word was hurled through the alley opening as Noah worked to set up a new barricade, three deep. Curses flew as the chaos of rolling barrels sent members of the mob into multiple directions, some crashing into walls of other barrels, others squarely set onto their backsides—creating a melee of outraged yelling. Gunfire popping, Noah ran toward the end, setting barrels across the exit before escaping into the night.

"I TRAINED YOU WELL."

She had waited for him. Gideon. *Some kind of woman, that Gideon.*

The group backtracked per Gideon's instructions to baffle the mob. Noah looked toward the man whose name he still didn't know.

"Not a bad idea, using them barrels." The man grunted his thanks.

Noah brought up the rear as Gideon zigzagged them for what seemed hours. Until—breath spent, several shoes missing, and the smell of fear dictating like a fieldhand overseer—the few beleaguered outlaws finally reached a house with a front door so red it seemed to glow in the dark. They disappeared toward the back. Oddly, the house itself was dark, too, but the sounds of the mob were fading. Praise God.

The faintest tremor overlaying her voice, Gideon whispered. "If anyone believes in prayer, pray we haven't come to a station that is no longer manned. I dare not call out. Not yet."

They crouched beneath the high and wide back steps, the baby girl still limp in her father's arms, though the mother had sworn she was breathing. A rush of feelings nearly unmanned Noah. This might well be July, his precious little mouth open in contented sleep, his curls flattened to his head. Bleeding from the meanness of a slavecatcher.

In New York City.

Had he been wrong to hope all these years? Was Sunny right, after all? *Is we hated everywhere, God? Please don't take the life from this little girl 'cause of my meddling.* A door opened above the steps. A cautious whisper.

"Is anyone out there?"

A swoosh of relief escaped Gideon. "It's me, Hiram. We're coming in."

———

Near the site of Eliza Borden's Kentucky farmhouse, same night

THE THICKET WAS SO dense Clayton hardly knew north from south. He leaned against a tree, fumes from a recent burning somewhere setting his teeth on edge, along with the knowledge that he and Jess were being followed. He struggled to maintain his bearings. He hadn't made it to the Great Dismal Swamp all those years ago without knowing when he was being snooped, but he didn't plan to give fear the upper hand.

"I reckon we done picked us up a tail, Jess."

"I know. Been behind us for a while now."

"Don't know if he's inside the forest or not."

Jess sat beside another tree cracking and munching from a sack of nuts they'd "borrowed" from a storage shed a ways back. His ankles crossed, he looked like a gentleman out on a hunting trip. "Interested to see what he'll do when we start moving again."

Believing their collective memory had placed them within a mile of Eliza Borden's farmhouse, they had decided to wait in the woods until sunset. Never had Clayton thought it would take this long to get back to the other end of Kentucky. But they were here, and the sun was setting. Snooper or no snooper, it was time to move.

"Don't know, but we 'bout to find out."

Clayton and Jess walked in silence toward the clearing he hoped would hold little July. The smell seemed stronger. No question about whether something near had burned.

"Just not July. Not the little boy I took on as my responsibility."

Jess coughed. "I'll be a happy man when we get that odor behind us."

"Me too. I'm getting a li'l worried about you and that cough."

Jess waved away the worry. "All I need is a good night's sleep, some fresh air and a warm bed. I'm thinking that'll do us both good. Maybe Miss Borden will let us—"

Voices ahead hushed them. "Sounds like slaves. I overheard somebody say since the war started, they're beginning to walk off plantations in numbers."

"Just up and walk off?"

"Just like that."

Clayton leaned in to listen to the voices, Jess so close on him he was about to knock them both over. "Watch it, man!"

One booming voice out of what sounded like a goodly number of slaves silenced the rest. "There's nothing left here, I tell you. Use your noses, your eyes." He sounded like he was about to mount a pulpit. Had that preacher voice. "It's all burned up, the house and everything."

Clayton fought the urge to scream. He'd hoped that stubborn smell had come from a barn or shed or something. Not the house itself. A baby cried. Clayton shifted, surprised at the way his heart leapt at the possibility of seeing July again.

"We know you got a li'l book learning, Brother Ben, but we ain't stupid," said another of the men. "Just thought maybe it'd be worthwhile to stay here the night. Might be a smokehouse out back or a cellar or something what's got some food hid away."

A female voice, soft but fearless, interrupted. "Can anybody tell me where we going? Where *is* that northern army y'all talking about us joining up with?"

"It's not just one army, Pearl ... well it *is* just one army but—"

Enough. Clayton couldn't listen to this fussing any longer. He had to know what had become of Sunday's child. He crashed through the woods, the smell near suffocating ... *Achoo!* A scream split the darkness. Preacher Ben picked up a limb— more like a tree trunk—and pivoted toward Clayton's and Jess's direction.

"Who's there?" He stood rigidly, his voice seamlessly moving into a kind of preacher-like sing-song mode. "I'm ready to di-i-i-e before I go back into Egypt."

Clayton raised his hands. Stepped from the woods. "Whoa there, brother. No need for that. I be a slave just like you. Looking for a baby left here by mistake." The half-truth chafed him, especially told to a preacher. But he wouldn't take time to ponder that.

"We don't know anything about any baby," said Ben. "Only one we have belongs to Pearl here. Not looking for no trouble either."

"None found," said Jess through a coughing fit.

The big preacher relaxed his stance. Studied them for long moments. "I'd like to invite you to supper, but I'm afraid all we have left is rations for tomorrow's breakfast."

Borrowed nuts notwithstanding, Clayton reckoned he was still hungry enough to insist on the upside-down offer but thought better of it. "Thank you, but we just ate."

"Good. Then you're just in time for our nightly devotion."

16

Same night

Noah's breath hitched as the mother pushed past the group toward her baby. Somewhere in the last hour, he, too, had thought the child had moved against his chest. Running scared, he might have willed it to be.

"Give her to me." She lifted the little girl from her husband's arms as Noah and the rest of the group held their breath. The baby whimpered, and relief flooded the group.

They clambered up the steps, through the red door, and into the kitchen of a two-story house. Though quite old and dimly lit, it was well-maintained. An elderly black couple, both snow-headed, greeted them. Another station, run by Noah's own people.

"Gideon, we've been expecting you for weeks." They smiled at the rest of the group. "We're Hiram and Susanna Kelson. Welcome."

"We need a place to lay the baby," said Gideon. We think she might have been hit."

The mother stood trembling. "Please, won't you hurry?"

"This way," said Susanna. She moved like a woman of barely forty years, the group at her heels. "We just sent another couple with a little one on their way, so we are set with supplies." She pulled back the covers of a crib. "Now then, put the precious one right there. That's it. Easy now. Would you let me have a look?"

The mother wrung her hands. Looked at Gideon who nodded. "These are people of the cloth. You can trust them."

As though she handled one of the Lord's chosen jewels, the woman began peeling off the child's clothing. The baby's crying increased, her objection to being shuffled about mixing itself with her mother's groans as Susanna Kelson finished examining her. Slowly unfurling her body, the woman turned and smiled.

"Nothing here but dried blood. And somebody else's at that."

Noah felt lightheaded. The child's mother rushed Susanna Kelson, crushed her with an embrace before swooping up the now screaming child stripped down to her napkin. Prayers, laughter, and tears lit up the room until Susanna exclaimed, "Good heavens! Where are my manners? You all must be starved. Hiram, get water so Mrs. ...."

Noah chuckled, realizing neither he nor Gideon knew the couple's names. "Oh," said Gideon, turning toward the parents who cooed over their child, "would you mind introducing yourselves? Hiram, Susanna, this is Noah Duval, and this delirious couple here is ..."

"Horace and Esther Phipps." Horace extended his hand. "Mighty pleased to meet you, all of you. And very grateful."

Susanna beamed as though service to any of God's children was the height of her life. "Come along, now. We have fewer passengers these days—probably due to the war—so there's plenty of supper." She made her way back toward the kitchen. "Oh. And there's mail for you, Gideon, on the table in the vestibule. Been here for weeks now. The rest of you just follow me."

Noah decided to wait in the hallway until Gideon read her letter. He owed her an apology, and he wouldn't be able to eat a bite until he offered it. He owed Sunday one, too ... *What's the matter with you, Sunny? Don't you want to be free ...?*

Aw, Sunny, I got so much to say to you.

Had the only difference between North and South come down to the foe you know and the foe you don't? Was Noah truly a free man, when he couldn't even walk the streets without—what was the word Gideon used back in Pittsburgh— "predators"—sniffing after him? After tonight's narrow escape, he had begun to seriously wonder.

But there was still Canada. Things would be different when he and Sunny and little—

"No-wuh." Gideon called to him, her voice barely above a whisper. He turned to see her facing him, a letter in her hand. She looked like a graveyard hain't.

"What's the matter?"

She pointed toward a settee. "You'd better sit down for this one."

"I ain't sitting down. Tell me what's wrong."

"Miss Maggie back on the plantation. She wrote ... it's Sunday. She's been sold, and July is missing." Noah stumbled toward the door. Laughed. Heard the insane guffawing coming from his own mouth.

"That's a Ananias-and-Sapphira lie. Miss Maggie can't even write."

"Apparently, she had another conductor to write it for her. He signed his name."

Noah stared at the trembling letter in her hand. She paused. Swallowed hard. "That's all the letter says, except that Mama Tullie was supposed to be keeping your baby while Sunday washed, but there was a fresh shallow grave behind her cabin. She was in it. They don't know what became of July."

"Well, I do! I know what became of my little man. He made it. Just like his daddy go'n do. He made it." Noah turned away from Gideon, unexplainably angry with her. He fought to keep from shouting at her, picking her up and moving her from his presence. He struggled to hold back the tears. "Go 'way. I need to by myself."

"What have I done, No-wuh?" Gideon's throat constricted as she moved to face him. "What on earth did I ever do?"

She turned and left the entryway, Noah watching her move unsteadily for the first time. He eased himself onto the settee. Placed his head in his hands and wept.

At length, he looked up. Rubbed his damp hands down the sides of his face, fighting to rein in the little terrified boy inside who had watched his parents being sold so long ago. The child who, that day, had vowed he would die somewhere other than the spot of Duval land upon which he stood. Now, after all he had dreamed about, sacrificed for, still Noah Duval had *not* "made it." He was *not* free. Would never be free.

And the price he was paying for even trying was unbearable.

The following day

CLAYTON WAS the first to find them. A woman, identifiable as such only by the attempt of her jewelry to fuse itself with her bones. Though sorry for whomever the poor woman was, he was heartened by the jewelry. *Eliza Borden didn't wear nothing like that. Maybe she moved on—her and li'l July.* He'd been with her only a short time, but the thought was something to hold on to.

Until the sun's rays broke through. Probed further, cutting off Clayton's ability to breathe.

Smaller bones which, unlike the jewelry, sought no place on the woman's frame, lay beside her, next to a small skull that Clayton had cajoled wild berries into a few months gone ...

"Pa-pa?"

July's giggles, as Clayton wrestled him down to change his napkin, rose up in a chorus of accusations. A little baby was dead. His little cousin. Because of Clayton, Noah's child was dead. The child Sunday claimed Noah loved so much. *Aw, Father.* He would still be alive had Clayton not brought him here. Left him here—

Naw. Clayton himself would not be here in this inferno of death if not for Noah. If Noah hadn't run away and left him. If Noah hadn't run away and left July ...

"Boy, do you understand that that little cousin of yours is getting farther and farther toward freedom while you try to protect him? Why, he's go'n be up north pretty soon—going to school with a pocketful of peppermint candy while you still holding back from telling me which way he went? What did he promise you anyway that's making you so mule-headed? That he was coming back to get you?" Master Handley roared before he pulled Clayton's earlobe with such force that he thought the insides of his ear would come tumbling out ...

Clayton reached for the comfort of his hate. Pulled it closer like an old blanket. "Noah was getting what he deserved."

But was July? Sunday?

A shaking took hold, as fierce and unexpected as the distant quakes he had heard about while in the Swamp. Eyes on the scorched bones, he staggered backward.

Remember. You got to keep on remembering—how, for years, he had awakened every morning with the fear that sleep had robbed him of the hate he needed to go on. Checked to see if it was still there. Coddled it through the bruising fields and beatings until he'd finally run. Captured and used by a man named Buck Riley until he finally escaped to the Dismal Swamp.

Forcing himself to recall what had sustained him all these years, he turned. And stumbled into a wall of sweaty male flesh, long dirty blonde hair adding to the potential for dread.

"Can I help y'all?"

Clayton wished he could go into Miss Maggie's jam cellar and cry. The stranger's drawl confirmed the fear that had leeched his spirit for months. He and Jess had finally been caught.

"Y'all looking for something?"

Preacher Ben ran toward his battering ram. He was back in a breath. "Hope you've got a gun, mister, else you're about to be clubbed to death."

Clayton lifted his shoulders. Now that Ben had squared off, the man would pull his weapon. If Clayton was about to be jailed, whipped, or even shot, groveling wasn't going to help.

"Yes, sir, true enough. We looking for something."

Ignoring Ben, the man crossed his arms over his chest. Nodded for Clayton to continue.

"A few months back, a woman by the name of Eliza Borden took me into this house for a few days. I came back to thank her, but ..." Clayton gestured toward the skeletons ... "this is what I found." The man paled before moving toward the remains.

"I've been checking on this place for the last couple of days. First time the embers haven't been too hot to try to get through." The man stooped, his voice barely coming through. "This is her, I'd wager."

Clayton steeled himself against another wish for Miss Maggie's cellar. A skeleton was a skeleton. Though he'd just seen the tiny damming bones of a child, he clung to his jewelry theory.

Sorrow shadowed the stranger as he battled to collect his

own sense of manhood. "Though I've never known her to wear this much jewelry, couldn't be anyone else." His Adam's apple dipped. He stood. Seemed to find the presence of mind to reach out his hand. "Name's Taylor Mack. Everybody calls me Mack."

Ben dropped his tree. "Good to meet chu." Clayton and Jess said nothing.

"I'd hoped she'd been out visiting somewhere. But what with the happenings in her life years back and the baby she'd recently taken on, she rarely showed up in public anymore."

Clayton wouldn't be rude enough to dig into the "happenings," but Jess did ask a question. "You live around here, sir?"

"Used to, up until a few days ago. Had a railroad station." He searched the eyes of everyone, obviously trying to see if anyone knew what he meant. Ben spoke up.

"I'm thinking we all knows what you mean by station, and we thank you." The man seemed buoyed a bit.

"That's how I got to know 'Liza. She'd been widowed young but was a part of the Railroad for years until her ten-year-old daughter was abducted, killed, and much worse for being the child of a 'nigger lover.' 'Liza hadn't been right in the head since, though she still carried the cause of freedom in her bones. Hardly no one came to see her, black or white." He worked the ashes with the toe of his boot. "My house was burned four days ago—a message left for me, calling me not just a nigger lover but a traitor because of my Southern roots."

A hard-edged quiet ensued. "I'm real sorry," said Ben.

Clayton said nothing—though Ben couldn't have been more sorry for this man than he was.

"Don't have much," said Ben, but such as we have ..." He gestured toward the spot where the group had started a fire before the man arrived. "This be the last of what we have before hopefully we catch up with the Union Army."

Silently everyone moved into a circle and seated themselves. Two baked sweet potatoes were laid on a tin plate which someone whose name Clayton didn't know yet blessed and passed around. The soft-spoken girl called Pearl, thinner than a whipping switch, shifted the weight of her baby and offered the plate to the white man. Looked on him with unveiled awe.

"Here. You eat. I ... I ain't hungry." The man glanced at her large sunken eyes, belying her need for food. He nodded his head, bit the slightest piece from the potato, chewed slowly—deliberately—as though each movement of his bearded jaw attested his deep appreciation.

"What's your name, young lady?"

She smiled so brightly that Clayton's heart thudded out of rhythm.

"Pearl. Ain't nobody ever called me young lady before." She drew a deep breath. Pulled at the hem of her rotted dress. "What chu planning on doing now, Mister?"

"I plan to continue doing what I'm called to do."

"As we all should," said Ben.

Clayton scowled. The silly notion of a black man being "called" chafed him. The only thing he was called to do was avenge his heart of Noah's deed and mimic the greed of every planter he'd ever known. Whatever it took to become rich, slaves and all, he would do it. Hoping to catch the man's eye, he stretched his neck into the circle.

"And what would that be?"

"How much time you got?" Taylor Mack warmed to the question. "I consider myself a missionary—of the Pauline sort, if you will—called of the Lord Jesus to offer His redemption and whatever else I have to the ones so many think not worthy."

"Like colored folks?" Pearl seemed enrapt by the man. Though Clayton drew up inside at the sound of her near worship, he was strangely drawn to her. Couldn't help noticing how fetching she was.

"Exactly."

"But what 'exactly' will you do for us colored people?"

The man seemed stopped—not puzzled but simply stopped, as though waiting for the answer to come outside of himself. "Whatever is in my power."

For the first time in a half hour, Jess spoke up again. "Uh, you ever been to Charleston?"

"I have. As a matter of fact, twice. Beautiful place."

"How'd you like to lead me and my friend here back to Charleston—acting as our owner, of course."

"You mean to tell me you want to go back into the deep South in the middle of the war?"

"I realize it's a risk, but I've been stolen from my wife and family for months now," said Jess. Haven't let myself think how crazy with worry they must be. Now that me and this boy here got answers, though they ain't the ones we wanted, I need to go home." He sent a plea toward Clayton. "I'm hoping Clayton will go with me. Help me get my life straightened out."

Pearl shot to her feet. "I want to go too."

Clayton leaned back, evening out the circle, his mind spinning with all that had happened within the last hour. He wasn't ready to deal with the death of July, but he knew he would soon have to. He would have to at least find a way to get to Sunday— be man enough to tell her then take the blame on himself. He would not desert her to a cruel hope the way Noah had. The way Noah always did.

But going to Charleston was out of the question. Clayton's next stop would be a place in the deeper south. A place called Vicksburg, Mississippi.

17

Vicksburg, Mississippi

Sunday bolted upright, her frame forming a perfect *L*. Though tattered, the homespun rug she sat on was pretty. The tiny single-window space around her foreign yet bright. Where was she, and where was Jess 'nem? And ...

Where is July? Lord, where my baby?

She blinked against the encroaching purple of the belfry that never left her for long. How could she be thinking in that hateful color when she still didn't know where she was? *One, two, three ...*

Pressing her fingertips to her chest, she counted toward twenty. Nearly half the numbers her parents had taught her before freedom killed them. Would a day ever pass when she didn't think of how useless she'd been to her mother and father that day?

She scanned the strange place from rug to rafters. Through the haze of dust motes, she spotted the shift she had worn for five months.

"Four, five, six ... Vicksburg."

Vicksburg. She was at a house in a place called Vicksburg owned by a man named Smithmore. She glanced sideways at the window. Goodness gracious. What time must it be?

Hefting her stiff body from the floor, she scrambled into her shift. Why had Nonnie not wakened her? The girl's cot looked as though it hadn't been slept in. What if Sunday's own late-sleeping had caused the new master to change his mind about sending her to the plantation? Heart wobbling like the spinning top Noah had made July, she tiptoed toward the door and opened it. Bare dark walls and a set of unpainted wooden steps greeted her. Where were the other steps Nonnie had used to lead her to this room last night?

Seven, eight ... She breathed deeply. She had to find her way to something she'd seen before so that she could escape this big scary house. She saw no choice except to follow the steep narrow steps that seemed to disappear into a dark hole. She began her descent. She would run if she had to. Hide in one of those buildings along the river. Anything except stay in this—

"Oomph."

She crashed into a wall with a wide squat door that fit so well it took moments before she saw it for what it was. Should she open it? What if she ended up inside the part of the house where a smelly black girl like her had no business? What if she ran smack into the mistress? Back pressed against the wall, she slid to the floor next to the mysterious door and pulled her knees to her chest, memories of the only other mistress she had ever served having their way with her ...

"You'll open your mouth and speak, or you'll end up living without a tongue"—

The clomp of uneven footsteps accosted her coming from the direction of the attic rooms. "Nonnie? Is that you?"

"Shhh." Nonnie held a small lamp in the dark space. "I thought I heard something in here. What chu doing anyhow? We don't hardly use these short stairs a'tall, 'lessen we called for over in the night. Come on. Breakfast for Massa 'nem done been served long time ago. I 'spect they been waiting for you for a while."

"Where you been? How come you let me sleep this long?"

The lamp revealed Nonnie smiling. She flushed—sheepishly reliving something Sunday had neither the time nor desire to inquire about just now.

"Been helping Miss Lelia get dressed for breakfast. That's all. Now come on." She grabbed Sunday's tender wrist.

"Ow!"

"Oh! So sorry. I forgot." Muttering under her breath, she frowned at the open skin. "Looks like the kind of meanness Missus Lelia'd be right proud to be a part of. Anyhow, t'aint nothing for you to study on since the master as good as said he go'n send you to the plantation."

Nonnie's voice faltered, overriding her attempt at light-heartedness. Leaving Sunday with a sense of unexplained guilt and regret. "Something wrong?"

"Naw. Time to see what's goin' on down there. Find out just what Massa got planned for you." She twitched her nose and puckered her brow. "Too late to get you cleaned up. The missus won't like the smell of that shift, but I reckon it can't be helped. You just too tall and full-bosomed for my things."

Nonnie opened the door and motioned her to pass through first. Sunday stared at the soft green walls surrounding her, sunlit by a ceiling to floor window. Painted framed images, perfected with countless colors she had only dreamed of, hung all around. Two sets of endless polished stairs—one above her and one below—captured her side view, separated by the honey-colored wooden space she stood upon as large as her dirt-floor cabin back in Virginia. One set of steps curved upward to another level while the other plunged straight down into what would surely be more framed beautiful shapes and colors.

"Go on, now. Move on off the landing." *Landing? Is that what this small room is called?*

And then she saw it. A framed picture held up by a three-legged stand positioned near the wall at right angles to the window. A wonderful dreadful image so shockingly alive that she felt the need to jump in and help the desperate people. She lunged toward the image.

"Nuh uh. Don't touch that easel. Only thing Massa really particular 'bout is them pictures, most 'specially that one right there—"

But didn't Nonnie see? People were drowning, thrashing in the deep gray waves. Black people—thrown overboard or trying to escape?—chained as she had been up until yesterday. Chained like her mind still was. Yet she sensed they continued to fight.

Nonnie wrinkled her nose again. "Here. Let's me and you step back toward the attic for a minute. Maybe I can find something not quite so strong-smelling for you to wear after all." Nonnie practically pushed her back to the other side of the door.

"Stay here. I be right back."

"Uh-huh."

The safest thing to do was to stay put like Nonnie said. After all, the girl had been nothing but nice to her. But what if Sunday never got to see that picture again? What if Nonnie took her another way—the other stairs perhaps—and the master sent her straight to the fields? The pull was too strong.

As soon as Nonnie disappeared, Sunday was back onto the landing. She stared at the painting. Who would dare turn loose such anguish? Cruelty? Images equally as powerful frequently took root in Sunday's mind, but once she had drawn them into the dirt between the tobacco rows, she didn't have to worry about anybody seeing them. Nature and the feet of slaves destroyed them all too quickly. She looked to the lofty ceiling and back, allowing her eyes to scan the entire space, then took several steps downward. Just as she suspected, there along either wall, were more framed pictures. Every color, shape, and texture imaginable—some shiny and textured with what had to be oil. Others flat but so rife and fruity with blurred color she could taste them. She felt dizzy with hidden hope. Could it be possible that the images in her head might be brought to life like this?

Bare feet unable to stop themselves, she continued to descend into a world of more and more images until she reached what must be the main floor. On every wall along the vast and deep hall, people and places beckoned to her. Until finally she stood before an open door.

And a very white woman.

"Mercy! Who in heavens name are you? And how did you ever get into my house?"

New York City

NOAH COULD HARDLY FEEL his hands clasped and dangling between his knees. Numbness had crept into his soul. Seated on a piano bench, head down, he wished he were out there in one of those ships on that water he'd glimpsed. Or down in some biblical valley like the ones talked about in the hush harbor. He wished he had a chance to hold his family once more. See to it that the cabin they shared was warm—but not overly so.

He wished to be alone.

The Phippses had offered deep condolences before risking the trip across town back to their temporary home. Hiram and Susanna, seeming to understand the numbness he felt, moved about quietly, unobtrusively. But despite how he had injured her, Gideon was having none of the unstated privacy request. She stood next to him, her hand resting lightly on his shoulder.

"Would you like to talk about it?"

Lord, help him, he didn't want to hurt her again. But why did all women—except Sunny—believe talking about hurtful things would help? He stood. Walked toward a window.

"No."

If he talked at this moment, it would be ugly. Never before had he uttered a word about how shaming it had been to see his life become a slip of paper pulled from a hat. Nor had he talked about the promise he'd made to Clayton when he himself hardly understood the sacredness of the words. And never, ever had he spoken the word "reclaiming" to another soul. The keeping-quiet, like a man ought to, had served him well. Gideon didn't know what she asked of him.

"Please, No-wuh. Let me help you."

He rounded on her in a way he'd not thought himself capable.

"All right, Miss Fix-all, you want to talk about it?" He shook one of the finger stumps Handley Duval had left him after the Reclaiming in her face. "Let's talk."

"I don't mean to upset you. I only want—"

"No, no, no. I'm go'n talk, and you're go'n listen." He felt the numbness melting, heating up into a boiling rage. Gideon wasn't the true target, but he couldn't help himself.

"I seen—oh, pardon me, Madam Teacher, *saw*—my parents sold when I was five to the highest bidder right there on Duval Plantation. Why Handley and the rest of the heirs decided to sell most of their dead father's grown slaves and keep the children, I don't know 'til this day. All I can say is after they sold off the grown folks, they lined up the rest of us, dropped scraps of paper in a crazy looking clown hat, and drew names, giggling and drinking all the while like it was Independence Day. Like their father's grave wasn't still mounded yonder in plain sight.

"My little cousin—two years old at the time—and I were both drawn by Handley Duval, the oldest son who also inherited the big house. He told me I was to look after Clayton, keep him alive from that day forward. Think about that. Five years old and suddenly responsible for your two-year-old cousin." He paused. Fought against the choking sensation about to force the tears. "Cutest little fellow you ever saw. Everybody said we could be brothers."

"No-wuh, I—"

"Hush. I ain't nearly through with this story. But don't worry, you'll be able to fix it all, I'm sure, when I'm done." Hating the bitterness with which he accosted her, Noah started pacing the floor.

"To say we was treated badly would be like saying there's a few grains of sand on them seashores I hear tell of. Clayton and me, we was passed around from week to week among the few grown slaves Duval had kept—sometimes sleeping in cabins with a dozen or more other people, Clayton on my belly because there wasn't no more room. We learned the ways of tobacco farming before Clayton could talk. And if the driver said we hadn't done so well at whatever job he put us to, Massa took real joy in blistering us with his own special rope. Needless to say, we lived for Miss Maggie's jam and biscuits. And more often than not, when she hid us in the cellar, she slipped us a piece of bacon to share.

"'Have to be careful sneaking this off,' Miss Maggie would say, 'cause the new mistress would like nothing better than to send two little young'uns like y'all to the purple belfry to pray 'til she forgives you.' Miss Maggie protected us from that woman. I loved her. She was like a real honest-to-goodness angel to us."

Gideon sat down on a worn floral chair beneath a window. Noah had never seen her look so small.

"But I always had this itch to see how it felt to live life the way I wanted to. If Handley Duval's children was free to play all day, why couldn't I? When I was eight, I decided to run away. The only thing that had kept me from running earlier was Clayton, who, by then, had moved from a burden to a brother. I told him my secret—promised him, man to man, I'd return soon as I got us a place we could live. I didn't know where I was going nor who might take me in. I just figured anywhere was better than Duval Plantation, and when I found that place, I'd come back to get my brother. But after a week of eating bugs and leaves and fighting off snakes and drinking bad water, one day I just lay down in the middle of a field, curled up between tobacco rows, my little body in spasms from exhaustion. When I awakened, a stranger stood over me, lantern light pouring into my eyes.

"'Wonder who he belongs to?'" the man said aloud, like I wasn't even there. Didn't matter, though. I would never tell him who I was. I took a new name on the spot. July, after the name of the month in which I had experienced my first freedom. Wasn't long before he traded me for two sacks of meal to a young man who was about to get married. And the groom, deciding I was a pleasant-looking child, gave me to his bride for a wedding gift.

"They kept me for five years. Fed me, worked me, taught me Scripture. But when they learned from a peddler that Duval owned me, they decided to take me back. I begged them not to, but believing themselves to be doing the Christian thing, they packed my bag. They sent word to Duval to meet them halfway, and the only thing that kept me from running again was the idea of seeing my brother and explaining to him why I'd broke my promise. When I got back to the plantation, I learned Clayton had run away a week earlier."

"Rotten timing," said Gideon.

"I was thirteen. Duval thanked the couple—even offered to pay them for my upkeep—but they refused. They waved goodbye to 'July,' and so did I. Little did I know how much I would become Noah again. Then came the Reclaiming.

"Duval called it 'a formal Reclaiming' of what was rightfully his. As soon as the couple was out of sight, he forced me to strip to my underclothes before he tied my feet together and roped me to the back of a horse. 'No need wasting a good set of clothes,' he said. 'Only reason I don't strip you naked is that I don't want to have to look at you for five miles.' He beat me at the end of every mile. When we got there, I was near unconscious, my backside raw from being dragged by the horse. But I remember all the faces of the slaves, remember shrinking back from the terror coming from each of them forced to line up and watch. Then came the crosstree."

Gideon shot up from the chair, speaking in her most authoritative voice. "Enough. I shouldn't like to hear any more—"

"It was hog killing time. The new mistress despised that undertaking, so the crosstree on which the hogs were stretched and gutted was put off a ways from the big house. I could smell the scalded hair from the most recent hog as Duval dragged me through the woods. I pleaded with him. I didn't know if he would cut me open like the hogs or not, so I begged. He laughed and said I would live. Said this was a Reclaiming not a killing. Said I was money to him and he was formally reclaiming what he owned. He strung me up on the posts that had recently held hog meat. And he cut off my finger."

Ashamed of his maimed hand—as ashamed as what he was doing to Gideon—Noah trembled like July had at birth. "I know ... I know you can't fix it. Nobody can."

But she had asked, and he had told. And if he were truthful, he did feel better—if better meant simply alive. He jumped at the feel of her arms around his waist, her cheek pressed into his back.

"I am so sorry."

Turning to look into her eyes, he saw the same longing he'd seen earlier on the street when she'd tried to protect him. Pulling away as gently as he could, he kissed her forehead and walked back toward the piano. He had once more made a promise he couldn't keep, only this time it was simply allowing her to hold him. How could he tell her he could never love her? The sight of a girl named Sunday bent over in a tobacco field had taken that spot long ago.

18

Vicksburg, the morning after Sunday's arrival

Johnston paced the study of his hilltop home, waiting for the entrance of his wife. Thankful that, at the least, Nonnie had been able to contain the disturbed girl throughout the night without Lelia finding out she was in the house.

But what now? Now that Gillie had arrived before breakfast and flatly refused to take on the new slave Johnston had purchased? Saying he already had enough crazy niggers to deal with, which, in truth, he probably did.

Halting his circuit, Johnston stared out the window at the river below. Sometimes even he wondered if all slaves weren't indeed a little touched. The way so few of them ever complained, never seemed to give up on life the way he often wanted to, singing mournful songs in the hellish heat of the fields and then belly-laughing with each other at the end of the day when in all likelihood they should simply shrivel up and die. Or pound every one of their owners into the soil. Either they had the weakest minds of any race of humans on earth or they were a people with one of the strongest constitutions God had ever created.

Now if he could just get through this talk with Lelia Rose without revisiting that art piece on the stair landing that he had paid a fortune to secure on loan for a few weeks. This morning, he simply wanted to get to the point with his wife. No new maid. Nonnie or nothing. Then he could figure out what to do with the slave called Sunday. Now that Gillie had said no, should he try to sell the girl? With the war on, he wasn't quite sure how easy that would be. One thing for certain, he must do everything possible to keep Lelia from finding out Sunday was in this house. Insistent knocking eclipsed his thoughts.

"Enter."

Lelia Rose Smithmore floated into the room in a lavender morning dress looking every ounce the Southern lady.

"Well, good mornin', husband. You sound a little out of sorts. I missed you at breakfast. Are you all ri-i-ight?"

Ah, but he hated the deception—the practiced pout, the overdone accent. "Fine. Had to meet with Gillie, is all." Lelia stepped toward the window leaving the doors ajar. Always a sign she expected to say what she pleased while he tried to shush her.

"Did you read the paper this mornin', Johnston? Says we're whipping those Yankees left and right. I expect the war'll be over before cool ni-i-ights set in."

Johnston pursed his lips. He'd not been in favor of Mississippi's hasty secession. Had used Lelia Rose's "fragile" condition to justify his not volunteering. But since his state had insisted on seceding, the orders pouring into the foundry interested him the most. He moved toward one of the matching chairs on either side of the window, nodding that his wife should follow suit.

"Have a seat, Lelia. I need a word with you."

She ignored his suggestion. "Speakin' of the war, I tell you, the world would be such a better place if people like the abolitionists simply understood the order of things. Grace and mercy. I hate to even think of how monstrously they've painted us to the rest of the world. It's getting harder and harder for me to navigate that landing upstairs without thinking of the pernicious painter who set that to canvas. He has to be one of them and the mess they've all made of America. How did you come by that ill-conceived piece of riffraff anyhow?"

If all the weapons in his foundry were pointed at his head, Johnston could not have explained how or even why he had finagled that painting into his home. He only knew that, had it come to it, he would have paid twice the amount he did just to have it in his possession for a few days. To study it, rail against it, be petrified and terrorized by it.

"I tell you, after passing it on my way down, I could hardly swallow a bite of breakfast."

"It's only a painting, Lelia Rose."

She pivoted, gray eyes cold as January. "It's an abomination is what it is. I declare Johnston, sometimes you astound me with that silly hobby of yours, collecting pictures from all around the world like some wide-eyed schoolboy looking for marbles. Doesn't our new nation have enough on its hands right now without one of its upstanding citizens leasing and placing in his home a reminder of what so many of those misguided people up north think of us already?"

"That's quite enough, Lelia. We agreed days ago that the painting would be placed out of the sight of your society mongers until it's returned to the museum that I leased it from. I've kept my part of the agreement."

"Ha! You've never kept your part of the agreement, not during this entire marriage. Never lifted a pinkie finger to raise our status to the level you promised when you asked for my hand in marriage."

Johnston struggled against a nasty retort. He had never

really courted her. Her father, Richard Rose, had been so enamored of the Smithmore name and money until he'd not given Johnston the chance. Rather, he'd thrust her at him like a toy for the sharing. But Johnston wouldn't say that now, wouldn't pull the scab from a sore that had never healed.

"How many times do I have to tell you, Lelia? You're free to chase after my grandfather's legacy as much and as long as you want. Run after the Smithmore glory until your little heels harden. But legacy can't be deposited in the bank. I've worked hard to keep you in luxury, and the one fulfillment I get is art. As for my other failure, I had enough of being the Smithmore society heir to last for a lifetime when I was younger. I have no desire to—"

"To what? Simply perform like a responsible human being? Well, *I* do! Even Gillie—"

"Gillie. Always brother Gillie. Why didn't you marry *him*, Lelia Rose?"

Lelia Rose paused. Headed toward the open doors. Unwittingly offering him hope that she might leave without going down that road about her childlessness. About it being his fault. Even if it meant putting off the discussion of a new maid, Johnston wanted to avoid that subject at all costs. Nearing the fourteen-foot doors she so loved, she turned to face Johnston.

"If you must hear it again, Gillie understands the importance of plantation upkeep to the Smithmore name." Her eyes glossed over with a mixture of sadness and bitterness. "And Providence has rewarded him for his stewardship." Johnston's chest squeezed.

"Don't, Lelia Rose."

"Don't what? Don't lie in bed every single night and wonder why I, the wife of the Smithmore heir, don't have a single son after twenty years? While my husband runs around the country looking for obscene, stomach-turning drawings—like the one upstairs of darkies dumped from a slave ship in a storm—instead of acting the Southern gentleman he was born to be?"

His wife re-crossed the room. Stared out the window. With all her beauty, did she not see anything worthy of capture on canvas or in poetic words anywhere on this planet? A building, a little child, a flower, a destitute family? The majestic river below? Or, like so many others he knew, was the river for her only a means to carry slaves and cotton to enhance the Southern aristocracy? He counted the seconds until she would cross the threshold on her way out. A strange yet vaguely familiar odor assaulted his nostrils causing Lelia Rose to look over her shoulder. She moved toward the door, disbelief marring her usually unflappable beauty.

"Who in heavens name are you? And how did you get inside my house?"

SECONDS DROPPED off the tall clock in the hall like chilled sorghum. Every fiber in Sunday's body vibrated. Lord. What had she blundered into now?

"M-ma'am?"

"I asked, who are you?"

Sunday took a step backward. Grabbed hold of a shiny table with a marble-looking top. She had only meant to see every speck of every drawing and painting she could before going to the safety of the fields. And now, after all these years, she faced another white woman, clearly the lady of this big house. Something she had fought so hard to never do again. Her own stench assailed her afresh as she took in the impeccable dress and delicate scent of the woman whom she had barely escaped as a mistress.

"Sunday?" Johnston Smithmore's voice drifted in from a distant place in the room. "What're you doing here?"

"I-I got turned around tr-trying to find y'all. I never meant to ... Nonnie. Nonnie thought y'all wanted to see me."

"You ... you know this girl?" The woman pressed her fingertips to her bosom. "Oh, please don't tell me this is the one—the gift that is to be Nonnie's replacement. You wouldn't be so callous, so stupid, as to try to foist off on me ..."

"She stinks. Whyever did you bring her here? Why didn't you just leave her out there with the dead parents ... ?"

"You would call me stupid?"

Sunday sensed a shift in the man she had met only yesterday.

He closed the distance between him and the woman. Anger disfigured his face. "After all the trouble I've gone through for you?"

"Get her out of here, Johnston. Now." The woman spoke through clenched teeth, her face a florid mask of revulsion. "She smells like a pigsty."

"When and only when I see fit." Sunday's new master rose a notch in her thinking. "You forget yourself, Lelia Rose. Let me remind you of whose house this is and who it is that rescued you and your drunken father when you were teetering at the edge of poverty."

Images of rage, not hers but of the man in front of her, crowded Sunday's head, blinding her with red angry strokes. Pushing her toward wanting anything—a scrap of cloth, a paper bag—and red coloring, to try to re-create what she was seeing. A half second before the woman swung the flat of her bejeweled hand toward the master's jaw. Master Smithmore caught her wrist.

"Don't." His brows dropped to a scowl, as the sound of offbeat running unraveled the tension somewhat. Nonnie limped to a stop at the study's threshold, anxiety radiating from her like August heat.

"Sunday, I g-got chu a clean shift."

JOHNSTON CONTINUED to hold his wife's wrist, as Nonnie inhaled so loudly he wondered if she would faint, and Sunday shook so violently that the vases on the table next to where she stood made a tinkling sound.

"I won't tolerate another slap, Lelia. You've stung my jaw for the last time. And I warn you, don't ever call me stupid in front of my servants again."

He thrust her back and stared at her. He really didn't love her anymore. Hadn't for quite a while.

"And if I hear another word from you about that painting, I'll have it brought to the foyer so every one of your friends can appreciate it as much as you do. Oh, and one more thing." He nodded toward the new girl. "Come closer, Sunday."

"Suh?"

Johnston lifted his hand in caution. He was in no mood for questions. Her head held high, the girl managed to get her foul-smelling person to within four or five feet of Johnston and Lelia Rose.

"Lelia Rose, meet your new lady's maid. Sunday, this is your new Lady, Mistress Smithmore."

Lelia Rose shot daggers he could have sworn caused pain. "I simply won't accept her."

Johnston's hand went up again. "You will or I'll call in every dress shop account, every millinery account, every bank allowance you have." He waited for his wife's response. None.

"Sunday?"

To her credit, the girl he had thought crazy up until minutes ago dipped her head in understanding. But her sable visage showed pure torment. Johnston felt a stroke of conscience. What had he just done? *Heavenly Father, Lelia will make that girl's life a living hell.*

He strode from the room feeling as though he would retch.

He had thrown Sunday, "July's mother," into the mouth of a predator just as surely as the captain of the slave ship in the painting above stairs had cast those souls into a shark infested sea.

The following day

IF NOTHING else good ever happened again, Sunday would always remember the second bath she'd had since leaving Virginia. Heavenly.

Somehow there had been a compromise between the master and mistress. Now, wearing her new gray uniform, as scratchy as Noah's morning whiskers, Sunday stood just inside the door of Lelia Smithmore's bedchamber. *If she could like me just enough to ignore me.* She watched Nonnie's awkward movements as she scurried about, Mistress Lelia's volume rising with each new order.

"Hurry, O incompetent one! At the pace you're working, there'll be no room left on Sky Parlor Hill when I get there."

"Yessum. I'm getting it right now."

The mistress, her corseted waist causing her thin hips to flare somewhat, glared at Sunday from a mirror's reflection, as Nonnie swept up a gown from a flowered chair.

Sunday watched her roommate wrestle with a colorful fabric-logged, day gown which seemed unwilling to slip over Lelia Smithmore's head after the woman refused to stand and step into the gown.

"You go'n watch me do the lady's maid thing for a few days 'til you get the hang of it," Nonnie had said earlier. "Be careful not to try to help. Mistress might think you getting 'head of yourself. Rest of the day you go'n help out with cleaning. Them's Massa's exact words."

"Ouch!" The woman's muffled voice shrieked from beneath the folds covering her head. "Something's caught in my hair. Owww! Don't just stand there, dimwit. Help me."

Nonnie's eyes glassed over, but she managed to control her voice. "Yessum."

"And you, back there! Friday? Monday? Whatever you're called. Do you see yourself as some kind of privileged apprentice? Get around here and help get this dress over my head before I die of suffocation."

A welcome thought.

Sunday moved to help as Nonnie frantically mouthed, "Stay back!" The woman yanked the neck of the gown over her head, taking with it a snatch of her hair. A scream followed.

"Oh, my beautiful hair! What have you done?" Yellow strands streaming from the coif Nonnie had labored over, empty sleeves drooping from Lelia Smithmore's shoulders, she lunged toward her slaves. Nonnie jumped from her path, leaving Sunday unguarded, the back of her mistress's hand connecting with Sunday's jaw before she could muster a clear thought.

"Would you just stand there while your mistress suffers this kind of indignity? Get out. I cannot bear any more of you. Go look beastly someplace else."

Sunday continued to stand like a statue, except for the one treacherous tear escaping the corner of her throbbing eye. She had vowed to never get close enough for a white woman to slap her again. Somehow soon, she would get back to working somebody's field, loving July, and savoring her times near a stream—asking for nothing more except dirt in which to draw.

"Out! And I will be checking to see if you clean better than you serve your mistress."

Nonnie's pained expression urging her to leave, Sunday fled the room. Until she could escape, her time here would be even worse than she thought.

19

November, 1861

Twenty-two times. Sunday's eyes had skimmed the cover of the sketchbook twenty-two times over the last few weeks. *Why it look so different from the other books in here?* Why was it always on his desk? Ever since she'd been thrown out of the mistress's bedchamber and assigned the cleaning of Johnston Smithmore's study, among other spaces, she had lingered each day in front of the massive desk, hovering between caution and curiosity. The book was huge, and if some of the pages happened to be empty, perhaps she might borrow a page or two—

And be caught by Lelia Rose Smithmore?

Couldn't chance that. Not while she was getting so close to striking an uneasy rhythm in this household while waiting for a chance to get to the fields.

Twisting the dust rag into a knot that matched her gut, Sunday indulged in a long loud sigh. The strain of the last few weeks—being slapped, emptying slop jars, dusting, shining, washing—hadn't left much time to think. But this morning the pierce of separation from July ran her through as though it were one of the decorative swords she had just finished polishing.

"If I could just have a few pages and one of them lead pencils, I could get these pictures of July out of my head. Get a little relief."

She stared at the book and the pencils before her. If it indeed had empty pages, what would it hurt to tear off one or two? Take a pencil—just one—up to the attic room where she and Nonnie slept? No. That was stealing, and she had never stolen before. She had lied to Noah—much too easily—and where had it landed her? She would not add stealing to her sins. She was still a good person, even if she hadn't quite come to terms with Miss Tullie 'nem's God.

Placing the lemony cloth at the hearth's edge, she moved to one of the bay windows looking out onto the river. The fading colors of fall hit so hard it made her heart hurt. She had barely noticed the season change, what with becoming an underfoot-nuisance to the other house slaves, while staying out of Mistress Lelia's way.

Her head felt swollen with images of home, bringing with them a dull ache. How she longed to paint like the person who painted the picture on the landing. Glancing back at the desk, she trembled with a new conviction.

"I'm go'n go crazy if I don't do something. I got to do this."

She lifted the book from the desk. She hadn't even known what it was called until Master Johns had referred to it as a sketchbook. Hands shaking so uncontrollably she had to slap them against the desk for a moment, she finally lifted the cover. Her heart sank. It was full of pictures. Beautiful penciled pictures. She thumbed through the first few. Mercy! Had her master drawn these?

No matter. His fascinating drawings were not what she sought right now. She needed clean paper of her own. She fanned through the book. Drawings and more drawings. The river, streets, children—lots and lots of children—filled the pages. Were there no unused sheets at all? Finally. The last few pages came up empty. Would her master miss one? Had he counted how many were left?

No. It wasn't in his nature to be quite so strict.

Overcome with excitement, she didn't think to tear out a sheet. Instead, she eased into his desk chair—a chair with rollers that never ceased to astound her. Had he lived, would Papa have made chairs like this?

Seizing one of the pencils, she let the stored images in her head travel through her fingertips. July. The plump of his cheeks, the light of his eyes. Feeling more lighthearted than she had in months, she tilted her head and sized up her work. So much like Noah. More penciling? Less curve? ...

"We've had this conversation before, Lelia."

Lord, have mercy.

Sunday tried to get to her feet, but her hem caught in the roller. Her skirt severed from the bodice, she fell back into the chair, mouth open as wide as the sketchbook. Heat and cold plied her body by turns. If she could untangle the skirt, maybe she could—

Too late. The door swung open. Heaven help her, there stood the master, his glaring wife by his side.

Charleston, South Carolina

CLAYTON AND PEARL sat on the back steps of Jess's barbershop watching Pearl's baby play in the sand. Taylor Mack had been the best of scouts, risking his safety more times than Clayton could remember in order to get his charges into Charleston. But it was time for Clayton to move on.

Not counting his brief time with Eliza Borden, Clayton had never stayed in a house before. Had never known the feel of family—except for the few years he had adored and depended on Noah and these last few weeks spent with Jess's family.

And with Pearl.

Like everyone else, he knew a war was on. Had seen signs of it everywhere on the way from Kentucky. But sitting here in Charleston—which to him seemed practically untouched by the war—he could almost believe there was no conflict, no trouble anywhere. Whispers, which he didn't truly believe, that the war was being fought over slavery were getting louder every day. And a thought, fraught with adventure and purpose—one he had not allowed before—was inching its way toward the front of his mind. If this war really did have the least little thing to do with freeing the slaves, shouldn't the North be allowing slaves to fight?

He startled as Pearl touched his arm, her curious eyes lit with hope. Something about this girl—much more than her lithe attractive body—intrigued him.

"I think, if I was white, I'd build me a house on this ocean," she said. "A house with so many windows that no matter where I was inside it, I'd always be able to see the water."

Clayton chuckled. "Might be a little hard to do since most houses can't front everything at the same time. Looks like you go'n have to buy a small island." She swatted him.

"Hush, boy. You know what I mean."

"Yeah, I do. But all white folks don't have them kinds of houses."

"True. But most white folks is born with a chance to have one—no matter how slim—and that's what counts."

Clayton put a bit of distance between himself and Pearl. Wasn't sure he liked the meaning of what she was saying. He would have a chance, too—just like white men—once he could show he could run a plantation as well as the next man. But if freedom came with this war ... No. No need thinking about that.

"Black folks done had a few opportunities chances, too, like Jess. He wouldn't be sporting that free badge—him and all the other free men in Charleston—if this wasn't so."

Pearl dropped her arms from her knees and faced him. "See, that's what I mean. How you go'n call that free if you forced to wear a badge to prove it?

Clayton frowned at her. He didn't like this argument. But he liked talking to Pearl. She stirred his thinking in ways his mind had never set upon before.

"What chu trying to say?"

"I ain't trying. I'm saying. Being forced to wear a badge is exactly what freedom don't mean."

Clayton palmed the crown of his head. Pearl didn't understand what being forced really meant. Hadn't been beaten silly by a man like Handley Duval or Buck Riley, his second master before he found the Swamp.

"Badge or no badge, Pearl, a man needs a job. A paying job. And, uh, what about the blacks who own slaves theyselves?"

"What about 'em?"

"I mean, wouldn't you say they was free?" She glared at him like he'd sprouted a single eye on the bridge of his nose. She moved from the steps. Pacing, she finally answered him.

"Naw. They worse off than those of us who still b'longst to somebody. Talk about being in slavery! Now that's the worst kind of slavery 'cause no matter how much money you make, when you climb up on your brother's back like that, you as much of a slave as he is. Only you a slave to your own greed. And the money you making—whether you want to think on it or not—is cut from your own flesh, so if your brothers and sisters go down, you go down."

Clayton's beard started to itch—scalp, feet, soles—Pearl's words flying right into everything he'd built himself up in, trained himself to believe in. Where was she when Clayton had watched Buck Riley go from ground-scratching poor to rich overnight—on the work of Clayton's ten-year-old back and others like him? Couldn't this girl see that this was just how it was done, how a man got to be powerful in this country?

Tough as it sounded—and to Clayton's dismay, it had begun to sound tough—you *had* to buy human beings, maybe even punish them sometimes, to produce the kind of crop you wanted. It wasn't a matter of right or wrong—or church talk that had nothing to do with reality—it was just the way it was. It had to be this way. Didn't it?

It had to be. Or else Clayton just might rise up off these steps, go out into the streets of Charleston and choke the tongue out of every slave-owning person he thought he saw.

"Hush up, girl. You don't know what chu talking about."

"I know enough to know you either free or you ain't. No two ways about it. And nobody, black or white, what owns other folks is free."

His shirt was at his feet before he knew it, the cool air doing nothing to deter the sweat pouring from his neck, back, thighs. He gave Pearl his naked back, the long welts scarred over but never healed—welts he'd touched but never seen.

"Tell me what chu see. Then tell me if there ain't more than two ways about it."

He heard her gasp. She moved closer.

"A man named Handley Duval set the foundation lashes— just 'cause he wanted to. And when I ran away and was caught by a dirt farmer named Buck Riley, he finished piling them on. One way or another, I'm go'n own one of those freedom badges one day. No matter what I have to do to get it. It's the only way I can live with these stripes."

The warmth of her body clinging to his made him think of Miss Maggie, the last hug he'd got. The circling of Pearl's fingertips soothed his throbbing back.

"So, what are we go'n do now? We can't stay here on poor Jess 'nem forever, even though Jess didn't leave you much choice in coming."

We? Clayton tried to continue. "I ... well I really have appreciated having you as my friend."

"I think maybe I want to be more than yo' friend."

Clayton tensed. What about Sunday? What about seizing that place which Noah once possessed? Pearl eased from his embrace. Scooped up her baby still playing on the ground. "Well, what's we go'n do?"

Sadness set in, the sparks they had created moments ago dying down like a wind at sunset, bringing in a lonely calm. He would miss their backyard talks, her haunting beauty. Her stinging wisdom. Why did she have to start including him in her plans? He looked at her. How was he going to tell her? Still Clayton knew what he must do. And to do that he had to go to a place called Vicksburg.

"I ain't go'n be taking you."

20

Master Johns slid into a stunned drawl. "Sunday? What're you doing sittin' at my desk?"

"Oh, you poor silly naïve man. She's not sitting. She'd plundering. Stealing, as her species is wont to do." The mistress started toward the desk, but Master Johns grabbed her around the waist. Set her outside the room, shrill protests filling the hall.

"She is to be whipped and sent to the fields. Do you hear me? If you don't have the guts to do it, then Gillie will—"

He clicked the lock to the door. "I asked you a question, Sunday."

Sunday's brain urged a number of lies, but words failed her. Why, when she needed it most, did her tongue always refuse to help? Master Johns walked slowly toward the desk.

"Sunday?"

"I-I'm stuck."

She placed her forearm to the gaping hole at the waist of her uniform, resigned for whatever would come. Braced for the pain of another slap, she squeezed her eyes shut as he leaned over her shoulder.

"Did you do this?"

"Suh?"

"These sketches, did you do them?"

Odd how her fear fled. Heart slowed. Mind cleared, as though the wind reversed its direction. Yes, she had done them, and she would not take it back. And if he threw her into the river, so be it. She had to draw like she had to breathe, and she would no longer try to do one without the other.

"Yes. Suh. I drawed 'em."

Since she would likely die anyway, she maneuvered until she could look him in the eye as she had done the first day they met. The look she found there was strange. Not ugly with lust, like Silas's or Hartley's. But probing to the marrow.

"Who is this child? Is this July?"

"Yessuh. That be July. My heart." Massa Johns turned his back. Ran a hand through his yellow hair.

"Well, dog my cats." He paced the room while Sunday continued to sit imprisoned by the hem of her skirt. "That's good work for a novice. Astonishing, really."

Though mostly he talked to himself, she nodded at his back. Afraid to move, to breathe. No idea of what a novice was. Palming the back of his neck, he stopped and stared ahead.

"I'd like it if ... that is ... would you like to see my studio?"

"I reckon I can't tell you if I would or not."

He whirled on her. "What do you mean by that?"

"Don't know what a studio is."

The man smiled, seemingly relieved she hadn't rejected his offer. "Oh, yes. Of course. Well, it's the place where I do my own drawings—paintings actually. As you probably saw in the book, I do a lot of sketching in here. In any case, I'm wondering if you'd like to learn more about the gift God has given you."

God? Sunday had never thought in terms of God giving her these images. After all, some of them were dark—as dark as the painting on the landing where slaves had been thrown into the ocean of big hungry-looking fish. This must be some kind of trap, one she hadn't the power to resist.

"Yessuh."

"Do you know how to read?" He chuckled at his own question. "Of course, you don't—"

"A word or two what my mama and papa taught me before ..."

"Before what?"

"Uh, I just meant to say before they died. That's all."

"Well perhaps we'll continue that—reading, I mean—along with the art lessons, on the day after tomorrow, once your duties are done. Nonnie will show you where my studio is. Tell her it will be part of your job to clean my studio and deliver supplies to it from time to time." He stared at her again as though he was in as much wonderment as she was.

"Oh, and Sunday?"

"Suh?"

"Not a word to anyone else about this, especially not the mistress. Understood?"

"Yessuh. I do."

Two days later

DOG MY CATS? Had those words actually come from Johnston's mouth? He cocked a half-smile. He hadn't used that phrase since he was a boy running around in his cousin's yard in Yazoo County. And even then, he'd used it only because he wanted to sound manly—to keep Gillie and the others from calling him a girl because all he ever wanted to do was draw pictures.

He paced the studio like an injured bear. Hadn't been this nervous since the day he wed Lelia Rose, though by then she had beguiled him. What had possessed him to ask a slave to his studio? Teaching one of them the rudiments of art—not to mention how to read and write—was no small undertaking. He didn't even know how possible it was. In fact, it was running afoul of everything he had ever been taught. Including the law. He stood to lose his business, if he were found out, and perhaps even his own freedom.

"Ouch!"

He bumped his knee against a table holding a covered tray of sandwiches. He'd gone so far as to order sandwiches. Had he lost his mind?

Whatever. He had to know if there was more of what he had seen on that sheet of paper the other day. And the best way to do that was to make her comfortable.

"She belongs to me, and I can do with her what I please," he said aloud, trying to make his own self comfortable. A soft knock followed, so tentative the fear seemed to radiate through the door.

"Enter." He turned to face her, the servant's uniform hanging from her shoulders like a sack thrown over a fence. Yet she seemed to fill in the extra spaces of fabric with a dignity— at once, familiar and foreign. *Foreign?* He was guessing. Hadn't been to Africa. Didn't want to go.

"Come in, Sunday."

"Yes, suh." Her voice was low. Hoarse. Plain to see he was not the only one whose nerves were strung tight.

"Careful, don't bump that easel."

She smiled and the room caught fire. *Ellen?* His daughter Ellen certainly would have been about Sunday's age. On the cusp of life—its wonders, disappointments, cruelties. But there was absolutely no further resemblance.

So why did he think of his daughter each time he was near this girl? Perhaps because he wanted to paint her. Just as he had planned to paint Ellen. Would she agree to sit for him? Of course, she would. Hadn't he just reminded himself she was his to do with whatever he pleased?

"You may sit at that table right there." She looked at him, uncertainty flooding her posture. "Yes, right there."

The wrist cuff of her uniform lifted slightly. Johnston flinched at the scars. Scars that spoke a language far different than the cusp of life he'd just imagined for Ellen.

"Now before we do anything else, I want you to draw something." She looked up, a wordless question on her face. "Anything. You may draw anything. I just want to see more of your work." Her fingers grasped the pencil. Hard, uncertain, the way a two-year-old might.

"No, no. You must relax with it—the way you've always done. Here, let me show you."

Leaning over her shoulder, he was struck by the nuances of her skin color. He hadn't thought she could get any darker than her face, but there it was, a deeper dark just below her cuticle. Could it be—this great divide between Union and Confederacy —all just a matter of an array of ... pigment—like the ones he often mixed to attempt a night sky or some other of God's endless spectrum? He reached to position her fingers. He'd not touched a black woman—well, not in this innocent way—since his mammy faded from his daily existence so many years ago.

"Sunday?" The more he said her name the more he liked it. Her hands shook. Perhaps it was a good thing he'd had the sandwiches brought out after all.

"I have an idea. Let's refresh ourselves first. Sandwich?"

"Sandwich?"

Sunday followed his gesture toward a covered tray. He had food waiting? For her? Of course, it was for her. Hadn't Hartley done the same thing? *A sick trap for a starved slave.* Miss Tullie's words crowded past the fear and resentment. *Don't turn down food folks offer. T'aint kindly nor proper."*

She lifted the cloth from the tray filled with bread slices filled with ... something.

"It's liver pâté. Different but good."

She bit into the tiny sandwich. Good? It stuck in her throat, its foreign taste colliding with the fear clambering up from her belly. She struggled to swallow.

"Did you know there's a war on?"

"Y-yessuh."

"Yes, *sir,* Sunday—sir with an r. Although many Southern-ers, educated or not, leave it off, I want you to know it's there." He seemed awkward in his new teaching role, searching for a safe topic. "As I said, there's a war on, but the North won't win. Especially in a place like Vicksburg. It's impossible. Too much of a fortress."

"Yes—sir."

Awkwardness stalked the room, making Sunday long for the tobacco fields, hard as they were. Hand splayed across her chest, she knew beads of sweat were popping up over her face.

"Massa Johns? I'm wonderin' if we could just—"

"I have an emergency meeting with a cotton factor in my study. I'll return in say an hour? Be sure you have something for me when I return."

"Yes. Sir."

A delay? Or could this man truly only mean to teach her to draw?

THE SKETCH WAS OF HIM, every inch Johnston Harrison Smithmore. Though the sandwiches were untouched, the pencil held between dark cuticles had probed the far reaches of his soul. *So, this is the kinship I've felt. She's an artist.* The air popped with excitement while he tried to drag his gaze from the image lying before him. He should look at her—expel the apprehension she was feeling. But he simply could not. The scowl he felt everyday but never really stopped to consider, the longing, haunted eyes which he refused to pay attention to in his mirror—eyes which the right color could express even deeper—the pain of a life squeezed into an insufferable mold, all there. He didn't know whether to praise her or kick her out. With a simple lead pencil and a square of paper, she'd turned him inside out as though he were a soiled glove.

"Very good," he said. He never looked up. "Take the sketch-book and pencil with you. Practice when Nonnie's not around."

"Yes, sir."

"Oh, and take the sandwiches."

She frowned. "Yes, sir."

21

Late November, 1861, Vicksburg

She had taken to arriving early. Knocking softly and entering when she heard no answer. Not since her Sundays at the stream in Virginia had she felt such joy, such anticipation. She scanned the space—the orderly disarray that was her master. The easels of unfinished people and wild landscapes. Brushes, aprons, and tunics all in their places. Colors in tins and palettes along tables and shelves, or caught in dried streaks and puddles on the varnished floor. She smiled.

"And there's them sandwiches again."

That glorious variety of new delicacies that had so rapidly conquered her palate. She lifted the cloth and popped one in her mouth. She closed her eyes and savored the chew—mild fish massaging her taste buds.

"July, baby. One day I'm go'n fix you one of these sandwiches." *Noah, I'd like to fix one for you too.*

Daring to wipe away a tear with the napkin provided, she sat down and began the magnificent task of sketching whatever she pleased. That was the way they always began. "With whatever you please." Imagine that! Whatever *she* pleased.

Lost in the wonder of pencil and paper, she didn't notice when he leaned over her.

"What's this?" She nearly knocked him over backward.

"I ... it's a ... a chair."

"I can see that, Sunday." He laughed out loud. "What I meant was where did it come from? Whose chair is it? How did it get into your head?"

What? Why, she hadn't taken time to think. It was ... just a chair, a child's rocking chair.

"It's July's chair."

"Oh? Who'd give an—uh—enslaved child such a work of art?"

Her brain registered his stumble over the description of July. But the rest of the question was too consuming for her mind to linger elsewhere. The chair *was* a work of art.

"What I just said, it ain't—that's not—true, sir."

She was about to cry. In front of this white man who had treated her these last few weeks like he might treat his daughter, she was about to lose every shred of pride she had fought to display within the walls of this studio. For the loss of Papa and the freedom he had taken with him, she was about to cry. Papa who had made that chair so long ago.

"My papa, he made that chair."

She sniffed like July and then asked the dumbest question. "Do you happen to know why my papa would let his self get kil't when he knowed he had a li'l girl depending on him?"

JOHNSTON SEATED HIMSELF. Pressed his fingertips to Ellen's empty locket. Studied this girl before him. This was pain. Paintable pain. But how could she be crying like this? Slaves

216

only cried this hard when they were being whipped or sold or something, didn't they?

"Tell me about your papa."

She fluttered her lids at the tears, used the backs of her hands to wipe them away. "If-if he'd j-just not throwed the coffee in the man's face."

"What coffee, Sunday? You're not making sense."

"The coffee that made the white man mad, the coffee that took my tongue. If only Papa had just kept quiet, not slung the hot liquid into the man's eyes, maybe we—him, Mama, and me —maybe we could've worked something out with the man. Stayed free a while longer."

The sound of a steamboat cut the silence. Johnston crossed an ankle over his knee. The thing his beloved South was fighting *for* this very moment, this girl—barely more than a teen—was fighting *against* in her heart, every whit as hard. He barely heard his own whisper.

"Tell me."

New York City, the same day

NOAH TRUDGED hatless through last night's snow, not caring two figs and a dead flower whether he was seized by a slave snatcher or not. The sky was so blue—the sun so bright— causing an ache past his pitiful word bank. Gideon had fought against his going out like this.

"You're much too easy to capture," she argued, "especially in your frame of mind."

Eventually she had succumbed to a much-needed after- noon nap, and Noah had finally escaped. Cold tears lined his face.

Sunday and July were gone.

His wife of three years didn't understand what freedom meant to a man like Noah—how it practically owned him. She had never really wanted to escape that cabin. He'd always known that. Yet, so driven by the need to be accepted as a man, that he had jumped at the chance to embrace the promise she'd made about joining him later. He looked down at the layer of the first snow of the season. Muttered to himself.

"What good did it do to go to that hush harbor week after week? What good is faith when the possibility of utter loss always hangs over a man's head?"

"Faith doesn't always mean happiness. Faith is surrender, and surrender is faith."

He shook his head. Ignored the puzzling words intruding upon his thoughts. Blindsided by the many places on Duval's land where he and the rest of the slaves slipped away to worship, he paused in the snow, oblivious to the annoyed afternoon walkers forced to go around him.

Truth be told, he hadn't gone to the hush harbor just to honor his faith in God. He had gone looking for a way to escape the clutches of slavery. Hoping that someone from the mysterious, exciting Railroad or some brave educated preacher like that Nat Turner man from the thirties would show up and lead them out from under the foot of Handley Duval. But week after week, Mama Tullie and the rest of them seemed to put praise and worship first.

He couldn't quite understand that. How had his fellow slaves not realized how precious that secret time together was? Always praying, moaning, singing before getting down to the business of organizing themselves, freeing themselves from that murderous lot called slaveholders. Many times not getting down to business at all. Though the services often pulled at something deep within his soul, just as often Noah had railed inside, screaming within himself the urgency of coming together as a people ready to fight. They needed to make plans, before Duval, and all the God-forsaken scoundrels like him, decided one day to simply sell them all farther south. Why had they been so blind?

"No one wants your freedom more than Me. Not even you. But first, you must surrender."

Noah's brow wrinkled. Where was all this inside talk coming from? Standing in ice, to him it felt like the middle of July. The words he'd just heard could not be described as audible. Yet they rang as clear as the church bells he'd learned to appreciate. He beat the heels of his hands against his ears. Blew into his sweaty palms.

"Thou shalt have no other gods before Me. Not even the justified desire for freedom."

"The justified desire. The *justified* ..."

It didn't matter that he was talking to himself on a busy street. Didn't matter that he'd be carted off any minute as a lunatic. "So, what chu sayin' is you want me to be free, but ..."

Noah dropped to his knees, the ultimate futility of any quest outside of God as clear as the sun that glittered the afternoon snow.

"Oh, God, forgive me. I never meant to set You to the side. I just wanted ... Oh, Jesus, have mercy on me, a sinner."

All those times in the hush harbor, had been so simple. It was never true that the slaves hadn't wanted freedom. It was just that they wanted God more.

"My papa, he was free. A woodworker, don'tcha know. A free person of color. Free."

Johnston had never seen her quite like this, not even on the day she arrived. She was rambling, repeating herself. Yet to interrupt her with his eagerness seemed sacrilegious.

"He promised I'd never be a slave, said our family had been

granted a gift from God—would always be free. That's why come he named me Sunday, you know, to honor the bit of freedom slaves often stole once a week to prophesy of what was to come. 'One of these days,' he said, 'everyday will be Sunday.' But then one day that white man came.

"'Don't you know there's no such thing in this country as a free black?' he said. And he was right, because after his horse killed my mama and his gun killed my papa—after he stared down at them on the ground as though they were two dead dogs—he took me to the plantation and made me ... No, not him. It was Silas who made me a scarecrow." True to her habit, she looked at him dead on. "And that part I don't aim to talk about."

He wanted to force her to tell him, but she had said enough today.

"I was a father once, for a short twenty-four hours. But when I looked at Ellen for the first time, I knew I'd take any risk to keep her safe." His cheeks were as wet as Sunday's, but he didn't care. "I think perhaps your papa felt the same."

Of a sudden, he was aware of his hands and arms. Didn't know what to do with them. Hugging her was out of the question, so he clasped his hands behind his back and smiled. Let go of the broadest smile he had offered since he'd looked on that frail bundle of squirming pink so long ago. No matter the risk, he would keep on working with this girl. For the simple joy of it.

December, 1861

As MUCH AS she appreciated Nonnie's presence, her slipping out tonight to meet Pete proved a real blessing. It wasn't taking long to relearn the alphabets Papa had taught her and Mistress

Duval had scared out of her, but it was hard to find the time to practice writing them. Careful not to tip over the tin can holding the candle atop the cot, Sunday squinted at the letters.

"*T, U, V, W* ..."

Why was that last letter called a double *U* when clearly it was a double *V*? Silly question. She needed to keep her mind from dallying with useless stuff and practice her letters. She was grateful for Master Johns. Very much wanted to learn to read. But drawing was so much more fun. At the sound of the door opening, she nearly set the cot afire. Wild-eyed and with one hand behind her back, Nonnie burst through the door.

"Sit."

Scrambling to place the paper, pencil, and reader beneath the cover, Sunday gave her a sharp look as she swung her legs to the floor.

"Thought you said Pete was go'n—"

"Sit, I said. On the floor." Sunday swallowed down her rising annoyance. It wasn't like Nonnie to be this bossy. Something was out of whack.

"I ain't sitting nowhere 'til you tell me what ails you. And why is your hand stuck behind your back like you done stole something from the high and mighty Lelia Rose?"

Nonnie smoothed her apron and tittered, brought her hand forward and opened up a palm to reveal a tiny box. 'Cause I did steal it from her. Can't keep nothing from you, though. You a smart one, you. Now sit."

"Nonnie, I declare if you don't hurr' up and tell me something, I'm go'n—"

"All right, all right. Here's the thing. I'm so tired of looking at your hair I could just cry. Thick head of hair like that, and you treat it like a pile of dead grass. Ain't bothered to braid it in a week. You know how many womens out there picking cotton would love to have your hair?"

"Nonnie—"

"So, since Pete didn't show up, I decided to borrow some of 'Lelia's' pomade and work on your hair." She giggled, as though Sunday's idea of calling their mistress by her given name in the confines of their space was the finest gift Nonnie had ever received. "I'm go'n make you so pretty you ain't go'n be able to stand yourself—make you look like a proper citified house slave ought to. 'Sides, it'll take my mind off Pete." Palm now loaded with pomade, Nonnie sat on the edge of the cot. Sunday sighed. Slid to the floor, her back between Nonnie's knees.

"All right. You've got that mulish look on your face. Might as well get this over with."

Reaching into her apron pocket, Nonnie produced a battered brush and began brushing out the tangled mass. A memory wormed its way into Sunday's thoughts.

"Ow, Mama. That hurts."

"I'm sorry, honey. I wish you'd not inherited such a mop of hair." Mama gasped at her own words, causing Sunday to wonder what she'd found in her hair.

"But Mama, your hair is not a mop. Papa's neither."

"Shush. Stop talking about it. I've told you you've other kin, haven't I?" Mama turned near peevish. "I wish I had some oil for your hair. I never have enough oil ..."

Why had Mama soured so fast? The scene had always haunted Sunday. "Can I ask you something, Nonnie?"

Giggles filled the small space as Nonnie set about her task. "Uh-huh. Anything you want."

"Why are you so happy all the time?"

Nonnie paused the brush. "Well, I reckon it's like this. This here way you see me ain't happy. This is joy. I hate being a slave, but I love having Jesus as my Master."

Sunday would have to ponder that.

Nonnie parted her hair. Swabbed pomade between the rows, as a sense of the long-forgotten familiar overshadowed Sunday. Months of tension uncoiled, her shoulders following the downward pull of the brush as she relaxed beneath the steady strokes.

"I ain't set 'tween nobody's knees since my mama." Tears pooled in her eyes. "Miss Tullie always stood up when she combed my hair. Said I was too tall, even sitting down."

The only sound was bird-chirping. Just Nonnie's hands massaging Sunday's scalp and working the oil through the thick tresses.

"I got to say it, Nonnie. This is a mighty good feeling. Even if old Lelia Rose kills us tomorrow, I'll die a happy woman."

"And old longheaded Gillie will raise us from the dead and put us in them cotton fields."

Sunday closed her eyes, tried to regulate her breathing. "Longheaded?"

"Longheaded."

That was it. The best description she'd come up with yet to describe Master Johns' strange-looking brother whom she'd glimpsed only once. No wonder he resented Master Johns. Johnston was a handsome man with a head of hair while Gillie had a sprigged head that sat on his neck like the wide view of a potato. A gurgle started in Sunday's belly, her body convulsing as laughter slowly worked itself up through her mouth and exploded so loudly Nonnie startled.

"Shhh! You go'n wake up the whole house."

But Sunday couldn't have stopped if the town of Vicksburg had rushed to the door. When Nonnie could take it no longer, she joined in until they were both stretched out on the cot. "Get back in your place, girl, so I can finish prettifying you."

"Noah used to say I had pretty hair."

"Umm-hmm," was all Nonnie said as the brush fell back into rhythm.

Once more, Sunday settled herself. Gave in to the regularity of the brushstrokes, calming her into the sweetest sleep she'd had since arriving in Vicksburg. Sending her into a half-dream about the oh-so-special, yet elusive, comfort of a mother and a father. And perhaps, at long last, a sister.

And Noah.

"What about this Noah?"

Sunday jerked awake. Shifted her weight. "What about him?"

"You love him?"

Here we go again. Why did everyone keep asking her that question? "You mean like you and Pete?"

"Zackly what I mean."

"We jumped the broom—more like fell over it—is all I can tell you."

Liar. Sunday had lots more to say. Was finding more sweet memories of Noah Duval squirreled away in her heart every day. She tried to wipe her eyes without Nonnie knowing it.

"I ain't believing that. Not with that water dripping from your eyes."

Sunday grunted. She wasn't quite believing it herself. Truth was, she was missing him more keenly than she could've ever imagined. She closed her eyes. Snuggled in closer.

"Just wondering if he's all right, is all."

"Umm-hmm."

PART III

22

And [Israel] ... made them the dens which are in the mountains, and caves, and strong holds ... And [the Midianites] encamped against them, ... and left no sustenance for Israel.
~ Judges 6: 2, 4

April, 1862

Sunday slipped into the smock Master Johns had bought for her. Glanced at the cloth he had draped over the many sketches she'd done of July. Thought of his explanation.

"But for the small chance that Lelia Rose could happen by, I might leave the sketches uncovered," he'd said.

She didn't care about that. She was too thankful for the window of peace she peered through each time she was allowed to release the images of her baby from her head. Sleeping. Cooing. Crawling. Walking. And now, at last, she was to be given the chance to find the colors that would speak of his tender wheat-colored skin. Colors that would reflect his sweet soul.

She picked up the palette she had been practicing with for weeks. Words she'd never heard of a year ago—intensity, texture, shading, hue, tint, depth—knocked against her brain. Choosing the brush she had decided best, she lifted a bit of color from the palette. She caught her bottom lip behind her teeth and leaned toward the easel, wondering if the color and canvas would combine to birth what she had imagined in her head. Oh, how she wanted to please her master in this. How could she ever have suspected him of trying to use her in Silas's beastly way?

Easily. Knowing the stories of how slave women were used —stories she had heard both here and in Virginia—not to mention what she had experienced in her own ordeal in Cincinnati. Thank goodness she had been wrong about Johnston Smithmore. And she truly had been. She knew that now.

He'd seemed a bit down last time they were here together. Something about the possibility of Confederacy conscription, whatever that meant.

"I never thought this war would come to forcing men to fight," he'd said. Sunday didn't care. Couldn't afford to, having loaded her thoughts up with July and Noah.

Engrossed as she was in the choices of colors before her, she barely recorded her master's entrance. Finally, she noticed him sitting in his favorite chair. He was staring again, but she was no longer bothered by it. Had grown to realize it a comfort, not a threat. She thought of Papa's lap and smiled again. Johnston Smithmore would have made a fine papa—

"I want you to move on from July."

Sunday looked up, her brush suspended in midair. "Sir?"

"It's time to move on," he repeated from the other side of the studio. It seemed the distance across the room had grown, though the pain on Sunday's master's face was clear.

"I hate saying this, but you've become obsessed. I've never seen anyone more obsessed."

She didn't know any more about what the word "obsess" meant than she did "conscription," but it sounded too much like Mama's use of the word abscess. Something that attached itself to the body and slowly poisons it.

"'Fraid I don't know what you mean, sir."

"I think you do, Sunday. You're strangling your creativity by not exploring other subjects. The world is full of other things, you know."

No, she really didn't know. Outside of tobacco fields, her stream, and her cabin, she had seen practically nothing except that horrifying trip with Silas and the speculator.

"July ain't no thing. He my life. You can't know how hard I've worked to keep him safe."

He looked at her as though she spoke a foreign tongue. What was the matter with this man? Wasn't education supposed to sharpen your understanding?

"Safe? Safe from what?"

Sunday seized his blue eyes with her own. Never before had she been forced to make a list, nail down one by one what she'd tried to do for her son. But she would do it now so that Massa Johns would back off.

"Safe from playing with other slave babies—like they go'n all grow up happy. Safe from being sneaked into the woods to worship and hear white folks' words that make promises as far from my baby as the moon is from that river out there. Safe from even looking toward that big white house with all its fine stuff that would only keep him up at night like it did Noah, dreaming 'bout things that ain't never go'n happen. Safe from seeing his heart ripped from his little chest while blood shoots from his papa's head." She grasped the side of the easel.

"Safe from that big lie called freedom that these warmongers supposed to be fighting over."

Master Johns stared. Took an eternity to recover. "Sunday,

you're better than that. You're a thinker. Can't you see that trying to keep your baby safe from life is a false existence?"

"Don't say it, Massa Johns. Don't chu dare say that to me." She had just crossed the invisible line between master and slave. Might as well go the distance. "How you go'n talk about something being false, anyhow?" She loosed the easel. Stretched out her arms. Dizzied herself with the speed of a twirl. "You think all this is real? All these soft couches and fancy sandwiches? Flooped-up carriages and padded wagons you ride in? Well, it ain't. It's what you—and Lord knows how many more like you—think you have to do to keep up in this greedy world you done created on the backs of folks like me and Nonnie. Naw. Don't chu tell me what's real and what ain't when that locket you always fingering is the only real thing in your life, and you don't even know it."

All traces of color in Johnston Smithmore's face fled, leaving a sallow stricken mask. Sunday felt the last breath leave her body. She truly had gone too far. The familiar cramps of fear and dread claimed every inch beneath her navel as she waited for him to slap her, stomp her. Oh, Lord, was she about to repeat that scene of so long ago when she soiled herself at the door of her parents' porch?

She watched him walk across the floor of his studio and take out the locket. He looked at it with such anguish that Sunday thought she might actually rather be stomped than see this kind of longing.

"Perhaps you are right. It just might be the only real thing in my life. Except maybe for my art." Now he was looking at her— his turn to lock eyes with her. "My art. And you."

He closed the door, softly—as though she were a sleeping baby nestled into a springtime afternoon nap. Guilt covered her as she remembered the same slump of defeat in Noah's shoulders as he walked away from her last Spring. Somehow, she had become the consummate dispenser of pain, even when she didn't mean to. Still, first chance she got, she would paint July again. And again, and again. She had to, or they both would die.

23

June 28, 1862

S unday's neck swiveled toward the movement. Of its own volition, the door was closing, the comfort of her cabin oddly shifting to biting cold. Her four walls—mostly the same measure of space she had lived in since she was six—becoming much too close. She looked to the rafters. Soot. Cobwebs? *Naw.* Not in Sunday Duval's spotless house. She sat up on the side of the bed, a squeezing sense of loss crowding her.

Where I'm at?

Fighting to draw breath, she redirected her eyes toward the door Noah had built and tried to stand. She needed to keep the door from shutting her in completely, but her legs wouldn't move—had become posts pounded into the dirt floor. She vied for one last breath as the door slammed closed, colliding with her scream as she turned to check on July.

July. On his knees. *'Cept he ain't in the belfry chapel tied to no pew* ... but inside a damp insufferable cave ...

Boom!

She wiped the perspiration from her neck, face, thighs. *A*

nightmare. The strangest one she'd had in years. Those Northern fighters, responsible for the explosion that had awakened her, were close by on the river. Had been for several days. What had Master Johns said the leading man's name was? Flag Officer David Farragut, she believed. She glanced at Nonnie, still asleep. Day would dawn in an hour or so with its war talk, but fleets and guns and batteries notwithstanding, she had just experienced a vision she had to put on canvas.

"Where you think you going this time of night?" Nonnie's fingers dug into her arm. "I know what Massa 'nem say 'bout Vicksburg being too strong to bring down, but they don't know everything. I'm worried 'bout Pete. What if Massa sends for him and he get caught in the middle of some fighting? What if some of them big guns hit us? This house near 'bout *in* the river, you know—"

Sunday smoothed her friend's forehead. "Go on back to sleep. Pete don't come up here by way of the river, you know. And that's the only place there might be danger right now."

SUNDAY HAD IGNORED the girl until she chattered herself back to sleep. Now, standing inside Massa John's studio filled with anxiety about last night's dream, her mind was as colorless as the blank canvas before her.

Until she touched it with a brush.

Amidst a perfect dawn, explosions of browns and grays and blacks flooded the canvas. Hours passed. A suffocating space emerged from her brush, not unlike that of her cabin in the nightmare, its floor crawling with bugs, its walls made of earth. Earth beneath the earth. Earth Sunday had smelled in the dream. She shrank back from her own work.

The space beneath the ground had peopled itself. *Lord.* She moaned like Miss Tullie. Couldn't seem to stop herself, as though her guttural sound was needed to complete the foreboding space. July—older—was on his knees. Or was it Noah? Mostly it was white people. Long-faced. Fearful. Huddled together in the cave—

"Johnston? Johnston, are you in there?" The door of the studio banged against the wall.

"I hope you're not hiding out here with these pointless drawings while we all may be about to die."

Lord, ha'mercy. Lelia Rose, in flowing satin nightdress, not six feet from Sunday's work.

"You again."

Sunday used her body to cover as much of the painting as she could. She glanced at the window. What time was it? She scrambled for a passable lie.

"I was just wanting to know, is all. M-massa Johns told me to clean up in here today, and I was just wanting to know what it felt like—t-to paint."

Lelia Rose's laugh came almost as a girlish giggle. "Do you take me for a complete fool? Wanting to learn to paint while the Yankees threaten to bomb the devil out of us?" Lelia Rose examined her, head slightly tilted. "Why, you've been sneaking in here all along, haven't you? Have you been with my husband? I saw that stance, heard those disgusting sounds you were making as I came in. No way you could have gotten this comfortable in a day." She moved toward the canvas and pushed Sunday to the side.

"Merciful heavens! What is this?"

Sunday opened her mouth to speak then realized she could no more answer her mistress's question than she could swim the length of that river outside.

I don't know what it is. Please help me, Lord. I don't know. She crept backward toward the door. "I don't know."

"You don't know. You don't know why you've painted these ghastly pictures of white people, in some sort of cave, surrounding a kneeling nigger boy, as though he were a prince at prayer and his betters were some kind of magi?"

"No'm, I ..." *Massa Johns said don't say no'm.* "No, ma'am, I was just—"

"Did I not warn you last time what I'd do if I found you near my husband's space?"

Said you'd have long-headed Gillie whip me and send me to the fields. Fine. Long as he take me 'way from here, you.

"Come here to me."

"Ma'am?"

"Come here, I said!"

Sunday moved toward a nightmare she could never paint.

"Put my husband's brush down."

Crack! Sunday withstood the blow from Lelia Smithmore, the hand holding the brush flying outwards in defense.

Crack! Sunday slapped her right back. With every ounce of tobacco-field muscle she had built up over the years, she slapped Lelia Smithmore so forcefully that the woman's eyelids fluttered. Clearly, Lelia Rose was stunned. Until every curse word in Mississippi, louder than the noise outside, seemed to infuse her, fueling her mouth like a set of demons.

"Oh, no. That's it. Get your rags. You're going to the plantation today, where Gillie will whip every bit of that evil black skin off your—"

Johnston Smithmore rushed through the door, his face red. His breath thin and rapid. "Finally. Here you both are. What are you doing out here? Don't you know we're under attack? Our big guns have successfully held our ground, but this time it's different. Some of the Yankees actually ran the batteries and made it north."

Rochester, New York, the same day

HAVING ACCEPTED the invitation to winter with Hiram and Susanna Kelson in New York City, Noah had said goodbye to Gideon. She had begged him to come with her, but he'd insisted she travel upstate alone to see her family. Her father was ailing, and Noah's grief would only be in the way, adding to the sorrow. Not only had the Kelsons fed him until he was more robust than he'd been in his twenty-five years, but Hiram had nurtured his soul to a place he hadn't known existed—not even in the hush harbor. A place that challenged and defied logic. That was what he had needed, and the Kelsons had given him that. Complete healing from the pain of Sunday and July would take a lifetime.

Now, his first train ride about to end, he had missed Gideon father's funeral. But he was here, for this woman he'd come to care about very much. So far, this city called Rochester looked somewhat foreign. Though the two places bore the same surname, from what he was seeing through the train window, Rochester was quite different from the city of New York.

He stepped from the train to the platform. Where was summer? Though the trees had begun to fill out and the land-scape was bursting with color, the air felt like late March and so did his insides. Then he saw her, running with the same grace with which she had baffled those hounds last year when she led Noah through places he had only imagined. He opened his arms, and she flew into them.

"No-wuh."

"Gideon, I'm so sorry about your papa. So sorry I wasn't here."

HE STOOD beside her at the steps of a brightly painted two-story house beneath a single gable. Noah loved the look. Three slender windows dominated the top floor front while, on the ground floor, two identical windows and a centered door mimicked the arrangement. He felt the squeeze of Gideon's hand as she leaned into his shoulder.

"We're home, No-wuh." He nodded, his heart swelling at the hope in her eyes. "Are you ready to meet everyone?"

Holding fast to his hand, she mounted the steps. Squeals erupted as Gideon put the key into the lock of the fairytale house. Three young girls—white as any plantation owner Noah had ever seen—latched onto their mother with glee. Babbling. Shrieking. Jumping for joy.

"Mama, Mama! ... when can ... where did ... may we—?"

"Girls, girls. Remember what I told you before I went to the station? I told you we would have a guest, didn't I? And what does that always mean?" They quickly quieted themselves.

"We're sorry."

Smiling shyly, the beautiful dark-haired little girls began lining up to the side of the entryway in what Noah assumed would be the order of their years, but the tallest took her place in the middle. Noah's eyebrows lifted in surprise. Gideon chuckled.

"Mr. No-wuh Duval, meet April, May, and June."

What? July's face sprang to Noah's mind. He fought to regain his focus. "Nice to meet you young ladies."

"Mama said you were handsome," said the tallest of the three. Gideon colored and looked toward a distant wall. Noah—partly amused, partly embarrassed—cocked his head to the side.

"Oh, for true? And what do *you* think?"

"Yes!" All three girls at once. Lovely precious ones spawned by a monster.

Obviously intent on recovery from her mortification, Gideon took her place behind the girls, placed her hands on the middle one's shoulders.

"May has decided to outgrow everybody—very soon including me, I suppose—but is, in fact, my middle princess. Be warned. She talks a lot too." Gideon shooed the children farther into the small entryway and closed the door behind them. "Girls? I suppose August is having his nap?" A woman descended a set of simple straight stairs, every whit as lovely as Gideon, though older.

"He was until those shrieks."

A boy, perhaps five, straddled her hip. Like his sisters, he was dark-haired, pale, painfully shy. Adorable. He cowed at the sight of Noah, and although his mother smiled widely, pain showed up in her eyes. She reached for the child.

"He's still missing Father," she said snuggling him close. So like Sunday and July. "No-wuh, I'd like to introduce you to my mother, Angel. Mother, Mr. No-wuh Duval."

"How do you do, Mr. Duval. I've heard so much about you. My husband very much wanted to meet you."

"I wanted to meet him, too, ma'am. You all raised some kind of daughter here." He glanced at Gideon who seemed to dissolve, like so much sugar, beneath his praise. Seeing the boy's eyes had never left him, Noah reached out his hand.

"Can we shake hands—man to man?"

August tightened his grip on his mother's neck and shook his head before clearly stating his answer. "No."

Gideon flinched, seemingly at a loss, causing Noah's heart to reach out. He owed this woman his life. And clearly these wonderful children were her life. Noah ransacked his mind. What might have won July at a moment like this? Remembering his leisure at the Kelsons, he searched his pockets. What he found there he had carried around with him for months— had actually made for July when he thought he was going crazy faced with the idea of never seeing him again. Aided by a strong throat clearing, he willed the tears to remain where they were.

"Hmm. Seems like you're having a bad day of it, huh, Mr. August?"

At the handle put to the lad's name, a small smile broke through before young August quickly averted his eyes toward the back of his mother's neck.

"Well, Mr. August, I'm thinking maybe this li'l trinket might make a man feel a bit better." August side-glanced him. With a hint of a flourish, Noah pulled July's gift from his pocket. He extended a tiny wooden wagon, complete with tongue and rolling wheels and painted with bright red paint left over from the Kelson's front door.

"A gift for you, my man. All I need to do is finish the horse."

The boy's sisters watched as August slid from his mother's hip and took the gift. He dropped to his knees and instantly began to roll the wagon. Laughter broke out.

"Hear, hear!" Angel's voice bested the laughter. "Is this any way to treat a guest? This poor man must be starved. Come children. Let's see how things are going in the kitchen. Gideon, you entertain Mr. Duval," she said, from down the hall. "Of course, you know the girls are going to demand equal treatment at some point. Too long in the town of Susan Anthony, I suppose."

Gideon rubbed her hands together and shrugged an apology. "Thank you. That's the first sign of childhood play we've seen since his grandfather died."

Noah nodded his understanding.

"Father—Gramps, to them—was the only father they knew. Thinking it might someday become a precious memory, I made the mistake of allowing them to see my father lying in the coffin, and now it's as though August is afraid of every man he sees. Wonders if they are 'real' or just ghosts. He clings to Mother and me most of the time. Demands we lift him like a two-year-old. Sleeps with one or the other of us every night.

Poor little guy." Gideon convulsed—all signs of the fierce scout Noah knew erased.

"His whole existence has become one big nightmare while he waits for someone else he loves to die."

Knowing Gideon's vulnerability as well as his own, Noah hesitated to move toward her. Still, he took the space between them in two strides. He stopped short, breathing in the familiar scent of her. Then, abandoning knowledge of the age-old danger of grief taken for far more, he enfolded her in his arms.

Early July, 1862, Sky Parlor Hill
Half Past Three in the Morning

SUNDAY MADE her way up the steep steps. *Flat out dangerous, this here hill I done started sneaking to.* Lelia Rose had called the seven Union vessels that made it past the batteries last month "Farragut's Little Foray," as though the enemy boats' successful breach of the city's security was no more than a fly on a horse's tail. Sunday's gut said otherwise. But it was another trip to this forbidden hill, not a Union attempt to put Vicksburg on its knees, she feared most.

She was getting better at sneaking away from her mistress's banishment, though her master had to know that his exiling her to his art studio was like putting a hummingbird in a flower garden. Further, she suspected he knew she was stealing away now and again. He just didn't know where she went. *Probably don't care.* So long as he didn't have to deal with her. That hurt more than she thought it would. Yet she had no regrets about slapping Lelia and living in the studio where Nonnie brought her meals while Massa Johns decided what to do about her.

It had been a big mess that morning. He'd had to physically restrain his wife, while he not so much as glanced at Sunday.

They had struck another deal, Lelia Rose and Massa Johns. Sunday would be permanently banned from the big house—provided the priceless artwork on the landing that he so loved to gaze upon was shipped back to its museum posthaste. He'd not visited Sunday since the incident, and simply knowing he wouldn't take the few steps to the studio cut her desire to paint. Made her lonelier than she'd ever been except in the belfry. Meanwhile, the cave nightmare continued.

She paused her walk up the hill. Allowed herself to remember a question she'd asked Master Johns—before the slapping contest—about the future of Vicksburg.

"Where we go'n go if the Yankees ever get hold of the river?"

Like everyone in Vicksburg, Sunday had learned to live with the fact of troop buildup around the river—white military men whom Southerners called Yankees, the very name always embedded in a helping of hatred and consternation. Master Johns had chuckled at her bluntness.

"You do get to the point, don't you?" He'd stood there, hands on hips, looking and laughing at her. "That'll not happen. The bluffs are too high. But I have to admit, these visits from the Yankees—gunboat runs and the such like—are beginning to be worrisome, though we still have the backdoor to the city. It's not like we're besieged or anything."

"What does that mean?"

Master Johns primped his lips. "Besieged? It means your enemy has surrounded you—is strangling you, cutting you off from your basic needs and demanding you see things his way before he reopens access to the world around you."

Exactly the way she felt tonight—the reason she'd had to escape the studio again.

She continued until she eased down onto the place where she knew the well-dressed white women sat each day when they came to watch river and sky. She envied the constancy of the stars. Knew—had always known deep down—that a power greater than her ruled the entire canopy. Wondered if the same power anchoring the stars might possibly want to do the same for her. She found herself mumbling another of Miss Tullie's Bible sayings. She was doing that a lot lately.

"The heavens declare the glory of God."

Yes, but sometimes stars fell. Why did He let things fall? Why had He allowed her perfect parents to drop to the ground like heartless rocks?

Could that be what she and all blacks in America were? *Fallen?* Mama, Papa. July, Noah, Georgie—all of them. Fallen. Torn loose from their moorings.

She felt confused, as though she was being hollowed out before the elements. She tried to lift herself from the white-woman bench she had no business on in the first place. Couldn't. Even as the hot summer night left her cold and shivering.

Sunday sensed movement far below at the bottom of the steps. Probably some lusty drunk stumbling around in the graveyard hours. She tried again to move but was ... *besieged?* Besieged. By her own thoughts, bracing for she-knew-not-what.

The word, "fallen," continued to hold her, prod her toward two ways to be labeled such: "Fallen" into the arms of something or someone better—like Mama and Papa had—was one way to think of it. For all Sunday's grieving, she had always felt her parents ensconced in a place of rest. But then there was that other "fallenness" of the soul that rendered a person dead before she died, and it was directly tied to a word she'd never wanted to face up to.

Sin.

Was it possible that, after all, sin and repentance were not something Mama Tullie and the hush harbor people had conjured up? If sin was real, then perhaps freedom was real. And if they both were real, then no matter the outcome of this war, this country was in trouble with its Creator—had committed a collective abomination called slavery, a carbuncle on its very soul that would stretch its tentacles into generations to come.

But sin was not just a grouping. It was one person at a time too. It was Handley Duval, Jed Hartley, Silas Duval, Lelia Rose Smithmore.

Sunday Pennington Duval.

Gripping the edge of the bench, Sunday felt reduced before the presence of the One who made those stars—seized by her own insignificance. Yet, she sensed within her reach the indescribable love of Miss Tullie's God.

"Stars do fall, Sunday." The sound of her own voice startled her. "Beautiful stars. All the time." Stars like her parents, seemingly for no reason at all. But the Creator knows what He does. What He allows. And still, the heavens go on declaring His glory. His wonder. His mystery.

As certain as she was that the images, which had to be put to form, lived within her soul, that's how sure she was at that moment that there was a God. Her body stilled, leaving only her shoulders to heave as she buried her face in her hands and wept.

JOHNSTON QUIZZED himself aloud as he looked up the steep steps. "So, why is the girl practically still under my roof?"

Comforted by the certainty there would be no one up there this early, he started the climb. No matter for days he had itched to slap his wife more times than Sunday could imagine, Lelia Rose was still a white woman, due her God-endowed respect, and the clash of feelings with rightness had robbed him of sleep.

"Why haven't I just sent her on out to Gillie, no matter what he says, out there where she should have been in the first place?"

Heading straight for the bench where Lelia Rose and her friends had taken to meeting every day, he heard sobs. A woman. So caught up in her plea she didn't hear him. He moved closer.

"Pardon me," ... Sunday?

He didn't want to see her. Had planned—once he made up his mind—to simply send someone to remove her from the studio. She was too confusing. Flew in the face of everything he had ever been taught about the order of things. But could he just walk away? Like the slave ship on his landing, the scene was too compelling. The draw toward comforting her, as he would have Ellen, too strong. Her cupped palms jerked away from her face.

"Master Johns! Master Johns, I think I've been saved! Are you saved?"

He stared through the darkness. She'd thrown him completely, with the last question on earth he expected her to ask. Like many he knew, he'd dabbled around in church life all his life but never had he steeped himself in God. He believed in Him. Admonished others to do so. But saved? Something about that pointed question disturbed him. Sunday didn't move, but she spoke.

"Come, sir. Please sit with me."

Sit with her? The request was most unseemly. And his fault. All of it. He'd given her license to ask such, and he was the one to have to undo it. Clandestine meetings in the studio were one thing. But the heir of the Smithmore legacy on a hilltop with his slave in the darkest of night? Some might even say he was defiling the place of quality Vicksburg ladies by just standing here with her. Still, he took a step. Two. Three.

"What are you doing here, Sunday? Did I not confine you to the studio?" He ran his hand through his hair, noting that, at his age, its thickness rivaled hers. "I-I mean, I could have had you whipped for assaulting my wife. Do you understand that?"

He could hardly see the purple of her skin. But the brightness of her eyes matched the stars ... *and something—someone—else.* They flashed anger then quickly cleared.

"Don't matter none now, I reckon." She choked up. "Though I can't say I'll ever be able to stand a whipping like Miss Tullie said Jesus took for me, without bad feelings against the one what whipped me. That's what makes Him so special."

Johnston sat down. Never had he heard the desire to follow the Lord put more succinctly. He inched his arm along the top edge of the bench. Splayed his fingers against her upper arm. Sensed the sun beginning to rise—more in his soul than upon his body. *Pat, pat.*

"Time to get on back to the house." *Pat, pat.* "Everything's going to be all right."

"Massa Johns?" She was so lovely. So innocent. So much like someone he'd known before.

"'Til you decide what to do with me, will you stop by the studio to help me learn sometime?"

He stood. Turned toward the steps that would take him back down to the town where black and white never openly assembled together.

"I will," he said over his shoulder. And he would find a way to keep her here too.

Mid July, 1862
"Grant's Ditch," near a segment of the river below Vicksburg, Mississippi

"THIS AIN'T nothing but the Great Dismal Swamp all over again."

Clayton slowed his shovel. Just in time to watch a fat lazy rattler slide alongside him. He held still, surprised that one of the scores of snakes he'd already seen hadn't chewed him to bits in this useless gulley. *Whomp!* With the shovel's edge, he decapitated it then back-stepped to be sure there would be no aftermath.

Hate this place.

He shaded his brow against the sun. Tried to look the length of the unwieldy, fever-infested canal in which he stood —a colossal ditch which a Union General named Thomas Williams actually believed, when completed, would bypass a bit of the Mississippi River. Some of the other ex-slaves with which Clayton labored went so far as to whisper that the ditch could possibly leave the city of Vicksburg—a few miles north— totally cut off from the mighty river itself.

Clayton, though, was antsy. Needed to get away from here. Get on with the business of why he was in this part of the country in the first place. Sunday Duval. How close was she to where he now stood? And how would he ever fix his mouth to tell her July was dead?

Questions hounded his every step, but no one seemed to believe it worth explaining to a black boy from Virginia why the Union Army was bent on capturing Vicksburg. A town which it had taken forever to reach, Taylor Mack posing as his master and dragging him in chains through unheard of places like Chattanooga and Tallulah, just to end up digging a vermin-infested ditch.

At least now he was close—attached to General Williams's brigade after getting caught hiding on a Louisiana plantation. But, truth told, this stretch of land they were now digging out between two strands of the river—having diseased or killed most of the 3,000 white soldiers General Williams had brought here before Clayton and the rest of the thousand or more

Negroes were conscripted—was worse than the swamp life he lived in North Carolina.

He lifted his shovel and began to dig again, just before he heard him, yards down the ditch. A young buck growling at an officer who had just called him all things imaginable.

Georgie?

The sergeant stomped away, and Clayton sneaked a glance to see if the other military bosses, who were turning out to be not much friendlier than a plantation overseer, had moved away for a moment. Yes.

"Georgie?"

Clayton blinked away the sweat from his lashes. Slogged around the men separating them. He thought he would never be this glad to see someone again in his life. Not even in the dreams of Noah's return when he was a small boy. He caught up to the young man. Touched him on the shoulder—

"Get cho hands off me, man. Name ain't no Georgie. What's wrong wit' chu?"

"Sorry. I thought you was somebody else."

They stared at each other for a long moment, Clayton seeing his own bitterness reflected in another man's eyes. He couldn't be more than four summers past a dozen years. Yet his anger was old and wouldn't be going away. If the South won the war, numbers upon numbers of stirred-up angry black men would be a part of the landscape. Did Clayton really want to own some of those men? Because he knew that, like himself, deep in the hearts of many blacks lurked that same rage he was looking at.

"Sorry," he said again. He turned back down through the mud toward his shovel.

And as long as men are mistreated, them feelings go'n keep breaking loose.

24

Rochester, weeks later

Noah scolded himself for the surliness he had radiated throughout the day. He hadn't been able to get Sunday and the baby out of his thoughts. Couldn't quite understand this war between the states.

Gideon's newspapers put the battles between the North and South in full swing. But to Noah, the whole idea of a country killing itself was a morass of questions. What exactly were they fighting about? Was it "maintaining economic advantage" under the guise of preserving the Union as some were whispering? Or was it some "amorphous idea about a way of life," as Gideon said the South claimed?

Or, at its core, was it to keep him and Sunny in Handley Duval's tobacco field?

Exhausted from cleaning fireplaces, repairing the roof, and cutting back shrubbery, he burrowed beneath the light blanket Angel had supplied. He was mostly comfortable during the day as he found ways to earn his keep, but he was surprised at each day's end by the chill that crept into his room as western New

York clung to the edge of winter. He had found kindness here. Yet the fact that it would be months before Gideon could lead him to Canada, made him feel boxed in.

A faint knock sharpened Noah's senses, causing a different war to break out in him. Since the first day he arrived here, when he'd almost lost himself in Gideon's beauty as she poured out her heart about August, he had worked hard to keep his distance. Prayerfully, this knock wasn't signaling the moment he had partly hoped for, mostly dreaded: choosing between one woman—alive and worthy of any man's love— and another, most likely dead from grieving the loss of the one person who was her everything. A woman whose nonexistent love for him still held him in its grip. He rolled over and faced the door.

"Come in."

The door seemed opened by a small-draped ghost.

"Mr. Noah?"

"Mr. August."

The boy crossed the room, a child-sized blanket wrapped around his shoulders. He handed the scarred red wagon toward Noah. "I thought you might be having a bad day."

Noah's heart sped up, every ounce of flesh and bone God had used to make him pulsated with feelings he didn't know he still had. He patted the edge of the mattress.

"You. Come up here."

Dropping his blanket, August climbed into the bed. Noah sat up. Swinging his legs over the side, he swooped the boy onto his lap. Held him close.

"Nope. Can't take your offering, man. No matter what my days are like, that wagon's yours to keep. It's even starting to look like you. Look at those eyes just as shiny as yours but lots more red." He tickled the boy's ribs, and a string of giggles lit up the room.

"Mr. Noah! You know a wagon don't got no eyes—"

"Doesn't have any, young man." Gideon leaned against the door frame. "August, may I ask what you're doing in here?"

Noah held the little boy's back close to his chest. "He's sleeping with me tonight. Ain't that right, man?" A rapid up-and-down shake of the head let Noah know he was indeed on the right track. And suddenly he knew something else. He loved this precious little boy but not his mother, not in the way a man loves a woman. Another major step toward healing was about to take place. He longed for Sunday and July, and he feared he always would. Gideon deserved to be told, and he would tell her. Soon.

Vicksburg, October 25, 1862

JOHNSTON WAS surprised at how pleased he was to see his brother.

"Here to rub it in on an old man, are you?"

Gillie knotted his fists against the slight dips on either side of his thickened waist, his long head shining with sweat as though it was August, his drawl as deep and muddy as the river.

"Happy birthday, Johns."

"Come on in, Gillie. We'll have a cup of coffee together like we used to behind Daddy's back."

Johnston was five and forty today, and if his instinct still worked, Gillie was not just here to celebrate. He was subtly reminding Johnston of last month's Confederate Congress's amendment to raise the conscription age to forty-five. Still, Johnston was happy to see his brother on his birthday.

"You do remember how old you are today."

On target. But he hadn't and wouldn't enlist, justifying his actions to himself on the superstitious notion that his fortune had turned when he'd brought Sunday into his life, and he was under a moral compulsion to bypass combat. Meanwhile, he told Gillie and everyone else in his circle it was because of Lelia Rose's fragile constitution.

Neither reason was true.

"I don't want to go back across this ground again, Gillie. I've already told you that I paid for a substitute to register in my place so I can ensure Lelia Rose's protection. And, of course, there's the day-to-day business of the foundry, essential to the war. Besides, I hear there's to be a new amendment exempting planters with twenty or more slaves. So, let's drop this once and for all, shall we?"

Gillie scratched his head, his lips pulling to one side in that superior smile of his that always made Johnston want to slug him.

"You haven't been hearing me, have you, Johns? We barely have fifteen slaves anymore. They've all either run away or been snatched up by Yankees to work on leased plantations on the Louisiana side. If something's not done soon, we'll lose everything Daddy worked for."

Understood. So that was the reason brother Gillie was here just the other side of the crack of dawn. Just once a year could they not put aside their differences and celebrate each other's birthday without money being the honored guest? Not the Smithmore boys. No, sir. They bare-knuckled it out three hundred and sixty-five with no time off for leisure. Suddenly, Sunday's face—her expression for the need for something Johnston hadn't quite figured out—warmed him. Filled the hole Gillie had just gouged.

"And what do you expect me to do about it? I didn't start this war. And, for certain, I can't end it."

"Maybe so. But you sure in blazes could fight in it, like I would like to do. For once, just tell the truth about it, Johns. You're resisting helping the Confederacy preserve our God-given way of life, and I'd like to know why."

Johnston gritted his teeth. He had to do something to keep from tearing his brother's lips from his accusing mouth.

"Are you daft? I just went over with you why I'm not fighting."

"I know what you say. But there's nothing wrong with your wife that a good old-fashioned spanking wouldn't cure." Gillie turned and made for the door. "The sorriest reason I ever heard for not fighting, and I'm plumb ashamed of you."

Johnston stood there, shaking, for how long he couldn't tell. He, too, was ashamed of himself. But try as he may, he couldn't make up his mind to enlist.

Early November, 1862

"How it feel to have a baby, Sunday?"

"Why? You planning on having one anytime soon?"

Nonnie's eyes stretched to saucers before she quickly started to examine her bare toes, eliciting a hearty chuckle from Sunday. "Well, do you?"

"Me? Naw! It's just that every other word that come from your mouth since you got here been about July. July this. July that. All the time it's always Jooo-ly."

Sunday quashed her giggles. If she didn't know better, she'd think her friend was jealous. But she did know better. Nonnie was prone toward a little deceit when it was convenient, but not jealousy. Didn't know how to be jealous. Sunday had wondered for weeks if the girl was in the family way. Now she was fairly sure.

"My talk about July what's bothering you? Or is it something else?"

"W-what? 'Course not. Ain't nothing bothering me. I ... well, I was just wondering. You never talk about the pain—how it supposed to rip a body apart—like so many of the womens back over on the plantation."

Sunday studied the girl. There'd been no throw-ups in the mornings that she knew of, and unlike Sunday—after only two months into Sunday's pregnancy—Nonnie's middle was as flat as a flapjack. But there wasn't a man on the place that she could've been sparking. Except Massa Johns.

No.

"You right. I haven't talked much about the pain 'cause there wasn't enough to talk about. Miss Tullie said I made one good push, and July just slipped out like a little greased egg. 'Bound to be a handful when he grows up,' she said, 'cause he come here so easy.'"

Nonnie sniffled. Then made for the empty syrup bucket used for a chamber pot. Forehead in Sunday's hand, Nonnie vomited until spasms set in, each pull and jerk tearing into Sunday like it was her own. Whose child was this?

Pete's? *Or Master Johns'?*

Was Nonnie's admiration for Master Johns more than just that? Had the master's strict order that she not tell Nonnie about the art lessons—even as she hid in the studio—been rooted in something between him and Nonnie? *I can't paint with a man who might be using Nonnie.* She groped around inside her head, trying to find something to stay her fears.

Maybe it ain't from being big, because she ain't got a inch of fat 'round her waist. And she throwing up at nighttime, so maybe ... aw hush, Sunday. Time to coax Nonnie into talking. Only don't let it be Massa Johns.

Nonnie limped toward the tiny window. "I ain't done nothing wrong, Sunday. I swear."

The tension in the room was a live thing, sucking up the air like a cyclone. And though Sunday couldn't quite put her finger on the severity of Nonnie's distress, she knew her own was rooted in the potential loss of the fragile bond between her and

Johnston Smithmore. Ruining a trusting sixteen-year-old girl was past what she could make peace with. And if Master Johns had compromised her sister-friend, then this new life source for Sunday—time spent together with Johns Smithmore in the art studio—was ruined too.

Nonnie's eyes held terror. "You go'n t-tell? You go'n tell Massa Johns on me?" Wringing her hands, the poor girl rattled on. "Please, Sunday. I ain't done nothing wrong. You go'n tell. I know you is. Then Lelia Rose go'n ... oh, lord, please help me. What am I go'n do 'bout Pete?"

Sunday's throat constricted, her voice sounding small to her own ears, her breathing a line of ragged wisps.

"What chu mean by that, Nonnie? You saying this baby don't belong to Pete?"

"Pete, he be the sweetest boy ever, even stuff my sack with his own cotton when I couldn't keep up 'cause of my leg. Took lashes from old Gillie for me."

Old Gillie—that tiny piece of freedom Nonnie still received when she could drop the titles from her owners' names.

"That first night you came, a few hours after, I sneaked out to see Pete. We almost lost our heads that night—almost got in trouble with the good Lord, but we didn't. We knowed we had to marry, but who was go'n take out time to marry us? Who here in town even cared enough to watch us jump the broom?"

Sunday cringed a little. Smiled a little. She and Noah weren't able to complete that action. But was it really about the broom, or did it have more to do with the heart? She had pledged herself to Noah, not just to conceive, but to stand by him. How had she taken that so lightly? Noah Duval. Handsomest man in the state of Virginia. They had become one flesh. But in her fierce determination to keep her world safe, she'd never allowed them to become one spirit.

"So, I started praying to the good Lord. I put my whole heart in that prayer, and the Lord told me it was all right—that if we could, we would do better, but since we couldn't ...

"It was a long time before we got a chance to see each other again, but next time Pete came, I borrowed a broom and Massa Johns' Bible. We snuck as close as we could to the river. Neither one of us can read, but we knew the words was holy. So, with the Bible in our hands and it being cleared with God, we jumped the broom—at least Pete did. I just rested in his arms."

Sunday thought her heart might give out. Pete was the father after all. "Then how come you so scared, Nonnie?"

Nonnie stared at her for what seemed a quarter of an hour. "Have you done forgot 'bout old Lelia Rose?"

Never taking her eyes off her friend, Sunday removed from the windowsill the old hairbrush, near bald from use, that had so soothed her months ago. Then she sat on the cot again.

"Sit."

"What?"

Sunday grinned. "I said, sit. And you know what it means to order a body to sit."

Nonnie limped over to the cot and squatted to sit down.

"On the floor." Sunday pointed her feet, spread apart. Nonnie lowered herself between Sunday's knees as best she could, her bad ankle turning inward. Not a word, as Sunday picked loose each braid of sandy-colored hair, brushing each sectioned-off plait one by one, before gently grasping the mass of hair in one hand and running the brush through it with the other.

"We are friends. I would never tell on you. But you know this is something we can't keep secret forever. You mustn't worry, though. We be figuring something out long before that sweet young'un start showing up." Sunday made a point of looking at Nonnie's nearly nonexistent midsection. "If she ever do."

Sunday heard the start of a giggle. Felt when Nonnie

relaxed. She had never asked about the limp before. Selfishness? Or perhaps the time hadn't been right. Either way, she knew—just like she'd always known that Someone somewhere much bigger than she was running this whole thing—that it was time.

"How did you get your ankle hurt?"

"I ain't ready to talk about that."

Sunday smiled. All right. So maybe it had been time to ask. Just not time to push.

25

Christmas Eve, 1862
Six o'clock in the evening, Vicksburg

R ain lashed the windows of Lelia Rose's bedchamber
until the leaves of the carved wooden pineapples atop
the four-poster bed seemed threatening to droop. Nonnie laid
out the toilette for tonight's ball and moved to gather the jewels
for her mistress's hair, while Sunday stood as far in the corner
as she could, resewing a button onto tonight's elaborate dress
that had shown up loose and dangling at the last minute.

"Oh, you two are a pair, aren't you? And as for you, Miss
Tuesday, heaven only knows how I let Johnston talk me into
letting you back into my bedroom tonight. But this is such a
special celebration—our boys whipping the Yanks upriver like
they did—and the Balfours are such wonderful people to do
this. I must look my best."

Lelia Rose sat at her dressing table tapping her long fingers
on the polished top, speaking over her shoulder at Nonnie.
"When are you going to get around to my hair?"

Nonnie was an expert hairdresser, and Lelia Rose knew it.

But never once had Sunday witnessed the slightest compliment.

"Are you deliberately trying to make me late for the Balfours' ball?"

Sunday wanted to remind the witch of how much she worshiped the idea of being fashionably late. Instead, she pierced the needle through the button opening. In and out. *In-and-out* until she drew blood. Not the blood she wanted to draw, however. Conscience pricked her for such a thought as Nonnie tried to appease Lelia Rose.

"Yes, ma'am. I mean, no, ma'am. It won't take me long."

Nonnie limped toward her mistress—her shapeless shift becoming more and more useless as a hiding place for her child—trying to keep distance between herself and her owner as she'd been doing now for weeks since her midsection had seemingly swelled overnight.

"Hurry, then!" Lelia Rose squirmed. "Wait. Get the backscratcher first. My back itches."

Nonnie did as she was told, starting near the small of her mistress's back as she had been ordered in the past. "Not there, imbecile." She reached around to swat away the backscratcher, fingers glancing off Nonnie's belly.

"What in heavens name? ..." Like the hands of a clock, she slowly turned and met the eyes of a frozen Nonnie.

Move away from her, Nonnie. Move, girl!

Lelia Rose squinted, measured every inch of the girl with a hatred so pure that Sunday thought she could actually find a color for it. "Have you been lying around with someone? Under my roof?"

Still, Nonnie said nothing. Simply opened her mouth, closed it in horror. Watched—as did Sunday—the wheels of Lelia Rose's mind turning faster than that of a mail coach.

"Whose bastard is it?"

"Mine."

Sunday wanted to shout. Nonnie had finally found her voice. Her answer was brilliant. More courageous than any Sunday had heard come from her own mouth. But it was kerosene to the flames of fear and hate already burning bright in Lelia Rose's eyes.

"It's Johnston's, isn't it? ISN'T IT?" Lelia Rose Smithmore blanched as white as the lacy undergarments she wore, her stays expanding and contracting like bellows. A shadow of something fell across her face before the woman erupted in rage.

"Cursed whore, get out!" Hands fisted, she stood and struck against Nonnie's jaw, bosom, abdomen with all her strength while the poor girl tried to cover her unborn child with her forearms. "Do you dare mock me? My inability to conceive? Do you think you can mix your half-white blood with my husband's and win his affections?"

Sunday's breath came in puffs. *Ha'mercy. So that's what's been making her so crazy all this time and making Nonnie so terrified of her.* The poor thing must have thought Sunday knew.

"This accursed thing will die. Never live to shame my Ellen's name. I'll see to it." She ran from the room, Sunday and Nonnie behind her. At the landing, next to the place where the drowning slaves had been, stood Johnston Smithmore.

"Johns! Oh, what have you done now?"

"Lelia Rose? What's the matter? You're not even dressed."

Master Johns, in his ball attire, looking plumb beautiful in the handsomest way Sunday had ever seen him, pushed a hand through his thick hair. "What's the trouble this time? You'll bring everyone in the house to the foot of the stairs."

For a moment, Sunday felt pity. She doubted the pain on Lelia Rose's face could be captured, not even with a brush.

"How could you, Johnston? Are you hoping it'll be white so we can pretend we finally have a Smithmore heir? Do you expect me to accept that?" The old Lelia seemed to fight through the pain, back to her comfort of hate. "Never."

Eight forty-five, the same evening

DISGUSTED by the outlandish interior of the carriage, even more than he'd been before Sunday arrived, Johnston turned up his collar against the damp chill and settled in for the short ride to the Balfours' home. He'd rather imbibe a shot of strychnine than go to this party with Lelia Rose.

My baby, indeed. What kind of monster did she make him out to be?

But Dr. and Mrs. Balfour were good people, and they deserved his respect toward their attempt to lighten the mental load of the war that loomed larger over Vicksburg every day, though to hear Lelia Rose and Gillie talk, there really was no war in Vicksburg at all. Just a silly show of Yankee foolishness that would never get any further than a bluster of maritime power on the river. From the corner of his eye, he saw Lelia Rose patting her hair, pursing her lips as though nothing out of the ordinary had happened between them just over an hour ago.

"That Sunday girl is as arrogant as she is black."

Johnston's jaw tightened. He could do this. Say nothing. Only minutes remained before they were plunged into a crowd where he wouldn't have to listen to her.

"And those addlepated abolitionists, as I'm sure Susan Coatsworth has become since her husband died, talk about freeing them? A bunch of airheads, all, if you ask me. And one of the silliest notions Yankees have ever come up with is that they can actually take Vicksburg. It's the talk of Sky Parlor Hill. Why, Susan almost lost her footing the other day arguing against the good sense of the rest of us about what could possibly happen if the Yanks got the upper hand. Had the nerve to bring up all that malarkey about the battery run back in the summer which we all know amounted to nothing. She's betting on them making another of Farragut's Little Forays one of these days. She got so worked up that she ended up grabbing hold of us to prevent what was sure to be a nasty fall. It would have been no less than she deserved. Well, I'll just say it. A little more clinging from her, and all our petticoats would have tumbled down the hill."

Images of a legion of underskirts toppling from Vicksburg's loftiest and most scenic view gave him a private chuckle. Not that he truly wished harm to the town's bored elite ladies, but a short harmless drop and a few torn unmentionables might quell some of their daily gossip.

"Yankees, with the upper hand on Vicksburg! Can you imagine such a thing? May Providence bless people like the Balfours who show the Susan Coatsworths of the town what the truth really looks like around here."

The carriage finally rolled to a stop in front of the head-quarters of General John Pemberton—who had recently situated himself one door over from the Balfours—and waited its turn. Johnston did a harrumph. He didn't have much for the new general, given he believed Pemberton to be a Yankee at heart besotted by and married to a Southern woman—that lady being the true reason he'd sided with the Confederacy in the first place. The Pennsylvania-born general had only been heading up the Vicksburg campaign resistance for a couple of months, so time would tell. And who was Johnston to talk anyway, since he'd done everything in his power to stay out of the line of fire—from buying a substitute soldier to claiming a concern for a marriage which didn't exist.

Inside the gaily lit home, the usual greetings and pompous announcements—followed by dining, feigning, and dancing—

went on for hours. One more dance and Johnston ought to be clear to go home without being fully labeled a Union sympathizer as many suspected. He waited impatiently while the musicians took a short respite. Lelia Rose smiled, fanned, carried on with the officers' wives—and the officers themselves —as though she were the queen of the South.

There. The music began again, thank goodness. Lelia Rose slid into his arms for a popular waltz, her flawless features a portrait of marital contentment.

"You will send that whorish cripple *and* your artist to the plantation tomorrow, or I will tell all of Vicksburg where your true sympathies lie." Johnston glanced across the room to find Susan Coatsworth staring at him. Could it be that Susan had already guessed?

"You will do no such thing. Even if you contacted my brother, he wouldn't take them. There's nothing for them to do out there right now. Except for Pete and one or two others, all the slaves have run off, and Gillie and his family have moved into the guest cottage."

She seemed to consider what he'd said before coming at him from another angle. "I'm only dancing with you because I'm afraid to leave you alone with anyone else, especially Susan Coatsworth who's been eyeing you all evening. Those Yankee sentiments that everybody has always known you possess have been pushing to the fore of late, and I'm afraid Susan's becoming enamored of you." She smiled her most enchanting smile at one of the senior officers. "Tell me, Johnston, are you trying to punish me for not producing an heir? Just tell me. Is the little bastard yours? Have I been wrong about you and Sunday? Is it Nonnie you're disgracing yourself with?"

He wanted to slam her to the dance floor. In his entire life, he had only "disgraced" himself with one woman. A beautiful funny intelligent woman that, under different circumstances, could have brought such joy. But what he had done—the way he might have damaged the woman's marriage, even though at the time he himself was an unmarried man—was unforgivable. *That was a long time ago. Has nothing to do with Sunday and Nonnie.* It was past midnight. Johnston was beyond exhausted. He would not dignify this foolish blather.

Abruptly, the dancers halted. Parted. Cut a clean pathway, as a windblown mud-splattered fellow identifying himself as Colonel Phillip Fall barged in, dripping across the partly-shining, partly-scuffed floor. With little or no apology Johnston could discern, the soldier marched straight toward General Martin Luther Smith, said something to him just before Smith announced in a voice loud enough to wake up the town, "This ball is at an end. The enemy are coming down the river, all noncombatants must leave the city."

Like everyone else, Johnston collected his wife and did as he was told. But at this, the oddest time, the reasons he'd been giving himself all these months for paying another man to do his fighting bobbed up in his mind unbidden. Sunday's fortuitous arrival and Lelia Rose's craziness had nothing to do with his decision. Both of them, unadulterated lies. Though he wanted the South to win, Johnston Harrison Smithmore's reason for not fighting was that he didn't believe in this war. He never had.

February, 1863

CLAYTON HID beneath a shapeless tattered hat. Kept his head toward the ground. Sneaked a glance at the hilly town called Vicksburg and quickly ducked again, trying to blend in. His labor, along with all the other men's—to dig General Ulysses S. Grant's ditches—had been a dismal failure. They had dug in icy mud, slogged through brush and swamp trying to turn the

Mississippi River in the general's favor, so that he could ship thousands of men past the bluffs of Vicksburg without massive harm, only to be reminded that the Creator still has the power to appoint and disappoint in mankind and nature.

But with the help of Taylor Mack, who had signed up as a Federal spy, Clayton had been able to wheedle his way into Vicksburg. And even though he'd not been able to become an official soldier yet, Vicksburg was worth it all. Now came the tricky part. Finding Sunday Duval in this town and telling her the news about July.

And claiming the place of Noah in her life.

Cramming the wilted crown of his hat farther against his head, he stooped his back and walked toward the nearest mercantile. Playing the role of a mindless slave wasn't hard, just infuriating. And he knew he was playing it well. Thank goodness Mack had found the most threadbare clothes he could find for him. Hat in hand, he gingerly stepped into the store. He spotted one other black person, a woman examining something in the corner. He waited until every white person had been served.

"He'p you, boy?"

A rotund redheaded man about Clayton's age—a friendly sort as far as he could tell—greeted him from behind the counter.

"Who sent you, and what can we get for him? Or her." He made light of his error. "Never can tell about the ladies. Find out you've slighted one of 'em, and that's a year's worth of business dumped into the slop jar."

He roared at his assumed cleverness as Clayton joined in, making sure he laughed just loud enough for the man to believe he appreciated the humor, but not so loud as to assume he could laugh on the level of a white man.

"Well, what can I do for you?"

"Well, suh. Uh, thank you, suh. I be trying to find a woman."

"You and everybody else."

The man guffawed again as Clayton produced his pass accompanied by Mack's note. This game was aging fast, and Clayton was running out of patience. He screwed up his face as though the idea of what he was about to say gave him a stomachache.

"She a runaway—chasing in behind them Yankees you know. Once she done heard about the 'Mancipation Proclamation, she run away from the farm near Bovina. Massa sent me looking to see if she might be here in Vicksburg, seeing as how old Grant's army is so close."

The man frowned. "Watch yourself, boy. I despise *General* Grant as much as the next fellow, but he's still white. That there alone ought to let you know your place."

Clayton scrambled to recover. "Oh, yes suh. Yes, suh." He bowed profusely. "No disrespect meant. None a'tall."

The man studied him, obviously trying to decide. He read the note a second time. "All right. Now what did you say her name was?"

Clayton hadn't said, but far be it from him to point that out. "Sunday is what we call her out at the plantation. Just Sunday." A crash split the air.

"Oh! Oh, mercy me. Look what I done did."

Clayton turned to face the woman he'd spotted earlier waiting in line behind him, her basket of goods scattered over the floor. Seeming a bit lame in one foot, she scraped and scrabbled to pick up the goods while he helped her.

"Outside," she mouthed. "Wait outside."

"Move along now, boy. I don't know no nigger named Sunday, but I do know the one behind you. Belongs to one of my best customers. Move along, now."

"Yassuh. Thank you, suh."

HOURS TURTLED by it seemed before the girl emerged from the mercantile. She did in fact have a slight limp, and unless he was badly mistaken, she was well into the family way. Neither seemed to matter to her as she plowed straight ahead.

"Jes walk along behind me. Don't act no different."

Clayton followed her until they reached the back of a stately white three-storied home with a view of the river. The girl fisted her hands to her chest. Nervous and determined at the same time.

"Okay now, who is you, really? You Noah, ain't chu?"

"I sholy ain't named Noah." *Careful, man. No need for that now.* "Name's Clayton. Clayton Duval. Do you know her? Do you know Sunday—?"

"Nonnie? Who you talking to? Why you back so quick?" ... *Clayton?* "Clayton, is that you?"

He spun in the direction of his name, his heart making a mockery of his effort to remain calm. Knees that had slogged through swamps for weeks now liquefied.

"What in the world you doing here?" He stared at her as Sunday cocked her head to the side and stared right back.

"And did you just say your name was Duval?"

THE ANSWER to her question could wait. Sunday grabbed Clayton's arm, dragged him behind the walls of the mostly dormant garden back of the house. Full-hoping, half-praying Lelia Rose didn't catch them, she flung her arms around his neck. Squeezed him until it turned awkward.

"Pardon me. I'm just so glad to see you 'til it hurts." She pointed to a bench. "Sit. Tell me everything. What happened to Jess 'nem? How'd y'all get away? Where you been staying—?"

"Whoa!" Clayton put his hands in the air, laughed, and took the seat she'd indicated next to her. "One question at a time."

Sunday glanced toward the upstairs windows, reality setting in that it was mid-afternoon and she couldn't afford to be seen by her mistress. Nonnie pulled back Lelia Rose's drapes, nodding that everything was fine for now.

"All right. Talk."

She drank his words like water from her Virginia stream, thrilled that Silas had unwittingly freed the coffle, though he never mentioned it to her before releasing her to a man in Memphis to be shipped to Vicksburg. She wondered about the price he'd have to pay for losing the slaves. Shuddered at what Duval would do if he ever saw him again—

"I'm Noah's cousin."

It took seconds for Sunday's conscious mind to catch up with what her brain had just registered. She jumped from the bench.

"You're *what*?"

"Noah Duval. He my cousin."

"But how ... why, Clayton? Why would you keep something like that from me? What did I ever do to make you not tell me? I mean ... I know I'm not the friendliest person in the world, but how could you not tell me something like this?"

She took in the images of struggle on his countenance. Pain and anger. Deep remorse.

"I got something else to tell you. I'm here because I found July."

Instantly, she was cold, Clayton's voice having thrown her into dread. She tried desperately to coax her heart toward relief, but it wouldn't play the game.

"Tell me what you got to say. Make it quick."

"Miss Borden, li'l July, they both gone."

"Gone? How can he be gone? You just said you found him. Is he sick? What—?"

"No, Sunday, not that kind of gone. Him and the woman, they both dead. Saw it with my own two eyes."

A whirring seized her chest, and she was a dumbstruck child again—squatting, stirring a heavy mud pie in front of Miss Tullie's cabin. Her eyes drifted upwards. Lelia Rose stood in the window, fury riding her scrunched brow, just before Sunday slumped onto Clayton's chest and into a world of purple.

It was simple, really. Death would be better. Even Lelia Rose had complied when Master Johns saw Sunday's state and demanded she be left alone for a while. A while turned into weeks.

Through it all—the horror of being stolen, the threat of rape, the abuse of yet another demon-possessed white woman —she had managed to fan the spark of hope. Hope that her son —whom she had tried to spare from life's by-and-by lies about freedom for black folks—was still safe. But now that fragile flame had been doused beneath a weeks-long cloud of continuous tears that she was powerless to halt. She sensed Nonnie in the room, smelled something savory that only served to sicken her more. *July. My baby. My life.*

"I am the Way, the Truth, and the Life."

But it's too late—

"It's too late. I done failed. God, my parents, July, Noah. Even you, Nonnie."

"Hush now, 'cause I don't feel failed. I'm glad you talking again, but you didn't do a thing to make this happen to your baby and none of the rest of it. Slavery did it—that monster that keeps swallowing up our souls, so's rich white people, from Vicksburg to wherever Manchester, England is, can live better and better. Don't chu worry, though. Nonnie's here. Go'n be here 'til things get better."

And each day Nonnie *was* there—quietly absorbing Sunday's rebuffs, waiting with open arms when the fear of living overwhelmed Sunday to the point where human touch was vital to the ability to draw another breath. Nonnie, selfless Nonnie, the sibling Sunday had never had.

Unable to answer, she leaned into her sister-slave and wept. And wept some more.

26

Rochester, New York
March 2, 1863

Noah adjusted this thing called a cravat as he covered the blocks toward the building for which Gideon had given him directions. He must not be late, she'd warned him, for this once-in-a-lifetime orator would change his life. But Noah had lost track of time shoveling snow.

"Just about the time my poor muscles get over the last snowstorm, another one blows in."

He chuckled to himself. During his months in this cocoon with Gideon, shoveling snow had worked muscles that the tobacco fields had seemingly never heard of. Branches on the loveliest trees he'd ever seen drooped like sullen white-bearded old men while hills of snow and ice, backed up into every inch of available space, seemed to stake out permanence with each passing day. This town in upstate New York saw more snow in one season than all Noah's previous winters put together. Would spring ever come again?

He mounted the steps to the cavernous building. Spotted

Gideon and eased his large frame into the tight space next to hers. She turned toward him, mock displeasure riding her brow. "You're late, sir."

"Yep. But you go'n be mighty happy when you see the dry steps at your house. Won't have to worry about li'l August' backside being bruised by another fall—at least for today."

She smiled. Patted Noah's knee. Seeking space to stretch out his cramped legs, he blew on his hands. Touched the tip of his nose to see if it was still there. Looked up and was immediately and completely hypnotized by a man named Frederick Douglass.

"Gideon?"

"Shh. You won't want to miss a word."

But Noah had questions. Dozens of them. No way this man could have ever been a slave. It was all Noah could do not to gape like an idiot. From his earliest memories, his and Clayton's hair had been cropped short—having been told their hair was created too wild looking to ever be allowed to reach past the length of their thumb joints. But this leonine man named Frederick Douglass unabashedly wore his thick hair long—each wiry strand shouting to the world of his pride in its strength and texture. Gideon had called him the most handsome man she'd ever seen. In truth, his carriage was regal. At once fierce and compassionate. Noah rubbed his hands together and leaned forward.

"When first the rebel cannon shattered the walls of Sumter and drove away its starving garrison, I predicted that the war then and there inaugurated would not be fought out entirely by white men ..."

A line of tiny prickles marched across the scars on Noah's back. Handley Duval's whip snapped in his mind like the frozen branches of this fascinating yet raw Rochester winter. He needed the outside air, which, moments ago, he'd been so ready to escape.

"There is no time to delay. The tide is at its flood that leads on to fortune. From East to West, from North to South, the sky is written all over. 'Now or never.'" ... "Liberty won by white men would lose half its luster." ... "Who would be free themselves must strike the first blow." ...

The smell of scalded hog. The powerlessness of a thirteen-year-old to strike out in his own defense—his youthful muscles aching with pain and anger—was beginning to overwhelm Noah. He twisted in his chair, his skin pouring sweat like a Southern summer.

"By every consideration which binds you to your enslaved fellow countrymen ... by all the ties of blood and identity which make us one with the brave black men now fighting our battle in Louisiana and in South Carolina, I urge you to fly to arms and smite with death the power that would bury the government and your liberty in the same hopeless grave ..."

Fly to arms!

Noah shot to his feet, Canada fading like yesterday's dreams. It would not be to Massachusetts to join with a set of black soldiers that he would go, as Douglass was suggesting. Nor would he cross the line into another northern country. He would go back south. The new nation—where he first collected the scars—would be the place where he would fight for healing.

"BE REASONABLE." Gideon paced softly in front of Noah's chair. "It's still only March. Way too cold. You'll never make it."

Noah stiffened. Circled his palms against his knees and looked out the window, straight ahead at the snow that had fallen all evening. Hadn't it been Gideon who'd insisted he be there for Douglass's speech?

"Try to understand, Gideon. I *have* to do this."

"It'll hurt August something awful."

"I know."

And the girls, they love you. Even my grieving mother is more like herself since you've been here."

"I love them too."

"So help me, I wish I'd never invited you to go with me to see Mr. Douglass. I thought you would connect to him in a sensible way. Thought you'd appreciate how brilliant and logical he is. He wasn't telling you to do something foolish like plowing down into hostile territory."

The man's passion—had she not seen that?

"Plowing into hostile territory? Isn't that what you do all the time, Gideon?"

"But you haven't been trained. You need to join up with the army first before going south. Mr. Douglass was talking about Massachusetts—able-bodied colored men joining up with the 54th there—not Mississippi."

"I never said Mississippi, only that I heard General Grant has been down that way for some time now and that, despite the rumors, he's a really good, really determined soldier. And I do plan to join the army—just not in Massachusetts."

"Doesn't matter. Mississippi, Georgia, Alabama. They're all of a piece. Despite what the president has proclaimed about freeing slaves, you know nothing about the mood of the Confederate army down there. The Union either, for that matter. It's quite likely some of them are just as resistant to colored men joining as the Rebels are."

"So, what are we arguing about—?"

Gideon sucked in a breath and began again before Noah could edge his way further into his defense.

"It would be utterly foolhardy. You've never even traveled alone. How would you even know if—"

Noah held up his hand, unable to stand any more of the desperation coming from this usually calm woman. This was shaping up to be even harder than he had thought—the idea of deserting August—as he'd done July—the hardest. Nothing to do except face her like a man. He turned toward her. Cradled her face in his palms.

"First off, even though it didn't turn out too well, I have traveled alone."

He stroked along her cheek with the nub of one of the fingers Duval had chopped off as he tried to make light of his first escape. She stared, unblinking.

"All right, Gideon, let me try to explain." He kept his palms against her face, thinking again of what a fine person she was. "I've made too many bad decisions already, though following you wasn't one of them. I've spent my life chasing freedom without understanding it, not knowing that until everybody in this country is free, nobody is. I'm starting to see myself as chasing a bunch of ghosts running around under the name of freedom. But at last, I've got a chance at real freedom, the kind that I can almost feel between thumb and finger. Not for myself alone but for every African coming before, with, and after me, who never thought it would happen.

"Right now, to most Americans, I'm just a fugitive slave. But I could never forgive myself if I woke up one morning to find myself a free man, never having lifted a finger to help earn it. I don't know Massachusetts, but I know the South. And from Virginia to Texas, I'd wager the feeling of absolute ownership is pretty much the same. I counted on you of all people to understand."

She turned away from him, changing into every inch the scout who had so deftly gotten him out of the South in the first place.

"You are right, sir. And if you think that because of the war your owner, Handley Duval, has forgotten you're still out here, you are sadly mistaken. Win or lose the war, a man like that, even if only in his mind, will hunt you down until he dies." Face still between his palms, she placed her hands over his. Gazed into his eyes.

"Let's go to Canada, No-wuh. You've not seen beauty until you go up there. If I didn't have the fledgling school and my children to look out for, we could go tomorrow, but if you'll just wait a few months, I'll sell the house. Mother and I and the children, we'll all—"

"Aw, Gideon. You've taught me so much—how to give, how to be a man without it being at the expense of a woman's God-given ability. How to rest in my manhood, all the while amazed at that mind of yours. I'm never ever going to forget you."

She lowered her head. Flushed like a young girl on the precipice of her first courtship. He smiled at her.

"And by the way, there is no way I could have strung that many words together two years ago." He forced her to look at him again. "Please don't do this."

The silence was potent. He held his breath, praying he had avoided the big, dreaded question.

He hadn't.

"But ... but what about us, No-wuh? What about me and you? Can't you see it? Even our Children's names line up like the stars. I know it's too soon after Sunday and July, but ... just tell me, is there a chance? Just tell me, and I won't ask it of you again."

His heart shifted to another place. Right or wrong—for this kind caring woman—he would leave the door ajar. He owed her that much.

"I don't have the answers just now. All I know is that I have to go."

"Would it matter if I said I loved you?"

"It would. Still, I have to go."

27

Milliken's Bend, Louisiana
June 7, 1863, the wee hours of the morning

The African Brigade was ordered to be in line by two o'clock in the morning. Noah still couldn't believe he was here. It was as though the Union recruiters had been searching for him, steaming all the way to Arkansas to find black recruits. A week later, behind one of the levees facing the Mississippi River, he rehearsed in his head, the hasty training he had received.

Scattered fire rang from the far side of the levee, an officer quickly stepping in to calm the new, mostly ex-slave, recruits.

"Nothing to worry about quite yet. Most likely our pickets."

From a few feet away, Noah couldn't tell which of the all-white officers was speaking. Hadn't been in the 9th Louisiana Regiment of African Descent long enough to remember its full name, let alone the muted voices of its officers.

Tension crackled along the line. Noah squared his shoulders, trained his eyes on the ten-foot levee and the sporadic bales of cotton atop it. Spoke casually to a boy whom, until an hour ago, he had never before seen.

"Hear tell General Grant was here at Milliken's Bend a short time back."

Nothing. Not even a grunt.

"Who was that officer who just spoke to us from down the line?"

"Why you askin' me?"

Noah looked again toward the levee. "Sorry. Thought maybe—"

"Just got here myself last night. Don't know nobody or nothing."

Last night? Noah sucked up the fowl words which tried to claim his tongue. At least he'd been here a little better than a week. What kind of army would put a young boy—albeit a stout, angry one—on the line within the space of twenty-four hours?

A desperate, determined kind of army.

He tried to beat back the questions picking at his brain by concentrating on the formation of the half-mustered African Brigade. The 9th, 13th, and 11th Louisiana Infantry units of colored men had been ordered to array themselves from left to right, beginning with the 9th and ending at the 11th, with the 13th and the 1st Mississippi sandwiched in between.

So now it begins. The chance he'd coveted was finally within reach. A chance that had simmered during his every waking moment and boiled over into his dreams each night since he'd witnessed the passion of Frederick Douglass: "Liberty won by white men would lose half its luster."

Still, he had expected more training, more organization. *More men.*

The levee they were assigned to fronting the river offered Noah little comfort as he waited with the rest of the four regiments of Negro soldiers for whatever would be their fate in the predawn hours of June seventh. Minutes ago, he'd finally cajoled the sullen boy's name from him. Simeon Tuck, recently recruited from a nearby deserted Louisiana plantation, stood right of Noah, the smell of field hand still seeping from beneath his uniform, while the one officer whose name and voice Noah did know, Captain Corydon Heath of the 9th Louisiana Regiment, bent low to strike a match. He scanned his troops and spoke in low soothing terms before moving on. Despite the man's attempts, his words sounded like a death knell.

"Seem like a good man, that Cap'm Heath." Tuck muzzled a cough. "But I'm thinking he might be as nerved up as the rest of us. Ain't no joke—a few white men heading up a bunch of green, colored troops like us, 'specially this far south. Heard tell them Texas Rebs out yonder just itching for a fight. Showed up like ole Lucifer's twin a month or so ago down at Perkins' Landing but didn't quite get the fight they wanted, seeing as how the Yankee numbers was no match for them in the first place."

Noah laughed at the colorful description. "Lucifer's twin, huh."

"You heard me."

"No need to get all touchy now, son. We've practically already been thrown into the lake anyway. Any minute now, we go'n have to sink or swim. Me, I plan to swim."

"Just so it ain't the lake of *fire* we being throwed into. And don't call me son."

Deadness reigned once more, the heavy night sky seemingly in a heyday of sultriness. No fear of a sunrise anytime soon. Disease clung to Noah's uniform along with the sweat itself, as he held on to the musket handed to him several days ago, something he was handling for the first time in his life.

He dug his heels into the damp soil. Did he have enough training to operate this thing? Why hadn't there been orders to give the black troops a little longer to learn how to shoot? Had the white man's dread of what Gideon called "insurrection" made even the Union scared to teach black men how to use a gun?

You know better than that, man. You wouldn't be wearing this uniform if Mr. Lincoln hadn't needed you to kill up as many Rebs as you can ...

"Now, men! Fire!"

Noah aimed. He'd already loaded slowly, methodically. Forcing his brain to recall the list of steps from the days before, he had removed a cartridge wrapped in paper from the shabby container he'd been given. Ripped the top of the paper away with his teeth. Seconds ticked by. Time to fire. He willed steadiness into his fingers. He was a whittler after all. Made things even with two maimed fingers. He could do this. Won't do for a colored man to fail at the start.

Colored men. Always having to prove themselves—

Boom! He fired one off.

Too quiet. Weren't they all supposed to be doing the same thing? Everyone should have gotten a shot off by now. No time to think about it. He began reloading. Thankfully, getting the powder and the ball into the muzzle went smoothly. Now what? His brain skipped to the percussion cap. No! The rammer. That's it. The rammer. Pulling the long rod from its holder, he jabbed the powder and ball into the lower depths of the musket and replaced his rammer. Now the percussion cap. *Finally think I've got this thing.*

Pow! Somewhere on the other side of his brain he'd heard fire before his own. After his. With his. Thank you, Jesus. At least some of the other men had managed too.

He was about to fire again when he noticed Tuck still fumbling with what must be his first loading. Fumbling but not running. Good. The tip of the boy's tongue poised at the corner of his lips, he was determined. Didn't even see the white man approach.

"Great heavens, boy, don't you even know where your caps are?"

"Naw suh. Ain't nobody showed me yet."

Noah ignored the officer. Didn't have time to be angry. Didn't have time to help Tuck either. Or did he?

Perhaps he did. The Rebels' answer to the volley was weak, sporadic. Some had even turned and run.

"Here you go Tuck. Watch me." He began loading, Tuck straining to see in the darkness, hanging on his every move. Noah looked at the boy. Grinned. Though it seemed hours, only a precious few moments had passed.

Then he heard it. A keening screeching yell. A shout of "No quarter for white officers!" mixed in, as a rushing sweep of men charged the levee like a dumping of the Niagara Falls Gideon had told him about near Rochester.

In a long nightmarish minute, the men of the 9th Louisiana stared in disbelief then scrambled to use whatever half-cocked knowledge they had of guns, before the two opposing lines melded into one. The armies fought savagely. A bone-cracking melee where soldiers abandoned the shooting aspect of the weapons men so revered and swung wildly like cave men. Bayonets crossing. Black heads butting against white. White bodies falling atop black.

"Give it to 'em, boys! Give it to 'em!"

It was Captain Heath, loading a musket with the kind of quickness Noah could only imagine. Noah allowed himself another grin. It was the first time he'd ever been called a boy by a white man and not resented it.

"Yes, sir!"

Then time slowed, as a fresh curtain of Rebels fell upon the levee and surrounded the captain. And young Tuck. *And me?*

A bloodied soldier was upon him, the hate in his eyes—even in the darkness—as wild and rabid as any Nat-Turner-type slave insurrectionist could ever be.

"Say your prayers, boy."

Noah jammed the butt of his musket into the underside of man's chin shortly before he felt his senses rattle as something cracked into his skull from behind. He stumbled forward. After all the tries, all his life, finally a white man had killed him. He steered his mind toward the comfort of Gideon and the children then lost control of his thoughts as, of their own volition, they veered toward Sunday and July.

Sunny. I had so hoped ... prayed—

He jutted the point of his bayonet. "No quarter," they'd screamed, and he expected none. But in these last seconds, neither would he give any. Slashing and clanging, he fought on until his bayonet fell away. Grabbing his weapon by the barrel, he swung into a soldier's knee. Cringed at the shattering pop, so different from the pop of gunfire that had startled him at the outset. Straining for breath, he repeated his mantra. "I will not quit. I will not quit ..."

My Sunny. July. Clayton.

With three names on his lips, the piercing pain of a bayonet's tip rammed straight into his chest and laid him before the stars.

Eight hours later
In the camp of the 11th Louisiana Infantry, African Descent

EVERY INCH of Clayton's body screamed for some kind of balm. Still, the pain of fighting for eight hours hadn't come close to the ache he'd endured for the last several months each time he found himself alone with the thought of July.

He'd left Sunday in the hands of her friend—not that he had wanted to. Breaking her spirit like that then leaving the same night was the hardest thing he ever did—worse than waiting for Noah's return when he was a child. But sensing she hadn't wanted him there any longer, he'd determined to find something else—do something else—to make himself feel a little better about that precious little boy, though he was afraid the child's mother would never feel joy again.

He lay down on his back, keeping his distance from the rest of the battered exhausted men whose names he barely knew. For a few hours they had become the family he'd lost so many years ago. Rubbing his chin with the back of his hand, he realized how badly he needed a shave. Craved a bath. Clean clothes. None of which he would be afforded anytime soon. He thought of Pearl, how he left her standing stoic in Charleston. He was surprised he missed her so much.

Staring into the humid Louisiana midday, he allowed himself a bit of pride in the way his unit had fought today. Too many lives of young innocent soldiers had been lost. But no one who valued truth could ever again accuse black men of not being willing to fight, though most of those men had at some point been owned by another. A few of them, perhaps, by men of their own blood. Men who had decided on whatever it took to compete in a society built on profit.

Men like Clayton Duval.

Clayton shifted to his side. Thought of Georgie. Banished the thought. Could he really have owned Georgie? For the most part, untrained and definitely undermanned, Colonel Hermann Lieb's African Brigade fought the odds with valor. But it was the 11th who had somehow managed to hang on against the venom of the Texas unit of the Confederacy. Clayton had seen it in their eyes, a special hate reserved for him and all men like him—a near astonishment at the very idea that an ex-slave would pick up a gun in defense of the North. In defense of himself. Talk from a cluster of men nearby cut through his thoughts.

"Heard tell the 9th sho' did get it bad, though they put up a fight."

Clayton's ears pricked up. He knew the 9th Louisiana, holding the opposite flank from the 11th, had fought valiantly. He wondered how badly it had ended for them.

"Yeah, I heard the same thing," said another. "Heard, too, about a fellow who f'it like a wild man 'til he was captured 'long with his captain. Heard the colored man didn't make it."

"Oh, yeah? I know a few of them fellows. What be his name?"

"Name be Noah. Like the ark. Noah Du-something or other. Duvane, Duval—"

Clayton surged to his feet. Collared the man. "No, suh! You got the wrong name."

"Easy now. Just take it easy. You just still spooked from today's happenings."

Clayton's hands fell away, reached for his head. "My God, it wasn't supposed to end this way. It wasn't."

June 7, 1863, same day
During the Siege of Vicksburg

SUNDAY SAT by the narrow cot in the attic room, watching Nonnie sleep. A Negro child had died in the shelling this morning, mangled past resemblance, and she dreaded the moment when Nonnie found out about the latest horror into which her baby would soon be born. Despite the predictions of Lelia Rose and others, Vicksburg was now surrounded by the soldiers of General Ulysses S. Grant. No more harmless firing from the blue. No more boasts of invincibility from the gray. For weeks now, the citizens of Vicksburg had lived with the certainty of fighting nearby and increasing hunger and panic.

Sunday's eyelid twitched. It could so easily have been July, mistaking the shell for one of Noah's creations. Not knowing that lurking in that odd contraption was the sizzling path to certain death.

But July is dead. Your baby is dead.

She wiped the wetness from her cheeks. Smoothed Nonnie's hair. Thought of the move they were all about to make. Since the siege, Lelia Rose had become a nervous sniveling bag of bones—seemingly having forgotten her edict that Sunday never set foot in her house again, giving Sunday space to help Nonnie.

Master Johns had already paid, actually *paid*, Pete to dig out the caves—dark windows in the sides of hills that Sunday had only glanced at from a distance but had touched months earlier in a bizarre dream. One cave for a very swollen Nonnie, one for the other servants, and one for himself and Lelia Rose. Where would Sunday stay?

Old Lelia Rose might be right this once. Cave life with its threat of snakes and mice and insufferable closeness was perhaps more than even a slave could bear. But things were getting so scary above ground that there seemed to be little choice.

Moving to the small-paned window in the attic, she stared at the ravaged town, savoring the familiar sound of the girl's soft snores behind her. For days, she'd watched the light of the shelling turn Nonnie's caramel face into a lurid red. But not for long. She smiled, wondering if she'd had that special radiance Nonnie possessed before July was born. She'd been so consumed with his birth—had worried so about whether he would survive—that she had forgotten to savor the pregnancy, allow the beauty of its bloom to grace her. Next month he would have been four years. *Lord, why?*

She looked down at the studio and thought of the treasure there, numerous renderings of July. All she had left of the little boy who'd meant everything to her. Her chest pained as she turned from the window. Where was her little boy now? Could it be that the Creator might truly have him in his bosom? Oh, how she needed to believe that. The loss of her child, it just couldn't be borne.

I want to die, Lord. I need to die.

She wrestled down her emotions. Looked back out on the yard. If they remained cooped up in this house much longer, she probably *would* die of sadness—

Mercy! A mortar shell barely missed the corner of the widow's walk above her. Like so many others in this town, the conscious fear of shellfire and all its cousins of war had become short-lived. Not so with the stalker that lately owned her dreams.

She slumped against the window. Tried to suppress a yawn, her body craving sleep she dare not enter. Each night since the middle of April, when that line of what Master Johns called gunboats had pushed southward past the Confederate batteries, she'd not been able to sleep. A trail of floating iron monsters lit by the backdrop of oil-soaked mountains of cotton afire had laid claim on her dreams, a terrified July running from one of the monster's eyes to another—begging to be saved as firepower she could never have imagined boomed from the bluffs. She looked once more toward the studio that held the images of July. And found it ablaze.

Merciful Jesus.

Feet bare, oversized shift askew, she flew down the servant's stairs and out to the place where everything that still meant something to her was stored. Only a fool would try to go in. She was that fool.

The room was a miniature hell. It took only seconds to see that all was lost. Every sketch of July, every scrap of paper, every easel. Ruined. Screams backed up in her throat, she felt an arm around her waist. Master Johns. He dragged her back out into the yard. Voice choked with smoke and the likely loss of his own beloved artwork, he held fast to her as though she were the buoyant remnant of the slave ship like the one that yet haunted the upstairs landing. He turned to the stunned group of servants and neighbors. And Lelia Rose.

"We move now, or we'll be killed."

"I won't do it."

"Fine. I won't argue. It's been over three weeks since this dreadful siege began—months since we were warned to 'leave or prepare accordingly.' This wondering every day if the house will be blown to bits can't go on. You will sleep in the cave, or you will sleep in this dangerous house of yours alone. Or you can sleep on the streets. Your choice, Lelia Rose."

CLAYTON WAITED until the cover of night before sneaking into the space of the battered 9th Louisiana Infantry. He stepped around men, not knowing exactly whom or what he was looking for. All he knew was it wasn't Noah. *Not Noah.* Clayton's arms went up as a man's eyes flew open, awkward musket at the ready.

"Who you and what chu want?"

"I-I mean no harm. Truly."

The man fumbled for something. Struck a match while Clayton reached for any words that might make sense.

"I'm from the 11th." He pointed toward his uniform. "And I just—"

The man focused on the uniform. Held the match up toward Clayton's face. "Yeah, you is, ain't chu. Best you keep your voice low. I don't know as them sleeping officers over yonder would take kindly to being woke up after a day like this. Anyhow, name's Simeon Tuck. Y'all done some good fighting today."

"'Preciate that. So did you." Clayton breathed relief. "Mind if I sit down?" The man nodded while Clayton lowered his sore body to the ground. "I'm wondering about a cousin of mine"— Clayton hadn't thought of Noah as a true cousin in a long time —"who's supposed to have joined up with this unit. I've only been here a short while. Been so busy I've not had a chance to look him up."

"Know what chu mean. I ain't been here a good two days yet myself."

"You might know him. Noah Duval?" Tuck straightened his back and leaned forward, revealing how much of a youth he still was.

"You Noah's cousin? Well, I'll be. So, you Noah's cousin." Tuck reached his hand toward Clayton's. Nearly wrung it from Clayton's wrist. "Well, I'll be. In one day, he taught me all I know. Saved my life but wasn't quite able to hold on to his own. Bravest man I ever knowed. Most of what he said near the end didn't make sense, though. Kept calling the day of Sunday and the month of July. Only name that sounded like a man's was Clayton." Tuck paused. "By the way, I never did get your name?"

"My name Clayton. Clayton Duval."

28

They sat without words, Tuck seemingly realizing he had stumbled into something much bigger than his oversized frame. Something about this young soldier reminded Clayton of Georgie. The wide-eyed boy from the coffle stood out in his mind. Accusing.

"You wanted to buy me, Clay, or did you just want to steal me, or was it just somebody like *me ...?"*

"What did you make of Noah? Do you think he would've stuck it out after today?"

Tuck looked offended. "You asking me if Noah would've run?"

"Well, not exactly. It's just that it's been a long time since I saw him, and back then—you know how it is with boys—back then, he wasn't so good at keeping his word."

"Spill it."

"What?"

"G'won. Spit it out. Don't take much to see you itching to talk about something you holding 'gainst Noah."

Clayton shifted his weight. Never had he discussed with a

single soul the hurt, the sense of betrayal Handley Duval had injected into him—except maybe for that time with July who had simply laughed in his face. Maybe here by this river that so many men were losing their lives over he could bare his soul without unmanning himself.

"Do you know what it means to be left totally alone with a measly five years of living under your belt?" Clayton sensed Tuck searching for his eyes.

"Matter of fact, I do. Lots of slave children do, but now ain't the time for my story. It's yours we need to hear."

Clayton paused. Heard snatches of whining in his story. He'd never dwelt on the fact that for all plantation children, separation was a potential way of life.

"Noah was my life. He took care of me, patted my back when the nightmares about my mother's sale came. Gave me half of his biscuit when I didn't have enough. Though he was only three years older than me, he was as tough and smart as any grown man on Duval's plantation.

When he ran away and told me he would come back for me, I never questioned it.

"But he didn't come, and when he didn't, Handley Duval became like a man possessed. He saw it as spit in his face that an eight-year-old black boy had outwitted him. He believed I had helped Noah run. Month after month, he whipped me for it. Starved me for it. Swore I knew what I didn't. Day after day, he painted pictures of the good life Noah was living. Eating until his stomach poked out. Playing with toys that only white children had ever even heard about. He even painted across my mind a little red wagon Noah was being pulled in, so real until I can close my eyes right now and hear it squeak."

Clayton heard his own voice grow small. Pitiful. Desperate. He fought against the tears as hard as he'd fought the Texas Rebels.

"I looked up to him. How could he leave me like that?"

"Naw. You quit looking up to Noah long time ago. Seems to me you done lived your whole life making an idol out of your hate for a li'l boy who probably wasn't no better off than you. Listen, I ain't been a slave all my life without being able to tell good from rotten. I ain't very old in years, but I'm real old in hurts. There ain't nothing rotten about Noah Duval. All it takes is one good fight like we had today, and whatever a man's got in him will come out. Whatever you thought happened when y'all was little, we talking about a different man now."

Clayton coughed into his hand. Turned his head and let the tears flow. Tears that made him go inward. Could he have been wrong about Noah all this time? Had he used the hate to harden himself against the fear of facing life alone—used it to convince himself that all that mattered was to get ahead like the planters he had known, even if it meant enslaving his own?

He hefted his sore body from the ground. Heard Tuck push to his feet.

"You all right? You think you can make it back across to your side?"

Clayton stuck out his hand to Simeon Tuck. "I thank you, but I'm fine. I've got to find a way back to Vicksburg."

He had yet another message to deliver to Sunday, one that was sure to destroy what little heart she might have left. Noah, too, was dead.

June 8, 1863

NONNIE HAD BEEN SAFELY PLACED in her cave, one of the many projects Master Johns had thrown himself into since the studio burned. Now Sunday, still numb from the loss of July's pictures, stood back as Master Johns steered his wife through the door of the main cave, the faintest sketch of pride and hope on his face. Bright rugs, chairs, makeshift beds—even a looking glass—had been carefully arranged within the dark space now lit with oil lamps. Lelia Rose splayed a hand against her chest. Staggered backward against Master Johns, who had once called such play-acting histrionics.

"Do you really expect us to survive here? Niggers and all?"

Master Johns said nothing. Just looked crushed. As abruptly as his wife had swooned, she straightened. Shook her head. "I cannot live this way. We're going back to our house, Johns. Do you hear what I say?" She turned toward the door. "The Lord is on our side. We're going back."

"The Lord?"

"Yes. And if you'd been attending church with me these last months like a Southern gentleman ought to, you'd know it."

Sunday's fragile relationship with her Maker swayed beneath the crazy idea that a just God would be on the side of a hellion like Lelia Rose. The woman jutted her chin, smiled as if the most original thought had hit her.

"If Sue Coatsworth and her children of all people—Union sympathizers all—can brave this absurd war against our independence in her home, so can we."

"Good for them. But this is where I and my family and servants will be until this is over." He gestured toward the scores of freshly dug caves scarring the landscape. "This is the best I could do. There are much worse accommodations in these hills. A portion of the staff will have to make do near the opening of Nonnie's cave until I can figure out something else. Sunday can sleep inside with us."

Sunday, who'd not known until this moment, gasped as Lelia Rose took a full minute to answer. Her color shifted like an unsettled afternoon. Her eyes snapped with fury. Sunday expected the woman to explode.

"You had a cave dug for *Nonnie*?" She stamped her feet like the child she was. "That does it. You have embarrassed me long enough with that bastard-carrying girl. Humiliated me with your desperation to replace Ellen."

Master Johns face caught fire beneath his wife's reference to Nonnie's child. "I warn you Lelia Rose—"

"You've disgraced the Smithmore name with your love for a species whom it is clear to everyone else in the South were created to serve. And I have borne it all like the lady I was trained to be. But if I have to make my bed on Sky Parlor Hill, I will not live in this kind of closeness with neither your concubines nor the likes of them."

Finally, she looked at Sunday. "Her odor alone would kill me."

The slaves on the outside were hushed, obviously taking in every word. For a moment, Sunday prayed that every bit of her would dissolve right there in the door of the cave. Her body jerked, feeling the skin of a little soiled girl of long ago stretching tightly over her.

Get her away from me, Silas. Make use of her as a scarecrow or something. She stinks.

All the wicked treatment withstood by all those who had gone before her in the rice, sugar, tobacco, and cotton fields rose up to prod her imagination, the colors so hot and disturbing she could almost smell them. Taste them. For the first time since she'd become a woman, she doubted her own worth. Did she smell unbeknownst to herself? Was there some primitive odor that seeped from black skin that she wasn't aware of? Might all the labeling of black people, all the name calling, the accusations of stupidity—might all the abuse her people had taken over the years really be the true order of things after all?

A dry sob tore through her. She lifted her eyes from the shell-pocked dirt, moved back toward a vicious, still-nattering

Lelia Rose, ready to submit to what she must deserve to be called. Stupid. Stinking—

"Massa Johns, I—"

He stayed her with an uplifted hand. Begged her with his eyes not to worsen things. Turned back toward his wife. "I have said what I'm going to say. Beyond that, Lelia Rose, what is it you expect me to do?"

"I expect you to be the gentleman I thought I had married. Get that girl away from me."

June 10, 1863, nightfall

SUNDAY FACED the dank rear wall of her own cave—not half the size of the one occupied by the Smithmores, an unlit oil lamp in her hand. She felt no bitterness. Master Johns had done the best he could with the time he'd had. And one good thing about it, people were making money digging these caves—even though the amount was left up to the hearts of the men who either owned or hired them.

Ignoring her makeshift bed of boards, she lay down on the dirt floor. Pulled her knees up to her waistline. Waited for the next round of shelling to shower her with dirt. Fitful dreams overtook her. Pushed her back to the grounds of the hush harbor, Miss Tullie's words falling like soft rain ...

"He loves you, honey, but there ain't a lot of things He hates more than idolatry ..."

What had she done that was anywhere near idol worship? She *had* wrapped herself in July. But she had built nothing like the idols of the Bible. No statues, no golden calves.

"But you still live for your son, not for Me. July is the idol on the shelf of your heart."

She bolted upright, memories lining up before her in the darkness. The scheme to conceive a child, the rebellious times when she had rather tie July to his bed than send him to the hush harbor. The way she had dismissed Noah's plea to go with him as though it were a pesky fly. The way she had stubbornly denied Miss Tullie the one thing the sweet old woman desired. The word *Mama* before her name.

And then there was the dilly-dallying about whether she should enter the hush harbor and warn her people, save precious men, women and children from Handley Duval's whip.

Oh, Sunday.

All this time, the Jesus worshipers had understood the mystery she had rejected. They had known whom it was they worshiped better than the slave masters themselves. It wasn't that they didn't long to be free, protected from the horror of the whip. Indeed, Sunday would never believe that God sent Africans to this land to be enslaved so they could get to know Him. God was more resourceful than that. But on this alien shore called America, in their suffering, they had found Him, and they would not let Him go.

She looked over at the boards leaning against the wall which Massa Johns had provided for her bed.

"Trust Me."

She forced her mind toward the words and sentences she had learned from Massa Johns these last two years. There, floating across the sheet-covered boards were the words, "Trust Me." She didn't know if she'd gone crazy or not. Didn't care. If craziness brought this kind of peace, then give her crazy.

Remembering a set of paints and brushes she had found earlier, which her master had never bothered to move from study to studio, she clasped her hands over her chest. There they were, tucked away behind her apron bib. She lit the small lamp Master Johns had given her, and light flooded the cave. She pulled the palette and brushes from her chest.

Boom! Boom! The shelling continued on.

"Boom on," she said, scrambling toward the boards. She yanked off the sheet, smiled at the palette. "Boom on!"

29

Late June, 1863

Besieged.

Johnston stood outside the cave wondering where the next meal would come from. He wanted to bring down curses upon the useless money he still had while he and those for whom he was responsible starved in a stretch between Grant's army to the east of Vicksburg and the occupied Mississippi River to the west. He thanked the good Lord for the company of Sunday, whom he had managed to keep via the excuse of fallow fields due to the war. Without her, he felt sure he would go mad. Lelia, thank heavens, had joined one of her society cave friends to bemoan their restriction from Sky Parlor Hill and decry the fare of horse flesh.

"Master Johns?"

He whirled toward Sunday's voice, pleased at her articulation. Over the months, her speech had improved tremendously, except when she was upset.

"Caught me napping on my feet, I'm afraid. What is it, Sunday?"

The girl's uncertainty from two years ago was suddenly there again, and he wondered if she might be coming down with something until he noticed the glow of her velvety skin. Smiling, he tried to make light of it.

"Cat got your tongue?" His attempted humor thudded, causing her tongue to revert to its first language.

"Naw suh. I jes wondered ... I mean to say ... would you step inside with me?" She was truly a beautiful girl. And so obviously happy with herself today that it made his heart hurt.

"Of course, Sunday. You may always feel free to ask—"

He heard the embedded ... paternalism? Arrogance? ... in his voice, something he was working on where she was concerned. "Uh, yes. Yes, of course—"

"It be in my cave. It's the end of that story I started telling you a while back. You never did ask me to finish it."

He didn't answer. Followed her into the cave, wondering why he needed to go inside for the telling of the story's end. The boards he had provided for sleep stood covered with a cloth. She stared at him as if she hadn't invited him in. He was beginning to be a bit annoyed.

"All right, Sunday. Will you finish the story now?" She chanced a look toward the boards.

"Yes, sir. Well. Time crept along like turtle legs while I waited to see what my new mistress would do with me. 'What am I supposed to do with this little filthy thing?' she asked. 'Isn't it just like Handley to be away from the plantation when difficulty comes?'

"The man who'd kil't my papa didn't answer her. Just stood there twirling his hat while she knocked one of my teeth out for looking up at her. I didn't know I wasn't supposed to ... She was so tall. I just wanted to see how far up she went—study the whiteness of her face."

Johnston's discomfort swelled. Never had he thought about

what it must be like to see white skin through the eyes of a black child.

"I—I felt my stomach cramping again. Wondered if maybe I'd eaten too much breakfast with Papa. Lord, I wanted to hold it in so bad. But I ... well, my bowels started to run again—almost like water—and this time my underpants failed me even quicker. My body shook with fear as the foul smell of what was running down my leg seemed to suck up the air. I sensed what was to come.

"'You. Little. Animal. You dare to pollute my home?' Mistress Handley struck me again—with so much force that I truly did see something like stars winking at me—all the while screaming for the house slaves to come clean me up. I hoped, prayed she'd never want to see me again. But half-washed, my bottom pinned up in a tow sack, I was quickly hauled back in front of her. I must have stood as straight as a picket. I was that scared, but she took it as sass.

"'A prideful little thing, aren't you? Now, what's your name?'"

"I tried to tell her, but my tongue—maybe it was my mind, I don't know—wouldn't let me. Maybe my mind was telling me my name was too beautiful to share with her. Meant too much to my daddy, still lying a few miles away out there in the dirt, to say in front of the likes of her."

Desperate fingers, sticking out of the water in the art he'd had on loan, seemed to tug at Johnston's ankles. He crossed his arms over his chest. Had there been gifts and talents like Sunday's in those drowning bodies? He remembered what his father had told him once ...

"Niggers are made to serve. They're the underside of the bottom rung on the ladder of humanity ..."

Johnston fought for breath. Grabbed hold of his own mind as Sunday's words reclaimed his thoughts.

"'I asked you your name!' Still, I couldn't tell her. My tongue was as locked as a rich man's treasure. That's when she picked up the candlestick. She was go'n kill me. I knew it. I covered my head with my arms and fell to the floor. She asked me how old I was. I felt hope for the first time since I'd slid from my papa's lap. Maybe she wouldn't have to kill me after all, 'cause I could answer that. I held up six fingers, one handful plus the other thumb—the way Mama had showed me.

"'Don't you sign at me, you little she-devil!' She cracked my fingers with the candlestick. 'Get her out of my sight!' She looked at the pink-white man. 'On her knees in the chapel until I say otherwise.' She turned her back on me. 'She still stinks.'"

"The chapel was a broke-down old rat-and-bat house that everybody said had been a real place of worship back in the day when the first Duval mistress was alive. A so-called throne room had been built close to the ceiling next to a belfry, both painted purple for royalty. But over the years, Massa Handley 'nem had mostly give up on God. Now it was a just a place to punish slaves."

Sunday leaned forward, her forehead in her hands. "The man made me kneel in front of a bench, strapped my arms and legs so I couldn't stand. Told me to pray for a better heart 'til he got back, so I could grow up to be a fine house nigger or something."

Johnston barely breathed. Nothing worth saying would come. Sunday lifted her head until her eyes were level with his.

"I did pray. But not for a better heart, nor to be a fine lady's maid. I prayed that the man who had killed Mama and Papa and the woman who had hit me all be swallowed up like Jonah in the Bible. And I prayed that, like Lazarus, my parents would come forth. None of it happened.

"Day or two later, I was back in front of the woman, this time in the kitchen, where she'd sent for a new slave named Silas. He was young then but already as mean as a tangle of snakes. The mistress told him to find another way to help me see the light. He seemed to take a heap of joy in making me a human scarecrow in the hot sun of the tobacco fields. But Silas's first go-round at Duval Plantation didn't last long."

"A living scarecrow? What do you mean?"

"I mean, standing at the edge of a row all day, hands stretched out, dressed in loud-colored rags worse than the ones the field hands wore."

Field hands who might have had minds as sharp as Sunday's.

A scripture from the prophet Jeremiah—one that had haunted him for years—came to Johnston. "Woe unto him that buildeth his house by unrighteousness, and his chambers by wrong; that useth his neighbor's service without wages, and giveth him not for his work."

But these dark-skinned "others" from heathen lands, they couldn't be Johnston's *neighbors,* could they? Johnston railed against the senseless question he'd just asked himself, but his thoughts whirled like oak leaves, and that one had gotten away from him.

"Hands stretched out and everything?"

"Yes—sir. Only I had no hat. Stretched out for two long days, until I passed out into the arms of a woman named Tullie. I was six. They didn't know what to do with me. Nobody would buy a six-year-old addled mute, so they gave me to Miss Tullie to try to fix. I didn't speak no more 'til I was ten."

"What became of this Silas fellow?"

Sunday's midnight skin seemed to darken even more. "Like I said, he was new. But after Massa Duval found out he had murdered a piece of his property—a little boy who'd cried too loud for its working mother to do her job right—he wasn't there long after. Years later they brought him back because it's hard to find a sic-'em dog as mean as Silas."

Johnston said nothing as Sunday walked a few steps toward the boards, obviously nervous. "This be what keep me going after Missus said again about me smelling. She lifted the cloth and stepped away. It was July. He'd seen enough pictures of him to know instantly. A tall well-sculpted black man held him with so much love and pride it stung.

"That be Noah."

The hand of a young vibrant black woman dressed like a free person of color sat loosely atop the child's shoulder. Sunday?

No.

Sunday smiled, seemingly craving his usual praise. But he had none. Only shock. Fresh piercing regret for a decades-ago moment in time. *Oh, Lord. Oh, Lord. Oh, Lord.* A moment he had pushed so far into the back of his mind that he wondered occasionally if it really happened.

"That's my family. I don't know why I put Noah in Papa's place. But the woman, that's my mama."

"I know exactly who she is," said Johnston Harrison Smithmore before he abruptly walked away.

JOHNSTON WAS atop Sky Parlor Hill again, praying no one would approach him with talk about the meanness of the Yankees. He was still trembling, his chest almost a separate thing with a foreign gnawing sensation.

By the seven wonders ... "She was beautiful as I recall."

Except the innocence was gone. Taken away by Johnston himself when he was barely past his teens even though she was married already. None of it had been planned. Johnston's father had taken him and Gillie on something of a tour of the upper South and had insisted they go out with a hunting party. "Probably the last trip we'll take together before you're married," he'd said. "You two'll have to start thinking about a suitable mate pretty soon."

Truth was, Johnston hadn't wanted to go on the trip.

Further, he abhorred the idea of an arranged marriage. But when—in the decades of his life before his father's demise—had he ever had the courage to tell him no? Even in death, he honored his father's wishes by continuing the legacy of slaveholding.

The whole thing had an innocent start. Johnston had wandered off from the hunting group. Got lost—even more so as thick rain-clogged clouds had set in. She was in her garden next to a small neatly constructed house when he stumbled upon her, obviously hurrying through her vegetable gathering before the clouds burst.

"Can I help you, sir?"

She was beautiful, darker even than Sunday, reminding him of what he imagined Nubian might look like. More nervous than he could remember, he almost cackled.

"I suppose the plain truth is I'm lost. Don't know if I'm one mile or ten from my father and the rest of our hunting group. Can't seem to gather a notion as to how to find them."

"How long has it been since you saw one of them?" she asked as casually as one asks about the weather.

"Not since around nine o'clock this morning."

She laughed, not scornfully but with a playful infectious vigor. "Perhaps if you'd shot that gun you have strapped to your person, they might have heard you."

It took him a moment to join in her mood, mortified as he was. But when he did, it was so very liberating—laughing at himself, without the condemnation of not being manly enough, of his love of art, of his distaste for cotton fields except as art. They both startled, as lightning, followed by an earsplitting round of thunder, lit the landscape. Covering her basket with her apron, she ran for the back door beckoning him to join her.

Should he? Where was her husband?

She made coffee, explained that her husband—"a

305

wonderful man, albeit a bit stiff at times"—was a few counties over purchasing lumber. She quizzed Johnston and chatted away as though they were equals while he answered as best he could. Obviously, she wasn't a slave, though her surroundings could hardly be considered a lot better. Perhaps things were a bit different up here from what they were in Mississippi.

The rain came in torrents setting up a hazy cocoon that intoxicated Johnston. He felt he could stay in this tiny space forever where he didn't have to learn to hunt like a man. Didn't have to go East to be schooled. Didn't have to learn the coded graces of a southern gentleman. Didn't have to be the sought-after Smithmore heir. If only he could paint her.

"You are so pretty," he said, as incongruous a statement as any fool had ever made.

But not to her. To her, as best he could tell, it seemed Johnston had sprinkled gold dust over her. All over the cabin. She beamed at him.

"No one's ever told me that before." She moved toward him, kissed his forehead. As though it was the most natural thing in the world, he encircled her waist then ...

Johnston yanked himself from the memory. "Lord, what have I done?"

Sunday Duval was not just his property. She was his daughter.

NONNIE'S SCREAMS rent the night as though fighting for a place among the screeching shells coming from the river. Sunday glanced at the doctor. Squeezed her friend's hand, certain the poor girl wasn't aware of the ear-splitting pitch of her incessant pleas for relief. Nonnie clutched Sunday's arm.

"D-didn't you say yours didn't hurt real bad, was more like a wide band around your belly? A-and didn't you say it was quick?"

Sunday's words, at the time meant to encourage, came back to haunt her.

"It won't be much longer. I promise."

"What in the world is going on down here? I can't sleep as it is."

Lelia Rose. So help me, I will strangle her tonight.

"Breech birth." The doctor spoke in clipped groups of words. "Must hurry. Or we'll lose them both. Most certainly the mother."

Master Johns had somehow persuaded another cave dweller—a doctor—to look at his slave, but what kind of doctor would say this in the mother's hearing.

Nonnie's eyes went glossy while Master Johns face receded into the deepest scowl Sunday had ever seen. The doctor looked sheepish—finally grasping, Sunday supposed, that a slave woman in labor could hear the same as all other women.

"Mrs. Smithmore, would you happen to have something that could serve as ... pardon me, ma'am ... a ... Would you have a petticoat, perhaps?"

Lelia Rose's gasp was as loud as the mortar shells. "Why, sir, I simply cannot fathom your asking me such a thing—and for the likes of her at that—"

"Lelia Rose! Get the petticoat. Now!"

She didn't budge. Master Johns grabbed her arm, yanked her through the cave opening and down the path, Lelia Rose whimpering like one of Vicksburg's starving dogs. Nonnie's screams subsided as an otherworldly kind of peace seemed to settle over her.

She don't care no more. She dying. What will I tell Pete when this siege is over? What will I tell myself without Nonnie here? Oh, Lord, please help her to care.

The doctor finally proved himself a healer, first. A white

healer, second. He accepted the petticoat Massa Johns poked at him, doing what he must to stanch the flow of lifeblood, the smell so sharp and threatening it took Sunday's breath away.

Lord, she dying. Please, Lord. Sunday gathered Nonnie's head to her chest, smoothed back the wild mass of hair. She would not let her die without a prayer. The doctor glared at her.

"What do you think you're doing?"

"What we all should be doing right 'long in here." Sunday buried her chin in Nonnie's hair. "Now say what I say. 'Our Father, which art in heaven, Hallowed be thy name. Thy kingdom come. Thy will be done in earth, as it is in heaven. Give us this day our daily bread. And forgive us our debts, as we forgive our debtors. And lead us not into temptation, but deliver us from evil: For thine is the kingdom, and the power, and the glory, forever. Amen'"

By the time she finished, the doctor and Massa Johns was praying right along with her.

NOAH OPENED his eyes to the light of day, having no idea how long he had been out. Hands afire with cuts and bruises, he tugged lightly at his bloodstained shirt. His jaw was a hammered anvil. Hot. Unyielding. He had been removed from the place near the levee where he'd been struck down, along with most of the men of Company B, including Captain Heath.

"You woke now, boy?" Noah's head exploded with pain. His tongue doubled its weight.

A boy again, replete with the embedded insult, he tried matching the hatred in his eyes to that of the high-ranking officer in gray. Failed.

"Good. Then maybe in a day or two you'll be able to follow the lead of your friends in offering free labor to the Confederacy." The man laughed. "Of course, we would want you to offer it, given how long the lieutenant has seen to your care. We wouldn't want to have to take it." He placed his hand on the hilt of a sword. Continued to measure Noah with a steady blue glare. "You'll want to know that your nigger-loving captain is hopefully hanged by now." The officer barked at a nearby soldier.

"Lieutenant!"

The man drew his ponderous body to attention. "Yes sir, Captain, sir!"

"Tell me again, now. Why did you bring this one into camp? Why didn't you just leave him to his fate?"

"I apologize, sir. I thought he was dead, but a closer look showed he yet breathed. We got him to the tent where the doctor said he had a 'mustard seed'-sized chance. Said his body, however—hearty as it was—might pull him through. And seeing the wound to be a knife wound rather than a bullet, he decided to treat him. Said the bayonet missed his heart, and we might get some labor out of him after all. I thought we could use as much free labor as—"

"Do you presume to tell me my job, Lieutenant?"

"No, sir. Not at all, sir."

"Then get him away from here. Throw him in the river if it pleases you. Just get him out. We have enough starving mouths to feed right now. I don't care what you do with him."

Noah drifted back into darkness thinking ... *I don't care either.*

30

Noah shuffled along in the dark, following a man he had never seen who seemed to hate him in a personal way.

"Know what I was before the war, boy?" Noah understood he wasn't supposed to answer.

"I was an overseer."

Just Noah's luck. But wasn't that the same word used in the Bible for the one who watches over your soul? He wanted to laugh. This overseer represented one of the most despicable symbols of the so-called institution from which Noah had fled over two years ago. An overseer. How ironic, as Gideon would say. Noah was about to be reclaimed. Again.

"That's right. An overseer. I know you know what that means. I can see it in every black crease in your forehead even in the dark. But you don't know the whole story. So let me tell you what this war has cost me. Every nigger I trained for fifteen years ran away. And that before the Yankees ransacked the whole place. Right after the plantation's manager thought it best to move out. And where did that leave me? What happened to my own little house I'd managed to build from the hard work of trying to make beasts like you productive? You want to guess?"

Noah watched the rage lather like a spent horse. Started to wonder if a single "yassuh" might be called for just now. Decided against it.

"So let me tell you. I found myself not only out of a job but a wife and two children scared crazy by a bunch of Yankee soldiers acting like loose cannons. You want to know what happened to my wife? She upped and left. Took all the young'uns and left me. Went up to Monroe to live with her mama. So, I enlisted, moved up quickly in the ranks. Who'd have ever thought a country-boy overseer like me would make a soldier? Ain't that much difference, though. Either job, you just beating the stuffing out of the enemy 'til he sees it your way. That's what slaves have always been you know. The enemy. And that's what we plan to do to the Yankees and every traitor-nigger like you that they put in a blue monkey suit. Meanwhile, I got me other plans for you. I'm gonna see what I can get for you in Vicksburg."

JOHNSTON SAVORED the moment alone as he walked near the river he loved so well. He'd had to get away from Lelia Rose. Needed time to think clearly about Sunday. How would he tell her? *Would* he tell her?

It was dangerous out here. He could be hurt or even killed. If not by one of the screaming shells, then maybe by some vagabond or Confederate deserter, crazed by hunger, hoping and praying for a scrap of food made of something other than pea flour. He paused. Looked out over the Mighty Mississippi at the ever-present, monster-looking gunboats that terrorized his hometown. If people like him were down to saltless biscuits, what must be happening to the ones who had already been hungry when the Rebel retreat into Vicksburg began? His thoughts recoiled. He had all he could do to reckon with Sunday and that purple belfry.

And her long-deceased mother.

Noises. He whirled around, deep groans progressing up toward him.

"Shut your trap before you get us both killed! I ain't supposed to be this far down the river no how, let alone on this side. Got to get back to camp 'fore my buddy ruins my cover and they think I've done deserted." A big plop of spit hit the surface.

"You'd better say your prayers, boy. I'm done wore out knocking on doors of empty houses and peering into dark caves. Nobody seems to be in the market for a big cheap nigger —not even the planters who've always walked around Vicksburg like the rest of us white men was horse manure—and I sure ain't taking you back 'cross that river to no prison hold. So what does that mean? It means if I can't get nothing for you, it's go'n be the bottom of that big muddy for you. I ain't leaving you to roam around a free nigger."

Johnston dabbed the back of his neck with his handkerchief and looked at the river. Whatever was going on behind him wasn't his concern. He couldn't get involved with a potential deserter trying to sell a slave in the middle of a siege. Scuffling and heavy breathing jerked him back toward town.

"You think you able to take me on, boy?" *Click click*. "Come on then. Might as well put you away right now. All the years I've spent keeping your kind in line, and a war strips me of everything I have. Ain't no reward in fooling with dogs like you. Mayst well kill you and be done with it ..."

"His horse killed my mama and his gun ... his gun killed my papa. He stared down at them as though they were two dead dogs." Johnston fought to erase the images that had plagued him for

weeks. *"Then he took me to the plantation, and Silas made me a scarecrow ..."*

"No appreciation for the poor hardworking man. Never has been—"

"Let him go." The man pivoted toward Johnston, pistol at the ready.

"And who might you be?"

Johnston walked to within a yard of him. "Doesn't matter who I am. I said let him go."

A new energy sprang from the man. "Wait a minute. Don't I know you? Yeah, I know who you are!" He kept the gun trained on the Negro who fought to stay on his feet. "You're Gillie's brother, ain't you."

Johnston stiffened. Hadn't heard from his brother since the siege started.

"And if I am?'

"No ifs about it. I know you *and* your brother—the one who just had to 'let me go' when all the niggers left. No bonus, no nothing. Just 'I can't afford to keep you any longer because my brother said so.'" Anger seeped from the man's pores like a long-repressed fever. What had Johnston stepped into now? The man looked from the Negro back to Johnston.

"I ought to kill you both."

"What is it you want?"

The man barked out a laugh. "I want to be thanked. I want to be paid for ever' bit of strength I wasted on half-animals like this one right here who murdered more Rebels than you can imagine a short time ago." Gillie's overseer was in tears.

"A feller like me tries for years to show them how blessed they are to be in a civilized country. Tries to train them in the right way—the way God laid out for their kind, and what do they do? First chance they see to follow a blue uniform, they run off chasing in behind them like wild dogs. They're untrainable, dontcha know. Unthankful! So, you want to know what

I'm after? I'm after selling this slave and getting something for my hard work."

The man was crazy. Nobody was buying slaves in Vicksburg. He needed to think fast. The shelling would likely start up again any minute, but Johnston needed to think. This man was definitely crazy. As crazy a fellow as he'd ever met. But ... wasn't Gillie crazy, too, for hiring such a man in the first place? And ... *aren't you a little crazy for believing you could go on forever riding the backs of these people?*

He snatched his mind back to reality, and reality was *now*. He wasn't afraid for himself. The man wasn't going to kill him. The ex-overseer's fear of what Johnston stood for had him as enslaved to the idea of the planter as the black man standing behind him. *So, you're free to go. Just walk away.* Johnston had been taught as a well-bred son of the Southern aristocracy that he was entitled to turn and stride back to his cave.

An entitled caveman. He wanted to laugh at the irony.

But he couldn't—walk away, that is. He simply didn't have the guts to let this other man be thrown into the river. Gillie was always the one with guts. So be it. Johnston's stomach wouldn't let him swallow this man's being thrown into the Mississippi.

"I don't have money on me now."

"Well, it's go'n be now or never. I won't wait."

Out of the blue, a portrait of Ellen—or was it Sunday?—seized his thoughts, sad eyes longing for her papa, defying Johnston's entitlement to walk away. A privilege which, at this moment, young poor innocent Southern soldiers, like the one fighting in his place, were dying for. He reached into his pocket. Smoothed Ellen's locket.

"I have a gold locket worth five hundred dollars when I purchased it." He heard the hoarseness in his own voice. "No telling what you could get for it now." The overseer spat a wad of tobacco on the ground.

"Been working for Gillie long enough to know how rich you are. I reckon that'll do."

The Negro soldier stared at the disgusting clump of wet tobacco. What must he be thinking right now?

Of course. What else? *Once more a slave.*

NOAH PICKED his way along the bluff behind the white man, looking down at the tattered uniform he'd worn forever. Vicksburg. He knew of the fight for this river town—knew the town was now belted by Union forces. Knew, wearing this uniform, he was likely to be hanged.

With his good hand, he nursed his jaw. He didn't mind the pain anymore. Pain had become his friend, signaling to him that he was still alive—still blessed with a chance to make it up to Clayton, if not July and Sunday. If only he knew where Clayton was.

The city had the feel of Mama Tullie's Judgement Day stories. Windowless houses pocked with shell shots stood precariously on hillsides—every now and then a house with a low-burning candle, some brave soul flaunting a mantle of defiance.

"I suppose you're from over the river in Louisiana. I've heard that a number of Negro units have been organized from runaways over there."

Noah couldn't figure out if there was hostility in the man's voice or simply curiosity. "Yes, sir." Already, he plotted how best to get away from this man. Two years now he'd tasted of freedom, tainted though it was. He'd find a way to die before he was enslaved again.

He wasn't shackled, and the man didn't seem to be armed. Immediately, the pain he'd just lauded became a problem. If he wasn't so badly maimed, he could lose him quicker. The man halted, abruptly deciding to walk alongside Noah rather than in front of him.

"And what's your name?"

Noah frowned. Saw no reason to arm his new owner with his real name in case he was able to escape.

"Gideon, sir."

"Good name. Excellent model from the Scriptures." The man turned east, away from the river, the hilly terrain looming in the darkness. "Gideon made sure, though, that it was God's voice calling him to do battle with the enemy. Do you know the story?"

"Yes, sir."

"Tell it to me, then?"

Noah's hackles raised. He recognized an order when he heard one, though the man's voice lilted with question. Was he testing Noah's character? Trying to see what kind of property he'd just purchased?

"From what Mama Tul—that is, from what one of the older slaves said—Gideon asked God for proof of his calling by providing a wet fleece surrounded by dry earth one day and a dry fleece surrounded by dew the next."

The sound of the man's feet echoed through the darkened hills. A couple of dogs howled in the distance sending Noah's thoughts spiraling downward.

"Yes, Gideon was fortunate to have questioned the Almighty with impunity. I suppose you must have such questions now—like where we are headed, and why I purchased you." The man released a troubled laugh. "And what am I going to do with you in this God-forsaken town."

Boom! Boom!

The river lit up with a menacing glow, lights whistling through the air like errant stars. Noah dropped to the ground. But the white man kept walking. Never once looking back, his steps fading quickly into the night. *Boom! Boom! Boom!* Noah ducked, sweat making a path between his shoulder blades as if it were noonday in the tobacco field—his every breath a prolonged pant as he struggled to master the hill. He scrambled to keep up with his thoughts.

How often was this town being shelled like this? Could anybody be left alive? Where were they living if they'd survived?

The idea of being trapped in this besieged town shook him. Pain shot through Noah's chest. He halted, slipped to his knees in a nearby ditch as a shell whizzed by his ear and landed in a yard across the way. Songs from the hush harbor outstripped the sounds of the shelling.

> *Do, Lord, do, Lord. Lord, remember me,*
> *Do, Lord, do, Lord. Lord, remember me,*
> *Do, Lord, do, Lord. Lord, remember me,*
> *Lord, remember me.*

> *When I'm sick and I can't get well,*
> *Lord, remember me,*
> *When I'm sick and I can't get well,*
> *Lord, remember me,*
> *When I'm sick and I can't get well,*
> *Lord, remember me,*
> *Lord, remember me.*

Noah glanced around him, a notion drifting in on the haze of the shells from the Union boats. Was the man who had just bought Noah trying to lose him?

Legs screaming against the possibility of more taxing hills, Noah hefted himself to his feet. He mustn't wait for a lull in the attack. He had to move now—find a scrap of shelter before he was reclaimed by his new master.

Turning onto another street, totally dark—the few lights

that had shone previously, put out at the onslaught of the shelling—he fought against the dizziness. Slapped at some of the largest mosquitoes he had ever seen. Wondered if this night would ever end. Still, this was his time to escape, while the Union boats were firing on the city. But where? The only direction he was familiar with was west, back toward the river. Should he try to re-cross? Or go north on this side where he might eventually reconnect with the Federals?

Do, Lord. Do, Lord. Lord, remember me.

He stumbled to the side of an abandoned house—elegant, three-storied. Totally white. He leaned beneath the eave. Whatever his approach back to freedom, it couldn't be just yet. He simply didn't have the strength. Right now, he had only the strength to try to rest. Come daylight he would keep himself hid until dark came again when he would try to somehow get back behind Union lines. A shell blossomed in the yard outlining the tattered gray of a uniform filled with a living skeleton who glanced at another wide-eyed skeleton on the ground slightly behind him.

"Well, now. What have we here?"

HOPING he had put enough distance between himself and the man, Johnston slowed his steps. He had done what he could for the boy. Hadn't he? Surely, even a traitorous heart like his wouldn't expect a Southern-bred man to take a filthy injured colored Union soldier to his cave—a cave already ringing with hatred and discord—after he had just bought the boy's life with his dead baby's locket.

He flinched at the sound of another shell, but it was only instinct. The fear that had flared back in April was now shriveled into a dull rhythmic caution—though at times, knowing he was trapped inside Vicksburg threatened to make Johnston as twisted as his wife. If not for the cave and hunger and Lelia Rose's constant carping, he might even be able to do some painting. Soothe his parched soul after all the work he'd lost in the fire.

But if it was true that Sunday and all the other slaves felt life's pains—as Johnston was sure they did—what might this poor devil he had just deserted be going through? Double-sided shame gripped him. Each day he was sounding more and more like a rabid abolitionist.

He picked up his pace to clear his head of the incessant rabble of thoughts, only to halt and stare down the hill that housed multiple caves including his own—the meager supper he had endured souring at the thought of what awaited him there. He turned around and headed back up toward the river. The back veranda of his battered mansion was still intact. He would sit there for a while, block out the shelling and try to find himself.

"LET HIM GO."

Johnston couldn't believe he was repeating the same words he had said an hour ago about the same man.

"He belongs to me."

Two Confederate soldiers, as thin as a pine needle, looked at each other and laughed. One, obviously too weak to stand, sat on the ground. He held a knife.

"Yours? Then why's he wearing a blue-devil uniform? You some kind of Yankee sympathizer?"

"He ran away. Must have joined the Federals. Now he's back. Let him go."

"All right then. Let's play pretend. We'll pretend he ain't wearing that uniform, and you can pretend we ain't wearing these grays. We'll pretend like he belongs to you, and you can pretend we're slave catchers. That way, you can pay us for his return. Ain't that the way it goes with you planters who look down your noses at the rest of us who're just as white as you? Why, I'll bet my boots—" The soldier looked down at his bare feet and laughed. "Let me put that another way. I'll wager money what I ain't even got that the reason you ain't suited up yourself is 'cause you've paid some clown like me to starve and die in your place."

Johnston's heart was the target for the oncoming knife had the Negro not lurched at the man from behind, knocking the wind out of him and sending his rusty knife flying across the yard. Johnston seized the knife while the Negro put the spitting soldier in a bear's grip, giving Johnston time to place the blade to his throat. With his free hand he pointed east.

"Now get yourself and your half-dead friend back to your units before I summon the Federals." Johnston squared his shoulders and shook himself. That felt pretty good. Except the man on the ground started to tremble.

"We slipped away just a few hours ago knowing they'd be likely to round us up and hustle us back 'fore long. But even then, we won't be in them ditches much longer. I just wanted to have a chance to see old Pemberton—tell him face to face that everything a man can eat, even the mules, done run out. So we can't fight much longer if we die of starvation."

Johnston shuddered. Could any good ever come from this war?

HE WALKED down the slope ahead of the Negro, still hoping that the man would not follow. Cave life looked eerie at night with people huddled inside, fervently praying this night might be the end of the mud. Mosquitoes. Fear.

Johnston let loose a loud sigh, not caring that the man

could probably read his thoughts. He dreaded taking this man to Sunday. How could he ask this of her after all she had been through? But what else could he do? A fierce protectiveness tightened his chest. How did he know this man wouldn't harm her? Ravish her? But there was nowhere else. And the poor fellow looked like he hadn't enough strength to ravish a bowl of gruel.

"I DON'T HAVE any room. No space for him to sleep."

Sunday tried to reason with Master Johns who stood just inside, his face inscrutable. His presence radiating desperation.

"They'll kill him out there. Is that what you want?"

"No, sir. I don't *want* anything. I just hope you won't make me take on a stranger in a cave like this."

In shadow, the man stood at her threshold. He filled the doorway before he swayed, nearly dropping to his knees.

"Maybe he ought to come in. Sit on the floor for a minute until we can figure out what to do."

She retrieved the nub of a candle she had squirreled away. Lit it. Stared at the doorway. Squinted. Stared again. Warmth suffused her, all the way to the ends of her braids.

Noah.

It. Can. Not. Be. She made her way across the cave space, miles of treading water. He grasped a doorpost as she explored his shoulders, chin, hairline. So hot with fever.

"You're hurt." She snatched the boards he was painted on without ever totally releasing him. "Here, lie down. I'm gonna see to you. I'm gonna always see to you."

He didn't argue, just blinked and leaned into her as though he'd found a rock. She let him down to the painting. She hadn't known how much she loved him, missed him, until she saw him hurt.

"Master Johns, you still there?"

"I'm here."

"Could you go get the doctor again please, sir?"

"I suppose," he muttered. He sounded stunned, but she could hear his footsteps fading.

"Noah?"

Clearly, her husband had succumbed to whatever awful sickness had finally demanded he enter another sphere somewhere between life and death. Kneeling, she pressed her cheek to his.

"You have to live, Noah, because I have to tell you that our little boy—your son—is alive out there somewhere. I know he is."

31

A few days later

Noah was either dead or out of his head, because the woman sitting beside him, her smooth dark skin as inviting as ever, was his wife.

"Sunny?"

"It's me, Noah."

"And July? Is he all right?"

A flash of agony darkened her eyes, quickly replaced by a steely confidence. "July's all right."

Then where was he? The Sunny he knew would never be this comfortable without him, even tending Noah. But he wouldn't ask further, too afraid of the answer.

He looked at her, drank from her features, thinking he would never get his fill of the near-purple hue of her skin. The piercing molasses-colored eyes filling with tears and the delicate crease above her upper lip so, like July's. Voice croaking, he reached for her face.

"My sunshine."

She leaned in closer. Smoothed his hair. "I see you still have that mixed-up kind of hair, like you couldn't decide what side you wanted to come down on—your mama's or your daddy's. Hope you don't mind. I've been helping myself to the feel of it these days."

"I don't ever remember minding." It hurt to smile, but he did it anyway. "You sound different, Sunny. More educated."

"Funny, I was thinking the same thing about you."

"I've had a good teacher."

"So have I."

Enough of the small talk. How was he to begin? *I almost slept with another woman. Your thoughts on that?* He tried to swallow only to find his throat on fire from the need for moisture. His heart afire with the need to explain.

"Water?"

Her hands shook as she poured a sip and put the brackish taste to his lips. Was she glad to see him or simply overwhelmed?

"I'm sorry. The water's not very good these days."

"Sunny, there's so much I need to say—"

"Not yet. The doctor said, when you came out of it, you didn't need to tire yourself."

"When? Or *if* I came out of it?"

"Doesn't matter. You're out now." A tear splashed against his forehead. She gentled a trembling thumb through the wetness. "There is a God, Noah, and He has brought you out."

He tried to lift himself, and she caught him before he fell back onto the makeshift pillow. "Sunny? Did you say God?"

She smiled. "And His Son, Jesus, and the Holy Spirit."

Memory intruded, causing Noah to think of how thankful he'd been to open his eyes to the caring of another beautiful woman in a Pittsburgh Underground Railroad station two years ago. Beneath Sunday's touch, he felt the scowl of his forehead and the guilt that accompanied the truth he had always known. From the moment he had seen the skinny little girl alongside

Mama Tullie, timidly trying to rid the tobacco leaves of worms, it had always been Sunny. He'd missed her terribly. He would tell her right now—"

"There's somebody else, isn't there, Noah."

SHE WAS sorry as soon as she said it, but it had to happen. Throughout the delirium of the last several days and nights— mixed in with the noise of the shelling and shots both from the river and the far side of the eastern Confederate earthworks— she had heard the name mixed in with her own. Gideon. A man's name, but the softness of it was attached to a woman.

"Yes. There's been someone."

She held her breath as he told her of a remarkable woman who had been his scout through Virginia, Pennsylvania, New York City, and finally to a place near the edges of America called Rochester. He told her how this woman with the strange name had nursed him back to health. Seen him through the darkness when he thought he'd lost her and July. A woman whom, when he'd heard of openings for black soldiers, he had walked away from to come south.

"And she loved you."

He tried and failed again to lift himself up. "She did."

"A-and you? Do you love her?"

Sunday knew what the answer was. She had earned it. In her desperate need to fence in a little piece of the earth for herself and July, she had tossed the love of a good man to the wind. Yet, she had to hear him say it. He took forever, but she would wait him out on this one. If it took until this time tomorrow. As a surrendered woman to the One who would see her through, she was called to wait.

"I do love her, and I always will."

THE STRUGGLE TO accept with some shred of dignity what Noah had just said was written across Sunday's face as plainly as those words on his pretzel sign near the alley in Pittsburgh. Plainer, given his reading skills at the time. Whatever the consequences, he'd had to give Gideon her due. Honestly and with force. But then he took a moment to study his wife, reveled in the fight that had always been Sunday, seeing for the first time that she did care for him after all. With much straining, he finally rested on his elbows.

"But not the way I love you."

She turned away. "Don't say that if you don't mean it—"

"Adore you. Always have." Even after I received the letter from Miss Maggie saying you were forever lost to me, deep down I was always looking for you."

She reached for him. Gathered him to her chest. Held him for a long minute.

"So, you say Gideon loved you, huh?"

He said nothing, just let her hold him.

"Well, Mr. Duval, I think I understand what won her over. Any woman who didn't love a kind, good-looking man like the one I'm holding would be a fool. I was that fool, though now I think I've got her beat since you're in my arms. I love you, too, Noah Duval. Think I always have. No, I *know* I have. It just took God and hardships to let me know it."

Finally, the words he'd waited for since he was thirteen—

"Sunday? You in there?"

Sunday froze. Noah's stomach knotted. The man was sounding too familiar with his wife, as though he knew her well. And how could this male voice that he could not have ever heard somehow sound so familiar to Noah himself?

SHE COULDN'T BE SURE. Despite the candle, the cave was dark and oppressive. Maybe she was hearing things. It couldn't be Clayton. The last thing Sunday needed was to have Noah's fragile progress damaged with Clayton's news about July. Noah's effort to breathe ticked up. He loosed himself from her embrace. Propped himself up further on his elbows.

"Sunday, who's out there?"

"Is it all right to come in?" It was Clayton, all right, and he seemed rattled.

"Boy, what chu doing back here?" she asked.

"Who ... who this fellow you holding onto?"

A sliver of anger pricked her. She'd not taken the time to examine the resentment of the way Clayton had dropped the news about her child and then left without a word of comfort.

"Never mind that. How did you get into Vicksburg in the middle of a siege, and why in the world would you even want to?"

It struck her that Clayton still clung to the threshold. For the last two years, it seemed her life had been plagued with undecided men at thresholds on the verge of trying to make her do something or tell her something she didn't want to hear. Noah, Master Johns, and now Clayton. She shifted the candle, inadvertently shining it on Noah's face. Clayton crossed the threshold. Bent to get a closer view.

"Noah? That chu?"

CLAYTON STARED. Who was this man that looked so much like Noah? Clayton's senses were taken prisoner by the half-illuminated face. It had been a long time, but beneath the scarred visage was a version of the eight-year-old who had deserted him.

Noah.

His older cousin had always been larger than life, dwarfing Clayton in every game, every escapade. And now here he was again, filling up this damp, scary, cut-out space of earth with his very presence. Even in his obviously weakened state, Noah Duval was as handsome as ever. The spit of July. Or was it the other way around? He had to have known it all along. How on earth could he have missed July's heritage? He saw the moment it hit his cousin.

"Little Clayton? Is that really you?"

"It's me."

That wasn't enough. He needed to say more. Couldn't think of a single thing. Found himself backing up on unsteady legs.

"C-come closer, man!" Noah seemed ... *moved?* Where was the arrogance—the gloating—Clayton had expected all his life? "Why you backing up, man? Come on over here."

"I ... I thought you was dead. I mean, that's what they told me when I went to the 9th to see if it was really you they was talking about."

"Are you talking about the 9th Louisiana? What do you know about them?"

Clayton finally got his legs under him. Moved toward the only relative slavery had spared him. "I reckon that would be it since I fought with the 11th. A young buck named Simeon Tuck told me you'd been killed." He glanced at Sunday. "I come to give the news to Sunday. Lord knows I didn't want to, not after—"

"Not after all we went through in that coffle."

Sunday's words cut through, sharper only than her stare. Noah looked thoroughly confused but not much more than Clayton himself. Obviously, Sunday hadn't told him about July, adding to the swirl of thoughts in Clayton's head that would soon get the best of him if he didn't sit. He lowered his sore limbs onto the dank earth while Sunday, her face now in full glare, accosted him.

"Did you desert the army? Black folks can't afford a bunch of deserters."

"I didn't desert. I managed to get a twenty-four hour pass. I had to beg hard to get it—make promises I'll never be able to keep. But I'm here."

Sunday's face softened. "I'm sorry. It's just that so much is happening. We don't have food. Don't know when we'll be able to get any."

She looked at Noah—the light of love in her eyes if Clayton had ever seen it. And though, in truth, he *hadn't* seen that kind of glow before—except for Pearl?—there was no mistaking where Sunday's heart was. She propped Noah onto a pillow. Stood and moved toward the door.

"Something tells me an old account needs to be settled. I'll be right outside."

"I waited for you, man. Waited and waited, but you never came back."

Noah prayed for strength. He knew he was nowhere near out of the woods. Even if the doctor didn't know it, his body was telling him the fight was not over. But this was the chance— perhaps the single opportunity the Lord was granting him before he left this world—to explain, and he would do it. No matter what.

"I was eight. That's not an excuse. It's the truth. The plan I told you about was a child's imagination. I wanted better for us. Believed I was man enough to find it. But it only took a week's worth of mosquito bites and hunger before I was captured."

Clayton's brow lifted, as if the idea of Noah's being captured had never entered his mind.

"That ain't what Duval told me. He said you'd made it to the North. Said you'd found one of those 'nigger-loving' families.

Said someone had seen you with a pretty red wagon. Not long ago I did hear you was running again but—"

"Listen. The first time I set foot on northern soil was two years ago—and that over sixteen years after I'd been captured the first time, shortly after I left you. Yes, I was caught, bartered, then kept by an over-religious couple for five years, and finally returned to Duval when I was thirteen for what he called the Reclaiming."

Noah told the shame of the Reclaiming. The courting of and marriage to Sunday and finally the Underground Railroad.

"Don't you know I have lived for this minute? Not a day has passed when I haven't wondered what became of you—prayed you bore up under the meanness of Handley Duval." Noah laughed through uncontrollable tears. His fever had spiked again. Still, he laughed.

"I should have known you'd make it. You've always been so much stronger than you'd let yourself believe." He reached out his hand. Couldn't control the trembling.

"Shake?"

"No."

His cousin did better. He encircled Noah in a fierce hug.

CLAYTON WAS CRYING, something he had not done with this kind of abandon since he was a boy. Crying. For Noah, and Georgie, for himself and every other wretched black boy still facing the far-reaching tentacles of slavery. All the anger had not been against Noah. It had been against Handley Duval and all the Handley Duvals, before and after, across God's green earth.

June 30, 1863

SUNDAY SAT in the door space of Nonnie's cave listening to today's fight between Grant's and Pemberton's armies as it gradually died down. She'd just bathed Nonnie and the baby, delighted in the very act of it. Behind the cave, the sun was setting, but the damp suffocating Mississippi heat hadn't noticed. She swiped a mosquito, mixing the blood it had drawn with her sweat. Noah's fever ebbed and raged while hunger stalked the town like a ravenous dog.

"Help us, Lord Jesus."

Starving soldiers had appealed to General Pemberton. The citizens had resorted to eating mules and rats, and no one seemed to know for sure when it would all end.

A few feet behind her, her sister-friend laughed. Lusty cries filled the space as Nonnie prepared for a feeding. Eternally grateful to see Nonnie survive the difficult birth, her health blossoming like the June roses in spite of the siege, Sunday smiled at little Queenie, sweeter than one of Mama Tullie's rare molasses cakes.

Noah was another matter. He slept incessantly, the deep need for healing protecting him from the maddening wounded-animal sounds of Lelia Rose's crying, about which everyone in the vicinity of the Smithmore caves was complaining.

Master Johns hadn't visited today, most likely seizing the opportunity to distance himself from his little compound by joining the various knots of other cave men who had nothing else to do except discuss the siege and make irrational predictions—often loudly enough for Sunday and everyone else to hear—of how "Pem's boys," would emerge the victor very soon. She startled at the figure that had appeared out of nowhere.

"Master Johns? You scared me." It tickled her to see him at

Nonnie's door again. She hadn't figured out who was more foolish when it came to Queenie, her or her master.

"Mind if I join you?"

Despite the amount of times, she was always amazed that he talked to her like a person. "No, sir." He positioned a chair from his own cave. Crossed one leg over the other, clasped his foot, and gestured toward the inside.

"How's the little one this evening? It's mighty quiet in there."

"She's wonderful, Master Johns. I've never seen a happier baby. She has Nonnie's spirit if I ever saw it. By the way, have you heard anything about Pete? Nonnie's so worried about him."

"Not directly, but I have reason to believe he's still on the place out there. Hopefully, if this siege ever ends, he'll find a way to get into Vicksburg."

"Any word on when it will end?"

"No, but the town is dying of hunger. Those poor starving soldier boys trapped in those ditches and those of us huddled together in these caves—we all know it. Surely Pemberton must know it too. It's just a matter of time."

Sunday shrugged. Having eaten rations most of her life and slept in a cabin not much larger than her cave, she didn't view the hardship in the way of the privileged. At the moment, hers was a different nightmare.

"I worry about Noah. He ain't out of the woods yet. Sleeps nearly all the time."

"I ask your pardon, Sunday, but what's happening between you two?"

"Noah a good man." She was back in her slave tongue. "All them years, his love done seeped into me without me even knowing it. Wouldn't let myself know there ain't no separating him from July. But I done got scared now. I know I'm new at being a believer, but I'm wondering if God go'n punish me. Take away from me what I didn't know I loved until now."

She looked at Johnston Smithmore, all signs of a Southern plantation master erased from his face and replaced with painful sympathy.

"God doesn't work like that, Sunday. If Noah dies, it will simply be that his number of days is up. Nothing to do with you."

How she wanted to believe him. She made to remove inside to check on Noah but took another look at Master Johns. He looked as disturbed as she felt. Probably pining for his art. She reseated herself.

"What about you, Master Johns? What you go'n do afterwards?"

He studied on what he was about to say as though he was a learner, and she was the teacher. "I can't say for certain though I've thought of little else. Thank God I didn't turn crazy and give over everything I've amassed to the Cause. And, of course, the foundry will hopefully still be able to produce."

An abrupt break in Master Johns' talk ensued. Sunday said nothing, sensing there was more he wanted to say. They sat quietly, taking in the noises of slaves pretending to fix a decent supper while children played to the end of the swiftly decreasing sunlight.

"Sunday, I must tell you something. "Something very, very important. Something I never truly regretted because I didn't know to regret it before now."

She stiffened, suspecting whatever he was about to say would be life changing. Did he mean to sell her in the middle of the war?

"Do you remember showing me the painting of your little boy, your husband, and your mother?" Sunday nodded.

"Well ... that is ... I know—knew—your mother."

"Sir?"

"I said I knew your mother." Fear and excitement assailed her. This was no sell-off.

"But how?"

"I knew her because I'm your father."

Sunday folded her hands in her lap. Felt her eyelids flutter. Purple overtook her as she found herself glued to the door of the cave. Memory washed over her of the barely perceptible tension between Mama and Papa from time to time. Mama's sheepish look that morning when Papa challenged her about the number of white men who had visited them ...

"I wouldn't worry too much about all those speculator rumors running around, William. We've been on this spot of land for a good many years now, and no white men have set foot out here unless they truly wanted to buy something ..."

"No white men?" Papa had said. And he'd been peevish about it.

"Sunday? Are you all right?" Master Johns' desperation fought through the swirling purple. "Sunday, please."

She sensed the cave dwellers gathering around her. Nonnie had come to the door with Queenie. "What's wrong, Massa?"

Queenie sighed as the purple receded from Sunday's mind, leaving in its wake the stark empty gray of Johnston Smithmore's grief-stricken face.

"Let me have Queenie. I need her warmth." Nonnie passed her the sleeping baby, milk curling from her pink lips. Sunday thought of July and smiled. She didn't know where the joy came from. Only that as long as God made babies, there would always be hope.

32

Friday, July 3

Sunday dug near the edge of the caves for a bit of sustenance. Perhaps she could find an herb or two like the ones Mama Tullie had taught her to spot in Virginia. Rumors flew like flocks of birds, a murmur moving along the line of caves as she conducted her futile forage, the words coming more from the mouths of the underclass than the gentry.

"Pemberton done sent one of his generals with a white flag this morning."

"T'ain't so!"

"Well, if it ain't, one of his very own is the one what said it."

She listened. Knew her place as a slave was to hold her tongue. Believed no one. Still, she couldn't have lived this shelling, burning, starving nightmare along with the rest of Vicksburg's cave people without knowing what a white flag could possibly mean. Food. But even if the Rebels surrendered, how would the town restock itself? Would this General Grant be able to rescue them from the brink of starvation? She sighed, dug deeper into the dirt. She had her own truce to consider.

"Lord, I don't know if I can forgive Master Johns, and if I do or don't, what difference does it make? He owns me, bought and paid before I even knew what he looked like."

She wiped away the perspiration stinging her eyes. There would be no flinging her arms around Johnston Smithmore's neck like a long-lost child. That simply could not be between master and slave. She felt her tears washing away the sting.

"Mama, how could you?"

What if it's not true? What if Master Johns is wrong? It wouldn't be the first time a woman found herself in that predicament and the child turned out to be her husband's—

But it was true. Sunday knew it the moment her master said it. Not only was the timing too precise, but Sunday's features, albeit her coloring was her mother's, were too sharp—her hair too thick and shiny—to have come from Papa's bloodline.

She'd avoided Master Johns ever since, and to his credit he'd given her space. She had spent all her time with Noah. Hovering, holding his hand, speaking sugar-coated nonsense to him that she didn't know existed inside her. Burying herself in trying to find leaves, roots, injured birds—anything that might heal her husband. Still, as she whispered sweet pleas to Noah, pictures of Master Johns invaded, mixing in sweetness of their own. She fought it, kicked and screamed in her mind against the way he had defiled her perfect image of family.

But while she made fires outside the cave to boil and prepare whatever scraps Master Johns had come up with for the evening meal—or while she aired out Lelia's Rose's ridiculous dresses or tried to find a way to wash little Quee-nie's rags used for napkins—too often the image of father-hood that Papa and Noah had planted was quietly joined by another. Here, moving in to balm the shock of Lelia's words. There, leaning over her as she tried to perfect a form on canvas—listening and correcting as she pronounced what seemed more words than was needed for any language, bringing her sandwiches that explored taste buds she didn't know she had, lightly patting her on the shoulder as they both basked in her accomplishments—was the face of Johnston Smithmore.

"And all this before he even knew."

It's time to tell him.

Still, James Pennington, the man who had loved her unconditionally for the first six years of her life, was not to be set aside. Not for all the art and language in the world.

"Papa, oh my Papa, no one could ever take your place—"

"Nor would I ever try."

Sunday rose from her knees, turned and looked him in the eye. "How long have you been here?"

"Long enough."

Sunday examined his face. Everything had changed. Nothing had changed. He was still as free as she was slave. As white as she was black. "I took very little after you."

"Oh, I'm not so sure about that. I'm determined to take responsibility for the art talent." Deep sadness grooved his features. "Though I have nothing left to prove it."

Time to show *him too.*

Sunday battened down her smile. Sensed how much he needed it, wanted it. But heaven help her she wasn't ready to give him that yet.

"I'm not sure I even believe your story. Maybe you've mistaken the woman I sketched for someone else. My mother was the purest, kindest woman I've ever met."

"That she was. And perhaps, other than you, the most beautiful." Master Johns looked even more stricken, staring through the hill of caves as though he were tunneling for some truth or other. "In those precious few hours, your mother gave me new eyes. Helped me see another beauty—one as strong and pleasing as any I'd ever been taught to admire. She changed my life."

He cleared his throat, obviously trying to stem the tears without the dead giveaway of using his hands.

Pity surged through Sunday, pity she did not want to feel. She tried to steer herself around what he was saying, all the while realizing that God-infused human emotion had no map. Followed no prescription. Knew no race.

"You know, ever since you showed me that painting, I've realized I married Lelia Rose for reasons not at all clear to me at the time. I wonder if I used her classic western beauty to re-anchor myself into the young planter I'd been trained to be before I met your mother. To remind myself of the kind of woman I was supposed to love. To reinstruct my confused heart in the ways of Southern aristocracy and the path and legacy already laid out for me before I was born."

"Yes, sir," was all Sunday could manage. But she knew—and she knew that he knew—a deeper bond was being formed in that moment. Vocabulary she'd never heard before he taught her had joined with old emotions still aflame in his heart to speak the unspeakable. He patted her hand. Offered a weak laugh.

"How's Noah these days? I purchased him with my little girl's locket, you know." Anger flared. Purchased? No, she hadn't known. Didn't know how she felt about it even now. Still, there was no denying a part of her bruised heart was for Johnston Smithmore.

"He's fighting. I'm praying nothing's gone too bad that some nourishment and medicine and lots of rest can't repair."

"I'm thinking this siege will be over in a matter of hours. And when it does, I want to talk to both of you about working for me as free people of color. The way the war is going, the question of slave or free will probably be moot in a year or two."

Rising abruptly, she asked—no, commanded—her master. "Stay here." Within minutes, she returned from the ghostly mansion on the hill, laden with a floral carpet bag over her shoulder. *Time to show him.* Without a word, she handed the bag to him.

"What's this?" The flush across his face was pink as he examined his work. "Wh-where did you find these?"

Inbred fear took over, making it near impossible to face the man who owned her. "I didn't steal them. I swear. I only meant to borrow them overnight—to look at and study."

He was crying again, this time openly and hard. "I thought I'd never see my work again."

"Of-of course, it's not all of it by far, but the night before the fire, I chose what I thought was your best, meaning to put them back after a day or two, hoping you were too busy thinking on whether or not you should have caves built to notice. After the fire, when you said we were moving, I hid them beneath the house." She lifted her shoulders, her own eyes now spilling tears for a man she ought to hate. "I'll understand if you s-sell me. Just please sell Noah with me."

He stood. Dropped the carpet bag. Trembling, he leaned in and kissed her forehead. "Indeed, you are your mother's child."

She watched as her master climbed the short distance back to his cave, her own personal truce flag taking shape in her mind. Small and tattered, but a flag of hope nonetheless.

July 5, 1863

"Say it again. Say the word."

She fought to keep from laughing. "Freedom. Master Johns says he's going to free us."

Since the day before yesterday when Sunday had told Noah

of Master Johns' words, he'd had her repeat them at least a dozen times. She hadn't minded a bit, because even with the non-existent food, he'd immediately begun to gain strength. Sunday had wept into the night, praising the Savior for His miraculous power.

Yesterday was frozen in her memory. They had already begun the move back to the house. And though she had despised the war—which was to keep her enslaved whether the white folks admitted it or not—she couldn't stop her heart from lurching toward the breathing skeletons dragging themselves from the pits they had survived for forty-seven days. Blue and green eyes robbed of hope—gray uniforms reduced to strips of filthy cloth—stumbled into the city of Vicksburg. They looked ready to eat anything. Everything. And she suspected a great many of them weren't even as old as her. Noah's words swung her back to the moment.

"Wonder what became of Clayton?"

"Oh, not to worry yourself about him. He left that same night. Kept talking about a Pearl he'd left in one of the Carolinas." Sunday giggled. "I have a feeling it's going to take more than a war to keep him away from that gem whoever she is."

THE LOFT in the carriage house seemed the logical place for her and Noah until Master Johns figured something out. It hadn't taken long for Grant's army to begin putting food on the table of Vicksburg's citizens. Sitting on the steps to the mansion's back veranda, Sunday worried over what the bedding for Noah would be like until he grabbed her wrist, pulled her to his lap.

"I knew you were a fussy woman, but I do believe you're taking it to the other side of the river right now."

She threw a playful jab. "I just want you well. Lord, Noah.

I'm beginning to believe we might all be free pretty soon." Noah gave her a pained look and quickly tried to mask it.

"Noah? Something wrong?" Silly question. It was July. He hung between them like a delicate web.

"I know," she whispered. "I want it, too—to raise our July into a free man."

She'd worked hard every second—even when she was asleep—to hold to the hope of July's return which she had been sure she'd received from the Lord weeks back. But with each passing day, she wondered how much of it was God, how much her desperate heart.

She slid from her husband's lap and picked up the broom she had borrowed from Nonnie. Descending the steps, she started toward the door of the carriage house. There was still so much to do to make the main house livable again, and with Lelia Rose's mind daily slipping into permanent fantasy and Nonnie not quite healed, Sunday had had to help out in the big house today, from dawn until after supper. She stepped into the twilight toward the carriage house.

And into the sounds of a child.

The low complaint sent a sweet little alarm through her. *Don't do this to yourself, Sunday, every time you hear a child's cry.* She cupped her hand over her eyes and squinted as though that would help in the encroaching darkness. The only thing she saw clearly was the long blond hair of a tall man and two shadowy figures next to him. One holding a little boy's hand.

"Help you, sir?"

"Hope so. It'd be mighty nice of you." He laughed. Dragged out the drawl he possessed. "We're pretty worn out—my friends and I—trying to avoid two armies bent on annihilating each other. But with the ending of the siege, things have gone better. Eliza?"

Sunday turned the name over in her mind. Rejected the

possibility of the lunatic woman from Kentucky. Sensed it was time to get Master Johns.

"Yes, sir. Just let me get my master—"

"We're looking for a man named Clayton Duval. You happen to know him?" Sunday sped up her steps toward the back of the house. *Why are they looking for*—

"Or perhaps a girl named Sunday?"

She pivoted. What would you be wanting with—?"

"Mama?"

Sunday felt warm again—not the warmth of the month of July. But *her* July. As though all the words Master Johns had taught her had been put to shame by that one word. *Mama.*

"July? Is that my baby, July?" She dropped the broom. Stumbled over it. Almost fell thinking of how she and Noah could never get that part of the marriage ritual right. She righted herself. Flung herself at the woman holding her baby. Without a hitch, Eliza handed her the child. Looked at the ground.

"Thought that might be you." Eliza nudged July toward that 'mama' he'd just called. 'Fraid I have some explaining to do."

Sunday didn't hear her. Didn't hear the other strange-sounding woman trying to greet her. All she heard was her own voice shouting back toward the house—running—her baby clasped to her bosom.

"Noah! He's back. God has given us our baby back."

EPILOGUE

June, 1866

Sunday stepped back from her easel in the cozy quarters she shared above the carriage house with Noah and July and looked at her portrait of Gideon. A fine person who had accidentally met Mack at a Railroad station and joined with him to find Eliza and July after Eliza fled the farmhouse.

Turned out, Mack had been the object of the fire which everyone thought killed Eliza. After failing to destroy Mack in his own home, a few pro-slavery men had hired a mentally broken woman who resembled Eliza to occupy Eliza's deserted house for a few days—to sit near the window—hoping to lure Mack who sometimes looked out for her from the woods. The hired woman, who'd brought a child with her, must have accidentally set the house afire. And according to what Mack told Sunday and Noah, during his and Gideon's search for Eliza and July, it hadn't taken long for Mack to recognize he was "besotted."

Sunday chuckled, thinking of how Mack laughed at his rare use of a word like besotted. "The strangest-talking, strangest-walking, smartest—and perhaps the prettiest woman—I ever saw," he'd declared.

Sunday agreed. Gideon was quite a woman and, last she'd heard, desperately in love with Taylor Mack.

Thank God.

She cocked her head to the side and closely examined her work, still unable to believe that Mister Johns—they agreed she should no longer call him master—had actually sold a few of her pieces. She had made her peace with purple and pink, recognizing the former in her own skin and the latter in her father's. A father whose identity she had never revealed to a soul. But a father who, in his own way, worked hard to heal the wounds.

Sunday touched her swollen belly and smiled. Thought about the life blossoming inside. Wondered if it was a little girl. Wondered, too, how a man like Silas could ever have harmed such a gift. Taylor Mack had sent word that Silas was dead now, found in a Memphis alley robbed and beaten to death in the riot last month. The God in Sunday wouldn't allow her to rejoice, but her flesh was relieved that he could hurt no one else.

She put away her supplies and eased herself into her favorite chair next to the window. She loved this time of day when July napped and she had a few minutes before it was time for Noah to come home from the furniture-making business Johnston Smithmore had helped him establish. The work was hard and the pay was less than any white man would accept. But it was a start for Noah and the many other black people who had finally set out on the road to freedom. The war had left a bitterness that might take centuries to heal, but there would be no going back. Her people would continue to move in that hazy direction toward freedom. No matter the cost, no matter the time.

Reaching toward the Bible Mister Johns had given her,

Sunday knew she finally understood the meaning of Sabbath. That sweet restful gap between life's laborious days and weeks of pain. She'd had one of those "weeks" between April of '61 and July of '63, and she knew the odds were, she would experience another. But for now, she was in the sweet time. Her mother's long-ago words, so often used when she was weary of life's midweek trials, wrapped Sunday in hope.

Go day, come day,
God, send Sunday.

"Sunny? You up there?"

Her heart leapt, running to him as she herself had done over the last few years, but lately her cumbersome body was slow to follow. She frowned at her husband, standing before the threshold, and reverted to her slave language.

"Noah Duval, what chu doing home this time of day, standing there grinnin' like a boy who ain't tried his first kiss?"

Before she could set her balance, he had covered the space between them. Gathered her as close as their unborn child would allow. "I love my work, but it gets cloudy in that shop sometimes." He flashed another heart-stopping grin. "I needed some sunshine."

"Go on with you, boy."

But she didn't move, and her matching smile belied the protest. She closed her eyes. Relished the moment.

Thank God for life's Sabbaths.

ABOUT JACQUELINE FREEMAN WHEELOCK

Jacqueline Freeman Wheelock's historical novels share the narratives of African American women seeking their identities in the difficult setting of the old South. A former high school and college English teacher, her first novel, *A Most Precious Gift*, debuted in 2014 and ranked among Amazon's bestsellers in Black and African American Historical fiction. In 2017, she released its sequel, *In Pursuit of an Emerald*. Wheelock is a multi-published author whose works range from short stories and devotionals to a memoir of growing up during and after segregation. Published multiple times by University Press of Mississippi, she has been a member of the American Christian Fiction Writers for over a decade.

Her awards and recognition include the Zora Neale Hurston-Bessie Head Fiction Award at the 10th Annual Gwendolyn Brooks Writers' Conference in Chicago and honorable mention for "Alaska, By and By" in the William Faulkner

Awards for Short Fiction in New Albany, Mississippi. She and her husband Donald have two adult children and two grand-daughters.

ALSO BY JACQUELINE FREEMAN WHEELOCK

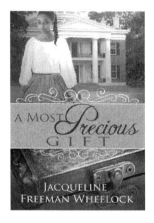

A Most Precious Gift

Dinah Devereaux, New Orleans-born slave and seamstress, suddenly finds herself relegated to a sweltering kitchen on the Natchez town estate of Riverwood. Having never cooked a day in her life, she is terrified of being found out and banished to the cotton fields as was her mother before her.

But when she accidentally burns the freedom papers of Jonathan Mayfield, a handsome free man of color to whom she's attracted, her fear of the fields becomes secondary. A gifted cabinetmaker, Jonathan Mayfield's heart is set on finally becoming a respected businessman by outfitting a bedroom at the palatial Riverwood—until a beautiful new slave destroys his proof of freedom and his fragile confidence along with it.

When the mistress of Riverwood orders Dinah to work alongside the sullen Mr. Mayfield, sparks fly setting the two on a collision course. Is their mutual love for God strong enough to overcome deep-seated insecurities and set the couple on a path toward self-acceptance and love for each other?

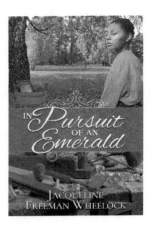

In Pursuit of an Emerald

All ex-slave Violette McMillan ever wanted is to see her troubled daughter Emerald grow up to be a better person than she has been, so when Benjamin Catlett, an old acquaintance, asks her to become his bookkeeper in 1869, in a business that is sinking due to southern backlash during the Reconstruction era, she agrees. But when his arrogance surfaces, their goals collide, and Violette wonders if she might be forced to renege at the expense of her daughter's future education.

Benjamin Catlett is plagued by his past as a free man of color whose African American father was a slaveholder. Renouncing his father's way of life, he moves to Natchez hoping to quietly atone. But his new hire, Violette McMillan, and her flirtatious teenage daughter, Emerald, test the limits of his good intentions one time too many, offending his straight-laced upbringing and tempting him to fire her.

Will the Lord who tugs at the heart of both Benjamin and Violette prevail in their efforts to tolerate each other and finally affirm the love already blossoming in their hearts?

MORE CIVIL WAR FICTION FROM SCRIVENINGS PRESS

Beyond These War-torn Lands

Wounded Hearts - Book One

By Cynthia Roemer

While en route to aid Confederate soldiers injured in battle near her home, Southerner Caroline Dunbar stumbles across a wounded Union sergeant. Unable to ignore his plea for help, she tends his injuries and hides him away, only to find her attachment to him deepen with each passing day. But when her secret is discovered, Caroline incurs her father's wrath and, in turn, unlocks a dark secret from the past which she is determined to unravel.

After being forced to flee his place of refuge, Sergeant Andrew Gallagher fears he's seen the last of Caroline. Resolved not to let that happen, when the war ends, he seeks her out, only to discover she's been sent away. When word reaches him that President Lincoln has been shot, Drew is assigned the task of tracking down the assassin. A chance encounter with Caroline revives his hopes, until he learns she may be involved in a plot to aid the assassin.

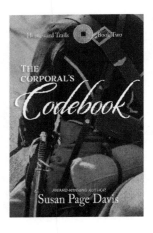

The Corporal's Codebook

Homeward Trails - Book Two

Jack Miller stumbles through the Civil War, winding up a telegrapher and cryptographer for the army. In the field with General Sherman in Georgia, he is captured along with his precious cipher key.

His captor, Hamilton Buckley, thinks he should have been president of the Confederacy, not Jefferson Davis. Jack doubts Buckley's sanity and longs to escape. Buckley's kindhearted niece, Marilla, might help him—but only if Jack helps her achieve her own goal.

Meanwhile, a private investigator, stymied by the difficulty of travel and communication in wartime, is trying his best to locate Jack for the grandmother he longs to see again but can barely remember.

Stay up-to-date on your favorite books and authors with our free e-newsletters.

ScriveningsPress.com

Made in the USA
Las Vegas, NV
18 September 2023

77774721R00203